Accolades for America's greatest hero Mack Bolan

"Very, very action-oriented.... Highly successful, today's hottest books for men."
—*The New York Times*

"Anyone who stands against the civilized forces of truth and justice will sooner or later have to face the piercing blue eyes and cold Beretta steel of Mack Bolan, the lean, mean nightstalker, civilization's avenging angel."
—*San Francisco Examiner*

"Mack Bolan is a star. The Executioner is a beacon of hope for people with a sense of American justice."
—*Las Vegas Review Journal*

"In the beginning there was the Executioner—a publishing phenomenon. Mack Bolan remains a spiritual godfather to those who have followed."
—*San Jose Mercury News*

HOME FRONT

The death toll had mounted, expanded by the questionable incidents that were thought to be linked to the attacks on Japanese business in America. Bolan wanted in on this one as soon as he discovered what was in the balance. He had pursued and fought terrorists all over the world; he wouldn't have hesitated at taking the chance to shut down terrorists operating on American soil.

Especially American ones.

"Mack Bolan stabs right through the heart of the frustration and hopelessness the average person feels about crime running rampant in the streets."
—*Dallas Times Herald*

DON PENDLETON's

MACK BOLAN®

SIEGE

A GOLD EAGLE BOOK FROM

WORLDWIDE®

TORONTO • NEW YORK • LONDON • PARIS
AMSTERDAM • STOCKHOLM • HAMBURG
ATHENS • MILAN • TOKYO • SYDNEY

First edition December 1990

ISBN 0-373-61421-7

Special thanks and acknowledgment to
Mel Odom for his contribution to this work.

SIEGE

The only prize much cared for by the powerful is power. The prize of the general is not a bigger tent, but command.

—Law and the Court (1913)
Oliver Wendell Holmes, Jr.

They say that power corrupts. I say that only the worst kind of savage would put into motion events that would kill scores of innocents. A man like that has no future, has no choice but to face the cleansing flame of his executioner.

—Mack Bolan

ng over the three men. (Jaily Vardeman was really so naive in this kind of civilian encounter. The other two were trained killers who had been involved in a dozen behind-the-scenes

PROLOGUE

"We're lucky this is one of the tallest buildings in the area," the helicopter pilot said into his headset as he angled his craft toward the target zone. "And we're lucky this damn smog isn't any thicker. I don't know which is worse—this time of night, or dawn or dusk."

Ross Tuley grinned. "Eric, my man, I've been listening to you bitch about LZ standards for the past ten years. Believe me, I'd be more worried if you didn't say a goddamn word."

He glanced out at the moonless night. Downtown Los Angeles was spread out below, and he could pick out Pershing Square to the southwest, fading behind them. Streetlights were dim flickers in the thick smog, leaving only the skyline to mark their progress.

"You and your glory boys got two minutes until the drop site," the pilot announced after glancing at his wristwatch.

Tuley nodded and unbuckled the seat harness, his gloved hands automatically making sure the Detonics .45 sheathed across his chest was still strapped down. "You give me the go."

"Red light above the bay," the pilot replied. "Same as always. You get a winnin' routine, you stick with 'er."

Tuley slapped the pilot on the shoulder as he dropped the headset into his seat, then went back to rejoin the crew he'd drawn for this mission. He paused in the cargo area, looking over the three men. Only Vardeman was really seasoned in this kind of civilian encounter. The other two were trained killers who had been involved in a dozen behind-the-scenes

international battle zones. He waited until they made eye
contact with him. "Quick in, quick out, just like we re-
hearsed," he said in a flat voice. "You get caught, you burn
on your own. I don't want anybody playing cowboy on this
operation. It goes down smooth, or it doesn't go down at
all."

They nodded, looking like three-dimensional shadows
against the metal wall of the cargo area.

He rolled down the hood of his ski mask and tucked it
into the collar of his knee-length Velcro-sealed poncho. The
ponchos were easily disposable and contained generous
pockets for the hardware they were carrying into the strike.
Each man wore one. Only two of them, Vardeman and
Johnston, had Uzis; all had incendiaries.

Tuley rolled the cargo bay door open and glanced ahead,
his eyes tearing from the wind. He waved the team forward
as the target building come into view.

Dwarfing most of the surrounding structures, the building stood twenty-four stories high. Most of the lights were
out in the top half of the building, which was primarily office space. Shops and restaurants made up the lower third,
with a mall area on the bottom two floors. The plan called
for them to achieve their objective, mingle with the resi-
dents of the building until confusion filled the hallways,
then get out.

If the Japanese didn't have heavy security on the scene,
Tuley thought. That was the one thing they hadn't had time
to scope out properly. In addition to the usual business run
by the Japanese on the top floor of the building, his information said they also received infrequent shipments of cocaine.

"Who'd have ever figured I'd be part of the team to kill
Galaxy Boy?" Ellison asked, then laughed. "I swear this is
one freaky fucking deal."

The red bulb over the cargo bay came on just as the helicopter glided a half-dozen feet above the building. Tuley

eased out the door. Vardeman was on his tail, just as he'd been for the past three years. The rooftop came up quickly, and he slammed into it hard enough to take his breath away.

Instinct took over, rolling him to his feet as his hand found the butt of the Detonics and drew it out from under the poncho.

"Clear," Vardeman called, heading toward the fire escape door. Ellison and Johnston checked in as well, dropping the rappeling lines off their shoulders as they headed for the opposite side of the building. Glancing up, Tuley saw the helicopter already gaining altitude as it spun back toward the rendezvous point on Catalina Island.

Tuley reached Vardeman's side just as the biggest man chugged a silenced round into the lock. Sparks spit from the metal as a ragged gouge appeared in the door. Vardeman slammed into the door, and it popped open at once. Tuley took point, letting his second-in-command bring up the rear.

The empty stairwell came to an abrupt end at a locked door leading into the offices that were their target. Tuley lifted a leg and drove his combat boot through the window, tearing out the metal mesh reinforcement. He reached in and twisted the knob.

Moving through the dark rooms, he ticked them off against the checklist in his head, leaving time-delay firebombs with seven-minute settings. He kicked open doors and raced through the maze of small offices, tossing the bundles, emptying his pockets as quickly as possible. Posters and pictures adorned every room, advertisements for Galaxy Boy, the latest Japanese-produced comic book to hit the American market. They were all different, all showing the same hero battling various space creatures and villains, zapping them with his trusty ray gun or chopping at them in martial arts stances.

Without warning, a security guard stepped out of a room, leveling his Colt .38 and peering over its six-inch barrel.

"Vardeman," Tuley called, dropping to one knee. He heard the sound suppressor on the Uzi whisper softly, then a line of bloody holes chased the security guard back against a fold-out wall that collapsed beneath his weight. The team leader stood up, pitching the incendiaries onto the floor as Ellison and Johnston arrived on the scene. "Have any trouble?"

"No," Johnston answered, holding his Uzi straight up from his hip.

Tuley indicated the dead man. "This guy might have pushed a silent alarm, so watch your ass." He led the way back to the fire escape, perspiring profusely under the poncho, mask and gloves as he held the .45 in front of him in two hands, still counting down in his head.

Another security guard was one floor down, carrying a white paper bag in one hand while holding his holstered weapon with the other, curiosity etched into his seamed face.

Tuley put two silenced rounds through the old man's chest. Then, ripping off his poncho, he dropped it onto the landing floor and charged down the stairs. The trick now was to put as much distance between themselves and the top floor as they could. He jumped over the guard's body, palming the security badge from the dead man's shirt just in case. Then he ripped the ski mask off with his free hand and dropped it onto the next floor.

The upper floor exploded in a series of booms, each one seemingly louder than the last. The building shivered from the force of the blasts. Tuley dropped his gun reluctantly and signaled the others to do the same. Five minutes later they were in a hallway ten more stories down, mixing with the crowd of confused people who wondered what had happened. Fifteen minutes later they were out of the building, watching as fire trucks and police cars lined the streets.

"Hey, Tuley," Ellison called as he peered upward with a large grin. "Now that we've offed Galaxy Boy, who do we do for an encore?"

"We go to Tokyo," Tuley replied as he turned to walk away. "Our intel has gotten wind of some hotshot the Feds are pulling in to help the Japanese Foreign Affairs people figure out who's been hitting the Jap holdings in the United States. We've got orders to intercept this guy before he makes contact, and see what kind of poop he's bringing to the meet with him."

"And if he doesn't intercept so well?" Ellison asked.

"We take him out."

Vardeman fell into step with Tuley. "One guy has the old man worried?" he asked.

"Yeah."

"Must be some kind of guy."

"His name's Belasko. Mike Belasko. He's done some on-again, off-again type of work for a handful of agencies from what intel has been able to dig up. He's strictly a loner and a pro, the kind of guy who doesn't even leave a shadow at the scene. And he's trouble."

CHAPTER ONE

Mack Bolan stared through the rain-dappled Plexiglas window of the water bus, then turned and glanced across the faces behind him, acting like an American tourist captivated by the sights. Two men, both Caucasian, both wearing sunglasses and dark suits, shifted their gazes away from him hurriedly, each finding something of interest on their side of the craft.

Satisfied that he had uncovered at least part of the force that had been pursuing him so quietly since Shimbashi Station, Bolan faced forward again. A simple message from Hal Brognola had brought the Executioner to Japan—no warnings, no details, just a quiet plea for him to come as soon as possible. The head Fed's reluctance to try for a meet outside Japan told him something big had been scheduled; the two men breathing down his neck told him Brognola's security had evidently been compromised to a degree.

He settled back in his seat, his warrior's psyche already outlining his choices of tactics. Brognola was taking care of his weapons, but until he made contact with the Justice man, he was unarmed and operating on thin papers that wouldn't stand up under the scrutiny of Tokyo police if this encounter turned bloody. And, judging from the tight-lipped features of the two men, it had every chance of doing just that.

The water bus rode low in the muddy water of the Sumida River, burdened by the large number of tourists aboard. Late-morning July sunlight left golden crescents floating on the river's surface. The pomp and many-colored splendor of Hamarikyu's waterfront gardens just a few minutes from Shimbashi Station had given way to fleets of old fishing boats in need of a new coat of paint, whose captains and mates were already at work bringing in the day's catch.

Tooting his horn, the water bus driver yelled at an over-zealous fishing boat that came too close. Waves rolled under the craft, causing the tourists to grab for loose handbags and camera cases that went skidding across the wooden deck.

Bolan pushed himself out of his seat and made his way to the back of the water bus at a dead run. The vessel pitched again, and he fought to keep himself on his feet, reaching the first of the two men as the guy grabbed under his jacket. He palmed the man's face as the guy stood up, powering it into the upper set of wooden casements holding the windows in place on that side of the water bus. The man's head made a hollow thunk, and he dropped, unconscious, to sprawl across the legs of the old woman he'd been sitting next to. She started to scream, drawing the attention of the rest of the people on the water bus. The gun spilled out of the man's nerveless fingers and thudded solidly against the deck. It went off, the report deafening in the enclosed space. The bullet ripped through a suitcase held by a man across the aisle before holing one of the Plexiglas windows.

The second man had his weapon in hand by the time the Executioner moved on him. Bolan reached for the automatic as the man pulled the trigger, jamming his little finger between the hammer and the firing pin, feeling flesh tear. Using his weight and forward momentum, he slammed the man back into his seat, grabbing a handful of hair as he lifted his knee into the man's face. Cartilage snapped, and the man went down without a word.

Pandemonium broke out behind him as the rest of the passengers realized what was going on. Bolan didn't hesitate. Still on the move, he jammed the captured .45 into the waistband of his jeans, under the loose folds of his knitted sport shirt. He broke through the small door to the rear of the water bus, moving up on deck.

The people manning the speedboat had spotted him. One man pointed him out from the prow, yelling, but his words were torn away by the confusion and the wind. Bolan paused a moment to take stock of the situation as fishing boats tried to avoid the swerving water bus.

The speedboat closed in. The pilot kept winnowing his craft between the boats, closing the gap to less than fifty yards. The two other men had assumed prone positions and shouldered automatic weapons. A sudden line of fire behind the water bus threw water over Bolan as the 5.56 mm tumblers chewed into the rear hull.

Glancing over his shoulder, the Executioner saw the Azuma Bridge coming up and knew from his map book of the area that access to Umamichi Street would give him at least two more options than he had at present.

Bullets tore into the back of the water bus, which started a whole new wave of screaming. Bolan dived over the side, knowing his evacuation of the craft would pull the attackers away from it. He hit the water off balance, turned and twisted by the water bus's speed and the churning wake created by the fishing boats. He opened his eyes and found himself surrounded by brown murk.

The speedboat zoomed by overhead, the screw turning the water foamy white as it passed. Bolan stroked for the shore, seeing the fishing nets spread out before him only seconds before touching them. His fingers pulled at the rough hemp, feeling the accrued slime come away on his palms. He charted the speedboat's course, watching the white line slowly curve back toward him for another pass, slower now.

Putting aside the questions of who the men were, why they would attack him and how they knew where to find him, the Executioner reached for the large folding knife he'd recently purchased and flicked out the largest blade. Lungs near bursting, the warrior sawed quickly at the thick hawser rope holding one end of a fishing net, then kicked out across the murky river when the last strand had parted. The speedboat cruised through the choppy water only yards away. He swam harder, tugging the heavy net after him. He stuck the knife between his teeth and hauled on the thick hawser with both hands, forcing it to the surface, giving it up to the whirling screw of the speedboat as the sandy taste of the river filled his mouth.

He heard a muffled thump, then the propeller yanked the rope through his fingers. He released it and broke the surface, gasping for air, twisting his head to watch the speedboat go out of control.

One of the men had fallen from the boat and become twisted in the net. He was dragged along until the hawser drew tight between the speedboat's forward momentum and the fishing berth's heavy immobility. The man screamed just as the speedboat caromed off the pilings and exploded into a fireball of gasoline that spread across the river's surface.

Bolan swam after the man tangled in the net, knowing the guy would drown unless he was able to cut himself free. Screams and yells of rage dogged him as the fishermen came to renewed life, piloting their vessels toward him, scrabbling around their stained decks with grim proficiency. Sunlight glinted off knives and boat hooks held tightly in their callused hands.

Bolan dived, following the bedraggled end of the hawser that floated on the surface, letting his fingertips guide him down into the murk. The trapped man wriggled and squirmed against the constricting strands of the net, eyes bulging when he saw the Executioner. The warrior reached for the net, and the man's hands slid through an opening to close tightly around Bolan's wrist. The guy tried to speak, his face pleading.

The blade was dull, but the strands of the old frayed net parted quickly.

Still holding the knife, Bolan reached out and seized the man by the collar, pulling him upward.

When the two men broke the surface, Bolan had to struggle to keep the man up, combating his captive's fear and poor motor control. He shook water from his eyes and locked an arm around the man from behind.

The fishing boats had ringed the area, and a hundred questions were being tossed back and forth. Bolan watched them all, backpedaling toward the flaming wreckage of the speedboat smeared against the piling. More people had gathered there, pointing excitedly. He couldn't help but wonder if there were more of the unknown assassins within their ranks. "Talk," he commanded gruffly, "or I'll put you back under."

The man waved a trembling arm in front of his face, weakly managing to lock onto Bolan's forearm at his chin. He hacked and coughed and spit out water. "I'll talk, I'll talk. Just don't let me go down again."

Bolan swam backward, watching the perimeter. The water bus had come to a final stop on the other side of the river. People were milling about on the deck in a state of confusion, some of them covered with blood. The driver was slumped over the wheel, the Plexiglas in front of him blown away.

"Who set this up?" Bolan demanded, grabbing on to a berthed rowboat behind him.

"Tuley," the man answered. He flailed weakly against the water as three small outboards closed in, filled with grim-faced Japanese youths carrying makeshift weapons. "Ross Tuley."

"Spell it."

The man did.

"Why me?"

The man spluttered, fighting against the water.

Bolan restrained him, struggling to keep them both afloat. The poppings and crackings of the outboard motors made conversation difficult. He shook his captive. "Why me?"

"Tuley had orders to talk to you, to find out what you were doing in Tokyo. You reacted too fast. Orders were that if you resisted, we were to take you out and worry about what you were here for later."

One of the outboards choked and gasped as the engine died, allowing the small craft to come drifting in sideways. Two young men wielding hooked fishing knives glided toward them, yelling in Japanese. Most of it Bolan couldn't understand, but there was no doubting their intent. "What name did they give you?" he asked.

"Belasko. Michael Belasko. We picked you up at Narita International Airport, stayed with you until you made the Shimbashi Station junction and set this up." The man's voice was stronger now. "Hey, look, guy, the natives don't appear to be very friendly. What do you say to us getting the hell out of here and figuring out what to do later?"

Bolan didn't answer. He wondered if this had anything to do with what Brognola had called him in for. The big Fed had set the paperwork in motion that allowed the Executioner into Tokyo under the Belasko name, but the security could have been penetrated at either end of the operation, and "Belasko" himself had made a number of enemies over the past little while.

A shadow crossed the warrior's vision, and he quickly submerged, trying to bring his captive with him. The boat hook slipped past his chin, burying itself under his prisoner's jawline. Crimson flooded the dark waters. The man twisted in pain, unable to speak because the boat hook had nailed his lower jaw to the roof of his mouth, his arms reaching futilely for his attacker.

Bolan saw them both tumble into the river in front of him just as the familiar sounds of a large-bore rifle thundered into his ears. A fist-sized hole appeared suddenly in the chest of the young man holding the boat hook. Splinters erupted from the rowboat just over the Executioner's head, scattering across the river surface as he went down. He palmed the .45 from his waistband, knowing there was at least one sniper on the Azuma Bridge, wondering what Brognola had brought him into. But that thought dissolved as something impacted brutally against his lower ribs, driving the wind from his lungs in an explosion of bubbles.

"WHERE THE HELL IS HE?" Ross Tuley barked into the walkie-talkie. He peered through the compact binoculars hanging from his neck rather than the telescopic sights of the Weatherby, scanning the river where Bolan had gone under. Two bodies, the Japanese kid's and Ellison's, floated up, locked in a bizarre death embrace.

"I'm looking for him," Vardeman radioed back. "For God's sake, keep your shirt on."

Tuley dropped the binoculars and slapped the top of the stone bridge with his palm. "I want that bastard found," he snapped into the walkie-talkie, "and I want him found *now*."

An old man dressed in a dark blue robe stepped forward from the crowd at the east end of the bridge, holding his hands up. "You must not do this," the old man begged in broken English. "There are women and children here who do not deserve the trouble you bring to them."

Tuley brought the sniper rifle to bear on the old man's chest. He smiled thinly. "Don't be a hero, Hito. Come any closer and I'll blow you away. I'm already having a bad day, and there isn't a thing you can do to fuck it up more except to make me mad."

"I got him," Vardeman's voice called out.

Tuley turned from the old man. "Where?"

"Nine o'clock from your position. Just got a smell of him before he dropped out of sight alongside one of those fishing boats."

Tuley watched a flurry of activity erupt on one of the vessels as the fishermen on board picked up everything they could lay their hands on. He thumbed the walkie-talkie. "Connors, I make that your target zone." He stared across the river, seeing Connors move into position on the roof of the apartment building. Then the man knelt, leaning into his weapon, ready to ride out the recoil. "Connors, get your ass down. I can see you from—"

Two shots banged out, echoing up from the river. Connors rolled from the rooftop and dropped onto the pier below.

"Son of a bitch," Tuley breathed. Another shot scattered sparks and brick fragments from the bridge less than a yard away. Tuley dropped automatically, rolling back to cradle his rifle. "Son of a bitch!"

"Ross," Vardeman called over the walkie-talkie.

"Here, damn it."

"Are you okay?"

"Yeah, so far, though it's not from that bastard's lack of trying." He scrambled to his knees, peering warily toward his target. He saw Bolan haul himself up a pier farther down the river, a dark stain spreading across the big man's lower right side. "Somebody got a piece of him."

"Yeah, well, he isn't moving like it."

"I noticed. Where the hell did he get that gun? I thought he checked through customs clean."

"He did," Vardeman said. "My bet is that he picked up one from the on-site team. There's a handful of guys down in that water who won't be needing theirs anymore."

"Close in on him," Tuley ordered, pushing himself to his feet and trotting toward a waiting Subaru. "I don't want this guy to get away." He clipped the walkie-talkie to his belt, then clambered into the small 4X4, barely seating himself before Marashanski took off.

Tuley tried to keep Bolan in sight as they rolled down the side road along the river, watching the man make the leap from the deck of one fishing boat to the top of another. Then the scene was swept away as Marashanski took a hard left into a covered alleyway that was scarcely large enough to allow the Subaru through.

Tuley grabbed the walkie-talkie and keyed it up. "Vardeman!"

"Here."

"Do you see him?"

"Yeah, he's still here."

"Still moving?"

"You got it."

Tuley unslung the binoculars, focusing on Bolan as he made the leap from the top of the last fishing boat he'd landed on to the side of the bridge.

"You should have stayed where you were," Vardeman said. "He's doubling back."

"He knows the area, damn it. I figured we'd have our best shot here, where he'd be cut off from whoever he's meeting. He's heading for Nakamise Street. You can bet your ass on that. Once he gets lost in those shops, he can be lost as long as he wants to."

"Time's on his side and he knows it. We aren't dealing with some babe in the woods on this one."

"Yeah, I figured that from the start. I just didn't figure on the guy being this good."

The Subaru hurtled back toward the covered alley. Tuley held on to the rifle in his lap. Assuming his quarry had taken a pistol from one of the guys below, that gave him eight shots in the .45, and he'd fired three of them. At least three of them. That would leave five. Then Tuley remembered that assumptions had left a lot of good guys dead. He gripped the rifle tighter.

The 4X4 roared out of the alley, preceded by screams of the people standing in the street. Tuley held on to his seat, not believing his eyes when the first thing he saw was Bolan standing in the open with a pistol leveled in front of him.

The merc ducked, already hearing the bullets smash through the windshield, listening to Marashanski die beside him, feeling the Subaru skid wildly out of control as the driver fell forward.

Ten yards away, Bolan finished the .45's clip, spacing the bullets across the 4X4's windshield, knowing the passenger had ducked too soon to remain in the line of fire. He threw himself out of the way of the uncontrolled vehicle, and the Subaru smashed through the railing above the river, toppling end over end to crunch through the top of a fishing boat.

Autofire skipped across the street, seeking Bolan. The warrior moved, still holding the useless .45. The wound in his side didn't feel as if it were life-threatening, but he'd learned a long time ago that death could come quietly for a man on the battlefield. He felt the sticky warmth, diluted slightly by the wet clothes, trickle down his side.

Faces blurred past him as he ran. His feet hit the street solidly, pushing him on, propelling him up to clamber over a stalled rickshaw, dropping to the ground as autofire ripped the bright green material that covered it into tatters. His breath whooshed out of him as he hit off balance, bracing himself on his hands as he recovered. Disembodied screams and wails pursued him. An old man driving a bicycle fell to the ground, forcing him to leap over the tangle of flailing arms and spinning wheels.

He landed in a shoulder roll and came up into a screaming forest of arms, legs and bodies.

"Over here!" someone yelled. More voices picked up the cry.

Bolan guessed there were at least a half-dozen armed men on his backtrail, but he had no time to check. Bullets kicked off the wrought-iron patio of the apartment above his head, driving the frightened people around him to the ground and leaving him exposed. He ducked into the first alley he came to, scattering the metal trash cans behind him. He bounced off the walls with his hands and headed into the next alley, which would keep him headed in the direction of Kaminar- imon Gate.

Darting back out onto the main street, he saw the large and ornate Kaminarimon Gate less than twenty yards away. People moved in a constant flow in both directions through it, dressed in conventional suits and business attire as well as the white robes of the Shintoists going into the temple at the end of the street. He pressed a hand to his side, then pulled it away to gaze at his bloody fingers. Ripping off a sleeve of his shirt, he folded it and tucked it inside his waistband as a pressure bandage.

A man cradling a CAR-15 sprinted around the corner, looking both ways, paying no attention to the people that scattered from him. Pressing himself back against the alley wall, the Executioner reached for the broken mop handle that jutted up from a nearby trash can. He swung its three-foot length in a short arc by his leg to get an idea of its weight. Then he froze, listening for the quick steps of the approaching man, hearing even more coming up the alley after him. He tightened his grip, waiting until the man drew even with the corner of the alley and swung.

CHAPTER TWO

"Papa Hosaka is a real ball buster," Alan Tucker said as he signaled for the right-hand turn that would take the car toward the underground garage of the Ministry of Foreign Affairs building. "He's been screaming since the first that he's the victim of an American conspiracy, and that the CIA people heading the investigation—meaning me—are doing nothing more than staging an elaborate cover-up."

Hal Brognola shifted his unlit cigar from one side of his mouth to the other as Tucker expertly cut off an oncoming car to make his turn. He caught the younger man's attention and lifted an eyebrow. "Are you?"

The CIA man laughed good-naturedly.

Brognola decided he liked the sound. It made the prospect of working with Tucker easier to accept. When the President had suggested pairing him with someone from Langley, he'd almost turned the request down—until he looked at the reports that crossed his desk immediately after his conference with the Man.

Tucker moved into the lane for the underground garage. "The front office warned me about you."

"Yeah?"

"Yeah."

Brognola chuckled. "And what did they say?"

"That you were the most tight-fisted, uncompromising, distrustful son of a bitch to ever jockey a desk at Justice. That pretty much sum it up?"

Brognola crushed the wet cigar into the gleaming, unused ashtray, enjoying the look of dismay that flashed across the CIA man's face. "Pretty much," he replied, relaxing back into the seat.

"They also said you were a good man to depend on when the going got rough. And that you could be counted on to get the job done right in the clinch."

"The people in Langley must be getting generous of late."

Tucker laughed and moved up one more space in the line through security. "They are where you're concerned. I was told to stay on the level with you concerning everything I do while we're together."

"You'll excuse me if I pause for a guffaw of disbelief."

"Guffaw if you want, but I'm being honest here."

"I've never known the Company to run anything on the level with an outside agency in all the years I've been associated with them."

"Me, neither, and I've been involved in some shitstorms." Tucker smiled, looking younger than the early thirties Brognola had him pegged at. The CIA man was lean and good-looking, with a nice, even tan, capped teeth and unruly dark brown hair. He looked as if he'd be more at home on a tennis court or as a news anchor. He looked comfortable in the expensive suit he wore.

"Them telling you that only means one thing," Brognola said as the shadow of the underground garage slid over them. "Either you're telling me that to make me feel good and get me to open up, or—"

"Or they're telling me that because they know I'm the highest profiled member of the Tokyo-based team and they plan on keeping me in the dark with you."

Brognola grinned without mirth. "Pleasant company you're doing business with, Tucker. Where do you plan to be in five years?"

"Alive, my man, and still playing the game because it's gotten into my blood. The same way it's gotten into yours." Tucker reached into his jacket and pulled out a pair of Foster Grant sunglasses. "Excuse me a minute," he said as he thumbed down his window.

The air was cooler in the underground garage, but tainted with auto exhaust and the mildewed smell of large air-conditioning units. Yellow-bulbed security lights were mounted every few feet on the concrete wall. An old man was pushing a broom down the left side of the enclosed parking area.

Tucker spoke in Japanese, dangling his ID out the window. Brognola picked up the names of Hosaka and Fujitsu, the man in Foreign Affairs they were meeting with. The CIA man nodded, put his ID away and continued into the lighted recess of the garage. Then he took the sunglasses from his eyes and held them toward Brognola. "Lots of moviegoers in Tokyo," he said. "Get all our best stuff through the black market. It's how they learn American culture. You show 'em a pair of Grants, and they figure you for CIA immediately. Lends credibility when you flip out the ID. I don't wear them unless I want to be known or noticed." He pulled into a slot and they got out.

"Tell me about Joji Hosaka," Brognola said as they walked toward the bank of elevators.

"You received a package on him, didn't you?"

"Yeah. One from Langley with your John Hancock on it, and one from my research people."

Tucker smiled. "And did they jibe?"

"Almost line for line."

"So what do you want to know?"

"I got the paper on the guy, and I know his birthday and what he likes to do when he's not busy making money, but you've talked with the guy."

"You're looking for a handle on him."

Brognola nodded. "Something like that."

"I can't give you any easy answers. If there were any, I'd be on top of this situation by now." Tucker came to a stop in front of the elevators, reached out and tapped the Up button. "Joji Hosaka is a clever little animal with more strings to pull than a textile worker. Other than that, I don't have much."

"I don't want to run my people in here blind," Brognola told him. "You lose too many of them that way."

"I know."

Tucker's voice was soft, and Brognola believed the man was speaking from experience. The doors parted to reveal a handful of male and female office workers talking among themselves. The big Fed felt tall and bulky as he stepped inside, like an oversize ape next to the two small Japanese women left sharing the elevator with them.

Tucker said something and smiled. The two women replied and returned the smile.

Brognola felt even more uncomfortable and out of place when they looked at him and he could only shrug.

"I take it you don't speak the language?" Tucker asked.

Brognola gave him a sour look, knowing the CIA man's obvious expertise in the situation he was expected to help control was part of the irritation he felt. "A few words. I've seen bits and pieces of *Shogun*."

"Ah, *Shogun*," one of the young women said, nodding her head slightly. "Very good cinema."

Her accent struck Brognola as being so atrocious that it was charming. He smiled and she smiled back.

Tucker was grinning when he looked back. "You'll discover many Japanese speak English over here, so getting around won't be a problem."

Brognola nodded, knowing the man also intended the information as a warning against eavesdroppers.

The elevator rose smoothly with almost dizzying speed, discharging the two young women four floors up into surroundings of clean whiteness, Oriental rugs and large green plants.

"I want you to form your own opinion of the guy," Tucker said as the elevator continued on. "Then we'll get together and compare notes. Hosaka is a hard, abrasive son of a bitch with an intelligence guided by nothing less than pure ruthlessness. His sons are chips off the same flint block.''

"Will the whole family be here?''

"Yemon probably will, but not Saburo. From what I understand, papa Hosaka and his younger son aren't exactly on the best of terms. Saburo has a small problem with nose candy, both using and selling, that pisses the old man off since he's tried to point the family more toward legal business interests.''

"That wasn't covered in the documentation I received.''

"That's because it's not something real well-known at the moment. I know because I have a drinking buddy in the Metropolitan Police Department. I kept it out of all my reports as a favor to him. They're working on a few schemes of their own to nail Saburo Hosaka. I don't want to see them messed up because Langley decides we need to take an active role in what's going on. We're not here to ring down the curtain on an internal drug problem. We're here to figure out who's making an effort to destroy Japanese investments in the States, and why. Your own people didn't know about Saburo, either, so don't get your nose out of joint. I'm only telling you now because I want you going into this thing with both eyes open. In case you haven't noticed, we're going to be taking care of each other's back on this one.''

The elevator dinged and the doors opened to a spacious lobby filled with plants and colorful prints. The air-conditioning smelled clean, with traces of perfumed carpet cleaner in the air. Three women and two men were busy behind the counter to the left, offsetting the almost empty waiting room to the right.

A man sitting in the waiting room stood nervously, drawing Brognola's attention. His trained cop's eye flicked through details at once. The overcoat the guy had on was too heavy for the day's weather, even considering the rain earlier.

The big Fed was reaching for Tucker and the .38 holstered on his hip as the man braced himself and dragged a sawed-off shotgun into view. Brognola yelled a warning to the people behind the counter as he triggered a round from his weapon. The shotgun boomed and something smashed into his leg, knocking him off balance.

Brognola went down, automatically throwing out his empty hand to cushion the impact. The .38 in his other hand tracked onto the shotgunner's face, centering between his attacker's narrowed eyes. He stroked the trigger again, and the piercing crack of the .38 in the confined space of the waiting area seemed deafening. Third and fourth shots followed in rapid succession as he went down. He saved the last bullet for when he landed on the tiled floor, wanting to be sure of its effect, realizing it might be the last thing between the killer and the innocents around him.

The shotgunner stumbled to one side as his head jerked back and his arms and legs went rubbery. His weapon hit the floor with a hollow thump, audible above the screams that reverberated from every corner.

Still in the prone position, Brognola kept the downed man covered and looked past him into the waiting room. People lay scattered in refuge behind the overturned chairs, but no one made any hostile moves. He forced himself up as he kept the .38 on target.

Tucker knelt in front of the reception desk with a big Charter Arms Bulldog .44 in both hands. He looked calm, but his face was paler than it had been a moment ago. Directly behind him, the imitation wood finish of the desk had been ripped away in two places by the shotgun loads, leaving holes big enough to shove two or three fists through.

"You okay?" Brognola asked as he moved forward to lay the .38 against the shotgunner's throat, then checked for a pulse and found none.

"Yeah." Tucker's voice didn't sound all that sure. He didn't put the pistol away.

People spilled out of doorways down the hall. They approached the dead man with trepidation. Even though they weren't speaking a language Brognola understood, he recognized the familiar signs of shock as the crowd moved in to take stock of the situation.

Brognola knelt beside the body and began checking the pockets for identification.

Tucker joined him. "Security will be here in a minute. Leave this to them."

"Maybe you didn't notice it during the confusion, pal, but this son of a bitch was waiting for us," Brognola growled as he turned the body over after the front pockets yielded nothing. "And maybe I'm a tad bit old-fashioned when it comes to getting shot at, because I'd kind of like to know who pulled the trigger."

The CIA man knelt down to take a good look at the corpse.

Brognola noticed the rubber bands wrapped tightly around the butt of the Bulldog. The blued metal showed bright spots where the finish had been worn away. The big weapon wasn't just an affectation; it was a working tool that had been used for a number of years.

"I don't know this guy," Tucker said.

"Neither do I, but the bastard knew us." Brognola was disgusted when he found nothing in the back pockets, either.

"Anything?" Tucker asked.

"No. He probably ran out of calling cards at the last stop." Brognola was irritated at the CIA man's aplomb. Did Tucker really act that cool under pressure and see the attack as being a matter for the Japanese police to handle? Or did it come as no surprise? He took his Visa card out of his wallet just as the elevator doors popped open and security people walked into the reception area with drawn guns. Wiping the credit card across his pant leg, he pressed the first three fingers of the dead man's right hand on the front, then repeated the operation on the back as Tucker began talking to the security people. When Brognola finished, he slipped it back into his wallet between other cards and stored it inside his jacket pocket.

"They want you to get away from the body," Tucker said.

Brognola looked beyond the CIA man at the stern faces of the guards. He got to his feet slowly, ignoring the quickening throb in his leg. Tucker still held the .44 at his side.

One of the security guards stepped forward and began barking orders to the rest, making emphatic gestures with his white-gloved hands.

"Tell him I want a report on this man as soon as possible," Brognola instructed.

The leader of the security team turned to face him with hooded eyes. He asked something in Japanese.

"I don't think this is the time to start pushing the issue," Tucker said.

Brognola broke open the .38 and dumped the spent casings into a big palm. He tucked them away in a pocket and thumbed in fresh cartridges from another pocket. "You try pushing it any later, kid, and this body won't be so accessible to us."

Tucker shrugged and spoke to the man. The leader's eyes registered a brief flicker of anger. He opened his mouth to speak, but another man's voice drowned out his reply.

Brognola turned carefully to take in the new speaker. The man was small and compact in his immaculate black suit, his spine ramrod stiff, his head smooth-shaven.

The security man nodded obediently and moved away, while the bald man stepped forward and held out his hand to Brognola. "As soon as he has anything of value, you will receive a copy of it. Fair enough?"

Brognola nodded and shook the man's hand.

Tucker smiled. "Hal Brognola, let me present Goro Fujitsu, our contact in Foreign Affairs."

"A pity the meeting couldn't have been under more pleasant circumstances," Fujitsu said.

"If the circumstances had been any less pleasant," Brognola replied as he waved toward the shattered reception desk, "a meeting of any type would have been impossible."

Fujitsu nodded. "Did you know this man or what reason he might have had to attack you?"

"No."

"Then what makes you think he singled you out?"

"He looked right at me when he pulled the trigger."

"Could the target have been Mr. Tucker?"

"I don't know him, either," the CIA man said.

"Still, you have been in this country long enough to have acquired a considerable number of people who might want to kill you." Fujitsu smiled. "Your Agency is sometimes careless with its operations."

Brognola saw Tucker's lips compress into a thin, hard line. Maybe the agent wasn't as chummy with the Foreign Affairs representative as he'd tried to act. Brognola put the .38 back into its hip holster.

The security team busied itself with moving the people in the reception area into the elevators in small groups. Some of the women were still crying as others helped them along. One of them had a bloodstained sleeve, but the injury looked superficial.

Fujitsu walked forward to survey the body, quietly studying the bloody patterns latticed across the tile. "You are bleeding, Mr. Brognola." The little man looked up.

Brognola lifted his pant leg slightly, exposing the torn flesh along his calf. "It's not as bad as it looks."

"Still, it would be in the best interests of everyone concerned if you had it taken care of now." Fujitsu made a small grimace. "As you can see, I will be tied up here for some time. I'll leave word for Mr. Hosaka and his son that we will be contacting them as soon as another meeting can

be arranged." The man's tone made it clear that no dis-
agreement was permissible.

"Is there a room I could use while I make a few phone
calls?" Brognola asked.

"Of course, but shouldn't you have your injury taken care
of first?"

Brognola smiled. "Duty before comfort, I'm afraid."

Fujitsu nodded and headed back down the corridor he'd
come from. "I can arrange for someone to drive you to the
hospital if you'd like." He stepped inside the first office he
came to and said something in Japanese. The man standing
inside the door left without a word. The Foreign Affairs
man waved them in. "Please."

"Thank you," Brognola said as he stepped into the room,
"but Mr. Tucker can take me the moment we finish here."

Fujitsu nodded, closed the door and left.

Sighing with momentary relief, Brognola took the chair
behind the desk and pulled up his pant leg and pushed down
his sock. The wounds looked ugly and already showed signs
of bruising and swelling. Tucker went over to look.

Brognola grabbed several tissues from a box on a desk
and began to dab at the three puncture wounds in his leg.
None of them had gone through, flooding him with a new
sense of disgust as he realized a doctor would have to probe
for the pellets and injure the area even further. He applied
pressure with a half-dozen tissues.

"You weren't serious about having to call in before you
went to the hospital, were you?" Tucker asked.

He shook his head. "I did need to borrow this office for
a few minutes, though."

"For what?"

Brognola took another handful of tissues from the box.
The wounds were starting to throb. "Did you get a look at
the gunner's right hand?"

"Not really. I was more interested in making sure the security team knew whose side we were on before they came in and finished the job."

"The last joint of his little finger was missing."

"Are you working out some kind of Sherlock Holmes fetish here?"

"No. I just know that the Yakuza have a code of cutting off the last joint of the little finger when they screw something up. If the guy was Yakuza, that means he could have been an assassin hired by someone local to pop us as we came through the door."

"He could be a guy who went around the bend today and happened to have lost that finger in a childhood accident. You stay in Justice long enough, you start finding Mafia bozos everywhere. Even in Japan."

Brognola scowled. "Do you usually play devil's advocate, Tucker, or do they really not teach you to guys to think when you're in training? Do they just point you at an obstacle or a person and let you go?"

The agent smiled, seating himself on the edge of the desk. "I'll force myself to remember that you're a gravely injured man and not operating with all of your faculties at the moment."

"You do that." Brognola removed the tissues. He opened a desk drawer and found a small tube with Japanese writing on it among the other office supplies. He held it up. "Is this what I think it is?"

"If you think it's heavy-duty glue, it is."

"That's what I thought it was." Brognola set it on the desktop. "Do you think you could get me a bottle of Drano from the building maintenance people?"

"Drano?"

"Or an equivalent. Just so that it's ninety-five percent sodium hydroxide."

Tucker gazed at him for a moment in silence. "You're serious?"

"Yes."

"Shit. What have you got up your sleeve?"

"An arm." Brognola pushed himself up out of the swivel chair. "Find me a bottle of Drano, and I'll show you an old beat cop's trick."

Tucker moved for the door. "Anything else?"

"A cotton ball."

"Where am I supposed to get a cotton ball?"

"If the building maintenance people don't have any, ask one of those pretty, young secretaries out there. This looks like the kind of job that could cause a lot of headaches. I bet you'll find one of them who has an aspirin bottle. Haven't you heard of improvisation?"

"Sure. I can make a garrote out of a hair clip. I'll show you how when I get back. That way we can swap trade secrets." He left.

Walking more gingerly now that the pain had set in, Brognola limped to the door and out into the hall for a glass of water at the fountain. Fujitsu was supervising the entire operation, taking a 35 mm camera from a man who was snapping pictures of the corpse and doing the job himself. Watching as the man shed his jacket and rolled up his shirtsleeves before lying prone on the floor, Brognola realized the Foreign Affairs guy took his job seriously. Even as Fujitsu advanced the film for each successive shot, he was issuing orders to the men around him.

Brognola took his cup of water back inside the office and closed the door. He found an ashtray, standard issue and unused, on top of a filing cabinet and brought it back to the desk. Sitting down, he applied another handful of tissues to his leg. A moment later he rechecked it. Satisfied that he had stopped most of the bleeding, he took his handkerchief and wrapped it around the leg, tying it with a loose knot to keep part of the pressure on.

Opening the desk drawer again, he took out a paper clip and a pencil. There was nothing in the small rubber trash can beside the desk except a handful of paper, which he left on the floor when he emptied it. He used his pocketknife to make a slit in the side of the trash can near the bottom, then widened it until the pencil slid through and was held in place.

Tucker entered the room, carrying a small canister. "It's not Drano, but it is ninety-five percent sodium hydroxide."

Brognola took it and sprinkled a light dusting across the bottom of the ashtray, then added the water. "Did you get the cotton ball?"

Tucker rolled it across the table.

Uncapping the glue, Brognola squirted a generous portion onto the cotton ball after flattening it.

"Are you going to tell me what you're doing," Tucker asked, "or do I have to wait until you actually pull the rabbit out of the hat?"

Brognola put the cotton to one side and reached into his pocket for his wallet. He pulled out the credit card, carefully avoiding touching either surface. "I'm making a set of prints so that we can follow up on Shotgun Sam ourselves. If the guy has a record—and I'm betting he does because the missing little finger points to a screwup of some sort—Interpol might have him on file." He slipped the paper clip onto one corner of the credit card and hooked the other end of the clip over the pencil poking through the inside of the trash can.

"You're going to make a set of prints on your credit card?"

"It was the only thing I had handy at the time." Brognola set the trash can down gently.

"Why not American Express? You're not supposed to leave home without it."

"The Visa has a smooth surface above the imprinted information. American Express has a line between the two colors that would show up. Do you wear contacts?"

"No."

Brognola grunted and dropped the glue-smeared cotton ball into the mixture in the ashtray. A pink film formed over the cotton immediately. He set the trash can upside down on the desk over the ashtray and leaned back in the swivel chair.

"Why did you ask about the contacts?" Tucker asked.

"Because the chemical reaction I've just started releases cyanoacrylic esters in the fumes that would glue them to your eyes. At least it would glue them to your eyes until a doctor cut them off."

"Doesn't sound pleasant."

"I wouldn't know."

Tucker moved toward the windows and pulled down a blind to look outside. "It's raining again."

Brognola grunted, then studied the CIA man. There was nothing he could put his finger on, but his instincts told him something was bothering the man. He glanced at his watch—11:17. Bolan should have checked in by now. Thoughts as dark as the cloud outside the window crowded into his mind. He lifted the phone and left a message for Michael Belasko.

Thirty minutes passed in studied silence as he reorganized his line of thinking. He could tell from the brief emotions flitting across Tucker's face that the young agent was doing some reevaluations of his own. Lifting the trash can from the desk, he unclipped the credit card as Tucker came over to observe the results.

Three white latent prints stood out against the gray background of the card. The ones on the white back of the card didn't stand out as well, but he could feel the ridges. Putting the trash can away, he dumped the papers back inside and dropped the disposable ashtray into his drinking cup. On their way out he could dump the contents down the john.

"It doesn't look like much," Brognola said as he put the ruined credit card back into his wallet, "but it may be just enough to get us into the game."

"You still sure you want in on this?" Tucker asked.

"Oh, yeah." Brognola limped toward the door. "I want in even more now than ever." He wondered where the hell Striker was and how badly the mission had been compromised.

CHAPTER THREE

Brown water gurgled around Tuley as the Subaru continued toward the river bottom. It streamed in through both windows, rapidly filling the small car's interior. Marashanski was deadweight pressing against him. The man's forehead had all but been erased by at least one of Belasko's rounds.

He pushed the corpse off him as he moved toward the window and tried to fight his way through the water. Panic surged through him like the beating of a drum. His fingers clawed for purchase on the doorframe, sliding away as he felt his fingernails rip and tear. Marashanski floated up with the water to throw dead arms around his neck. He brushed the corpse away again and shoved himself upward, finding that the air pocket remaining inside the vehicle had been reduced to a matter of inches.

Flattening against the top of the Subaru, he sucked in the air greedily, tasting the taint of the river overriding everything else. Then the car shifted again, overturning as it struck the riverbank and finished filling the air pocket.

He tried not to let himself think how far under he was as he pulled himself toward the window. Desperation gave him strength. He stared into the filmy brown murk around him as he kicked free of the car, trying to figure where "up" was. Suddenly he was swallowed by the undertow created by the sinking car. The last few saucer-sized bubbles exploded from the vehicle, and it dropped from sight faster, sucking him down with it.

He fought to resist, knowing his flailing was burning up the oxygen remaining in his lungs even faster. Turning away from the pull of the undertow, he watched as a shadow took form in front of him and wondered if Marashanski's body had somehow slipped free. Then hard fingers closed around his wrist and pulled him upward. Free of the undertow, he swam for the surface, forcing thoughts of waiting Japanese police from his mind.

When he surfaced, he found himself almost in the middle of the river. He treaded water, panting, and checked to make sure he still had the .45 holstered at the small of his back.

Vardeman broke the surface beside him, shaking his head like a wet dog. The bandanna the man had tied over his bald head to protect it from the sun gave him the appearance of a pirate, especially with the long fringe he kept on the sides. "Marashanski?" the big man asked.

Tuley shook his head, still panting from the exertion. "Dead before we hit the water."

"Too bad. The kid was starting to show some promise." He started swimming toward an approaching speedboat that carried three knife-wielding youths. "We need transportation, Cap'n."

Tuley drew the .45, freezing as he went for his shot, barely having time to see the tillerman thrown backward and out into the water as the heavy bullet nailed the guy in the chest. Water closed over him for a moment as the recoil pushed him back down. When he resurfaced, Vardeman had a hand on the boat, hanging on to it as the motor died. The remaining two men rushed at him with their weapons. Tuley's .45 took another one out as Vardeman caught the remaining man's elbow in his hand and dragged the guy out of the boat.

Swimming toward the speedboat, aware that more of the fishermen were working their way toward them now, Tuley saw Vardeman take the smaller guy under. As he put a hand on the stern of the speedboat and pulled himself out of the water, a crimson cloud spread under the river surface. A moment later Vardeman came up holding the captured knife.

Tuley seated himself by the motor, and soon it roared to powerful life. He had to yell to make himself heard over the noise as Vardeman clambered aboard. "What about Ellison?"

Vardeman pointed at his own body with two fingers. "Two shots through the heart that you could have laid a playing card over."

"Did they get Belasko?" Tuley powered the craft through a narrowing gap between two fishing boats as the crews tried to cut him off.

"No."

Tuley scanned the riverbanks as crowds converged on the scene, pointing and talking. The insistent screaming of police sirens cut through the popping of the outboard motor.

Vardeman grinned and adjusted his bandanna. "We'll get him, Cap'n. At least one of your shots hit him. I saw the blood. McElroy's group is on him now. He can run, but he can't hide."

Tuley pulled the outboard against the east riverbank under the Komagata Bridge south of the battle zone. Gun in hand, he waved away the handful of people standing near the dock. Then he glanced back and saw the first police car roll into view, its pale blue cherry flashing. Doors opened and men got out just as another thunderclap of autofire rang out. The policemen took cover behind their vehicle, peering anxiously into the crowd. "Doesn't sound like Belasko's going to give up easily, does it?"

Vardeman didn't answer.

"You got your walkie-talkie?"

"No. I lost it when I went under for you."

Tuley felt the chill of the wind and glanced up to see dark clouds gathering.

"There's no sense in trying to call those men off," Vardeman said. "Some of those guys Belasko killed were friends of theirs, and they know he was hurt. Got that blood smell in their noses now. If they can get Belasko quickly, they'll still have time to drop into the arranged checkpoints and vanish before the locals get them. Speaking of which..." The big man indicated the crowd inching toward them.

Tuley lifted the .45 and watched the group fall back. Then he and Vardeman set off toward the dilapidated warehouse that covered their escape route.

"We need time to figure out that son of a bitch," Tuley said.

"We don't have a lot of time if we stick to Sacker's schedule."

"Sacker's original schedule didn't include Belasko. This guy was a write-in from out of the blue. We have dossiers on everybody else. Sacker's always been good at researching intel, so why can he only come up with a handful of rumors on this guy?"

Vardeman shrugged. "As long as he keeps the paychecks regular and the politics to the right of right, what have we ever cared? You and me, buddy, we learned how to fight and to kill a long time ago. It's what we do, and as long as we both agree that Sacker's the man to do the paying, I don't see that we've got a bitch coming. Sacker handles the details, but he doesn't do the hands-on research anymore. We've known that for years, and it didn't scare us away." He flashed a brief grin. "All this, and you still get to work for the benefit of the U.S. of A. at the same time."

Tuley kicked open the warehouse door and covered the scattering shadows in the big, empty room with the .45, feeling the other man at his elbow, backing him up, without ever seeing him. The crowd continued its pursuit at a safe distance as the police car slowly forced its way through them. The siren had been turned off, but the blue cherry continued to flash. There were no further shots fired.

"Sounds like it's over," Vardeman grunted.

"I don't think so." Tuley spread the contents of a jerrican across the wooden floor, then followed Vardeman down into the narrow tunnel. He took a flare from a recess beneath the first rung of the ladder they'd descended, popped it and tossed it onto the floor. Flames whooshed across the wooden planking. Satisfied, he pulled the door closed over him, leaving only the yellow glare of Vardeman's flashlight. He followed Vardeman down into the darkness of the sewer, still wondering who Belasko was and what the man's continued survival might mean to their mission.

THE MOP HANDLE splintered across the gunner's nose and forehead, knocking the man backward. Bolan dropped the few inches remaining in his hand as he knelt for the assault rifle. He fisted it in blood-slick fingers and winced when the wound in his side sent electric jolts of pain through his body as he cradled the weapon and rolled for the opposite side of the alley. Then, bringing the muzzle up, he regained his feet, still in a crouch.

Four men spread out in front of him, bringing their weapons to bear. The Executioner touched off a 3-round burst that stitched the first man from navel to neck and threw him to the ground. The second burst would have chopped through the next man's head except the CAR-15 clicked empty after the first bullet. The man still went down, but the remaining two fired on full-auto, driving chips of brick at Bolan as rock dust clouded his vision.

He dropped the useless weapon, knowing he'd never have the chance to check the other man for extra magazines. Pushing himself to his feet, he risked a glance around the corner before heading back into the street.

The man on the right dropped his assault rifle and used both hands to grasp the black-feathered arrow that suddenly filled his left eye. His scream was piercing, then faded to nothing as he fell.

The remaining man scanned the walls for the unseen enemy. A black shadow stepped from concealment on a second-story balcony, another arrow already nocked in the black bow that was held by black-gloved hands. The gunner tried to rake the figure from the balcony with the CAR-15 on full-auto, and a ragged line of pockmarks climbed up the brick wall toward the unmoving archer.

Bolan watched the bowstring slide through the archer's fingers, then made his dive toward the man he'd stunned with the mop handle. His fingers found the .45 in the hip holster and ripped it free, lifting it to cover the black-garbed figure on the balcony. The gunner was down in the alley, the black shaft of an arrow poking dead center through his chest.

Peering across the open sights of the .45, the Executioner saw that the archer had another arrow ready but wasn't pointing it at him. At that moment police sirens cut through the din of screams and excited voices behind him.

"There's no time," the archer said in a muffled voice, keeping one hand on the bow and arrow while shaking a length of knotted rope from a backpack. "Hurry."

Bolan released the hammer on the automatic and paused to grab the three extra clips the man at his feet was carrying. He jammed the .45 into his waistband, reached for the knotted silk cord and began pulling himself up as a police car roared around the corner of the alley and came to a stop almost directly below him. Two clean-cut Japanese plainclothes detectives tried to disembark.

As Bolan reached for the wrought-iron railing of the balcony, the archer fired and drew smoothly three times, keeping an arrow at the ready. Startled shouts, interspersed with the breaking of glass and the screech of torn metal, came from below. He looked, expecting to find bodies of the two policemen sprawled in the alley with the corpses of the other men, but he was glad to see the arrows hadn't been directed at flesh-and-blood targets. The detectives had taken cover back inside their car. Three arrows protruded from the white sheet metal, still quivering from the force of the bow.

Moving with an economy of motion, the archer removed the grappling hook of the silk cord from the balcony and flipped it toward the top of the building only four yards up. "Go," the archer commanded in a muffled voice, handing Bolan the rope.

The warrior hesitated, not wanting to leave his unknown companion unaided, not knowing if he was only leaving one firing line for another.

"Go," the archer repeated, bending the bow to send a black arrow crashing through the police car's windshield. "They're not going to stay there long, and I won't kill them. They're going to realize that in a moment, and we're going to be sitting ducks. You're wounded. I'm not."

Bolan grabbed the cord in his hands as authoritative commands in Japanese filled the alley. The warrior used his feet to aid him in his scramble to the top and felt the weakness in his side slow him slightly as his head spun. But he forced the pain and weakness away and reached for the battle edge that had kept him going since Vietnam. Then, rolling over the top, he drew the .45, peered back down and fired a shot that ripped off the side mirror on the driver's side as the archer threw the bow over one shoulder and seemed to flow up the rope.

The archer hit the rooftop running, dragging the cord while hurriedly wrapping it in a coil around one arm. Before they reached the other side of the building, it had been returned to the backpack. The archer didn't hesitate, using a hand to swing out onto a narrow canopy below, saying, "Walk where I walk or you'll fall through."

Bolan nodded, dropping to the canopy and feeling it bend under his weight where it hadn't under his companion's. He reached for the archer, laying a big hand on a thin shoulder. "Wait. I want to know what's going on."

The archer spun quickly, flinging his arm off, one hand filled with a black stiletto filed to a needle point. Bolan pulled his hand back but the stiletto stayed where it was in the clenched fist. The eyes, which were the only part of the archer's face revealed by the black ski mask, were moist and brown, delicately almond shaped. "Don't touch me," the muffled voice said hoarsely.

Bolan nodded, aware of the crowd milling in the alley at their feet, knowing they would draw the Metropolitan Police to the area quickly.

"There's no time to go into all of that," the archer said, making the stiletto disappear. "You can trust me to lead you to safety, or you can make your own way."

"I'm not wanted by the police," Bolan pointed out. "Those men tried to kill me."

"Suit yourself. But if you get yourself killed by any of those men who might still be in the area while you're trying to explain that to the policemen down there, it'll defeat my reason for saving you."

"And what reason is that?"

"Later." The archer leaped from the canopy to the rooftop of another building.

Bolan followed, landing more heavily. "At least those policemen below are in a uniform I recognize."

"Even then their intentions may not be what you think they should be. Nothing is ever what it seems." The brown eyes gazed at him speculatively. "I don't think the night or murder finds a stranger in you any more than it did in those men we left behind."

He returned the direct gaze full measure, wondering at the challenge he found there. He cataloged the weapons his companion carried, noticing the short Japanese sword sheathed between the guy's shoulders under the quiver, knowing the loose folds of the black coverall concealed even more. The split-toed black *tabi* on the archer's feet drew attention to their smallness, making him realize how small the man really was.

Pressing his free hand to the wound in his side, Bolan followed the archer across the rooftops, twisting and turning behind the higher buildings to lose anyone who might attempt to follow them the same way. His head was full of questions, wondering how much of what had happened to him in the past half hour had to do with Brognola's reasons for calling him to Tokyo. It wasn't his way to go into a situation blind, nor was it the big Fed's way to send him into a hellzone without a background workup.

He crouched beside the archer on a building ledge under a brightly colored canopy that waved in the rising breeze. Balanced precariously, they inched down the ledge, hugging the rough brick facing.

The archer knelt and lifted a window, then slid inside. Bolan eased through a moment later, hardly getting his feet on the floor before his rescuer threw a sash-bound bundle at his chest. He looked around the small hotel room, noting the sway-backed bed and the paint peeling from the walls.

"There isn't much time," the archer said, slipping out of the black coverall. *Her* body was slender, the color of dusky olive, more girlish than showing the full bloom of womanhood, but the warrior put her age at somewhere on the right side of thirty.

He unwrapped his bundle and found loose Japanese-styled clothing inside. "Get dressed," she said, pulling the ski mask from her face and letting her long black hair fall to her shoulders. "They'll be searching for us."

He couldn't help noticing that she kept her weapons within easy reach at all times, just as he did. He peeled off his bloody shirt, grimacing as it pulled from his side. "Who are you?" he asked, dropping the garment into the plastic bag she pulled from an inside pocket of her clothing.

She shook her head.

"What was that all about?"

"They were trying to kill you," she said, glancing at the torn flesh of his side. She produced a roll of adhesive tape and tossed it to him.

He caught the tape and glanced down at the wound in his side for the first time. There were two holes: one going in and the other, slightly larger, going out, less than two inches apart. Nothing vital had been injured, but both entrance and exit wounds would need stitches to heal correctly. Most of the bleeding had stopped.

"Can you manage?" she asked hesitantly.

He looked up, catching her staring at the accumulation of scars crisscrossing his body. "Yes."

A police siren sounded outside.

"Who were those men?" he asked as he tore generous swatches from the bed sheets and folded them into squares, taping each one into place.

"I don't know," she replied.

"How did you know they would try to kill me?"

"I didn't know who their target was. I just knew there would be one."

He stepped out of his blood-stained jeans, pausing to remove his passport and papers and tucking them into a pocket of the clothing he had been provided with. A fistful of yen followed next, split into three divisions in separate sections of his clothing. He dropped the jeans into the plastic bag, then stepped into the dark gray pants and cinched them so that they'd help keep the pressure on the makeshift bandages. "How did you know they'd be there?"

"That's not important."

Bolan used the tape to secure the .45's extra magazines to the backs of his calves, wrapping them in layers so that he could peel them free one at a time if the need arose. "It suggests that you had foreknowledge of their attempt on me," he said in a flat voice. Pain, dull and throbbing, hammered his body as he straightened back up. His head spun for a moment. He indicated the clothing. "So does this."

She faced him without speaking.

"Why didn't you go to the police?"

"I couldn't."

"Why?"

Her face settled into hard lines. "For reasons that are my own and don't involve you."

"They involve me enough for you to kill two men on my behalf."

"I had no choice after I discovered their intentions."

Bolan's voice became ice-cold. "You had plenty of choice, lady."

"Meaning the police?"

He nodded.

Her laugh was dry and bitter. "If you're that naive, then you have a lot to learn about the way life works over here. Some of the Tokyo policemen are no better than their American counterparts when it comes to taking bribes. If I had gone to them, you might be dead now, and me with you. No, thank you. I learned a long time ago not to trust anyone I didn't have to."

The woman dropped into a cross-legged position on the floor long enough to secure her weapons in a roll-up tote bag, tossing it over her shoulder when she had finished. The black bow had unscrewed when unstrung, each half not much longer than the quiver of arrows. A baseball cap featuring a Tokyo Tigers patch completed her ensemble.

"Now that you've got me, what do you intend to do with me?" Bolan asked as he followed her out of the room.

"I'm going to find you a doctor, then you're on your own," she replied. Her face was expressionless beneath the cap.

"You saved me only to let me go? Without telling me what's going on?"

"I didn't have any choice about saving you," the woman said. "If you could have gotten away on your own, I wouldn't have been distracted from my real target. Thanks to your involvement I've temporarily lost the only lead I had."

Bolan remained silent as they walked out onto the street, having deposited the plastic bag containing their clothes into a large trash bin inside the hotel. People flowed around them, moving in all directions. Uniformed policemen walked within the confines of the crowd, looking in every direction. "You're not a pro, are you?" he asked.

"If you mean, do I kill people for greed or government, then no, I'm not. I've been trained to take care of myself."

"Evidently more than most."

Her responding smile was slight, without humor. "As you say. I had a most demanding teacher."

A policeman crossed the street in front of them, walking against the flow of pedestrian traffic. People grumbled and spread out around him.

Bolan moved more to the right, not wanting to cross the street to avoid the man, trying to shrink inside his clothes so that his height wouldn't be so apparent. His own dark hair would pass at a glance, as would his dark complexion. "Have you given any thought to what might happen if we're discovered?" he asked as the policeman came toward them.

"Don't be discovered." Her words were flat and final.

The policeman was less than twenty feet away when Bolan put an arm around her shoulders. He felt her tense, about to spin away from him. "Don't," he whispered. "They're looking for a man apart from the crowd, not someone who's here with a girlfriend. Put your arm around my waist and smile." The policeman looked at them briefly, then went on. They passed under the brightly painted gateway of Sensoji temple a few moments later, stepping into a courtyard ringed by tall oak trees.

She broke their embrace and moved a step away. The sky let loose with a sudden torrential downpour. The woman pulled her clothing tightly around her, moving quickly toward one of the smaller buildings clustered together on the east side of the courtyard.

She passed through the doorway without hesitation, calling out a name. The room was large by Japanese standards, at least sixteen tatami—traditional rush mats—covered the floor. Then a rice paper door slid open to Bolan's left, allowing a small man approximately the woman's age to step into the room.

"Akemi," she said, bowing slightly, then spoke rapidly in Japanese.

After a few moments, Akemi turned to look at Bolan, his gaze lingering on the Executioner's eyes before dropping to the general area of the wound in his side.

Bolan stood so that he could keep them in view as he watched the crowd thinning out of the courtyard. Every dry place available outside filled with people as umbrellas began to mushroom in increasing numbers. When he turned back to face the man and woman, he found that she had gone. He moved forward, intending to find her because she was his only lead to what was going on.

"You will not find her," the man said in heavily accented English.

Ignoring the words, Bolan stepped through a curtained doorway, finding a much smaller room on the other side with more knee pillows organized across the floor. Three blank walls greeted him.

"She's gone," he said, turning back to the man, who was now kneeling in front of a row of candles.

"Hai." The man nodded as he lit a trio of candles, then carried them toward Bolan. "She still has much to do." He waved toward the small room. "Please come. She has told me of your wound. I will tend it for you." He waited, holding the curtain open, his eyes alert and careful.

Bolan hesitated. "The police will be looking for me. It won't be safe for you if I stay here."

"She told me this, but she knew I would not turn you away if she asked. We have been friends many years, she and I. We have trusts between each other that will not be broken."

"She doesn't even know me."

"I know, and that is why she told me not to give you her name, but she has seen that you are aligned against her enemies. Please come and sit down. Your wounds are already bleeding through again. If you continue to ignore them, nothing I can do will keep you from the hospital."

Bolan stepped into the room, followed by Akemi.

"Please take off your shirt and lie down," the Japanese said, pointing to a cot.

When the warrior complied, the man knelt at his side, a shallow pan of water gripped in one hand, first-aid items in the other. His face was impassive. "There will be some pain."

"I know."

"I see that you do."

A lukewarm cloth swabbed at Bolan's side. He isolated the pain, breathing steadily to reduce the discomfort. "Your name is Akemi?"

"Hai."

"You know that she's in danger?"

"Hai."

Bolan remembered the taut, unblemished body that had been revealed to him in the hotel room. The lack of scars had told of a lack of knowledge of violence just as his own testified to many such confrontations. "There were at least a dozen men who tried to kill me back at the river. How can she expect to hold her own against something like that?"

"She feels she has no choice."

"She told you that?"

Akemi paused in his ministrations to look into Bolan's eyes. "I know that for myself without being told. Life is a series of trails, some traveled more, some traveled less so, each finding its own way. Some of these trails are not of our own choosing, yet we must follow them. It is a burden of honor, of duty. Were we unfettered to choose freely the substance of our lives, we might never encounter the crucible that transforms us into something more than we were."

"You could help her."

"No. I have given up the warrior's path."

"You'd sit here and let her throw her life away going up against the kind of people who tried to kill me?"

Akemi paused. "I have given my word."

"I could help her."

"Maybe."

"Help me help her before she's hurt."

"Name a way that I may."

Bolan looked deep into the man's eyes, finding a sadness there. He let it go, knowing if he continued to pressure the man he'd only be banging his head against a wall of silence.

Akemi's fingers probed and prodded, smeared medicants inside and over the two wounds. The salve had a sharp odor, pungent and stringent, stinging at first before settling into a warm and gentle burn.

"Do you know who those men were?" Bolan asked.

Pulling slender, black thread through the tiny jar of salve, Akemi said, "No. I know only what the radio has said of them. They were Caucasians carrying papers that identified them as Americans and Europeans." He passed one end of the thread through the eye of a needle, pulled it taut, then began to sew.

"The papers were probably faked," Bolan said, ignoring the bee stings in his side. "Those men were professionals and probably had police records."

"I think so as well."

"You're very knowledgeable for someone who spends his time locked away in a shrine," Bolan observed.

Akemi raised an eyebrow and flashed a quick smile. "I was not always here, nor did I always try to follow a quiet life."

"Would you know where an American with money might go if he needed false papers to get around Tokyo?"

"I have heard of people who deal in merchandise like that."

"I need their names."

"I will get them for you."

"As well as where they do their business."

"Hai."

Bolan watched the man's fingers move quickly and surely, joining the two ragged edges of flesh.

"You were very lucky. The bullet hit nothing vital."

Bolan nodded.

"Many people were not so lucky. I have heard that the rescue squads are still dragging the river for bodies."

"She could have prevented that by going to the police."

Akemi took up another stitch, nodding. "Maybe, and maybe she saved the lives she needed to. Perhaps things could have gone even worse with more guns there. Bullets know no morality once leaving the weapon. A sword cuts more true."

Bolan noticed the almost hidden trace of pain in the man's words, wondered briefly at its cause.

"What makes you worry about her?" Akemi asked.

Glancing at the man, Bolan said, "She might not know what she's getting into."

"And you do?"

"Not yet, but I will."

"Yet you were almost killed getting this far."

"The operative word is *almost*."

"And you are a professional in these matters?"

"Yes."

"So why worry about her and what she does?"

Bolan didn't answer.

"You do not think she is your enemy?"

"Not yet."

Akemi snipped the thread with a small scissors, then dropped the needle and the excess thread into the pan of water. He rinsed the wound again and applied more salve. "Sit up, please."

Bolan did so, grunting with the effort.

"There will be inflammation and swelling," Akemi said as he covered the area with a gauze pad. He took a roll of gauze and began wrapping it around Bolan's waist, taping it into place every few inches. "I have some penicillin tablets I can give you, but I suggest getting a tetanus booster as soon as you can as well as a penicillin shot to fight infection. I have cleaned everything out as well as I could, but it would be wise not to take chances."

"When I can," Bolan agreed, standing slowly. "For now it'll have to do."

Akemi cleared away his first-aid equipment. He returned with fresh clothing, a notepad and a pen and proceeded to write as Bolan put on the clothes.

The pants were a little loose but fit over the bandages with little discomfort. The shirt was enormous, with sleeves reaching well past his wrists. He rolled them up, peering through the doorway at the people still crowded away from the rain. He remembered the way the woman had reacted the first time he'd touched her, how she'd squirmed away from his arm on the street, the look that had been in her brown eyes after the bloodletting in the alley. "She hadn't killed before, had she?" he asked.

Pausing in his writing, Akemi answered without looking up. "No."

"I'm interested in her," he said as he tucked money into his clothes. "I'd like to preserve the innocence I saw in her eyes." He taped the .45 to his ankle, satisfied the loose slacks would conceal it.

"You might be too late," Akemi replied, handing him a list of names. "There is much more here than you know. You do not even know if the problem that brought you to Tokyo has anything to do with her."

"Those dead men answered that. It all ties in somewhere. I'll just have to figure out where."

"I wish you well on your quest then."

Bolan folded the list and put it into his pocket.

"Those men might not be the only ones who offer false papers," Akemi said, "but all of those listed there are dangerous men. You will be taking your life in your own hands if you attempt to confront them."

The warrior nodded and walked to the door. He tapped his wounded side gently and offered his thanks as he stepped out into the rain.

Locating a phone outside the shrine proper, he dialed the number that would put him in contact with Brognola. There were no policemen in sight, but he knew they wouldn't be far away. An operator answered him in Japanese and he gave Brognola's name. The voice went on, coming to a stop when he told the operator he didn't speak Japanese. A moment later another operator came on the line. "Yes?" the new voice said.

"I'd like to speak to Hal Brognola."

"May I ask who is calling?"

"Michael Belasko. He should be expecting me. I was calling to let him know I was going to be detained."

"Ah, I'm sorry, Mr. Belasko, but I'm afraid I have some bad news. Mr. Brognola was wounded in an attack only a few moments ago. I've been instructed to tell you he is en route to Tokyo Eisei Byoin Hospital."

"How badly is he hurt?"

"I wasn't told. I can arrange for someone to pick you up if you wish."

Bolan politely declined and hung up. He walked away into the rain, turning his thoughts to the list of names Akemi had provided. One way or another there was nothing he could do for Brognola now, but he could start shaking things up until something rattled loose. He was going to introduce the nightlife of Tokyo to the Executioner, and begin hunting the hunters.

CHAPTER FOUR

Mack Bolan kept a thumb over the bloodstained corners of his papers as he presented them to the woman at the counter of the car rental agency. She went through the motions hurriedly, writing down the credit card numbers logged in the Belasko name.

Once processed, he called Kurtzman at Stony Man Farm while his car was being serviced. Bear came on the line before the third ring ended after the connection was routed through the various overseas checkpoints and rerouted through local exchanges so that it couldn't be traced to its destination.

"This is Striker," he said into the mouthpiece, standing away from the wall so that he could survey the rain-darkened streets. "Something's gone wrong at this end of the ride."

Kurtzman's voice became clipped and professional. "Where are you now?"

"In the city."

"Alone?"

"For now. It got pretty chummy about an hour and a half ago. You should be hearing about it through the news services soon."

"I think I already have. The action down on the riverside?"

"That's the place." He shifted inside the new clothes he'd bought before going to get the car.

"Did you make your meet?"

"Negative."

"No brief?"

"No brief."

"Damn, Striker, I wish I could spread a little of the dirt your way, but we're on a tight line at this end. Lots of big doings in the air."

"That's what I was told."

"Without a secure line at your end, too, I can't say a word."

"Understood. I was just checking in to see if you had any messages for me."

"Nary a one. But I can tell you that you're smack dab in the middle of radioactive lands, guy, and could get burned from any direction. This property you're checking into is definitely not exclusive, if you catch my drift."

"Check." Bolan moved the .45 in his waistband, taking some of the direct pressure off his wound. Nothing was comfortable. "You might see if you can turn up the big guy over here and let him know I've still got a place in the game."

"Will do."

"The last I heard he was checking into a hospital."

"I hadn't heard that." Concern filled Kurtzman's voice.

"See what you can find out on the sly and I'll get back to you."

"You got it. In the meantime I'll see if I can set up a secure line to your neck of the woods, just in case the bottom has dropped out on this thing. You going to be around?"

"Yeah. I picked up an angle of my own to work."

"How are you set on hardware?"

"Making do. So far this mission has been anything but first class."

"I'll see what I can do, but I can't promise anything."

"Understood."

"Take care, Striker."

"You, too." Bolan broke the connection and moved toward the service area. His first scheduled stop was in the

Asakusa district, at a nightclub called Scoundrels, followed by two more in the same area. He'd grouped them geographically so that he could cover more of them in less time. None of them opened before 5:00 p.m. In the four and a half hours until then, he intended to see if he could upgrade his armament while maintaining a low profile and do some preliminary work on recon. Once he opened the play, there was no telling which way the action would run. If the opening numbers were any indication, it was going to be a hell of a horse race.

"GODDAMN IT," Brognola growled as he limped around on the wooden cane the emergency room had supplied him. "I've got a man loose in this shitstorm somewhere, Tucker, and that sandbag routine you're giving me is helping keep him out there." He cast a baleful gaze over the carnage spread out along the banks of the Sumida River and the surrounding streets.

A tugboat with an impressive winch arm was dragging a battered Subaru from the river bottom. The big Fed felt his jaw tighten when he saw the bullet holes stitched across the windshield and the dead man's arm flop in the window. A trio of yellow fire trucks sat in front of a burned warehouse on the other side of the river while a dozen men searched through the rubble. There were eight police cars on the scene at last count, and at least thirty police officers. Ambulances picked up the dead in an organized fashion, each one filling up before letting the next one move into the vacated space. The crowd still hovered on the edge of the police line.

"I saw Special Forces tattoos on a couple of those men," Brognola said in a hard voice when Tucker remained silent. "The kind a guy could pick up in Vietnam during the Phoenix Project. You remember that little operation, don't you, Tucker? You might be a couple years too young to have been there, but you've been around the Company long enough to know that was the CIA's prima donna bid in that Southeast Asian farce.''

Tucker jammed his hands into his pockets. The rubber-banded butt of his .44 stuck out from the folds of his jacket. He turned to face Brognola, his sunglasses a dark line across his eyes. "Yeah, I know about the Phoenix Project."

"What else do you know?"

"I know that some of these guys were once CIA, though I doubt Langley will give that information to the Japanese."

"Once?"

Tucker nodded. "Once. This wasn't a Company-based operation, no matter what you think."

"Then tell me what to think."

Clenched muscles showed in Tucker's jawline. "Langley was aware of some of this. I was working on it, quietly, before things went haywire in the States. These guys are like phantoms, Hal. They cross borders without leaving a trail or, sometimes, without anyone knowing they were there for sure. They have big money behind them. It would take a lot of financial and political clout to get these guys to places undetected, and they've had it. So far they've only been hitting the Japanese interests, but nobody knows how long that's going to last." He looked away. "Hell, I've got guys on my payroll I don't even know I can trust."

"How long have you been aware of it?"

Tucker shrugged and watched a gurney being carried away, the occupant covered by a single bloody sheet. "I've known for the past month, since I was brought into the operation to figure out what the hell was going on. I couldn't tell you how long Langley has known. They wouldn't want me to tell you that much." He flashed a quick, mirthless smile. "I guess it doesn't matter. One way or the other, I figure this to be my last posting where I go in blind and stay that way. I'm not going to ask you to do the same."

Brognola leaned heavily on the cane he'd gotten from the hospital, his insides churning from the unreleased anger.

"What makes you think the guy they were after here was your man?" Tucker asked.

"The fact that he's missing and that we'd talked briefly about how he was coming into Tokyo. We didn't mention the water bus, but he had to get through Asakusa somehow. The description the detective gave sounded right."

Tucker nodded toward the line of ambulances. "Must be a hell of a guy to survive this and manage to stay free of the police, too. I overheard one of the officers mention that a big, dark man with black hair escaped the area with a ninja who dropped two of these guys in the alley with a bow and arrows."

"A ninja?"

"I kid you not, an honest-to-God ninja."

"And you thought I was reaching when I mentioned the possibility of the Yakuza."

"Ninjas exist," Tucker said. "I've seen them kill. They're in and out in an eye blink. It's something you don't forget." He looked at Brognola. "So tell me, do you Justice guys have somebody over here working with ninjas?"

"No."

An uneasy silence sprang up between them, punctuated by the creakings and bangings the tugboat made as it settled the wrecked car on its deck.

"Who is this mystery guy you brought in with you?" Tucker asked.

"Michael Belasko." Brognola limped back toward the CIA man's car, hoping to end the line of questioning. "How long before you can know who these guys were?"

Tucker fell into step beside him. "A few hours, probably. A few hours one way or the other. I should get something back sooner than Interpol gets back to you on that credit card you expressed them. It depends on how generous the home office is feeling."

"You mean, how brave."

"Maybe I do. Who's Belasko?"

Brognola came to a stop and swiveled on the cane. "Surely you've read his file by now."

"Yeah, I've read it, and it didn't mention anywhere in it how this guy had the training to move through this kind of action unscathed."

"From what I understood the detective to say, Belasko didn't make it through this encounter unscathed. He was wounded. How badly remains to be seen."

"I've also heard that you have access to a pet shark you sometimes throw into situations like this," Tucker said. "A one-man demolition squad who lives by that old axiom of 'kill 'em all and let God sort 'em out.' I've also heard him called other names than Belasko, other names that summon up whole other histories."

Brognola didn't say anything.

"Everybody's got a little dirt on them. It's an occupational hazard. You might remember that when you start pointing out dirty hands in this business."

"I'll give it some thought."

"God, but you're a hardass." Tucker's look was open and honest. "I want to run this aboveboard if I can, and all the secrets I had just got passed on to you. So are we in this together or what?"

Brognola started toward the car again. "I don't speak Japanese."

"Terrific," Tucker sighed.

"Have you got anyone working stateside on this thing?" Brognola asked after the younger man got into the car.

"Yeah, an agent named Winterroad has a lead on the pilot these guys used for the L.A. hit involving the publishing house. I should be hearing something about that soon." Tucker started the car and put it into gear.

Brognola continued looking out the window, massaging his leg with his hand as the pain continued to wash over him in waves. The wounds hadn't caused any permanent damage, but they had made the cane a necessity for the next few days. Uniformed policemen were still taking statements from the crowd.

A police car drove into the area and Goro Fujitsu got out. The detective who'd talked to Brognola and Tucker ran over immediately, falling into step with the Foreign Affairs man and talking animatedly.

"Fujitsu may be a half step behind for the moment," Tucker said, "but don't ever make the mistake of underestimating him."

"I won't," Brognola replied. "Despite whatever he's doing now, that man used to be a cop. You can see it in him if you know what to look for."

Tucker pulled the car into the flow of traffic. "You're worried about Belasko, aren't you?"

"I got him into this without telling him anything about it. He could have been killed because of me."

"It's the situation," the CIA man said in a soft voice. "Everyone's playing this one close to the vest. People are going to get hurt this time around, and there's not going to be a damn thing you can do about it."

Brognola didn't reply, but he felt the same way.

CHAPTER FIVE

"You should come across him 'bout there, I 'spect," the gnarled old counterman said. His face was long and lean under his Dallas Cowboys cap. He tapped with a jagged fingernail, smudging a bit of oily dirt across the hand-drawn map resting on the stained Formica between them.

John Winterroad took a mechanical pencil from his shirt pocket and made a light X next to the creek bend the man had indicated. His eyes felt rough and scratchy from the overnight flight from Los Angeles, and the extra caffeine he'd been running on since this morning was beginning to give him the shakes. It was already going on midnight, but he was too close to his quarry to back off now. He gave the old man a smile as he rolled up the map. "I appreciate it, Pop. Appreciate the information and appreciate your opening up long enough to take care of us."

A gap-toothed grin twisted the man's features as he hooked his thumbs into the bib of his faded overalls and walked Winterroad back to the door of the little general store. "Ah, it weren't no trouble, young fella. You got the look of a man who's been down the road apiece today. Can't rightly say I'd have felt good about turnin' you away when you come knockin'."

Winterroad shook hands with the old man, then headed for the rental car parked next to the two ancient gas pumps. Night had descended completely hours ago, leaving only hard and bright pinpricks of stars scattered across the black sky, smoothing the rough Vermont countryside. Harry

Vachs, his latest partner, sat in the front seat watching him with a bored expression.

He slid in behind the wheel and turned the key over as the old man locked the door and shuffled off to the stairway that led to his rooms over the store. The engine caught smoothly, and he pulled onto the two-lane road.

Vachs chewed his gum, blew a small bubble and popped it loudly between his teeth. A chrome-finished .357 Magnum gleamed in his lap. "You and the old guy have a nice chat?" he asked in the flat, Midwestern twang Winterroad had learned to hate during the past four months.

Glancing in the rearview mirror and finding only the night, Winterroad said, "He more or less gave us De Luca's campsite." He unfolded the hand-drawn map and passed it over for Vachs's inspection. "Never underestimate what you can gain by asking."

"Sure, but did you ever think De Luca might have tipped that old guy to put people on the wrong track?"

"If De Luca had been that smart, we wouldn't have been able to tail him this far." He watched the road carefully because the twists and turns of the high country were tricky at this time of night. They were even more so with the fatigue he kept at bay through an effort of will. He was irritated that Vachs had been up at least as long as he had but wasn't showing signs of discomfort yet.

Vachs reached for the overhead light.

"Don't turn that on," Winterroad barked.

The younger man glanced at him sharply. "How the hell do you expect me to look at this map?"

"There's a penflash in that packet of stuff I stored in the glove compartment. Use that."

Vachs popped another bubble as he reached for the glove compartment. "You know what your problem is, Winterroad?"

He didn't reply, knowing the younger man would tell him anyway.

"You're a tight-ass. You need to loosen up a little, relax and have some fun. Working for the CIA doesn't always have to be cloak-and-dagger bullshit."

The penflash flicked on, throwing a bright haze over the paper resting on Vachs's thigh.

"Instead of using the interior light," he said with heavy sarcasm, "we could put a neon light on the top and advertise that we're in the neighborhood."

"You're worrying for nothing. De Luca doesn't know us from Adam."

Winterroad rubbed an eye with a broad, bony knuckle. "He might not know you, but he sure as hell knows me. He's run a few operations with me."

Vachs flicked off the penlight. "That wasn't mentioned in the dossier we got on him."

"These weren't the kind of operations you'd find in the files. De Luca's a free-lance pilot, just like the information says, but he's run more covert action for the Company than they have listed there. Bet on it. Part of the reason I was assigned to this was because I know the guy." He slowed, watching his odometer click over the final tenth of a mile the old man had said would take him to the first turnoff.

The turn was difficult to locate because it was almost buried behind a towering oak with warped branches and a thick stand of Johnson grass. He made the turn and switched off the lights. Gravel popped under the tires with hollow sounds that echoed inside the car. He switched off the radio and listened to the thick silence crowd out the last strains of a heavy metal guitar.

"Hey," Vachs said, "that was Bon Jovi."

"I know. They've played that same song at least a dozen times since we got here this morning."

"It's a Top Forty station. What did you expect?"

Winterroad stopped the car abruptly, catching the younger man off balance as it slid toward the bar ditch on the right. Dust swirled up around them.

Vachs pushed himself back from the dash, an angry look starting to form on his unlined face. "Hey, what the hell—"

Grabbing the younger man by the throat, Winterroad slammed him against the door. Vachs tried to struggle, then gasped as Winterroad closed off his air supply. He tried to kick. Winterroad slammed him into the door again, pressing his face close to that of the younger man's, breath sounding like a bellows through his nostrils. "Listen to me, you scrawny little sack of shit, because what I have to tell you may save your life." He took Vachs's .357 away effortlessly and threw it into the back seat.

Vachs stopped struggling.

"You're a stupid, punk kid, Harry," Winterroad said through clenched teeth. He kept his partner from moving. "Up until now you've been assigned zip as far as truly dangerous work is concerned. You've done baby-sitting jobs in a handful of countries, done courier work in the South American backyard. You've even done a little lie-swapping with the known Communist spies between here and Moscow, and maybe you've made it with a few KGB women because the other agents said you weren't a man until you hopped into bed with a piece of ass that might kill you in midstroke." He took a deep breath. "Now, until you actually lay your balls on the line, not knowing who's going to walk away the winner, you haven't done a goddamn thing. Do you understand me?"

Defiance gleamed in the younger man's eyes.

"Eric De Luca's been around the block," Winterroad went on. "He's been in more dustups than you've heard about. He was part of a Medevac team in Vietnam, reenlisted as part of the Agency's Air America program in Laos and flew with the Ravens in the Steve Canyon Program. When he checked out of that, he turned freelance and pulled contacts with a lot of merc units in South Africa. He's as good a flyboy as you'd ever want to pick you up in a hot LZ.

That's why the Agency still uses him even though they know he works other jobs on the side."

The younger man didn't say anything.

Winterroad put the car in gear and moved forward slowly. "De Luca doesn't know the Agency's looking for him. That's why only a two-man team was put on him. That's why that file on him wasn't as complete as it should have been. The Company has been burned on this, but I don't know how or why. We're supposed to bring him in alive, or bring him in dead. Either way he gets taken down."

"You talk like this guy is some kind of goddamn hero. What makes you think you can shoot him?" Vachs's tone was full of resentment.

"Because if he sees me here, De Luca will know this is Agency business, and that he's the business. If he gets a chance, I know he'll try to kill me because he'll be thinking I'm there to kill him. I won't have a choice."

"And this is all over that publishing house in L.A.?"

Winterroad shook his head. "There's more to it than that."

The resentment in Vachs's voice reached a new peak. "Is this in some other file you've seen that I haven't?"

"No. This is reading between the lines. If you stay around the Agency long enough, you'll learn how to do that, too. Otherwise you don't survive this business." Winterroad took the next turnoff, winding down a narrow road that led toward the small creek the old man had told him about. So far so good.

Vachs turned in the seat and reached for the .357.

"Leave it there," Winterroad ordered. He turned off the car's lights and continued on in darkness.

"What the hell's the matter with you?" Vachs demanded. "You surely don't expect me to go up against this son of a bitch unarmed?"

"No, but I don't expect you to go out there waving that chrome piece around in the dark, either. Reach up under that seat and you'll find an oilskin pouch with a Colt Delta Elite 10 mm inside. There's a couple of extra clips in there, too.'' Winterroad switched off the ignition and rolled down the window as Vachs set the pouch on the floorboard. He looked at his partner, watching the younger man fieldstrip the mat-black piece, then reassemble it, snapping the first round into place. ''Leave the safety off and keep it in your hand,'' he advised in a quiet voice.

Winterroad opened the door and stepped out of the car. The smell of the creek and the outdoors softly wrapped around him, bringing images to his mind that had been sharpened by the general store. Then the hardness of the SIG-Sauer pistol in his right hand distorted them, moving them from pleasurable memories to past killing grounds that had been just as dark and treacherous as this one promised to be.

He slipped on a black windbreaker and turned up the collar to cover the whiteness of his exposed neck. The navy blue polo shirt and charcoal-gray slacks he wore would help shield him in the night.

Winterroad moved quietly through the darkness as he circled the incline that would take them to De Luca's camp. For a moment he wondered how accurate their information had been so far. De Luca hadn't been an easy quarry to run down, but neither had the trail been filled with the twists and turns that might ordinarily follow in the wake of a professional who knew he was being hunted. He gripped the pistol tighter and kept moving through the dense forest.

''I'm not forgetting what happened back there in the car,'' Vachs promised in a quiet but rough voice.

Pausing to glance at his partner, Winterroad saw that Vachs was safely out of reach. He didn't say anything because he knew it would only escalate the argument. Vachs was still young enough to be hung up on the macho image that working for the Agency projected. The man simply hadn't been around death to know how easily it could reach out and take him.

Twenty minutes later they found De Luca's campsite located in the small concavity where the old man had said it would be. A fire burned in a generous pile of embers and painted garish shadows on two sides of the tent north of it. The eastern boundary was marked by the shallow creek. A line of trees farther down the incline the agents had climbed formed the western boundary, then circled around to frame the ragged trail coming from the south end. A Ford Bronco sat silent and still in the gap.

Winterroad shifted his pistol to the other hand and dried his palm on his pant leg. He glanced at Vachs, saw the question on the man's face and drew a quick line across his throat before the question could reach his partner's lips. Vachs looked sullen and turned away.

Winterroad crept closer, using the trees and brush to shield him. His partner started to follow, but he waved the man to a stationary position.

Then, glancing back at the campsite, he tried to put a mental finger on what was wrong. There was a cold spot between his shoulder blades that he couldn't ignore. He started to move forward again, duck-walking to keep a low profile so that he wouldn't be outlined against the night sky.

Then he froze instantly as an object was tossed from the tent. His left hand locked immediately under his right palm as he lifted the SIG-Sauer and pulled the hammer back. He tracked the flight of the unknown object as it started back down. It was cylindrical, short and stubby, familiar. It was—

"Don't look at the fire!" he yelled to Vachs. He turned his head and dived into the underbrush. "Don't look at the fire!" Maintaining a death grip on the pistol, he clamped his left hand over his eyes, kicked out with his feet and crawled toward the biggest tree he remembered seeing.

Even behind his hand he could see the green light of the tossed flare as it exploded into brilliance. Then the familiar stutter-bark of a MAC-10 ripped apart the silence of the night.

RAIN SPATTERED Mack Bolan's trench coat as he left the tiny Japanese café where he'd stationed himself for the past ninety minutes. The .45 was a solid bulk in his right coat pocket, and he was careful to keep it from being noticed as he threaded his way through the press of the afternoon sidewalk crowd.

Dark clouds had claimed the city, leaving the tall buildings wreathed in dull yellow that faded gray to black. The traffic on the streets was heavy, allowing him to keep pace with the metallic blue Toyota without breaking into a run.

His target, Kendo Morressy, kept a steady rhythm going on the steering wheel with his fingers while he studied the traffic. He didn't appear to be in a hurry when he flipped on the right turn signal to get into the fast lane.

Bolan moved at once, turning on his heel and streaking for the Toyota. A car horn bleated indignantly as a Nissan braked to avoid him. He put out an arm as the car rocked to a halt, then levered himself past it. Morressy had just begun to turn his head, eyes widening in surprise as he realized he was the goal.

Reaching the Toyota, the Executioner opened the passenger door and slid inside, hit at once by the intensity of the music rushing from the speakers. He brought the .45 into view, leveling it at Morressy and said, "Drive."

The lit joint tumbled from Morressy's full lips and landed on the car seat between his legs. He panicked and reached for the marijuana, scrabbling for the door handle with his other hand.

Bolan leaned across the seat and pressed the barrel of the gun into the man's neck. He thumbed the hammer back without a word. Car horns bleated behind them as the traffic came to a standstill.

His face white with fear and pain, Morressy raised his hands to his shoulders. He spoke in Japanese, his hands trembling faster than his voice broke.

"Speak English," Bolan commanded.

"I'm on fire," Morressy whined.

"Reach for it slowly," Bolan said, "otherwise I'm still looking for the man I need."

Morressy searched between his legs with one hand, keeping the other in plain sight. The sound of car horns picked up intensity, joined by cars in other lanes as the blocked vehicles made unexpected lunges into their paths. Morressy raised the joint between his thumb and forefinger.

"Throw it out the window," Bolan ordered, "and get this car moving. If the police become interested in us, you'll be the first to die."

"Sure," Morressy said. "You aren't going to have any problems with me." He flicked the joint away and started the car, pulling ahead at a sedate pace.

Bolan left the barrel of the .45 where it was as he glanced behind them. Traffic began to unsnarl. No one appeared interested in following them.

"Do I know you?" Morressy asked. He glanced nervously at Bolan, uncertainty flashing in his brown eyes.

"No, but I know you."

"What do you want with me?"

"I'm in the market for some merchandise."

Morressy's voice sounded more hopeful. "What kind of merchandise?"

Bolan studied the man, letting the silence build. The little finger on Morressy's right hand had been amputated at the second joint. The resulting scar tissue was rough and looked as lumpy as candle droppings. The man was dressed casually but expensively, and would have looked out of place with most of the sidewalk crowd. "Keep both hands on the wheel," the Executioner ordered. He reached across the seat and relieved Morressy of a Heckler & Koch 9 mm pistol from a hand-tooled shoulder holster. He dropped the weapon into his trench coat pocket.

"Look, you mentioned merchandise," Morressy said. "Maybe we have some business to transact, okay?"

Removing the .45 from his captive's neck, Bolan cradled the big automatic in his lap. "Turn left here. Stay in the outside lane."

Morressy complied, making an effort to keep his eyes off the .45. Bolan shifted in his seat as he tried to find a position that didn't stress the stitches in his side.

"Taking me down might not be such a bright idea," Morressy said. "I know a lot of people in Tokyo who'd love to have a chance at a guy like you."

"You're small potatoes to the Yakuza," Bolan said in a damning voice. "You know it and I know it, so don't try to confuse the issue by throwing threats at me. If I pulled this trigger once, you'd be history, and nobody you know could pull you back from that."

Swallowing hard, Morressy turned back to concentrate on his driving. Rain smashed against the windshield in a steady beat, swept away almost immediately by the wipers.

"I hear you're a guy to see about getting weapons in and out of Tokyo," Bolan said. He switched the radio off, letting the sound of the rain fill the car.

"You heard wrong. I don't do anything like that."

"We don't have time for games, guy. I'm on a very tight schedule here. You're Kendo Morressy and you've been living on the fringe of Yakuza activity for the past four years. You couldn't make it in the big leagues. That's why you lost those two joints on your little finger. The story I got was that you had to have help cutting the last one off."

Morressy's eyelids flickered rapidly.

"Turned out you didn't have the stomach for the bloody jobs," Bolan continued. "And you couldn't be trusted to keep your mouth shut about where some of the bodies were buried. Personally I think you're lucky you weren't drawn and quartered. The Yakuza normally run a tight ship."

"They needed me."

"They needed your connections," Bolan countered. "It's not the same thing. You're the son of an American soldier stationed here after World War II who developed a thriving business in the after-war black market. At least he was until SCAP put him in a military prison. You learned the ropes at an early age, and you had some of your father's acquaintances to work through. Most of those people are gone now, but you've maintained some channels of your own."
The information almost exhausted what he had on Morressy in his war book, but it was more than enough to get the man's attention.

"What do you want with me?"

"Like I said, merchandise."

"What do you want?"

Bolan showed him a thin smile. "Do you have a spring catalog?"

"It takes time to get things, you know? You can't just expect me to be able to get my hands on something right now."

"I'm not looking for an antiaircraft carrier," Bolan said. "Where are you going now?"

"Nowhere."

Bolan raised the .45 and shoved it against Morressy's temple hard enough to bump the man's head against the window.

"All right, all right." Morressy's voice was shrill, tight. "I'm going to see a guy about some machine pistols. Some Uzis, Skorpions, and maybe a half-dozen handguns."

"We can start there," Bolan said.

Morressy faced him as they stopped at a traffic light. "You can't go to this meet with me. Those guys will kill us both if they think something's wrong."

"Just tell them I'm the money man behind this deal," Bolan suggested.

"You don't understand the kind of men I'm talking about."

"I think I understand perfectly." Bolan took out a sheaf of crisp yen notes and tossed them into Morressy's lap. "Maybe money can't buy trust, but it goes a long way toward helping greed overcome it."

CHAPTER SIX

Three men waited in the narrow alley off one of the main streets leading to Tokyo Harbor. Morressy had passed Shinagawa station a few minutes ago and had almost succeeded in getting Bolan disoriented in the maze of tall buildings. The rain continued to fall, though in the form of mist now rather than solid sheets. Tokyo Tower rose spectacularly in the north, dwarfing Shiba Park, then disappearing from view as the walls of the alley closed in on them.

Morressy pulled to one side of the alley and stopped. His attention was riveted on the three men standing in the shelter of an iron stairway zigzagging up the side of the building behind them. All three were young, dressed stylishly and wearing sunglasses despite the weather. One of the leather jackets gaped open to reveal the butt of an automatic.

"Switch off the engine," Bolan ordered.

Morressy complied without a word.

"Give the keys to me." Bolan held out a hand, then dropped them into an empty pocket. "Get out of the car nice and slow. Remember, this is a business deal like all the others you've handled with these guys."

"This isn't going to work," Morressy said.

"Just flash the money."

"It's not enough for this shipment. I was just coming to look, not to buy. I haven't got a market for this stuff yet, and I never come to one of these meets to be robbed."

"We'll meet the price," Bolan assured him. He opened the door and stepped out into the rain. Morressy clambered out behind him seconds later. The arms dealer's face was pale, and his eyes blinked constantly. The sheaf of yen notes was balled up in one white-knuckled fist.

The alley was empty except for a scattered dozen trash cans and a Toyota van pitted with rust spots and dents. The windows in the vehicle were tinted enough to mask the interior. Fish odor from the nearby open-air market cut through the musty smells of the alley.

As Bolan walked across the alley with Morressy, he adjusted his numbers. The three men would take precedence until their buddies spilled from the van. He figured two, maybe three more inside. He kept his hands at his sides and an easy smile on his face.

The three men spread out as they were approached. The man in the middle looked like a Thai, but Bolan knew Singapore was a melting pot for Asian races, and whatever direction the arms shipments had to take from Tokyo, they were sure to cross near that country. The man on the left was Japanese; the one on the right was black and sported a Special Forces tattoo on the inside of his right forearm.

The man in the middle spoke in Japanese as Bolan and Morressy came to a stop in front of them.

"Speak English," Bolan ordered. He stood to one side of the small group so that he could still see the van.

Morressy started to speak, but the middle man waved him to silence. He studied Bolan quietly. "Who are you?"

Bolan returned the hostile gaze full measure. "I'm the guy who's putting down the money on this deal."

"Why are you here?"

"I go where my money goes."

"You're American?"

"Does it matter?"

The man gave him a smile that held no mirth. He held out a hand to Morressy. The arms dealer dropped the crumpled yen notes into it. He unfolded the currency as he stepped back into the protection of the other two men, then counted it. Finished, he straightened the notes and looked back at Bolan.

Dulled pain axed at the Executioner's side, and he could feel his shirt sticking to the bandages under the trench coat. It was easy to ignore when he looked into the flat eyes of the three men. All of them were killers, and the tension of the situation placed them at the edge of an abyss of violence that threatened to sweep them away. He focused on the center man, letting his peripheral vision take care of the other two and the van. All action would stem from the spokesman.

"It's not enough for the shipment we agreed to show Morressy," the man said. He didn't offer to return the money.

"I'm not here for a shipment," Bolan said. "I'm traveling light."

The man nodded. "What were you looking for?"

"Morressy mentioned machine pistols."

The man tapped the money. "And if this isn't enough?"

"I've got more."

A smile tugged at the corners of the man's mouth. "Good. Very good." He turned to his companions and held the money up, speaking in Japanese. The act was faultless. Only Morressy's sudden movement kept Bolan from being caught in a deadly cross fire.

The Executioner was in motion at once, drawing the .45 as the Japanese man came at him with a spinning reverse kick. He blocked the kick with his forearm, then got a grip on the man's leg and shoved them both into the wall under the iron stairs. He triggered two rounds from the .45 just before the impact. The hollowpoints lifted the center man from his feet just as he was bringing a chrome-plated pistol to bear. The remaining man fired three shots before he broke and ran toward the van.

Glittering steel slid toward the warrior's face, letting him know the man he was holding wasn't out of the fight yet. He stepped back as he blocked the knife with the .45, pulling the man's leg with him. Off balance, the guy had no choice but to follow him, waving wildly as he struggled to swing the knife again.

Bolan aimed at the man's face point-blank and pulled the trigger, smelling the cordite fill the air between them. The corpse collapsed as he tracked onto the rolling van.

The black man flailed at the sliding door on the van's side as arms reached out for him. The vehicle's engine screamed as it accelerated, rocketing for the mouth of the alley.

Holding the .45 in a Weaver's grip, the Executioner pumped the remaining five rounds through the windshield. One of the wiper arms spun away wildly. The van went out of control as autofire raked the alley in front of Bolan. He recognized the familiar stutter of an Uzi in full-throated operation as he threw himself over the hood of Morressy's car.

The van smashed into the car. Glass shattered in the windows of both vehicles and left them as intact jigsaw puzzles with only a few of the pieces missing.

The Executioner dropped the empty magazine and slammed another one home, thumbing the slide back into position. Someone fired through a window in the back of the stalled van, punctuating the hissing coming from the broken radiator with rapid-fire bursts and breaking glass. He blasted three rounds through the thin sheet metal where he guessed the gunner to be, then emptied the clip, blowing holes at waist-high intervals the length of the van.

A sudden burst of autofire sprayed out from under the car. Not hesitating, realizing he needed height for a moment to find out where his enemies were, he jumped up on the car, feeling the pain in his side soar to new levels as he vaulted for the top of the van. He landed hard, seeing black spots explode into his vision from the wound in his side, then rolled to the far side of the van. He pulled the .45 into position just as the gunner was getting back to his feet. A rapid drumbeat of two hollowpoints sent the man staggering backward, a scream dying suddenly as one of them crashed through his throat.

Still on the move, Bolan swung down and brought up an arm to level the .45 on the running black man as the guy turned with an Uzi blazing from his waist. The trail of 9 mm bullets left pockmarks along the brick walls and ripped long splinters from the privacy fences beside the tangled vehicles.

Bolan fisted the .45 as he pressed into the van, presenting the shooter with only his right profile. He became the gunsight as he brought the big weapon to bear on the man. When he had target acquisition, he let out half a breath, following the man's movements automatically, then squeezed the trigger. The pistol bucked in his hand, blocking the view of his target. By the time he had the .45 realigned for his next shot, the man was sprawled in the narrow street.

Bolan swiveled around the corner of the sliding door of the van. A dead man was crumpled against the rear section of the vehicle, a victim of the hollowpoints that had ripped through the thin sheet metal. He stepped inside, ducking under the low ceiling. The driver had been an instant casualty from the bullets penetrating the windshield.

Morressy started to get to his feet when Bolan looked back. The man immediately raised his hands over his head when he saw the Executioner aim the .45 at him. "Get over here," the warrior commanded.

The arms dealer was hesitant but quick to realize he had no choice.

Bolan kept the .45 in his fist as he inspected the contents of the two crates in the van. He removed the trench coat, slung an Uzi over his arm and donned the garment again. He found a gray-and-white duffel bag and unzipped it. "What did that guy say back there?" he asked as he shoved boxes of 9 mm ammunition for the Uzi into the bag.

"He told them to kill you," Morressy replied in a quavering voice.

"Thanks for the warning," Bolan said dryly. He lifted the top from another crate and found a half-dozen racks of hand grenades. Eight of them went into the duffel, two at each corner of the bag so that he could find them easily if he was in a hurry.

"I didn't know what to do," Morressy said.

"You ducked pretty good back there for someone who didn't know what to do," Bolan said. The blood smell of the dead pervaded the van. He looked through the smashed windshield at the crowd that had begun to gather, then blinked his eyes in an effort to clear them, feeling his system suffering from the adrenal payback his body was demanding. The pain in his side was no longer something that could be entirely ignored. "Why did he want to kill me? It couldn't have been for the money. That guy struck me as being a player, somebody who would have tried to string me along until he was sure he had me with all my ready cash on hand."

"He told his men he thought you were one of the Americans from the Sumida River confrontation this morning."

"Why would that matter to him?"

Morressy hesitated.

The Executioner gripped the man by his lapels and pushed him into the seat behind him. The corpse sprawled over the steering wheel and fell into the passenger seat. "I don't have time to waste on this, Morressy."

"Those men have prices on their heads," Morressy said.

"Who put it there?"

The man shook his head, looking frantic. "I don't know."

Bolan believed him. The panic was too sharp, too vibrant for Morressy to try to hide anything from him. He released the arms dealer. "How did you find out?"

"My connections in the Yakuza told me one of the big bosses wants these men. I have a couple of informants I keep in contact with so that I know the latest things I might be able to sell to them. I come across a lot of information in my dealings."

"How do they want these men?"

"Alive, if possible, but dead if it isn't."

"Why?"

"They didn't say."

"Do they know who these men are?"

"They're believed to be CIA agents. Some of the men killed this morning had files in the CIA. Others were mercenaries known to work sometimes for American intelligence. I believe they were sent over here to kill someone in the Yakuza. Someone big. Steps are being taken to prevent that. There was an attack made in the Ministry of Foreign Affairs building today that was designed to take out the Americans coordinating the CIA efforts in Tokyo."

Bolan raised the .45 as images of Brognola going down under an assassin's gun flashed through his mind.

"Don't!" Morressy screamed, closing his eyes and twisting his head to one side. "Please don't kill me!"

"Who ordered the attack?" Bolan asked in a graveyard whisper.

"Saburo Hosaka."

The big warrior lowered the pistol and turned the name over in his mind. There were a lot of connections to the Hosaka name, some of them dating back to the days of the American occupation after World War II. "Who is he?"

"Saburo's the younger son of Joji Hosaka, one of the founders of the new business consortium being gathered in Tokyo. Saburo's also a member of the Yakuza."

"Where can I find him?"

"I don't know. I've never seen him." Morressy licked his lips nervously, reading the disgust on the Executioner's face. "There's something I can offer you for my life, though. I know the name of the man who arranged the false passports for the Americans.''

''It's not going to do me any good if a hundred other people are looking for him, too.''

Morressy shook his head. ''No one else knows. I only came into possession of the knowledge because he was bragging to me yesterday of how much he was charging some Americans for false passports.''

''He has to know what went down today. What's going to keep him from running?''

''Where could he go? And if he did run, he'd be admitting his guilt. No, Shigeru's still in Tokyo. I'd be willing to bet my life on that.''

Bolan gave the man a thin smile. ''You might be doing just that.''

The thought settled uncomfortably on Morressy, shading his face as gray as the rain clouds.

''Where can I find him?''

''He hangs out at the Club Morena, down in the Roppongi, but it doesn't open till seven-thirty this evening.''

''What about a home address?''

Morressy shook his head.

People had filled the alley now, but maintained a discreet distance from the dead men. ''How will I know him?'' Bolan asked.

''He's known to the hostesses. Ask them.''

''Shigeru isn't going to want to see an American now.''

Morressy touched the top of his ear. ''The top of his left ear was slicked off by a knife, and there's a birthmark here.'' He rubbed the left side of his jaw.

Bolan riffled through the belongings of the two dead men, coming up with a Beretta and a Taurus. He claimed the Taurus and the three extra clips that he found on the driver. The .45's use was almost at an end because finding replacement ammunition for it would be difficult. The Taurus cut those difficulties down by using the same round as the Uzi.

He jammed the Brazilian pistol into the same pocket as Morressy's H&K. "If this information you've given me doesn't pan out," he said in a low, tight voice, "I'll be looking for you again."

Morressy nodded, unable to speak.

The Executioner shouldered his duffel and jogged from the alley, avoiding the people scattered around him. He paused at the corner of the alley to check on Morressy. The arms dealer leaned against the crumpled van, his hands covering his face.

Bolan touched his shirt to feel the bandages underneath. His fingers came away stained crimson. The wound was bleeding again, or perhaps it had never really stopped. In a way he was grateful for the pain because it kept the fatigue from his overnight journey at bay. He sprinted across the street, letting his combat senses define his territory and warn him of any threat. He wondered briefly at Brognola's fate at the hands of the assassin, then forced the issue from his mind because it was too emotional.

He glanced up at the next street, found Tokyo Tower and began plotting his course back to his rental car. It would take time getting there, but it would also allow him to find out how much his body could take before he put it to the test.

He hefted the duffel bag in satisfaction. At least now he had ordnance. The team of assassins this morning had been waiting for an unarmed man. Now he was ready, willing and able to take the war back to them.

"WHAT THE HELL is this?" Brognola demanded of the white-coated technician standing in the middle of the roomful of sheet-covered bodies. He leaned on the cane in a useless effort to take some of the weight off his injured leg. The chill of the morgue soaked into his bones and made his skin tighten.

The technician looked up in irritation, his pencil poised as he worked on a clipboard that he held. "You are Tucker-san?"

"No," Brognola growled. "He's Tucker." He pointed at the CIA man, who was lifting the sheet covering the nearest body.

"Ah, then you will be Brognola-san." The technician nodded in satisfaction, then checked off another series of items on his list. "Fujitsu-san asked that you wait here until he arrives."

"This is a morgue," Brognola said. He gazed around at the bodies and the bloodstained sheets as misgivings about the impromptu meeting stirred up dark thoughts.

"Hai," the technician agreed. He moved through the bodies, pushing up his glasses briefly to check one of the toe tags. "Fujitsu-san said that his business with you must be done here. I assure you, this place being used as a conference room is most improper, but Fujitsu-san felt its effect would be necessary."

"Hey, Hal," Tucker called.

Brognola glanced at the agent and saw that he had moved on to the next table. "What?"

"We've seen these dead guys before." Tucker lifted the sheet on the third table, cocking his head to survey the body. "About an hour ago, down by the Sumida River, they didn't look this good."

Brognola limped over to join Tucker. He didn't recognize the face under the sheet, but the chances of a Tokyo morgue containing this many Caucasians were too slim to give him any doubt from where the bodies had been brought. He reached out and snared the toe tag at the bottom of the table. Japanese characters covered most of it. "What does this say?" he asked the technician.

The man pushed his glasses up again and glanced briefly at the tag. "It lists height, weight, hair and eye color, and the approximate age."

"This line of characters is the same," Brognola said, pointing to another tag.

"It is what you would call 'John Doe' in your country. Even though these men are not known, they must be called something for our files until their true names are discovered."

Tucker let the sheet slide through his fingers. "I've got the feeling someone thinks a first-class reaming session is in order," he said quietly.

Brognola silently agreed. He leaned back against a table covered with scalpels, drills, saws and other implements of the coroner's trade.

Tucker thrust his hands into his pockets. His collar was unbuttoned, and his tie hung loosely around his neck. "What do you figure the chances are that we'll be shot out of the water on this one before we get a real break?"

"Real good," Brognola replied honestly. He gazed silently at the tattooed arm sticking out from one of the tables, recognizing it as belonging to the Special Forces in general, and the Phoenix Project in particular. He tried to remember if it was the same tattoo he'd seen earlier, then decided if it wasn't, it was another just like it.

The door burst open a few minutes later to allow Fujitsu's entrance. The Foreign Affairs liaison dismissed the morgue technician with a curt nod as he turned to Tucker and Brognola. Once the lab man was gone, Fujitsu walked to the table nearest him and yanked the sheet back. The corpse was sheathed in blood and a ragged line of bullet holes had been punched through the chest. The dead man's face was curiously devoid of any expression. "Do you know this man?" the Foreign Affairs man asked in a voice tight with anger and frustration.

Brognola shook his head.

Switching to Tucker, Fujitsu repeated his question. "Do you know this man?"

"No."

Fujitsu covered the body and moved on to the next one, deliberately choosing one that put him closer to his audience. "Perhaps you know this man?" He swept the sheet back, revealing a dead man with an arrow through one of his eyes.

"No."

"And you, Mr. Tucker?"

"No," the CIA man said after a pause.

"So, out of a whole roomful of dead men, neither of you can offer any assistance in identifying any of them." Fujitsu dropped the sheet back into place. "Yet both of you are highly touted in your fields."

Brognola kept a handle on his temper. Striker was still out there somewhere, and it wouldn't do any good to antagonize the people they were supposed to be assisting. "We were assigned to help your government find out who's attacking Japanese holdings in the United States," he said in a neutral voice. "If I knew who any of these men were, I would tell you."

Fujitsu looked at him speculatively. "I wonder how true that statement is."

Brognola returned the gaze but kept quiet. He shifted his weight again in another attempt to alleviate some of the pain in his leg.

"Have you anything to offer, Mr. Tucker? You have been in Japan a number of years now. Has this given you any insights you would like to share with us?"

Tucker's voice was harsh. "If you've got something to say, Fujitsu, spit it out and let's deal with it."

A slight smile tugged at Fujitsu's lips but lacked any sign of humor. "Yes, let us do that. You have been here a number of years, as I have said, Mr. Tucker, and during that time things between us have not always been seen the same way. We have had, should we say, our disagreements."

"Ours, and those of others."

"Yes, and sometimes we have found ourselves sitting on opposite sides of the fence as we faced the problems our respective governments have given us. Luckily we have always been able to sort things out in the past." Fujitsu sighed. "Now, however, that option does not appear to be possible. I have a roomful of dead men bearing tattoos of the American Special Forces, men who have served in the Phoenix Project in Vietnam. And, as we are all aware, that was a CIA project. Do you think it would be too far off base for me to assume these men, at least the ones with these tattoos, were once a part of that CIA operation?"

"That doesn't mean they're still with the Agency," Tucker said defensively.

Brognola unwrapped a cigar from his pocket and stuck it into his mouth.

"You would not know these men were a part of the CIA if your employers did not want you to," Fujitsu said. He encompassed the room with a gesture of his arm. "Your agency has a history of clandestine operations in my country as well as in others. My father was killed by a G-2 man during the occupation. He was on strike against the rightest government when MacArthur's SCAP soldiers were busy releasing Yakuza into the streets to help pull Tokyo in the direction the American government wanted Japan to go. You are too young to remember that, Tucker, but I remember. I was eleven years old the day my father's friends came to our home to tell my mother of his murder at the hands of the Americans."

Tucker opened his mouth to say something.

Fujitsu stilled the protest with a curt hand gesture. "Silence. There is nothing you can say about this. You will be trapped into telling me things are different now, or that the CIA has never done anything like this. Maybe you would even try to excuse it by telling me it was still wartime. I do not care to hear it. You will never know everything that was done during those times. Neither will I. But I do know that

your government worked with Yakuza members to rebuild
this country in the image they chose, the very same way they
did with the Mafia in Italy. I know how the black markets
and other crimes thrived under the leadership of Yoshio
Kodama. Your agency has tried to bend the rules in this
country many times, Tucker. Not in the least have been the
attempts to stockpile nuclear arms here, despite that being
outlawed in treaties. I know the kind of people you work
for, and you cannot really defend them to yourself because
you know those people, too."

Silence fell over the room as Tucker looked away.

"Before you get the idea that I am dismissing you from
this conversation, Mr. Brognola," Fujitsu said, "let me
address you concerning your man, Belasko."

"What about him?"

"Where is he?"

"I don't know."

Fujitsu nodded in satisfaction. "He's not on any of these
tables, is he?"

"No."

"Yet he was supposed to check in with you as soon as he
arrived in Tokyo, was he not?"

"You know he was," Brognola said, letting some of his
irritation show in his tone. "I had to clear his entrance
through your office, as well."

"Then where is he?"

"I don't know."

"Is this standard operating procedure for your office, Mr.
Brognola? Because if it is, I find it lacking in respect and
responsibility."

"Maybe he ran into the same kind of trouble that Tucker
and I had this morning," Brognola said evenly. "We were
almost gunned down in your office this morning by a street
punk with a big gun. If that is an example of your security,
I find that not only lacking in respect and responsibility, but
goddamn dangerous to boot."

The Foreign Affairs man's face tightened and grayed with repressed anger. "Both of you are here at the sufferance of the Japanese government," he stated, "yet neither of you seem willing to volunteer information that will help us find out who is attacking Japanese-held businesses in America and killing Japanese employees."

"It isn't just Japanese employees being killed over there," Tucker said sharply. "Whoever the assassins are, they're not prejudiced about political or racial issues when they're inside their targets. At the light truck factory in Detroit the American deaths to Japanese deaths was five to one."

"The principal targets are Japanese holdings, Mr. Tucker," Fujitsu said. "Let us not forget that."

Brognola took the cigar from his mouth and shook his head. "For three men who are supposed to be pooling their talents on this, we're not getting along very well."

Tucker didn't look at him.

"Until I am sure we all share a common goal," Fujitsu stated, "I do not intend to."

"That's your prerogative," Brognola said, "but I have a job to do and I intend to do it until it's done or my services are no longer wanted by your government."

"That may be sooner than you think," Fujitsu promised. "I am told your President's plea to let you work on things from this end was passionate. However, do not expect his words to carry you if you are unable to aid in this investigation."

Brognola resisted making a retort. Fujitsu wasn't a politician like many of the ones he'd been forced to deal with over the years, but his views were just as political. He leaned on his cane and began walking toward the door.

"And, Tucker," Fujitsu called after the CIA man, "I hope for your sake that these men really are unknown to you."

Brognola led the way into the narrow hall of the morgue, with Tucker right behind him. "Was it just my imagination," the CIA man asked, "or was Fujitsu really coming on a little strong?"

"It wasn't your imagination," Brognola replied, grimacing as he looked up the flight of stairs leading to the first floor of the building.

"I didn't think so. I was on the edge of my seat waiting for that old cowboy line about this town not being big enough for the both of us."

"The three of us," Brognola grunted. He wrapped a hand around the bar mounted on the wall and began pulling himself up. A woman's voice calling his name made him stop and turn around.

"You wanted on telephone," the young woman in a nurse's uniform stated with difficulty. "You come, yes?"

"Yes."

"I show you."

Tucker tagged along. "This private?" he asked.

"If it was, whoever's on the other end wouldn't be calling me over an unrestricted line."

The young nurse handed Brognola a telephone. He sat in the chair behind the small desk as she went away, grateful for the comfort. He stared at his reflection in the window overlooking the hallway. "Brognola."

"Just a moment, please." There was a click. "Your party is on the line now, Mr. Brognola."

"Thank you. Hello?"

"How's the leg?"

Brognola recognized Bolan's deep voice at once and some of the worry left him. He saw himself smile, and a couple of interns passing in the hallway glanced at him quizzically. "It's been better. I see you're still alive, too."

"Despite an almost overwhelming objection. You've heard about it?"

"I've seen some of your work. How soon can we meet?"

"Soon. At the moment I'm following up on some leads that this morning's activities generated. I don't know if this ties into what you've planned here, but the people I met this morning had to have picked me up somewhere along your trail. I came in clean."

"Yeah, well, that's entirely possible. There are some undisclosed players on this one." Brognola detected the fatigue in Bolan's voice. "What kind of shape are you in from this morning?"

"I've seen better days."

"Maybe you ought to consider coming on in now and letting some of the people I brought with me take over for a while."

"Not now, Hal. This one's hot and bloody so far, and definitely not for someone who hasn't been in the jungle before. I'll be in soon. Where can I meet you?"

Brognola gave him the address of the hotel the Ministry of Foreign Affairs had selected for the Justice team.

"I've also got a lead on the guy who tried to whack you and the CIA guy."

"You're ahead of me, but I'm working an angle that might pay off."

"We both know the CIA's going to run its own plays on this, but what's the home team like?" Bolan asked.

Brognola watched Fujitsu walk down the hall with an erect carriage, like a soldier going off to war. "Inscrutable," he replied softly. "Very inscrutable. Watch your ass on this one, Striker, because anything could come out of left field."

"I've found that out." Bolan broke the connection.

CHAPTER SEVEN

Winterroad came up firing, holding the SIG-Sauer in both hands as he emptied the clip into the tent. The flare still blazed in the campfire, throwing jade shadows over the trees, the camp and the Bronco. He whirled back down as the slide on the automatic locked back empty, then pushed himself onto his elbows to another vantage point as the gunner holding the MAC-10 ripped splinters from the trees and bushes he'd hidden behind. Dropping the empty clip, he shivered when he thought about the cost of replacing it if he couldn't find it in the darkness. The Agency didn't pay for everything. Finally he slammed the next magazine home and turned onto his side to look down the hill.

Gaping black holes flapped in the sides of the tent. The flare continued fizzling as it spread dozens of small fires in a rough circle around it. There was no sign of De Luca or whomever might have been manning the MAC-10.

Taking careful aim, Winterroad placed five shots across the front of the Bronco in an effort to hole the radiator and limit the vehicle's usefulness. Sparks flew from the grill-work. He pulled his head back down as a line of bullets scythed over his head. Branches and leaves tumbled across his back as he scrambled to another clump of brush and trees.

"Harry," he called softly, watching the campsite for movement. He didn't know if De Luca would take a chance on coming after them or if the man was alone. He still wasn't sure De Luca was even in the tent. He called again, louder. "Harry."

"Here, damn it."

"Are you okay?"

"I can't see."

Winterroad raised his weapon to his cheek as he glanced through the trees, wondering if his night vision had been affected enough to make him blind to an approaching enemy. "Are you hit?"

"No."

"Stay where you are while I go take a look."

"I can't cover you like this."

Winterroad eased into a crouching position, ready to fling himself back to the ground if it became necessary. "You just stay put for the moment and take care of yourself. If that was De Luca, he's going to be making tracks out of here instead of hanging around to see who's after him." He began to angle down the side of the hill, maintaining cover as much as he could. He wondered if De Luca normally carried something as lethal as the MAC-10 when he went fishing.

Branches crackled ahead of him and he went down instantly, falling backward and ready to roll as his gun arm draped itself over his knees. Something moved in the darkness, but he could tell from its outline that it was too small to be a man. An old fear of rabid skunks manifested itself in his imagination, and he struggled to keep from reaching for the flashlight in his pocket.

He eased up on the tent as the flare burned itself out with a final sputtering rush. The campfire reached for the remnants of the cardboard hull with greedy fingers. Smoke filled his nose and blocked out all other smells.

Taking a penknife from his pocket, he slashed one of the stake lines and steadied his gun. The tent collapsed with a gentle whoosh. There was nothing man-sized outlined under the drab olive cloth. Whoever had been in the tent was gone.

He stood as he released the drawn breath he'd been holding. The forest on the other side of the creek was dark and forbidding. He forced himself on, making himself remember the anger that had kept him working at the Agency the past handful of years. His feet sank in the soft ground as he neared the edge of the creek. Mud filled his shoes around his socks until he squished every time he took a step. Feeding on the anger, he paused long enough to untie his shoes and slip them off.

He paused to listen. Bullfrogs croaked, crickets sang, an occasional night bird took flight in a flurry of heartbeats. He listened for something that didn't belong, remembering how much easier it had been in Vietnam a quarter of a century ago. He'd been lean, mean and scared shitless, every sense alive to the slightest variance. It was funny how he had gotten older and seemed to wear that fear out. Even at the end of that war, he had used his anger to sustain him and push him back into the jungle.

He moved into the creek under cover of a spreading oak tree, squatting down until his butt was immersed in the cold, slow-moving water. Now that the smoke had cleared away, he could smell the dankness of the creek banks. He waited with his weapon held loosely. Nothing moved. The sounds of the nightlife continued unabated. A bullfrog to his right resumed its calling. He dipped his hand in the cold water and rubbed it across his lower face.

"Winterroad!" Vachs's voice exploded out of the darkness.

Winterroad ignored his partner. De Luca, or whoever the shooter had been, waited out there in the darkness. Before getting a chance at Vachs, Winterroad knew the man would have to cross his field of fire.

"Goddamn it, Winterroad, where the hell are you?"

Winterroad smiled to himself. At times he thought he was too old to play quiet, deadly little games in the dark, but he still maintained the instincts for it. Agents like Vachs would never learn how to be predators.

A shadow separated from a tree thirty yards upstream and made a dash toward the creek. Water spumed up whitely in the moonlight. The figure sloshed across the creek awkwardly, fighting the current rather than moving with it.

Vachs called his name again as Winterroad slipped an extra clip into his empty hand and waited for the running man to reach the middle of the creek. He squinted but couldn't penetrate the darkness enough to see if the man was De Luca.

When the man reached the midpoint of the stream, the water had crept up to his chest and his forward momentum had been almost stalled. Winterroad stood, leveling his gun arm before him as he sighted carefully down the barrel. He emptied the clip as fast as he could, putting all of the rounds over the running man's head. He took his time changing magazines as he moved deeper into the creek, then shoved the empty one into a pocket of the windbreaker.

The man had gone under in the center of the stream. Still gripping the SIG-Sauer tightly, Winterroad bent his knees and dropped into the water until only his head and arm were above the surface.

A head popped up almost twelve feet from where it had disappeared. The man threw himself across the remaining distance to the creek bank and fell at once into a prone position. The MAC-10 stuttered to life and the muzzle-flashes marked the man's position.

Bullets whizzed by Winterroad but none of them close to his new stand. Then the death chatter rattled to a halt as the bolt blew back dry.

Winterroad saw the shadow throw the machine pistol onto the ground as it charged into the forest. He lowered the hammer of the SIG-Sauer and followed, gaining the creek bank only seconds after his quarry and regretting his decision to take his shoes off at once.

The terrain was just as rocky and broken on this side of the creek as it had been on the other side. Winterroad used his free hand to pull himself up over an incline that the other man had chosen to run around. Locking his fingers around a gnarly tree root that stuck out of the sheer side of the incline, he shoved himself forward and up as sandy loam splashed across his face. He spit out a mouthful of dirt as his gun arm cleared the top of the incline, then used it to lever the rest of his body up.

Dodging trees as he sprinted down the other side, he glanced to his left and saw that he was gaining on the running man. His breath wheezed in his ears and pain stitched his side, but he refused to give in to it.

The fleeing man cut back under him, never seeing him skylined against the incline. Winterroad leaped to the top of a boulder the size of a compact car, then threw himself into the air. His lungs threatened to collapse from the bone-rattling impact. Then they were locked in a rolling sprawl that ended with Winterroad's back smashed into a tree. He knew he was still holding his pistol because he could see it in his hand, but he couldn't feel it. He lifted it anyway, centering it on his opponent's face as he pulled back the hammer. "Don't move," he gasped. Feeling returned to his back and limbs in an almost blinding jolt. The gun barrel trembled.

His quarry fell backward in exhaustion, arms spread well away from his sides and above his shoulders. Winterroad winced with the effort of sitting up. He searched his windbreaker pocket and found the flashlight unbroken. He gulped in air as he switched it on.

Eric De Luca blinked back at him. "Is that really you, John?"

Winterroad moved the light out of the man's eyes. "Hell, yes," he said in disgust. "You got any more guns?"

"No." De Luca's face was scratched and bleeding, and stained by muddy clumps. "Did the Agency send you to bring me in?"

"Yes." Winterroad dropped the SIG-Sauer into his lap and eased the hammer back down.

"If I'd known for sure that it was you, I wouldn't have pulled the trigger."

Winterroad didn't say anything.

"Can I sit up?"

"Yes." Winterroad gave him a hand, and they sat facing each other, breathing hard from the exertion. "You've never been on the wrong side of the Agency before, Eric. Why am I chasing you?"

"Because I flew in the team who blew up the Japanese publishing offices in L.A."

"How did you get involved in a deal like that?"

De Luca hesitated. He touched a finger to one of the scratches and studied the blood that came away on it. "Ross Tuley contacted me."

"Tuley?" The name went back a few years.

De Luca nodded. "Right. Your old partner, Ross Tuley."

"He was mustered out of the Agency over three years ago for personal problems."

"You mean Langley caught wind of the fact that he was doing unauthorized sanctions of people he considered to be enemies of the United States." De Luca's eyes were filled with sad humor. "Remember, John, I've palled around with the CIA for a good many years, too. I know where more than one body is buried."

Winterroad waved it away. "Why the hell would you follow someone as unstable as Ross Tuley?"

"I don't remember you saying anything about Tuley being unstable when the Agency came down on him. The way I remember it, you were in his corner all the way. According to you, Tuley was given the big green wienie by the Agency."

"Times change, Eric."

"Do they?" Vachs's voice rang out in the distance, and De Luca cocked an eyebrow.

"My latest partner."

"Real professional."

Winterroad nodded. "He thinks he's 007."

"He'll die soon with that kind of attitude."

"Yeah, but he'll die happy."

De Luca paused. "We aren't heroes out here," he said quietly. "None of us. Despite the propaganda Langley feeds you when you manage to come back off an assignment with your head and ass intact."

"They give you the same story, do they?"

"They don't bother learning any new ones, John. That's why I got tied up with Tuley after all these years. My head said no, but that goddamn red-white-and-blue streak that got pumped into my ass over in Vietnam told me yes, and yes it was. It wasn't until later, until I was reading about the explosion in the papers and saw it on television, that I realized those people killed in that building didn't even know they were in a war zone." De Luca's voice broke at the end.

Winterroad listened. He shifted his mind into neutral and refused to deal with the mixture of emotions writhing in the pit of his stomach. He'd seen the bomb site in L.A. himself—had found a woman's hand in the rubble that the cleanup crews had missed. He also knew that the man sitting across from him was a good and brave friend when the chips were down.

"It wasn't Tuley who decided me," De Luca said. "It was Sacker."

Winterroad felt the impact of the name. Sacker went back even farther than Tuley, as far back as his earliest memories of the CIA. "I thought he was dead."

De Luca shook his head. He spoke in a hoarse whisper. "The man's still alive. I've seen him, talked to him."

"Where?"

"We met in Peru. Tuley set it up."

Winterroad's thoughts rambled as he tried to fit it all together. The heavy weight of the SIG-Sauer kept him tied to the intensity of the present situation.

"His face is different," De Luca went on, "but, hell, guy, you can take one look at those eyes and know instantly that it's him. Do you remember the first time you met him?"

"Yeah. I was in Vietnam. I volunteered for the Phoenix Program in its early development." Sacker's eyes, centered in the long, hard face, peered at him from his memory, daring him to live up to their standards.

"I saw him my first time in Laos when I joined up with the Ravens in the Steve Canyon operation. I've never met a man who's impressed me more. You could tell by looking at him that he lived his whole life walking that thin line between patriotism and insanity."

"I know." Winterroad was surprised to find his throat dry at the memories.

"The publishing offices was Sacker's idea from the beginning," De Luca said. "He's got this plan to push the Japanese out of America."

"What?"

De Luca turned his palms up. "Look, John, I know it sounds crazy coming from me, but you should have heard it from Sacker. Sitting across one of those white tables with an umbrella keeping the sun off of you, holding a cold glass with one of those fruity tropical drinks with the little parasol in it, and looking into Sacker's eyes, you could believe the line of shit he was selling you." He shook his head. "Even now I'm not sure if it was shit. I only know I can't operate the way he's having his guys work. I mean, Jesus, blowing up buildings with innocent people in them." He looked at Winterroad. "It's different in wartime, you know? At least I always told myself that it was. Sacker said this was war, though, said the bureaucrats in Washington, D.C., had their hands so deep in foreign investors' pockets they didn't even care that they were selling our country out. He laid out the whole thing for me, gave me a presentation like he used to do in the old days. Pictures, graphs and a sense of duty. He told me I was the kind of man he was looking for, and that he had been waiting for the right moment to catch me away from my CIA connections.''

"Why is he after the Japanese? Why not go after the Arabs and Jews, too?''

"Sacker said the Japanese were the real enemy now, only we didn't know it. He said the next war was going to be an economic one, not fought on any battlefield like we ever saw. The Arabs, Jews, everybody else, they only have money, and money's only worth what you read in the paper. Sacker said the Japanese were beating us at technology, taking away the only edge we have left. They've found ways around trade agreements for the past few years, the same way they did with the car industry. He told me everyone here needed to be woken up to the fact that we're being quietly invaded.''

Vachs bellowed Winterroad's name again, sounding more frantic.

"Your partner's getting antsy," De Luca said.

"He'll keep." Winterroad put the SIG-Sauer into a pocket of the windbreaker. "You don't have any idea where Sacker is?''

"No. Like I said, Tuley set up the meet, and Sacker had his face changed. Hell, John, I never knew the man's real name to begin with.''

"Neither did I.''

"Guy must be sixty, seventy years old now, but when I saw him he looked as spry as ever. He might have gained five pounds. His hair was white that day, but it could have been colored. It was gray the first time I met him.''

"Where's Tuley?''

"After the demo job in L.A., I flew him into Tokyo. He'd ramrodded a Lear jet from somewhere and had cover IDs for all of us.''

"All of us?"

"He had eight guys with him, but I got the impression he was going to be meeting more. I assumed it was a take-out operation from the talent he had with him. I knew most of the guys. Not their real names, you know, but the kind of work they did."

Winterroad nodded. "You didn't hear any names of the targets?"

"No. This is still a Sacker operation, and you can tell it from the git-go. Everybody knows his part and that's it."

A bad feeling concerning Alan Tucker sent chills down Winterroad's back. "How did you end up here?"

De Luca shrugged. "My job was to drop Tuley in Tokyo and await further instructions. Instead, I took a few hours in London, still working under the cover Tuley had given me, and got my head together. I decided I wanted out by the time I set back down in L.A. Then I found out the Agency was looking for me in connection with the demo job. I grabbed all the ready cash I could get my hands on and split."

Vachs called out again, sounding nearer. Winterroad pushed himself to his feet, reached down and helped De Luca to his feet.

"You want to put handcuffs on me," De Luca asked, "or will you trust me if I say I'll go with you?"

Winterroad clapped the pilot on the shoulder. The flight jacket smacked wetly. He grinned. "Actually this is your lucky night—you got away."

"Langley will have your ass if they find out," De Luca said.

"Are you going to tell them?"

"Hell, no."

"I'm getting old and slow," Winterroad said with a bitter smile. "Haven't you heard? It seems to be all the new guys talk about. This is my way of saying thanks for that time back in Singapore in 1983."

De Luca put out his hand and Winterroad took it. "I'm not going to waste my breath trying to talk you out of this."

Vachs splashed through the creek on the other side of the hill.

"I'd better go identify myself before he shoots me," Winterroad said. "I'm going to have 007 help me beat the bushes out here for a while, so if you need anything from the camp, give me a few minutes, then go get it."

De Luca said his thanks, then melted into the night.

Winterroad trudged back up the hill with his mind filled by troubling thoughts. Sacker had turned up again after how many years? He wasn't sure. The man had almost become a myth around Langley, except to people who had worked with him. He was back and apparently declaring war on Japanese business interests in the United States. The real enemy, Sacker had said.

He paused at the top of the hill and called out to Vachs, aware the thing troubling him most was that part of him agreed with Sacker's line of thinking.

"WILL YOU REQUIRE the services of a hostess, sir?" the doorman at the Club Morena asked.

"Not right away," Bolan replied as he paid the cover charge. He glanced at the patrons, relieved at the number of Americans who were in the bar. Most of them were dressed in business attire and appeared to be with their Japanese counterparts. Dressed in a black blazer, black slacks and a blue turtleneck, he fitted in with most of them. The Taurus was a comforting weight at his back with the three filled magazines in his left coat pocket. He stopped at the mirrored bar to purchase a screwdriver before moving back into the crowd.

The decor was expensive, burnished brass and red carpet, with dozens of real plants in hanging baskets, huge and ornate pots, and low, tiled walls that separated a number of tables to give the illusion of privacy. Flowered plants were kept at a minimum so that it appeared as if a forest had invaded the club. Smoke wreathed the low-hung lights above the tables, and hostesses stayed in constant motion to keep the drinks flowing while others sat beside the businessmen.

Bolan paused and took a sip of his drink. A slender woman wearing a punkish aquamarine skirt and matching light jacket approached him from the bar. Her hair was long, falling past her shoulders, and for a moment he thought she was the woman ninja. Then she stepped into the circle of light from overhead that he had carefully avoided. She smiled at him. The effect was as put-on as the heavy mascara.

"You a big man," she cooed appreciatively as she trailed her palms across the breadth of his shoulders. "Shanna like big man." She clasped his hands in both of hers. "You need hostess, big man? Shanna very good girl. Take care of your every need. Many American come here. Many ask for Shanna to be hostess."

"Maybe later," Bolan told her with gentle smile. "Right now I have to find someone I'm supposed to do business with."

She took her hands from him, wrapping her hands around her upper arms. Her long aquamarine fingernails matched her outfit. She tilted her nose into the air. "Shanna help you find this person. Maybe it's worth something, big man?"

Bolan didn't hesitate. The club took up the bottom three floors of the building, and the large crowd made a search by him impossible to do without being noticed by the management or the people who might be looking for him. He took a roll of yen notes from his pocket and peeled off enough to encourage the woman without paying so high that she would talk about it to anyone else.

She took the yen with a bright smile that was no longer completely artificial, then made the money disappear somewhere inside the waistband of the skirt. "Who you look for?"

"Shigeru."

Her eyes narrowed. "Are you a friend?"

"No," Bolan replied honestly. If the bar was a frequent hangout of Shigeru's as Morressy had said, the staff would have a good idea of who met him here and who didn't. "We have some business through another friend." He rubbed his thumb and forefinger together in a more universal language.

"Ah." She nodded in a way that let Bolan know it wasn't unusual for Shigeru to conduct at least part of his clandestine business on the premises. "You come. Shigeru on third floor." She led him to an elevator secluded in one corner.

The doors opened and they squeezed inside with five other people. Bolan towered above the other occupants of the elevator cage and drew attention. No one was speaking English. He understood bits and pieces of the conversations going on around him, but the lack of full understanding made him uncomfortable.

"When you through with business," the woman said as she turned from pressing the third-floor button, "you come back to Shanna, okay?"

Bolan nodded as the cage started up.

CHAPTER EIGHT

The elevator hissed to a stop on the third floor, and the door opened onto a huge dance floor, a polished rectangle that glistened under the rainbow-colored lights that flickered on and off in a controlled sequence mirroring the music being played. Four mirrored globes spun and flashed over the corners of the dance floor. Couples writhed and shimmied to the disco songs that were still popular in Japan despite their extinction in the United States.

It took ten minutes of diligent searching to locate Shigeru. The man was long and lean, dressed in a black blazer with wide lapels and a crimson shirt, his hair swept straight back from a wide forehead. Gold chains twinkled at his throat, and a row of four diamond earrings glistened at the bottom of his mutilated ear. He sat at a table near the wall of windows overlooking the street below and whispered to his hostess. They both laughed, and he slid his left hand farther down the low-cut dress she wore until he firmly gripped her breast. Her mouth made a false O of appreciation as her eyelids fluttered shut for a moment. She stroked his wrist.

A big man with a drooping mustache bisecting an acne-pitted round face sat to Shigeru's right. He was beefy and broad and looked uncomfortable in the suit he wore.

Bolan loosened the button on his blazer as he stepped forward to permit instant access to the Taurus. Floating candles in a small bowl centered on the table gave off an uncertain light that flowed across the faces of the three people who looked up at him. Shigeru's flat, dark eyes gleamed like a cat's. The hostess kept glancing at Bolan, then back at Shigeru questioningly.

"Who are you?" Shigeru asked. He released the woman and settled farther back into the round booth.

Bolan placed a thin sheaf of yen on the table near the floating candles and tapped them out with a forefinger. "I'm a businessman looking to make a deal."

Shigeru licked his lips. "I don't know you."

"You wouldn't." Bolan indicated the fan of yen. "But you know these."

"It isn't so very much."

"This isn't a big deal. Less than five minutes' worth of work. I need some information."

The hostess reached out to touch the money, and Shigeru slapped her hand away. Smiling, she reached down under the table and whispered something in his ear that made him laugh. The guard on the other side of Shigeru never took his eyes off Bolan.

"What do you want?" Shigeru asked as he pushed the woman off.

"You forged passports for the men killed down by the Sumida. I want to know who hired you to do the work."

The smooth smile melted from Shigeru's face quickly, leaving only a chiseled grimace in its place. "I don't know what you're talking about."

Bolan made his voice graveyard still. "It's your choice, guy. You can take the money, or I can drop the message in the ears of a few people on the streets. Either way something starts to happen and I find out what I need to know. If you take the money, you might get to live."

"Who told you this?"

"Does it matter?"

"Whoever told you I was involved in that was lying."

"Those men have a price on their head," Bolan said. "I'm willing to bet the man who helped them get the passports they needed to get in and out of Tokyo probably has a price on his head as well.''

''You have no proof.''

''How much proof do you think the people you do business with need?'' Bolan saw droplets of perspiration glisten on the man's forehead.

Shigeru spoke in Japanese. The big man sitting beside him reacted instantly. A long, slim-bladed stiletto appeared in his hand from a sleeve of the jacket and streaked for Bolan's hand on the table.

Bolan moved his hand slightly, and the needle point of the knife slid by harmlessly to bury itself in the table. He thumbed back the hammer on the pistol as he slid it from his waistband. The guard froze when he saw the muzzle come level with his chin, his hand still locked around the quivering knife. ''The ante's been raised,'' the Executioner told the guard. ''Are you in or out?''

Eyes smoldering with fury, the guard took his hand from the knife.

The dancers kept gyrating out on the dance floor. The density of the flowered walls around the booth kept people in the adjoining booths from seeing what had happened. The hostess bit the fingers of one hand as she quivered in silent terror, and Shigeru had a sick look on his face.

Bolan ripped the stiletto from the table as he sat down across from the guard, the Taurus out of sight. ''Keep both hands on the table,'' he instructed the men. He put the yen back into his pocket. ''Tell him if he moves his hands from the table, he'll be the first man I kill.''

''Takei understands English,'' Shigeru said.

Bolan faced the man. ''There will be no hesitation.''

The guard nodded. ''Pray I do not find you again, Westerner.'' His voice was ponderous and threatening.

''Maybe I should kill you now and save myself the worry.'' Bolan kept his face neutral and watched the big man blanch. ''You need to get yourself a more experienced guard, Shigeru. One who knows when to keep his mouth shut. Otherwise this guy is going to get you killed." He faced Shigeru, keeping the Taurus centered on the guard's stomach. "Who arranged for the passports?"

"Hosaka contacted me three months ago and told me to have them ready. That is all I know. I was not told who would be using them, or why the men were coming into Tokyo. I—"

Something flashed toward Bolan and his combat reflexes took over, forcing him farther back into the booth. A razor-edged *shaken* skimmed by his face, barely missing his eye as it clipped a lock of hair from his temple.

Takei, the guard, scrambled under his jacket and withdrew a huge revolver. The dance floor erupted into sudden pandemonium as three figures dressed in black from head to toe forced their way through the dancers. Glittering swords flashed in black-gloved hands as the ninjas cleared the slower moving people out of the way. Blood splashed onto the polished floor, and screams ripped the air as the recorded music came to a scratchy halt.

Shigeru hadn't been quick enough to avoid the throwing stars. One had embedded in his broad forehead and left him sprawled lifeless on the table, his eyes staring blindly upward as if seeking what had killed him. The hostess had dropped beneath the table and started screaming.

The Executioner shot Takei as the big man tried to level the .357 in his hand. The guard still managed to get one shot off as he died. The large-caliber bullet exploded padding from the booth in a brief snow flurry.

Semiblinded from the foot-long muzzle-flash of the Magnum, the Executioner vaulted over the back of the booth as the three ninjas closed in. He spilled over the flowered wall, crushing the table of the booth behind his. He got to his feet, maintaining his grip on his gun as the first ninja leaped after him. Squeezing the trigger in rapid-fire, he put three rounds across his adversary's chest before the man could land. The body came down awkwardly, sword spinning from nerveless fingers.

When the warrior looked back for the other two attackers, there was no sign of them. People scattered before him as he moved out with the Taurus at his side. Blinking his eyes didn't help clear the spots dancing in his vision. The darkness of the club would give the ninjas another advantage.

He stayed with the glass wall overlooking the street at his back to limit the number of directions they could come at him. Screams of the injured and frightened people made hearing almost impossible. Some of them had crowded toward the elevator while others took the stairway on the other side of the room.

Glistening steel whistled at his head from nowhere. He blocked the keen edge of the ninja sword with the barrel of his pistol, saw sparks fly as metal met metal and felt the automatic wrenched from his grasp. The ninja stepped back and swung again.

Bolan went down, landing on his hands as he kicked out with his feet. His boots caught his enemy in the stomach and sent the smaller man spinning away. The Executioner got to his feet instantly, but the darkness had swallowed his attacker and his gun.

Emergency lights came on and washed away some of the blackness, showing him the Taurus lying in the open only a few feet from him. He went for it, fisting the stiletto in his pocket he'd taken from the guard. Movement alerted him, and he held himself back from the pistol as one of the ninjas stepped out of the darkness and made a throwing motion. Two *shaken* skated across the floor in front of Bolan, but the third stabbed into his thigh. He threw the stiletto underhanded as the black-clad figure rushed at him with the sword.

The stiletto caught the ninja in the throat and sent him staggering back. He dropped the sword as both hands clutched at the knife.

Bolan retrieved the Taurus, not pulling the *shaken* from his leg until he had the pistol safely in hand. He fired once, putting a round between the eyes in the oval slit of the ski mask. The ninja went over backward. The Executioner dropped the throwing star to the floor as he searched the darkness for the remaining man.

A smoke bomb exploded in front of him with a loud pop as running footsteps came at him from behind.

Bolan threw himself to one side as he jerked his eyes toward the attacker. The ninja was on top of him before he knew it, knocking them both to the floor. The warrior rolled, evading the sword as it flashed down at him to stab the floor. The ninja was on one knee, working the weapon with both gloved hands as he pursued the Executioner relentlessly.

Unable to bring the Taurus into line for a shot, Bolan lifted a leg and caught the man in the head with enough force to send his attacker sprawling. Head reeling from the impact with the floor, the Executioner forced himself to stand, squaring off against the ninja.

A gloved hand snapped forward and sent spinning death at Bolan. The Executioner ducked to one side as he brought his weapon into target acquisition. The parabellums drove the ninja backward, making the body jerk as each round scored in the throat and chest area. Some of the bullets passed through the man's body to fracture the glass wall behind him.

Reflected light from the whirling mirrored globes suspended over the dance area created a strobe effect. The glass shattered behind the ninja as the Executioner's final round pushed the man through the weakened area. The figure pitched over backward silently, spilling through the sudden opening.

Aching, the pain in his side a roused and angry beast, Bolan changed clips in the automatic as he walked forward. Blood trickled down his injured leg. The screams had diminished behind him, pierced by the strident wailing of police and emergency vehicles that pulsed through the shattered glass wall. Whirling blue cherries gleamed in the street below, flashing over the man who was spread-eagled across the crumpled top of a luxury car surrounded by people.

Bolan knew with a grim certainty that Shigeru hadn't been the target of the attack. The man had only been the bait. But he was still confused as to who had been the intended victim. No one was supposed to know about him, but it seemed he was the only one who didn't know why Brognola had called him to Tokyo. Unless someone had been covering the chance of the mercenary force from the Sumida River trying to get in touch with Shigeru again. And Hosaka's name had turned up once more.

A harsh, authoritative voice sounded behind him. Bolan turned slowly to face a handful of men in Metropolitan Police uniforms with drawn guns centered on his chest. The authoritative voice called out again.

He didn't understand the language, but the meaning was clear. Slowly he laid the Taurus on the floor and moved away from it with his hands locked behind his head. One of the men came forward and forced him to his knees, pressing a gun to his temple.

"DO YOU EVER get tired of living in paradise, Mr. Picard?" Senator Robert Dawkins asked.

Picard moved forward easily, seasoned to the rolling gait of the yacht. He handed the younger man a glass of wine and toasted him as they looked out over the Caribbean. "Please, Senator, call me Philip. All my friends do." He smiled gently.

Dawkins nodded. "Call me Bob." He yawned. "Excuse me, but even with the recent senatorial meetings, I'm not used to getting up this early." The senator cut a trim, boy-ish figure in his white shorts set, deck shoes and sailing cap. With his unruly brown hair, hazel eyes, square-cut features and soft Southern accent, he had a presence television cam-eras treated very well.

"I love the mornings," Picard said as he stared out over the glimmering emerald depths of the sea. Gentle swells lapped against the fiberglass hull of the sixty-foot yacht. The sun was still a crimson ball in the eastern sky, and some-where below it was his private island. "I feel challenged by every sunrise I see to go out and do something different every day. Breathe in that salt air." He breathed in deeply as an example.

Dawkins laughed as he glanced up at the full sails above them. "How can a man who owns his own chunk of heaven feel challenged? What could there be left for you to want?"

"A great many things," Picard replied. "Would I be getting too personal if I asked how old you are, Bob?"

"No," Dawkins answered. "In fact, it's a matter of pub-lic record. I'm forty-two."

"I'm a quarter of a century older than you are."

Disbelief filled Dawkins's features. "You don't look it."

Picard knew it and took pride in the fact. Part of it was due to his full head of white hair, and part of it was be-cause he took care of himself. Exercise had been a part of his life even before the sometimes grueling existence he'd had in the Agency. He'd made love to a beautiful young woman the previous night until the small hours of the morning be-fore getting back up at 5:00 a.m. to start his day with Dawkins. And it had only been four months since he'd killed his last man hand-to-hand. He sipped his wine and studied his guest over the rim of the glass. "Some men my age might be content to park their butts on a fishing boat to while away their golden years, but I'm not. I still look for those challenges out there, the same way you do. Only I've got enough experience behind me to temper my pursuit of those challenges with patience."

"So what could a man who seems to have everything possibly want?" Dawkins asked.

"Power," Picard replied.

Dawkins's smile this time was tainted with uncertainty.

Picard clapped the man on the back to reassure him, wanting to pursue his game one step at a time. "I don't think we're so very different there. Take these senatorial meetings you've been engaged with these past few months concerning the trade agreements the United States currently has with Japan. You began as a junior senator who just wanted to get involved. Now you're chairing the committee. I'd say you've done very well for yourself all things considered."

"I've been lucky," Dawkins said. "After Senator Deichart had his heart attack four months ago, they could have chosen anyone to chair that committee."

Picard recognized the disarming manner as being as fully affected as the Southern accent. "Not just lucky," he said. "You've been skillful enough to maneuver yourself through some tricky situations these past few months to get yourself where you are."

"Maybe it was just time for another strong politician from Alabama to take a stand in Washington." Humor glinted in Dawkins's hazel eyes.

"My boy," Picard said honestly, "you've done more than just take a stand. You've carved out a chunk of the Capitol terrain for yourself."

Dawkins sipped his wine as he watched the sails.

Picard knew the man hung on every word he said and was playing his current audience like a member of the media. The senator had learned to shine in the public eye over the past few months. "You're good in front of a camera," he told Dawkins in a quiet voice. "Actually, you're more than that. I've seen perhaps a handful of people who were better in live interviews than you are.''

"Don't you think it's time to introduce me to your company, Philip?'' a feminine voice interrupted.

Picard turned to find Cherie standing behind them. She was blond, had a curvaceous figure that stressed the red bikini she was wearing this morning and had an earthy sense of humor that never failed to delight and amuse him. Her one disturbing habit was her ability to walk up on him without being seen or heard.

"Yes,'' he replied. "Bob, I'd like you to meet Cherie Amsterdam. Cherie, this is Senator Robert Dawkins of Alabama.''

"Nice to meet you, Senator,'' the woman said as she smiled and extended her hand.

Dawkins shifted his glass, took the hand and bowed slightly. "Please call me Bob. Philip and I have been very informal this morning and I'd like to keep it that way.''

She released his hand and stepped into Picard's embrace, pressing sun-warmed flesh against him as she tilted her head up for a kiss. Picard kissed her forehead. She gave him a small pout and pulled the gray hairs on his chest to let him know she was aware he held himself in check because of his present company. Though he felt entirely at ease with the woman's open sexuality when they were alone, and enjoyed her company more than anyone's he could remember, he was still uncomfortable about showing those feelings in front of someone he didn't know. Then he remembered that that was going to change in the next few minutes, so he brushed his lips across hers. The pout went away.

"Can I get you refills?'' she asked.

Picard took Dawkins's glass and handed them to her. "Please. Only this time make it the Napoleon brandy.''

She arched an eyebrow with amused interest. "The good stuff?''

"We're starting an early celebration.''

"I still think good brandy is wasted on an old sod like you," she said with sweet innocence. "Hopefully Bob will appreciate it enough to keep from gulping it down the way you do."

Dawkins grinned.

"Will we have breakfast aboard the yacht?" she asked.

"No. I've already radioed Henri to have something prepared by the time we reach the island."

Cherie nodded and walked away.

"Very pretty girl," Dawkins said when he turned back around.

"And bright," Picard told him. "Surprisingly she's become a very large part of my life these past three years." He was even more surprised by the honesty in his voice.

"You're a lucky man."

Picard didn't say anything as he turned around to gaze at the bow. He caught hold of the rigging as he moved forward. "Come on. You're about to get your first glimpse of the island."

They came to a halt and hung on to the rigging together, rocking with the swells of the ocean. Verdant growth was the first thing visible above the waterline, immediately followed by beaches filled with white sand and encircled by brightly colored flowers.

"Breathtaking, isn't it?" Picard asked.

"Yes," Dawkins said.

"Four miles at its widest point," Picard recited, "and two and a half at its narrowest. It's taken a lot of time and money to get it to what I wanted. But that's what I was talking about when I mentioned patience."

"Are you gloating again?" Cherie asked. She stood behind them with brandy snifters.

Picard took them and gave one to Dawkins. He kissed the woman, and she wrapped her arms around his neck. "Now if you'll excuse us," he told her, "we've got some business to finish transacting."

She wrinkled her nose at him and walked to a point a dozen feet away. Without regard to either of them or to the yacht crew, she sat on the deck and removed her top as she lay on her stomach.

"Why did you come here?" Picard asked, ignoring the naked desire in Dawkins's hazel eyes. Jealousy didn't exist in the world he had built for himself because it was an emotion that denoted a lack of confidence. He owned what he owned because he could own it.

Dawkins blinked and focused on him. "Because you asked me to."

"What do you know about me?"

An easy grin formed on the senator's lips. "I know you own an island in the Caribbean, you have this fine yacht, you enjoy a good reputation among some of the cabinet members and you have enough political clout in the right circles to give a junior senator a leg up."

"Honest avarice," Picard said with a smile. "I like that in a man. However, our world views appear to be at loggerheads at present."

"What do you mean?"

Picard sipped his brandy. "I mean the present Japanese problem."

The humor oozed from Dawkins's face. "If you've brought me out here to try to convince me my position on the Japanese embargo issue is wrong, I'm afraid you've wasted your time and mine."

"Maybe not."

Dawkins seemed startled by the apparent sincerity in Picard's tone.

"You see, I know about the deals Joji Hosaka has offered you to represent the interests of his business consortium in Washington. And I know the kind of money he's been talking about with you."

"His people have every bit as much right to lobby as anyone else," Dawkins said defensively.

Picard lifted his glass. "To free enterprise under the American flag. As long as it's in the interests of the American people."

"I think you're being unfair by suggesting the policies I'm fighting for are against the American people," Dawkins said in an even voice. "We can't simply discontinue trade with them because they have a higher profit margin than we do."

"Nor do I want to see the country continue to be sold out to foreign interests in a piecemeal fashion that's being allowed through a lot of flag waving."

"As a businessman, you know foreign dollars are something every branch of government is after now. Even city planners are soliciting money to put projects together. This country has been borrowing against tomorrow to pay for today for decades now. That's not going to stop overnight."

"No, but there's no time like the present to start things heading in that direction. I've been working on the Japanese problem for a number of years."

"There's nothing you can prove," Dawkins said. "And there's nothing wrong with Hosaka's people talking to me. But there's plenty wrong with spying on a person, especially a Senator. When I get back to Washington, you can bet I'll start an investigation into this."

Picard set his brandy glass between his feet and applauded. "Very good, Senator. You're learning all the pomp and chest beating you'll need to take you far in your career. You're turning out to be even more than I expected."

The look on Dawkins's face told Picard that his reaction to the threat wasn't expected.

"Come with me, and let's talk man-to-man for a while."

Dawkins stood his ground. "I want the use of a marine telephone and I'll be on my way."

"Don't be a childish ass," Picard said. "Take a look at what I have to show you, then if you don't want to listen anymore, I'll have my pilot fly you back to the mainland in the Lear."

Dawkins followed hesitantly as Picard led the way down into the spacious living room filled with modern furniture and small oil paintings. "Have a seat," Picard said, waving at the plush couch as he walked to the entertainment area built into the wall. He selected the videotape he wanted and slipped it into the VCR. Then he crossed the living room floor and seated himself beside Dawkins. "There's more brandy if you'd like."

"No. I'm fine."

Picard picked up the remote control and switched on the television, then the VCR. "Hosaka wanted you for a lot of the same reasons I did. You're young, photogenic and will appeal to the women voters, especially when you keep throwing in lines about how Japanese investments secure jobs for their husbands."

"A lot of those women work, too."

"True, and it doesn't hurt to point out in interviews that Japanese businesses often hire American women as vice presidents to help with PR and staffing. No, you've got your spiel down perfectly, and I have to say I admire the ways you manage to get it into every interview you do."

The television screen cleared, showing a recent segment of *60 Minutes*. Dawkins looked immaculate.

"See, this is the image Joji Hosaka invested in, this clean-cut, wholesome representative of middle-aged, middle-class America. And it's the image I want working for me as we start turning your views around on that committee."

"I'm not for sale," Dawkins asserted.

"Aren't you?" Picard fast-forwarded the tape. "Take a look at this."

The scene was a motel bedroom. A naked young girl was on the bed on her hands and knees, her shrieks and cries of passion overly loud in the stillness of the yacht's living room. Behind her, thrusting vigorously, was Senator Robert Dawkins.

Picard laughed out loud as the television image of Dawkins gave a sudden moan of completion and collapsed across the girl's back. He slapped the senator on the knee. "Overall, the performance lacked in creativity," he said, "but it carried a lot of energy, and you were very photogenic." He looked at the man. Dawkins had gone ash-gray.

"The girl was fourteen years old, though I realize that's hard to believe with the way she developed early," Picard said. "Even without the statutory rape charge, what do you think your chances of political survival would be if this hit *60 Minutes*? Or even graced the pages of the *National Enquirer*? To say nothing of your marriage and three children."

"I haven't done anything like that in years," Dawkins said in a strained voice.

"That was taken a little over eighteen months ago," Picard said. "As I told you, I've been working on this problem for years. It's only now gotten to the point that something needs to be done, and can be done. That's only one of the tapes I have on you, but I thought it was representative of the collection."

"You're a bastard, Picard." Dawkins stood and paced the floor.

Picard could see the man's mind working. "Oh, come now, you can call me Philip."

"I can beat this," Dawkins said. "I've got enough media behind me that I can beat this."

Picard leaned back against the couch. "I think you're letting your ego run away with your reason. And, anyway, you haven't seen it all." He fast-forwarded again.

The scene this time was another bedroom. Picard was on camera himself, standing beside the bed with a flashlight in his hand. The screen-version Picard pulled the sheet back on a sleeping figure.

"Recognize the man in bed?" Picard asked.

"Senator Deichart," Dawkins said, hypnotized by the tape.

"Your predecessor as chairman of the committee," Picard acknowledged. "Now watch. This is where he has the convenient heart attack that puts you in control and into the limelight."

The screen-version Picard placed a pillow over the sleeping man's face and held it there tightly until the frantic struggling stopped.

"See?" Picard said as he switched the television and VCR off. "Heart attack. Of course, the diagnosis cost a little, but it was worth it. He didn't have any little habits that would be publicly embarrassing like you did." He stood and held out his hand. "Now, Bob, do we have a deal?"

CHAPTER NINE

Naked and handcuffed, Mack Bolan lay on the hospital table as the emergency room doctor cleaned his wounds. He rested his hands across his chest in an effort to find a comfortable position. Two uniformed policemen stood at both ends of the table, .38 revolvers holstered at their hips.

"This is going to hurt a little," the young doctor told him.

Bolan nodded.

"The cut on your thigh isn't going to require stitches," the doctor said as he swabbed on the medicine. "The one that concerns me is the wound in your side. Even though it's been treated and sutured, I think you have some infection there. How long ago was this done?"

"This morning," Bolan answered.

The doctor removed his glasses and cleaned them with a tissue from his pocket. He consulted his watch briefly. "It's almost midnight now so that would be fourteen hours ago, correct?"

"About that."

"So you were part of the Sumida River massacre as well," the doctor said. He put the glasses back on. His eyes were bloodshot and fatigued. "I was here this morning for the results of that myself. It appears both of us have had a busy day."

Bolan didn't say anything.

"I watched some very good people die this morning," the doctor went on, "and there was nothing I could do. Adults, children, apparently the men engaged in that activity didn't care who their bullets struck." He stepped back to the small portable table behind him and selected a scalpel from the tray. The thin edged glittered in his hand as he moved forward.

Tensing, Bolan readied himself for anything, staring at the doctor while keeping one of the guards in his peripheral vision. He twisted slightly without moving, shifting his weight toward the doctor.

One of the policemen spoke in an imperative tone. The doctor responded but kept approaching Bolan. The policeman didn't hesitate in drawing his side arm and pointing it at the doctor's chest. A whisper of leather at the opposite end of the bed told Bolan the other policeman had drawn his weapon as well. The guard repeated his order.

Looking at the men in disbelief, the doctor came to a stop and held his arms away from his body. One of the policemen came forward, holding his .38 in both hands. The scalpel clanged tinnily to the floor. Holding the .38 to the doctor's head, the cop produced another set of handcuffs and proceeded to lock them onto his prisoner's wrists. The doctor talked rapidly and angrily. The barrel of the revolver kept his face pressed against the wall. The cop said something that evidently went unobeyed because he grabbed a handful of the doctor's hair and slammed the man's face into the wall.

Bolan glanced over his shoulder, wondering if the other policeman's attention had strayed. So far no one had approached him concerning the papers he'd had in the Belasko name, even though some of the upper heads of the Metropolitan Police should have been aware of who he was. The detective in charge of the investigation at the Club Morena had asked him a few questions, which he had pointedly ignored and asked for Brognola instead, but nothing else had been done. For the past two hours he'd been locked up in a police van before being brought to the hospital for treatment. It was evident that someone was keeping him on ice, but he had no idea why. The other cop pointed the barrel of his revolver at Bolan's face and held it without blinking.

Bolan relaxed. If they were going to protect him, fine. If not, he couldn't make a move against them yet.

The privacy curtain surrounding the bed was whipped back suddenly as a bald man in a dark suit stepped through. The hard eyes glittered as they took in the scene. His carriage was erect, military. He turned his head slowly, glancing briefly at Bolan before moving on to the cop holding the doctor. He spoke softly. The policeman backed away immediately, holstered his weapon and stood at attention.

The bald man spoke again, and the policeman replied rapidly. When the doctor interrupted, the bald man silenced him with a wave. The cop finished, still at attention.

"Put the gun away," the bald man instructed the other policeman in English. The cop complied immediately. The new arrival stepped forward, hands behind his back. He surveyed Bolan's injuries dispassionately, finally looking into his eyes. "I am Captain Goro Fujitsu of the Ministry of Foreign Affairs," he stated in a clipped fashion.

Resting his hands on his chest, Bolan said, "Then you know who I am."

"Perhaps," Fujitsu said with a thin smile. "I know who your papers proclaim you to be." The doctor spoke again. Fujitsu stared the man into silence, then glanced back at Bolan. "Did you feel threatened by this man?"

Bolan thrust his cuffed hands into the air. "At the moment I feel threatened just being here."

"Of course," Fujitsu said with a small nod. "Doctor, would you explain the scalpel you approached this man with? In English, please, so he may get the benefit of your words."

"I was going to release some of the infection that has built up in his wound." The doctor pointed to Bolan's side. "You can see for yourself that it needs to be done."

Fujitsu walked around the table, carefully staying out of reach when he interfered with the policemen's line of fire, and inspected the wound for himself. He looked back at Bolan. "I believe him. Do you?"

"Yes."

"Perhaps everyone overreacted," Fujitsu said. "Kendo, you will apologize to Dr. Sasakawa before we leave." The policeman nodded at once. "And you and I," Fujitsu said to Bolan, "will talk when you are finished here."

"Not before I talk to Brognola."

All traces of softness left the Foreign Affairs man's face. "That may not be for some time," he said. "Apparently your papers have been lost. Mr. Brognola will not know you have been taken into our custody for hours. It will allow us to discuss how you have happened to be in the vicinity of at least two gun battles involving multiple homicides while in Tokyo less than eighteen hours. And perhaps during our discussion we will discover why you are really here."

Bolan felt the scalpel slice along the wound, then the pressure that had built up quietly oozed away.

"I do not think you need to go to any length telling him how to take care of his wounds," Fujitsu told the doctor as he scanned the numerous old scars on the Executioner's body. "He seems to have had a lot of experience with such things."

THE PIPER CUB CUT through the cloudless blue sky above the island under the watchful gaze of a helicopter gunship. Picard shielded his eyes from the burning noon sun as he watched the aircraft touch down with a gentle bump that sent sand devils spiraling in the wake of the tires. He remained with his Cadillac as a security team of his hand-picked mercenaries pulled to a stop beside the Cub. The men debarked with military precision, M-16s at the ready while the man in the rear of the Jeep manned a mounted M-60.

Air-conditioning continued to swirl from the luxury vehicle and caused Picard's skin to prickle. He took a pair of field glasses from the console and fitted them to his eyes. Adjusting the magnification, he brought the pilot into view just as the security team met him at the door.

The lead mercenary pulled the pilot to the ground at once, slammed him into the tarmac and pressed a 9 mm pistol to his neck. The pilot didn't resist. The other mercenary entered the Piper at a dead run.

Picard found himself holding his breath. He blew it out forcibly, then cursed his fears silently. It happened every time he was on hand for an arrival. None were ever a surprise, not with the radar systems and other security measures he'd gladly paid small fortunes for, and all expected arrivals were treated the same way. He didn't entertain on the island, except in specific instances as with Dawkins, and those who came to his island home knew to expect such treatment.

The merc inside the Piper came back out within five minutes after checking the plane for stowaways. Picard had no fears that the man might have missed something in his search. He had trained the security teams himself and oversaw the supervision of all replacements. All of them knew the penalty of failure.

He reached down for the two-way radio mounted above the console as he put the field glasses away.

"Sir?" a man's voice said after a burst of static.

Picard thumbed the button. "Yes, McMorgan?"

"All clear, sir. You may pick up your visitor."

"Thank you, McMorgan." Picard slid into the seat and hung up the microphone. He engaged the transmission and drove out of the thick press of jungle surrounding the airstrip.

The pilot dusted himself off as Picard rolled to a stop beside him. He thumbed down the electric window and said, "Get in."

"Your boys play rough, Sacker," Eric De Luca said as he dropped into the seat.

Picard pulled way from the mercenaries, making a slow circle around the Piper that would take them back to the mansion on the other side of the island. "Don't call me Sacker here," he said, referring to the code name the CIA had given him during the fifties. He'd been young then, and especially vicious in pursuing the different quarries they had given him to pursue. He had found his talent in counterattacks in the quiet and deadly little cold war that had blossomed in the wake of World War II. An expert in behind-the-lines assassinations, he'd become known in spy circles as "the quarterback sacker," though he doubted many of the young men who knew him by that name were aware of the reasons behind it. "Most of these men think I'm just an old fart with too much money and a closet full of paranoias."

"So what do I call you?" De Luca asked.

Picard looked at the man and smiled. "My friends call me Philip."

"Philip," De Luca repeated, attracted by the sight of the flora and fauna outside his window.

"This is your first time to the island, isn't it?"

"Yeah. I figured Tuley was pulling my leg when he described this place to me. Jesus, look at all those flowers. Did you have them planted here?"

"No, they're all common to the island," Picard replied. "How did the talk with Winterroad go?"

De Luca turned to face him. "I'm not sure. I gave it to him the way you suggested, told him I thought you were crazy with your idea of saving the United States from the Japanese business influence. The situation was kind of wild and crazy. He caught up with me in Vermont, just like you planned, dead tired just the way you said he'd be."

"Winterroad is like a bull terrier. Once he gets his jaws locked on something he won't let go. That's one of the reasons he's never advanced any farther in the Agency than he has.''

"Well, I promise you one thing. Winterroad hasn't lost anything when it comes to working in the dark. He took me out before I ever saw him, and I was damn lucky he knew who he was hunting out there or he would have killed me instead.''

"His knowing who you were was one of the things we planned on.''

"Yeah, well, I wondered plenty about that very thing while I dragged my ass around in the dark last night.'' De Luca scratched his stubbled face tiredly and yawned.

"How did he take it when you mentioned the Japanese problem?''

"Like I said, I don't know. It was dark. I couldn't read his face. He didn't try to convince me I was crazy for believing you, but that wouldn't have been one of the topics we were interested in. His partner was busy scouting around for us.''

"Harry Vachs?''

"That's the guy. I didn't know you knew about him.''

"I know about a lot of things, Eric, remember? I knew enough to send Tuley and his men down to El Salvador and have you busted out of that prison.''

"True.''

"I've got a file on Vachs. He's a nobody. Winterroad's the man I want. That same dogged determination that keeps him running afoul of Langley will be something I can turn to our advantage, once I convince him his loyalty's in the wrong place.'' Picard put the car into gear once more.

"What about Tucker?'' De Luca asked.

"I can't leverage Tucker,'' Picard said. "He's part of the new Agency section chiefs. His background is clean from what I've been able to find out, which is one of the reasons Langley has him stationed in Tokyo. They've known for some time that Japan was going to be a hot spot again.''

"Too bad,'' the pilot commented.

Picard nodded, but knew it was more Tucker's misfortune than his.

"COFFEE?" Captain Goro Fujitsu asked as he lifted the pot from the hot plate in one corner of the interrogation room.

Bolan started to shake his head, then nodded. If Fujitsu intended to try to drug him, it would have been done in the hospital. He declined sugar or cream.

The Foreign Affairs man poured two cups, one ceramic and the other plastic. He placed the plastic cup on the table in front of Bolan, staying well out of reach. The liquid was scalding, but he drank it anyway. The last thing a soldier griped about in enemy territory was hot coffee, and he had the feeling that he was definitely in enemy territory.

The interrogation room was small, continuing the overall appearances of the tiny, out-of-the-way police station Fujitsu had found to continue their one-sided conversation. The table between them was short and narrow, framed by four metal chairs. Fujitsu sat comfortably in his by the closed door. So far the Executioner had seen no weapons on the man, but two policemen stood guard just outside.

The pain in Bolan's side had subsided considerably, and the wound in his thigh only twinged when he moved. More than anything else he needed sleep. He stared into Fujitsu's hard eyes and sipped his coffee.

"How well do you know Hal Brognola?" the Foreign Affairs man asked.

"We go back a long way," Bolan replied.

"So you trust him?"

"Yes."

"What about Alan Tucker?"

"I don't know him."

The frown on Fujitsu's face was slight. "Tucker is the CIA section chief on this operation."

"We've never met."

"I do not understand. How could you be brought in on an operation and not know some of the key people?"

"That's the way this one worked out."

"You seem undisturbed by that. Is this a usual occurrence in your job?"

"No, but it happens." Bolan flashed the man a mirthless smile. "It doesn't bother me nearly as much as being told the Japanese police and Foreign Affairs people were working with us on this."

Fujitsu grimaced. "There are reasons that everything is not being, as you would put it, played completely aboveboard."

"There always are."

"You have a very caustic sense of humor."

"I'll take that as a compliment." Bolan sipped his coffee and wondered where the man was headed this time. Fujitsu had a talent for asking the same question nineteen different ways, then pulling a twentieth one out of left field.

"Would you be as ambivalent about the matter if I told you my government has reason to believe that at least one of those two men is a traitor to the mission you have been engaged on?"

Bolan remained silent. His palms soaked up heat from the plastic cup as he wondered how big the hornet's nest was that Brognola had invited him to invade.

"SO JAPANESE investments are definitely on the downswing in the markets?" Picard asked. He cradled the telephone on his neck while he typed commands into the computer keyboard on the teakwood desk he'd commissioned.

"Shit," Keith Caputo said on the other end, "the goddamn yen flow is drying up like a cow pond in a drought. The federal finance people are getting pretty tense about it, but, hell, you can't blame the Japanese for wanting to keep their investments close to home so that they can keep an eye on them. This shit that's been going on over in the States is really fucking everything up." The financial adviser sounded like a man with his back against the wall. "If this heart-break don't let up in the next few months, I wouldn't be surprised if they start scraping stockbrokers up from the streets like they did back in '29."

Picard studied the figures and quotes as they streamed across his monitor from the financial man's data base. "It can't be as bad as you're making out," he said. The figures didn't get as emotional as the man at the other end of the phone connection, but they bore his words out. Picard enjoyed the triumphant feeling building inside.

"Come on," Caputo said in mock derision, "the Japanese investors pulled us out of that economic disaster of 1987. The falling American dollar that year put the Japanese yen on the map as a viable international commodity. If I remember correctly, you made a pretty good lump of cash from their investments. Remember me asking you how you knew when they'd come across?"

Ignoring the question, Picard switched off the computer and blanked the screen. "So there's no telling how far down the market may go?"

"I'm trying to tell you that at the present rate the market may never get back up again."

"I think you're wrong."

"I'm praying I am."

Picard made a notation in a ledger culled from the desk. "I'm having some money wired to your offices from some of my Zurich accounts," he said. "Feel free to play it in the money market for Japanese interests however you wish to as long as it stays liquid and ready to sink into the market. I'll let you know the properties I want to purchase when I'm ready."

Caputo was hesitant. "How much money are we talking about here?"

"One hundred million dollars."

There was silence at the other end of the connection for a moment. "That's a lot of money."

"You're right. It is."

"Maybe you didn't understand what I said earlier," Caputo said in a hushed voice. "The market's taking a definite downswing because of the attacks on Japanese businesses here in the States. You could stand to lose all of it if you're not careful."

"I've got a hunch." Picard smiled as he waited for the man's coming outburst.

"Jumping Jesus! A hunch? Seriously, tell me you're kidding! God, we've never met, and already I'm going to miss you!"

"Don't worry. I've had all of the high windows taken out of my home. And I really do have a feeling about this. After all, we both got quietly rich during the fall in '87 when everyone around us lost their shirts." Picard soothed the man a few moments more, moving the conversation into small talk.

He left the expensively furnished den in a good mood. Everything was on course now. Soon there would be no way to stop the designs he'd put into motion since 1987.

He found Cherie in the indoor swimming pool in the west wing of the mansion as he knew he would. She was rigorous about her exercise, and the majority of her workout time was spent here. He made himself a drink from the large stock in the portable bar within easy reach of the chaise longue that he sank into.

"You look like the cat who ate the canary," Cherie observed as she stepped from the pool.

"I've had a good morning." He threw her a plush towel.

"Playing boy millionaire again?" she asked with a teasing smile.

Picard nodded and sipped the gin.

"Seriously, how much is too much? I don't know what your assets are, but I know they've got to be considerable.

Vhy do you remain so involved with making money?'' She traddled him with the towel around her neck, arms resting n his shoulders.

He touched her face gently, tracing a forefinger down the urve of her cheek. "It isn't the money, my dear. It's the ame. Dollars are only a way of keeping score."

The phone rang, and Cherie answered it. "It's for you. t's that man, Tuley." She handed him the receiver and valked back to the pool.

"Ross?"

"We've got a problem," Tuley said gruffly.

"That's why you haven't contacted me in the past twelve ours to let me know how your assignment went?" Picard sked with steel in his words.

Tuley blew out a breath. When he spoke again, his voice vas more humble. "The assignment is the problem. I've een dodging interested parties for that whole time and aking stock of our losses. Over half the team you detailed or this has been neutralized."

"How badly?"

"Most of them won't be rejoining us, sir. The others de-pend on whether they pull through and how hard the locals ean on them."

"I'd learned through CNN that it went pretty badly over here."

"It looked even worse from our side. A lot of good men vent down on this one."

"What about the men the local people have?"

"They know how to keep their mouths shut. You know hat."

"Good. I've already got three legal staffs working on utting deals for them with the Japanese government now. should be hearing about that soon. I don't expect any problems, but it may take some time. In a few days, as hings escalate over there, those men should be all but for-gotten in the media."

"Understood, sir." There was a pause. "If I could, I'd like to pursue this assignment solo."

"And file it yourself?"

"Yes, sir."

"No. Not at this point. Things have already been scheduled that we need to follow through on."

"But, sir, this guy's hell on wheels. We weren't expecting anything like—"

"All the more reason to be patient," Picard interrupted. "You're riding the crest of your emotions at the moment. That's bad enough, but trying to take the assignment on again without researching the subject further is foolish."

"Yes, sir."

"Let me do some more digging and see what I come up with on this end. You just stay with your present agenda."

"Yes, sir."

"And Ross?"

"Sir?"

"I'm counting on you."

"I know. I won't let you down."

"Good. You have another assignment coming up in a few hours, don't you?"

"It's about fifteen hours away."

"Are you staffed for that?"

"Yes, sir. We set up two different teams for the encounters."

"Right. Keep that in mind. Remember, this assignment's even more important than the first."

"Yes, sir."

"I'll get back to you about the other when you call in again." Picard broke the conversation, then dialed a Virginia number from memory. "Gene, this is Picard. I need research done on a Belasko, Michael, currently assigned to Hal Brognola of the Justice Department, and at present stationed in Tokyo. Have that ready for me in one hour." There was hesitation at the other end. "Can do, Gene?"

"Can do, sir." The man sounded reluctant.

Picard grinned. He still owned a few souls in Langley, and the knowledge was comforting. "And, Gene?"

"Yes?"

"I'll also need John Winterroad's extension number."

CHAPTER TEN

"I am the chief investigating officer of this operation in Tokyo," Fujitsu said as he poured Bolan a refill and placed it on the table. "I have agents in the United States working at that end, but I believe—as the CIA and your President evidently believe—that the root of this problem lies here in Japan." He tapped on the wooden door.

Bolan remained silent as he lifted the coffee cup to his lips and wished Brognola had been able to inform him about the purpose of the current mission before he'd set foot on Japanese soil. The course he'd set for himself since being ambushed had dictated swift reaction, yet it was hard to see how the two things were connected other than as an action to take him out before the opening play. He waited patiently for the Foreign Affairs man to continue.

The door was opened quickly and quietly by one of the uniformed policemen. Fujitsu said something in Japanese, and the man nodded and hurried away. He resumed his seat. "My immediate problem is finding out if the traitor in your ranks is Tucker or Brognola while maintaining protection over Japanese businesses in your country and searching for the supervisor of those actions here."

Bolan noticed the man took care to dismiss the American forces from his investigation except as suspects. "Why tell me this?"

"Because I have pursued the question as far as I am able. I am at an impasse. Do not make the mistake of believing I have told you this because I trust you." Fujitsu sipped his coffee. "I find an interesting paradox set before me. Apparently Brognola and Tucker have been placed together in this investigation by their respective agencies without their consent. And you seem both willing and able to choose your own path to follow, leading me to assume you are something of a free agent yourself."

"How did you arrive at this conclusion?"

"I bugged their rooms, of course, and I had directional microphones trained on them every chance I got. I have got hard copy of the first conversation they had when arriving at the Ministry of Foreign Affairs, as well as the one they had when visiting the homicide zones at the Sumida River." Fujitsu smiled. "As I understand it, Tucker is not convinced about the validity of your identity, either, and seems very concerned by it. After the display at the Sumida River this morning, I cannot say that I blame him."

Bolan let that pass.

A knock sounded at the door. Fujitsu got up and answered it, coming back with a slender file. "So, to flavor the confusion I find around me concerning American involvement in this matter, I want to impart some of the knowledge I have."

Bolan understood the reasoning Fujitsu based his actions on. During some of his own campaigns, the Executioner had found it necessary to rattle some cages to see what turned up just to keep the numbers in play. He sipped his coffee again and kept his eyes away from the manila folder the Foreign Affairs man placed in the center of the table. "Why me?"

"A fair question, Belasko-san, and I have only this to offer." Fujitsu made a fist and tapped his stomach. "Because, in here, I feel that this is the decision I must make. The head rationalizes the situation the same way, which is good, but for different reasons. I understand you to be apart from either Tucker's or Brognola's investigative efforts, yet working in conjunction with them. Evidently you answer more to yourself than they do, judging from the clarity of your decision to follow your own intuitions. You, I feel, will be able to deal with the evidence I am about to give you without resorting to following a chain of command as they will." He smiled. "If you are a free agent in this as I believe you to be, perhaps I can persuade you to help my cause, as well."

"And screw up the working relationship of the American team at the same time."

Fujitsu spread his hand and shrugged slightly. "You cannot make an omelet without breaking some eggs."

The old adage coming so unexpectedly from the Foreign Affairs man brought a wry smile to Bolan's lips. He set the coffee cup to one side and held up his hands. "I don't suppose I could talk you out of the cuffs."

"Sorry. I like you just the way you are. I have already seen the kind of violence you are capable of. I have no desire to see it up close."

"So you trust me even though you don't really."

"I find it needful if not truly comforting."

Bolan glanced at the folder. "If I look at the material you have in that, I might find myself needing to trust you."

"Perhaps."

"That's not very comforting."

"Now you appreciate my position in this."

"Maybe I do at that." Bolan took the folder and flipped it open, knotting the handcuff chain in his fingers to keep it from scattering the small pile of papers and photographs as he sorted through them. He identified Brognola immediately. One showed the head Fed coming down the steps of Justice with three men flanking him. Another showed Brognola and an unknown man seated at a booth of a restaurant Bolan recognized as the Howard Johnson's across from the Watergate Hotel where he'd met Brognola a few times himself. The last was of Brognola in an unknown parking garage talking to another man. There were four more pictures, but Bolan didn't know any of the people in them. He moved the pictures to one side and started going through the sheaf of papers that turned out to be English translations of coroners' reports on the men who'd been killed during that morning's firefight. Beneath that was another stack of eight-by-ten glossies. The faces revealed in these were of dead men. Some he recognized as having been in his gunsights, and some he recognized as having been in the first batch of pictures. He went back and matched them up.

Fujitsu tapped a calloused forefinger on the first pictures. "Here, here and here. See them with your friend Brognola? And here. This is Tucker. See them? Here, here, here and here. In all, four men are in the seven photographs we received. Four men who had their pictures taken with key American personnel working on an extremely delicate international affair. The same four men you later killed. One of those men has been identified as having been with the Central Intelligence Agency during the 1970s."

Going back to the coroners' pictures of the dead men, Bolan reflected grimly that not all of them had been killed by him. The fletched arrow shaft through one man's eye was a mute reminder of that.

"Assuming these men are known to Tucker and Brognola, why would they attack you?" Fujitsu asked.

"They might not be known to Hal or the CIA guy." Bolan returned the Foreign Affairs man's stare full measure.

"Someone knew. Just as someone knew at least some of these men would be killed in their engagement with you."

The memory of the woman ninja played through Bolan's mind again, followed swiftly by the three he'd killed at the nightclub. He wondered if this morning's help was just an effort to complete the confusion made by the pictures. It would have been hard to point an accusatory finger at Brognola or the CIA agent without the convenient corpses. "When did your department receive these pictures?"

Fujitsu settled back into his chair and said nothing.

"Have you got the negatives?" Bolan asked as he burned the details of the pictures into his mind.

"This is where cooperation on my part ends," Fujitsu said.

"It would be easier to find out if these pictures have been tampered with by checking the negatives."

"I am aware of that."

Bolan knew the man had already checked or was unable to check. He assumed the latter due to the way the Foreign Affairs man was putting the questionable intel into play in the mix of agencies. He closed the folder and pushed it back across the table. There wasn't a shred of doubt in his mind as to Brognola's trustworthiness. The two of them had been soldiers fighting the same war for far too long for that, but it didn't rule out the possibility that Justice had been compromised. The attack on the Sumida River proved that. The thought left him wondering how much he could trust his friend's organization with intel he gathered during the operation, recognizing the hesitation to share would limit Brognola's ability to help. A coldness spread through his stomach as he studied Fujitsu's impassive gaze and realized the reverse knowledge was already achieving its desired effect. Fujitsu had called the play with the skill of a master strategist because he'd read Bolan as a loner and provided stimulus that would keep the Executioner operating that way.

Whoever had engineered the photographs, whether partially true or not, had moved with animal cunning. Whatever quiet and deadly little game was being played out in Tokyo was building tension and suspicion as it turned the American investigative effort into a house of cards. Bolan had no doubts that the wind that came along to sweep it away would be an eruption of bloody violence that would leave no one in its path untouched.

TULEY CAME TO A HALT at the curb outside the nightclub where he'd called Sacker, and waited for Vardeman to bring their car around. Repressed anger still turned his stomach sour. The last thing he needed right now was for Sacker to tell him how to do his job. He blinked his eyes in vain to clear the bleariness that stained his vision.

He cupped his hands to light a cigarette, then shut the lighter with a quick snap. When he looked up, he saw two men step from the crowd leaving the back alley nightclub where he and Vardeman had spent the past two hours. The skin across the back of his neck prickled, and he crushed the cigarette under his shoe.

He dropped the lighter into a jacket pocket with one hand while the other reached for the .45 holstered on his hip. His fingers brushed against the butt of the pistol as a cold, blunt cylinder was screwed into the base of his neck.

"Don't," a thin, reedy voice cautioned.

Tuley took his hand away from the .45 and swallowed hard. He thought about trying a spin kick on the man behind him, then saw the two men in front of him bring Uzi pistols into view. The man behind him relieved him of his side arm, then pulled the barrel away from his neck.

"Hands on your head," the reedy voice commanded.

Tuley complied at once. Right now his captors held all the aces, but he knew from experience if he gave them a little slack, things could change in a heartbeat. He'd come out of worse than this. If they proved to be Tokyo police, he'd sit in the cooler for a short time before Sacker pulled him out of it. All things considered, he decided he'd rather come out of the present situation on his own. Belasko had already screwed the mission up enough as it was.

"This way," the man behind ordered, yanking him into the shadows of the alley.

Tuley stumbled and skinned an elbow on a brick wall. He cursed under his breath. The stench of rotten vegetables, fish and stale urine almost took his breath away. A round whiteness blurred in the distance. When he got up closer, he realized it was Vardeman's face.

Vardeman was on his knees in the alley. Two men stood on either side of him and held Uzi muzzles just under his ears. "Bastards got me before I even saw them, Ross." The big man sounded apologetic.

Tuley gave him a tight nod of encouragement as he recounted the five men that held them. The man behind him grabbed him by his collar and said, "Down on your knees."

Tuley dropped to the ground, wetness from the alley soaking the knees of his slacks. His adversary yanked his jacket down with a sudden pull, pinning his arms. Tuley started to come back up fighting, but one of the men stepped forward and smashed the butt of an Uzi into his face. Blood flowed from his forehead into his eyes.

"You stay put," the man behind him said. "Alive or dead, it doesn't matter to us. Hosaka pay us all the same."

Tuley recognized the name at once as being on Sacker's list of targets.

"Never figured it would end like this," Vardeman said in a resigned voice.

"Silence!" one of the gunners ordered.

Clamping his jaw muscles tight to keep in the fear and rage pummeling through him, Tuley watched the men. One mistake, that was all he was asking for.

There was a moment of conversation, then one of the men dug a set of keys from his pocket and ran back down the alley. Tuley shifted subtly, swallowing hard when both guns at his throat increased their pressure. At least they were taking him alive. He made himself wait.

A van rolled down the alley with the lights out and came to a stop in front of them. He and Vardeman were allowed to rise to their feet as the driver ran around the back to unlock the doors. The man fell back with a shrill cry of pain as the doors exploded open to reveal a man dressed in black from head to toe. A short length of dark steel glittered in one hand as the other flashed forward.

What looked like a kid's set of jacks suddenly covered the face of the man to Tuley's left and sent blood streaming from numerous superficial wounds. The man went down, clawing at the caltrops as he tried to trigger a burst at the black-garbed man. Nine-millimeter rounds ripped through the back of the van, but the target was no longer there.

Tuley caught an impression of movement in his peripheral vision, then the head of the man on his right jumped from the man's shoulders. He felt warm blood spray across his arm as the corpse fell away from him.

One of the men covering Vardeman thrust his Uzi at the masked man and squeezed off a burst of parabellums. Tuley hit the ground at once, reaching for one of the fallen machine pistols. The sword blurred, slicing through the gunner's forearms and dropping hands and weapons into the alley. The injured man had time for one scream before the sword swept across his throat and removed his larynx. The last man was too far away for the sword, and Tuley figured his unknown benefactor's advantage had ran out.

Then the black-clad man's arm snapped out. Something that resembled a railroad spike sunk into the gunner's forehead and dropped the man instantly. Vardeman had never moved, still holding his hands on top of his head.

Tuley pulled the Uzi into his chest as the man in black turned to face him. He stared into the man's dark eyes, barely visible in the oval of the mask, as he rolled over onto his back. The man in black clasped his sword hilt in both hands as he kept his eyes focused on Tuley.

"Hold it right there," Tuley ordered as he brought the Uzi into target acquisition. As he watched, the outlines of the man seemed to blur and become indistinct. He blinked and could see nothing at all of the man. He forced himself to his feet and moved in cautiously on the wall where he'd last seen the man. There was nothing there. He made himself reach out a hand to touch the bricks.

"Holy shit," Vardeman breathed as he dropped his hands. "I've never seen anything like that."

Tuley made a slow circle, letting his peripheral vision max out, keeping the machine pistol at his waist. A dozen people had spread across the mouth of the alley. "Get our pistols and let's get the hell out of here." Vardeman began searching the bodies.

Shifting the Uzi to single-shot, Tuley put a round through the blinded man. He checked the body of the man who had opened the van doors and found ropes of intestines covering the guy. He fought down the urge to be sick. He had seen death a myriad times before, had dealt it out himself on a very personal basis, but he'd never seen something like this happen so quickly. The back of his neck prickled again.

"Who was that guy?" Vardeman asked.

"I don't know."

"Where did he go?"

"How the hell should I know? You were standing here, too. You tell me."

"Hey, take it easy, Ross. We're in this together, remember?"

Tuley let out a tense breath. "C'mon." He jogged down the alley with Vardeman right behind, wondering the whole time how the hell he was supposed to look for somebody who could vanish. They reached their car without incident. He dropped the captured Uzi out the window as Vardeman engaged the transmission and pulled them into traffic. Then he glanced over his shoulder to see if someone was following them.

"Clean?" Vardeman asked.

"As far as I can tell." Tuley turned back around and took a cigarette from his pack. He stared at his shaking fingers for a moment.

"It wasn't an accident that that guy was there," Vardenan said. "He was there to take care of us."

Tuley nodded.

"You think Sacker put him on to us?"

"I don't know. Sacker does things like that. You know hat as well as I do. He gives you a piece of the operation ınd never lets you know exactly where it fits, and he doesn't ell you how many different angles he's playing it from." Tuley remembered the sword flashing and the man's head lying loose through the air. "God, I hope so, because if it vasn't Sacker, we're in some deep shit here."

'WHAT THE HELL are we doing here, Hal?" Tucker asked, mothering a yawn with his hand.

Brognola clumped around the Club Morena painfully. 'I've got a feeling about this," he replied.

Two paramedics staggered out of the club's elevator with ı gurney between them. The sheet covering the body was bloody. Out on the street a half-dozen uniformed cops vearing riot gear kept the crowds from crossing their offiial lines.

"A feeling?" the CIA man repeated. "Okay, never mind. can understand that, but tell me why I'm here."

"That's even simpler," Brognola said as he smiled at him. The hours were finally starting to catch up with the youner man. "You're here because I can't speak the lanuage."

A plainclothes detective was taking statements from the mployees at a corner table. Three coffeepots were at his elow. Brognola wanted a cup but refrained from asking. Tucker had made it very clear that their presence was barely being tolerated. Throwing Fujitsu's name around didn't appear to impress the regular cops.

He'd gotten a glimpse of the carnage upstairs before the vidence recovery teams had restricted the area, but it had een enough. He'd been on a number of sites of Bolan hits

back during the early days of the Executioner's war against
the Mafia, and it had gotten to the point that he could tell
it was a Bolan blitz just by the crackle in the air. That crackle had been there tonight. So where was the Executioner?

"What kind of credit do you have with the homicide
people?" Brognola asked. A uniformed officer came down
the stairs on the other side of the room carrying a plastic
trash bag.

"I've got a little pull with a couple of guys I've been able
to do favors for in the past."

"Let's give them a call and see if you can find out where
they put the guy they took into custody."

Tucker looked like he wanted to argue, then shrugged and
moved toward a bank of pay phones around the corner from
the bar. Brognola noticed the homicide detective watching
him while changing interviewees. The CIA man dropped
coins into the phone and said, "Look, I listened to the same
translated-news station you did. There are a lot of Americans in this city. This doesn't have to be Belasko."

"Humor me."

Tucker's eyes showed that he'd like to do anything but.
He spoke in rapid Japanese, waited, then spoke again.

Brognola listened, growing more and more irritated at
being frozen out of the information exchange. He wasn't
sure which irritated him more, getting the intel secondhand
or depending on Tucker to get it. He watched the agent's
face shift from nonchalance to full-blown interest. By the
time Tucker hung up the receiver, he was frowning.

"Looks like you're right on target," the CIA man said.
"Giichi tells me they've identified the pistol the prisoner
used as one of a batch that had been brought into Japan a
few weeks ago by some arms dealers. They found a sizable
chunk of those weapons along with the bodies of known
arms traffickers earlier this afternoon. And, wonder of
wonders, some of those people had .45 slugs in them that
matched weapons used at the Sumida River target range.

Giichi didn't mind telling me that more than a few people want to get their hands on your boy.''

"Who has him now?''

"Fujitsu.''

A hard knot formed in Brognola's stomach. "Did you find out where?''

"Yeah. After I told Giichi the guy was one of ours, he told me where Fujitsu had him, and that Fujitsu had clamped down hard on this one from the beginning. Evidently our guy in Foreign Affairs has pissed off a lot of police people with his hands-off policy concerning Belasko. Giichi said one interview with your boy could clear a lot of paperwork from his desk and lighten the load immediately.''

"Sounds like maybe Fujitsu knew this was about to fall.''

Tucker shrugged. "At this point, between his shenanigans and yours, I wouldn't put anything past either of you.''

Brognola limped toward the door, turning events over in his mind and trying to make them fit together. It got confusing fast, and he gave it up.

"I've got it all figured out, though,'' Tucker said with heavy sarcasm. "If Fujitsu objects to our liberating your guy, we just slip Belasko a gun and let him shoot his way out. That seems to be his answer to everything.''

Brognola let the comment slide uncontested, filled with questions about why Fujitsu felt it necessary to isolate Bolan, and how much the Foreign Affairs man knew about the events that had taken place at the nightclub.

BOLAN SLEPT sitting in the chair in the interrogation room, one leg drawn up with his cuffed hands over it and his forehead resting on his knee. His combat senses came alive instantly when someone turned the lock. He looked up as Fujitsu entered the room with Brognola and Tucker. The CIA agent favored the photographs he'd seen earlier.

Brognola clamped an unlit cigar between his teeth and gave the Foreign Affairs man a hostile stare. "Where are the keys to those handcuffs?" he asked in a cold voice.

Fujitsu pulled a key ring from his pocket and tossed them to him. Brognola limped over to the table and sat down heavily. Bolan lifted his hands and presented the cuffs. "How are you doing?" Brognola asked.

"Better," Bolan answered tersely as the cuffs fell from his wrists. He rubbed the circulation back into his hands and stood.

"There are still a number of questions that need to be answered concerning the deaths you have been party to, Mr. Belasko," Fujitsu said. "My government would not think well of your department, Mr. Brognola, if he were to disappear in the next few hours."

"I won't be going anywhere," Bolan said. "I've got a few unanswered questions of my own."

Fujitsu smiled. "Of course. I am sure you do. Perhaps we can answer them together sometime soon."

Brognola didn't say anything, but Bolan sensed the restrained anger surging inside the Justice man.

Twenty minutes later the three of them were back on the street in Tucker's car. Bolan sat in the back seat. He'd had all of his personal effects returned except for the pistol. He watched the neon-lit streets unfurl around them as stills from the photographs Fujitsu had shown him slipped through his mind. "Does the name Hosaka mean anything to you, Hal?" he asked. He watched Tucker's reflection against the windshield as a bewildered expression filled his face.

Brognola swiveled in the seat. "He's one of the people we've been assigned to protect," the big Fed said. "How did you tumble to him?"

Thinking back on the information he'd uncovered about Hosaka, Bolan said, "It's time we had a long talk."

CHAPTER ELEVEN

"As near as we can piece it together at this point," Brognola said as he turned out the lights, "the assault on Japanese businesses in the States began six months ago. However, most of the agencies assigned to this in one capacity or another believe it started a long time before that, with less aggressive maneuvers."

Bolan, washed and freshly shaven, sat on the floor with his back to the wall and a coffeepot at his side. Around him, seated on the various chairs and the sofa in Brognola's motel room, were the other eight male and female members of the Justice team based in Tokyo. Five of them were obviously of Oriental heritage. When they had filed sleepily into the room after receiving a summons from Brognola, the Executioner had studied each of the three women, looking for the one who had been at the Sumida River. She wasn't among them.

"There have been eleven attacks in those six months," Brognola went on. He glanced at Bolan. "What do you know about the publishing offices being hit in L.A. four days ago?"

Bolan put his cup down. "The international newspaper I had available just sketched the bare bones of it. I know that it was incendiary in nature, executed by what was thought to be a small group of professionals, and nineteen people were killed in the ensuing fire."

"Two of those nineteen were security people who went down under small-arms fire," Tucker added. The CIA man sat perched on a desk beside a curtained window.

"Right." Brognola thumbed the remote control of the slide projector placed on a coffee table and color splashed against the white wall. The picture cleared and showed the blazing top of a skyscraper against a black, smoggy night. "This is what's left of the skyscraper in L.A. owned by Hosaka Industries. As stated, there were nineteen deaths related to this incident."

The picture changed again, showing a Japanese-owned real estate brokerage. The colorful sign hanging in front of the destroyed building hung by one corner. Fire trucks were frozen in the frame, forever too late. The picture shifted to reveal corpses almost shredded by the explosion.

"As far as we know now," Brognola said, "it began here, in Denver, with the deaths of four staff members."

"Are explosives always used?" Bolan asked.

A few of the agents seated around the room turned to study him.

"No," Brognola replied. "There are enough differences in the attack sites to tell us the hits were made by different people, and enough similarities to tell us that sometimes the same people were used."

"Who owned the real estate office?" Bolan asked.

"Shoji Kokan, a major land developer for the Japanese in America. Even though that office was small, they managed to compete head-to-head against the Canadians in that market. I'm told Kokan's people were turning millions of dollars through that office every year."

"Were all of the target areas big money-makers for the companies based in Tokyo?" one of the Justice men asked.

Brognola shook his head. "No. In fact, the publishing office that was destroyed in L.A. barely broke even." He looked around the room. "Any more questions?"

Bolan poured himself another cup of coffee during the silence. He stared at the pictures, riffled the facts through his mind and tried to fit in the bits of intel he'd gleaned since hitting the ground running. None of it seemed to go together. He sipped the coffee and listened.

"Look, people," Brognola addressed his audience, "I know we're all tired and anxious about tomorrow evening's function, but we're taking a final stab at this thing before we're in the middle of it."

"Looks like you and Belasko have already been there, sir," one of the women observed.

Brognola turned to the speaker. "Things took an unexpected turn for the worse today, Janet, as we all know. In addition to looking for whoever's behind these attacks, apparently we've been uncovered by our quarry. The attempt on Mike today is clear proof of that."

"And we no longer enjoy even the sham of cooperation we started with where our Japanese counterparts are concerned," Tucker said. The CIA agent's words had a sobering effect on the group.

"Eleven hits in six months," Brognola said, tapping the white wall where the corpse-filled picture still showed, "that we know of." The slide changed. "This was one of the cement companies Nogawa Building recently bought out in Atlanta. You're looking at 3.2 million dollars' worth of damage. Eight employees lost their lives that night."

The head Fed continued the litany of death that Justice and other agencies had threaded together in the past few months.

A Japanese-owned and -operated investment agency in New York had been hit next. Six men wearing ski masks assembled at an arranged area inside the building, then cut a bloody swath through the offices with automatic weapons before rappeling to the street and making their escape. Blurred slides from a security camera of the men in action accompanied Brognola's narration. Ten people were left dead. Owners of a Suzuki motorcycle dealership in Nashville arrived one morning to find their buildings burned to the ground, and their stock reduced to rubble. Three people were left dead, two salesmen working late, and a man cleaning up the offices. A Japanese-backed think tank in Silicon Valley was ransacked by a team that had no problems with security designed to protect the building from industrial espionage instead of commando tactics. Files were burned in the cabinets. The slides showed people sprawled across heavily stuffed furniture and lying on the floor. Nine people were dead. And on and on.

Bolan pushed the empty coffee cup away. He'd had his fill an hour ago. He gazed at the pictures that continued flashing on the wall, remembering how the stories behind most of them had caught his attention at one time or another in the past few months. In fact, most of them were logged in his war journal for follow-up at a later time if the situations didn't resolve themselves. Even then, with the different bits and pieces of information set before him in his own hand, he hadn't seen a national pattern; especially when they were sandwiched between other stories. Now, with everything spread before him, he could see it starting to take shape. But he still couldn't see what it hinged on.

The slide projector clicked and shifted. A van, wreathed in flames, was canted on one side. A film crew seemed to be in fuzzy focus around them. "We're not sure about this one," Brognola said, "but we think it might be a twelfth attack. It didn't fit the MO on this case at the time because it was believed to be an accident. Diligent research by FBI experts have led us to believe someone set extra charges under this van, which was manned by the special effects people, and the explosion was triggered by the electronic detonation designed to bring off the climax of the film. At first it appeared to be possible negligence on the part of the special effects people. The film was a science fiction epic being filmed in Orlando and was under heavy pressure to finish. There were other accidents while the filming went on, and that led back to the original belief of negligence. The movie was produced by Japanese investors hoping to break into the Hollywood market." The Fed faced his audience. "For our part, we'll take its presence in our file under advisement. The bottom line is that the film won't be finished at present due to the adverse publicity. Seven people died in that van, most of them Japanese nationals, and the cost of lost revenues is expected to run into the millions."

The scene blurred, was whipped away, then replaced by an interior shot of an assembly plant. Bolan sat up straighter as he viewed the carnage that had been left behind. Bodies were draped around overturned machinery warped by explosions. Bullet holes staggered across coveralls, stitched as surely as the names of the employees who had died in the cross fire. Smashed, twisted and burned truck bodies lay everywhere.

"This is the case that brought Justice onto the scene," Brognola said gruffly. "Over eighty people were killed in the assault at this light truck assembly plant in Detroit."

The picture winked away, replaced by another of an office area with bullet holes through the windows. More bodies were inside.

"VICAP—the Violent Criminal Apprehension Program—was initially assigned to this," Brognola went on, "because they thought we were looking for a small group of individuals. It quickly became apparent that we were dealing with a small army. The whole hit lasted only minutes and details were nailed down with skilled precision."

The slide projector whirred. A montage of scenes followed, detailing the blood-slick floors, the increasing number of bodies and the helplessness of the assembly workers to defend themselves.

"The VICAP team started the ball rolling by grouping the Detroit hit with two of the others. The targets had been the same, and the people killed fell into a category of their own, as well. This," Brognola tapped the wall with his cane, "showed the willingness on the part of the attackers to add even more lives to the balance. Whatever the stakes are as these people view them, evidently they're working on some sort of timetable that's been moved up. The hit on the publishing offices in L.A. is mild by comparison, yet larger than most of the other sites."

"American deaths to Japanese deaths at the assembly plant ran five to one," Tucker stated.

"There were a number of Japanese Americans among the dead," said Ron Roberts, an agent who'd been at the scene. He turned around to face the CIA man.

Tucker returned the look. "Even so the split was sixty-forty. These people aren't as particular as they were when they started out."

"So there's not going to be any cooperation between us and the Japanese?" one of the Justice agents asked.

"As far as I'm concerned," Brognola said in a level voice, "this is still a joint effort. Fujitsu, their man in charge, doesn't seem to play the same way we do, but we can't afford to be standoffish at this point."

"Is this because of the action at the Sumida River?" Roberts asked.

"Yes." Brognola didn't hesitate.

"And we were involved?"

"Yes. That was the ambush attempt on Belasko."

Heads turned in Bolan's direction, and he could read new assessments flickering into the eyes of the agents.

"The news also reported there were Americans down at the scene," Roberts went on.

Tucker got to his feet. "That hasn't been proved yet. The IDs on the bodies were false. We don't know who they were."

Roberts turned to face the CIA man. "I was also told that some of those unidentified bodies carried military tattoos."

"Tattoos can be copied," Tucker replied, "by anyone seeking to frame the United States for this."

Roberts rolled his eyes. "Then these guys knew they were going to be shot out of the saddle, right? Land of the kamikaze and all that, so why not?"

Tucker started to respond, but Brognola cut him short. "Who they were doesn't matter at this point. Our job tomorrow is to make sure the Hosaka Consortium meeting takes place without a hitch."

The voices died away as all eyes returned to Brognola.

"The one factor linking all these attacks, besides the Japanese one, has been that all of these businesses were owned in part, or outright, by the people who are going to be at that meeting tomorrow." Brognola paused to let that sink in. "We're working security with the Metropolitan Police and Japanese Special Services on this one, and you can bet we're not going to know all of their players. So make your play close to the vest if something goes wrong. We're skating on very thin ice here."

"The Japanese government hasn't been able to talk those people out of that meeting since the attack this morning?" one of the female agents asked.

Brognola shook his head. "No. In fact, the government has given those people assurances that nothing will happen. If Hosaka, Kokan and the others are able to work out their differences, the consortium they form will have a major impact on Japanese trade strategies."

"So everything's spinning around the pursuit of the U.S. dollar," Roberts observed.

"Yeah, that's one way of looking at it," Brognola agreed. "But you need to keep in mind that there are a lot of outlets for Japanese investment over there, as well."

"All of which amount to a slow but sure buy-out of America as we know it," Roberts added.

"We're talking politics here, Ron," one of the other men said. Bolan could detect from the tired anger in the man's voice that the argument was an old one. "Not economics."

Roberts nodded. "With Japan in the picture, it's one and the same."

"Shit, Ron, come on."

"Enough!" Brognola's voice was harsh and commanding. "We're aware there are a number of views we can take on this. You people need to remember the only reason we're here is to prevent a schism between our government and the Japanese."

Roberts blinked behind his glasses, but Bolan didn't see the man backing away from the fight. Evidently the agent held strong convictions about the kind of role Japan's business section played in the United States. The warrior wondered why Brognola had felt compelled to bring the man along, then figured Roberts must have had his high points, as well.

Brognola looked at Bolan. "Anything you'd care to add, Mike?"

Before Bolan could respond, Roberts cut in. "One thing I'd like to know, Agent Belasko, is why those guys tried to cap you and not any of the rest of us."

Bolan rose to his feet and addressed them from the front of the room. "I don't know."

Roberts looked skeptical.

"Whatever the reasons," Bolan continued, "that attack showed us a number of things. It showed they've penetrated our intelligence-gathering resources. It showed they are probably not only aware of me, but of each of you, as well."

Most of the faces looked uncomfortable with that possibility. Bolan pushed it home, wanting them to respect the power and abilities of the unknown group. "It showed how well trained they are. These people moved with military precision and skill. They secured the area and set up the ambush as if they've done it many times before." His voice turned cold. "These people are professionals, and you're going to end up dead if you don't respect that."

Roberts smiled, his white teeth gleaming in the darkness. "I don't know about the others, but it makes me wonder how you managed to get away unscathed."

"I'm not entirely unscathed." Bolan lifted his shirt to display his bandaged side.

Roberts didn't appear to be impressed. "What about the likelihood that those people were Americans?"

"I think they were. At least some of them."

Roberts looked back over his shoulder at Tucker. "Makes you wonder where they got their training, doesn't it, Agent Tucker?" The CIA man remained silent. "And it helps illustrate why the Japanese government wasn't exactly willing to open their doors to a bunch of Agency people when Langley volunteered their services," Roberts added.

"Let's call it a night, ladies and gentlemen," Brognola interrupted, "before things get too tense." He directed a look at Roberts, then at Tucker, making sure they knew to pack it in. "Thank you for your time and get a good night's sleep. You're going to need it. Mike, if you've got some time, I'd like to have a short meeting."

Bolan nodded. He watched as Tucker and Roberts filed through the door with the rest of the team and wondered which man he'd rather have on his side if it came down to it. Then he wondered what made him think he would get a choice.

"HELLO," Michi Ransom called softly. She stood quietly on the hilltop as the slight breeze chilled her. Her dark jeans and black turtleneck made her a part of the night around her.

Near the tomb directly in front of her, she saw the robed and hooded man turn his head to face her. He kept his palms together in front of him, still on his knees. The sleeves of the robe were large and voluminous.

Moonlight speared through the cherry trees overhanging the hilltop and painted angular planes on the tomb and the robed man's face. Dark night spilled down the hill around them, shooting tendrils through the dense foliage that hid the trail the woman had followed. She had found the trail without effort because of the summers she had spent making sure it would continue to exist. Her fingers had blistered from tying back wayward branches and uprooting bushes and trees that first year. Even then the aches of her body never came close to the empty hollowness in her heart.

The robed man came to his feet effortlessly, as if gravity and old age had no laws for him. Slowly he shook back his sleeves and pulled his hood back. Gray hair less than an inch in length covered his skull.

Ransom moved past him, walking to the tomb and placing the cherry blossoms on it. They had suffered very little in the fifteen-minute walk from her rental car. She stared at them as they shivered in the breeze as she did. Tears slid from her eyes and ran down her cheeks.

The old man moved silently to her side. He gripped her shoulders and turned her to face him. Studying her, he slowly wiped the tears from her face. "She has been gone so long. Why do you cry?"

"For you," Ransom replied. "Because I know you can't weep for her."

"I thank you," he said in a soft voice. He bowed slightly. "It is a most precious gift."

Impulsively, knowing he wouldn't respond in kind because of who he was and what he represented, Ransom reached forward and hugged him. The lean body under the robe was as hard as a rock, and too many of the shapes beneath it felt familiar. He smoothed her hair, and it was more than she felt she had any right to expect.

"I've been gone too long, Grandfather," she said as she pushed herself back from the embrace.

His smile was warm and gentle. His hand was callused strength in hers. "It is a big world out there, child. We knew that when you went."

She nodded, wishing there was something else she could say to erase the guilt finding him there had brought.

"Your grandmother always liked the cherry blossoms," the old man said.

"I know."

"How did you know to find me here?" the old man asked. His arms were once more in the sleeves of the robe.

"I asked Hosaka-san. He told me I might try here." Ransom kept her voice neutral, the way she had trained it to be when she was on location reporting world news. Her grandmother had helped her put the old hurt away that was connected with the Hosaka family name, and to put away the harm that might come with it were everything to be revealed.

"I am sorry I was not at the airport to greet you," her grandfather said.

"I am sorry I didn't call before coming," Ransom replied. She hoped he didn't detect the untruth in her voice. Before, when she was a young girl, her grandfather had been almost psychic where her wants and secrets were concerned. "The assignment was sudden, and I was given no time to prepare." And those were even more lies.

"I have seen you on television," he said. His attention, as always, seemed divided between her and their surroundings. "I am proud of you. You have done well for yourself."

"Thank you, Grandfather, but much of what I have benefited from, I learned at your feet."

The old man smiled. "How long will you be in Tokyo?"

"A few days, maybe more."

"Have you a place to stay?"

"I hoped there would be room for me in your house."

"Yes, Michi, there will always be room for you, even when you try your best to be an insolent Westerner."

"Thank you. I want to spend time with you while I'm here, since it's been so long, and combine business with pleasure."

"Ah, a very old Japanese custom."

Ransom smiled. "The Americans think they invented the concept."

"A very old American custom."

She laughed at his wit by herself because he never laughed out loud. His joy showed in his eyes, the way all of his lighthearted emotions did, the way his love for her grandmother did. Memories made the empty place in her heart swell. She rubbed her arms against the chill.

"You are cold," the old man said.

"No, please. Finish your visit. I didn't mean to take you away from that."

"I am through for tonight. Let us go."

CHAPTER TWELVE

"Pictures of Tucker and me?" Brognola repeated.

Bolan nodded. They sat in the small bathroom tucked into one corner of the big Fed's bedroom. Water ran in gurgling streams from the taps in the sink, shower and bathtub. They'd already found two listening devices but had decided not to take any more chances.

"Are you sure the men in those pictures were part of yesterday's attack?"

"I'm sure. I recognized a couple of them, and Fujitsu showed me before and after pictures."

"Why would someone go to the trouble of faking evidence like that?"

"It's smear tactics," Bolan replied.

"Even so, what could they hope to gain? It might confuse the issue some, but that wouldn't be enough to pull Justice out of the investigation. The CIA has, on the surface, acknowledged that they're out of this one. The Man has all of his markers riding on us."

"A lot depends on who directed the smear. At least some of the heat's coming from our side, and it would be easier for a mole they have in our ranks to take pictures of you. But the Japanese investigators might not want us here, either. Fujitsu, or someone above him, might have had the pictures dummied to keep you out of this."

"Don't forget that Tucker does most of his work in the Orient. In that scenario it would be easier for them to take pictures of him." Brognola rubbed his temples. "This mess is giving me a headache."

"Don't forget the Yakuza angle."

Brognola looked at him sharply. "You've come up against that, too?"

"Twice. A Yakuza operative named Shigeru, last name unknown to me, gave Tuley and his men their false passports. Word on the street is that they were CIA agents sent over here to cap a Yakuza leader."

"Do you think someone in the ranks is looking to move up quickly?"

"Maybe. No matter what, the Yakuza's a definite player in the game, and they're dealing in blood. Those men, after being eased quietly into Tokyo, now have a price on their heads. Dead or alive."

"The attacks in the States have been expensive," Brognola said.

"The Yakuza could foot the bill," Bolan replied.

"But how could they make you? Everything concerning you was routed through my office with Kurtzman officiating."

"And routed through the proper people here. All they needed was an inside man there or here."

"You make the structure of this investigation sound like Swiss cheese," the big Fed growled.

"Isn't it? How well do you know the people you have with you?"

"They're a handpicked team. You couldn't ask for better people."

"And how well do you know the people we're helping guard tomorrow?"

The Justice man fell silent as he mulled it over.

"Tell me about Joji Hosaka."

Brognola sighed. "Joji Hosaka made his fortune in the black market after World War II. Unofficially the guy worked for MacArthur's boys during the occupation. Hosaka helped organize the street gangs to break up labor strikes and keep the Japanese government on a right-wing course. According to the files I have on him, that was all he did. But those files were conspicuously devoid of a lot of pertinent information concerning Hosaka's activities. I believe the guy had dirty hands, and I believe G-2 helped him get them that way. There were never any definite links to the Yakuza later, but you could tell Hosaka's and Kodama's boys had bedded down together from time to time.''

"The CIA was active here during that time," Bolan said, "and they used some of the Yakuza members to assassinate people who stood in their way."

"I know, damn it. You could make a mosaic of all the little threads left hanging after the war. But what could still be operative now forty-five years later?"

"A lot of groundwork. A lot of people who have had time to rise to the right positions."

"There are no solid connections between Joji Hosaka and the Yakuza, or anyone in the CIA. Hosaka went entirely legit in 1972, from what Aaron and accounting could figure. Hell, the guy could definitely afford it. There was no shortage of money available to him from that time on."

"And Hosaka's the principal mover and shaker in the consortium?"

"There were other people who came to him with the idea a few years back, but they made the deal sound sweet enough to interest him."

"He has a son?"

"Actually two. Yemon's the oldest and more inclined to follow in his father's business footsteps. Tucker's had dinner with him occasionally and says the guy speaks nothing but Dow Jones. Saburo's the younger one. According to Tucker, the cocaine found in the publishing offices in L.A. was a shipment Saburo had muscled through. He can't be that bright, though, because Tucker said the Metropolitan Police were already wise to his trafficking."

Bolan nodded. "Being wise and doing something about it are two different matters." Both men were aware that facet was the cutting edge that divided their worlds. Brognola knew, and strived to work within the law. The Executioner made his own law. "The man I talked to told me Saburo Hosaka hired the assassin who nearly put you away yesterday."

"How sure are you of that?"

"The guy thought he was bargaining for his life."

"Adds a new wrinkle, doesn't it?"

"More than one," Bolan said, replaying the scene in the Club Morena in his head. "I found the guy who made the passports for Tuley and his shock troops."

"At the nightclub?"

"Yeah. That was Shigeru."

"So Fujitsu probably knows the score, too."

"Most likely." Bolan paused. "Just before he was killed, Shigeru told me Hosaka had him make up the passports for Tuley and company."

"He didn't say which Hosaka?"

"No."

"So we have a choice?"

Bolan nodded. "What about the possibility that Saburo Hosaka is trying to move against his father and take control of this consortium?"

Brognola shook his head. "When you get a chance, take a look at their files. A back-door effort on Saburo's part wouldn't be out of line with his character, but the door prize would be. From what we've seen, Saburo isn't interested in his father's businesses and would certainly lack the social skills to keep them going."

"Maybe Saburo isn't unaware of the charges the Metropolitan Police are building against him. His part in this may be just self-preservation."

"But you don't think so?"

"I'm not going to play it that way. Until I find out the real score behind the attacks in the States and the attacks on us over here, I intend to trust only the people in this room."

Brognola nodded. "I can't blame you, but you realize that's what Fujitsu might have banked on when he showed you those pictures."

"I know. And I also know from experience that it's hard to go after a lone target." Bolan's thoughts turned to the woman ninja who had come to his aid. She was in danger, too, from what Akemi had said. Yet she was as big a question mark as any of the others. "I'm in this until the end, however it turns out."

"I know." Brognola used his cane to lever himself to his feet. "Let's get some shut-eye and see if things look any better in the morning."

Bolan turned off the water and moved back into the bedroom with Brognola. The big Fed pulled a small suitcase out of the closet and tossed it onto the bed.

"I forgot to give you your Care package earlier," the big Fed said as he kicked off his shoes. "I wasn't anxious for Tucker to see it."

Opening the suitcase, Bolan found a Beretta 93-R and an Israeli-made Desert Eagle .44 in holsters on top of boxes of ammunition and spare clips. A blacksuit lay underneath, its hidden pockets filled with garrotes, knives, a pair of night glasses and a collapsible grappling hook. He made quick work of checking the actions on both weapons, then filled a couple of magazines for each one and loaded them. He left the .44 in the suitcase and fixed the Beretta in a shoulder rig under his jacket. Things looked better already.

After saying good-night to Brognola, Bolan let himself out, mind still whirling with everything that had happened to him since touching down in Tokyo only eighteen hours ago. There were so many unanswered questions and so many unidentified players.

His room was at the end of the hall. Most of the other agents were on this floor, as well. Foreign Affairs had arranged for them to be together, but for what reasons really? A well-placed bomb could take out the American effort in one fell swoop. The thought made his feeling of unease return. Usually he picked his own targets, defined his own approaches. This time he had walked in as one of the targets from the beginning, and his approach had been set through Brognola.

No one else appeared to be awake on the floor. He took the key Brognola had given him earlier from his pocket and turned the lock. The bolt sounded loud in the leaden silence.

The room was small, a half-size edition of Brognola's master suite. He dropped the suitcase onto the twin-size bed and left the lights off.

The draperies were open, and the skyline of Tokyo was outlined in the upper portion of the sliding glass door. Staying out of the line of vision in the window, professionally aware of what one man could do with a Star-Tron scope across the street, Bolan pulled the cord that shut the draperies.

The sliding glass door shattered only a heartbeat after he'd turned back to the bed. He spun, reaching for the 93-R as a black-clad figure clawed through the draperies.

Before the Executioner could drop his weapon into target acquisition, the Uzi in the intruder's hands blazed into noisy, destructive life. Bolan threw himself into a slide toward the door to the hall, followed by a hail of 9 mm death.

The warrior dropped flat, arm outstretched as he triggered three rounds. The first missed its target by inches. The second and third scored in the gunner's midsection and punched him back as another man came flying through the window.

Judging by the sounds from the hallway, Bolan guessed his room hadn't been the only one hit. He pulled himself around the corner and into the hall as the Uzi stuttered autofire in his wake. Flattening against the wall and drawing the Beretta in close, he checked the rest of the action brewing in the hall.

Two of the women were outside their rooms, holding their weapons in both hands. Three of the men, one bleeding from a wound in the upper thigh, were spread out on both sides of the hall. Cordite swirled toward the fluorescent lights overhead.

Agent Ron Roberts stumbled from his room as autofire shivered through his door. Roberts got to his feet with a .45 in one hand and slipped his glasses on with the other. "Son of a bitch!" the man yelled as he slammed into position along the wall. The slide racked back on the automatic loudly in the sudden silence.

"Move!" Bolan commanded, pushing off from his wall. He glimpsed movement inside the room he'd just vacated. "The emergency exit! Now!" He dropped his weapon into target acquisition and put a round through the head of the man in his room. He glanced back to make sure the Justice agents moved in the direction he'd ordered, then ducked into his room for the suitcase containing the Desert Eagle.

Roberts and one of the women provided brief cover fire as Bolan made his way to the emergency exit. Brognola had joined them.

"Who's missing?" Bolan asked as he fed a new clip into the 93-R.

"Saunders and Jamison," Brognola answered.

"Anybody know anything about them?" Bolan asked.

"Kristi was in the room next to me," one of the women replied. "I heard shots go off in her room before they got into mine. I don't know about Jamison."

"He never made it out of bed," one of the men said. "I checked. That's when I picked up the bullet in my thigh."

Bolan stripped off his jacket. "Hal, get them out of here."

"What are you going to do?"

"Cut down the odds a little." The Executioner fisted the .44 and triggered a round that caught one of their attackers in the shoulder and spun him into the open. The next 240-

grain round put the man down forever. "And find out if we can salvage our personnel."

Bolan moved out into the quiet hallway, straining his ears. There was a rustle of movement behind him and he turned to see Roberts following him, the .45 in both hands.

The Justice agent gave him a crooked smile. "Backup, my man. I'm not going to let you handle this alone."

"How many rounds do you have left in that clip?"

"Three. I didn't have any time to grab extra magazines."

Bolan passed over the 93-R and the two spare magazines he'd filled.

Roberts dropped the .45 and took the Beretta, fisting the extra clips.

"Which room was Kristi Saunders in?" Bolan asked. Nothing moved in the hallway except the gentle eddies of cordite. Roberts pointed.

Taking the lead, Bolan moved to the room, alert for the slightest movement. He pushed the door open and whirled back out of the way. Nothing happened. Peering around the corner, he saw the woman agent sprawled on the floor, a large section of the back of her head blown away. No one was in the room with her.

Roberts hunkered down beside him, the folding stock of the 93-R in his forward hand. "Kristi?"

"Didn't make it," Bolan said flatly.

"Too bad. She was a sweet kid."

A few minutes later they found Jamison in bed, his face reshaped by the half-dozen or so rounds that had been fired point-blank. He was alone, too.

"I read this as strictly hit-and-git," Roberts said.

Crossing the room, Bolan moved the curtain and peered outside. "So do I." Blood pooled near the base of the sliding door told him that at least one of the attackers who had entered through this room hadn't escaped unscathed. Slim black nylon cords floated free in the breeze outside the tiny balcony. He reached for one and gave it a tug. It was still secure. Just as he started to climb the rope a helicopter rose from the top of the building with its running lights off.

The helicopter floated like a big dark bird against the neon lights scattered over the vertical lengths of the nearby buildings. Then it was gone.

The Executioner released the rope and stepped back. Whatever was left of the attack force was already out of reach. When he got back to the hall, Roberts stood over one of the dead men, holding the guy's black ski mask in one fist.

"What the hell is this?" the agent demanded. "I thought we were up against a bunch of CIA rejects, not refugees from a Chuck Norris film." Despite the bullets that had obliterated the dead man's forehead, the features were unmistakably Oriental. "Who the hell are we up against, Belasko?" Roberts asked, releasing the corpse's head to thud against the floor.

The Executioner gave him the most honest answer he knew. "On this one, maybe everybody."

"WOULD YOU LIKE some tea?" the old man asked.

Ransom nodded, then automatically walked to the kitchen cupboard that held the tea and ceremonial cups. She kept her eyes away from her grandfather, for the first time in her life uncomfortable in the house where she'd grown up.

She went through the motions of preparing the tea mechanically, letting the familiar routine shield her from her grandfather's eyes. Without looking, she knew he sat on his knees with his hands resting lightly on his thighs. His weapons, the *shaken*, knives and garrotes had been put away in the secret places he had designed for them when he had built the house more than fifty years ago.

When the water was sufficiently hot, she added the family tea and stirred. Leaving the lid on the pot so that it would continue to steep, she joined him wordlessly on the floor with the teacups. She set the pot to one side, then poured and handed him his cup after turning it the required number of times. She filled her own cup, turned it and left it sitting before her, waiting for him to drink first, as traditional respect dictated.

His bright eyes crinkled in silent laughter as he picked up his cup with both hands and drank. He set it back down. "So you are not as much the Westerner as I had feared," he said without looking at her.

"No." Ransom willed her hands not to tremble. She had never lied to her grandfather, but knew she would have to if he questioned her. Even seventeen years ago, when she had first thought of leaving Tokyo, she had never lied to him about her reasons. Of course, she had never told him the real reason she had to leave, either. Grandmother had helped with that.

She sipped the tea and wished she could have stayed away until everything that was before her had passed. Except that, even had she stayed away tonight, their paths would have still intersected tomorrow at the meeting. She wondered if Saburo would be there, then felt a chill race down her spine. She sipped again and let the warmth of the tea fill her.

The living room was small and close, overfilled with old furniture her grandmother had never been able to part with, rattan and bamboo constructions that smelled of the oils her grandmother had rubbed into them to prevent aging and cracking.

A dozen pictures framed in white bamboo and neatly arranged adorned the wall in front of them. The subject in the stills were of modern things that seemed out of place in the surroundings of the room. She stared at them, recognizing them a moment later.

"My pictures," she said.

"Yes," the old man replied, looking at the wall. "Only a few of the ones you took of Japan." Mount Fuji loomed close in many of them.

"Grandmother always kept them away."

"Yes, she thought that by seeing them there, it would remind me how very far away you were." He placed the empty teacup to one side. "In a way, they do. Yet in another they help me hold your grandmother close to me."

"I'm glad. I have others, of grandmother, if you want."

"No, Michi, these serve me well enough."

"But grandmother is in none of them. Those pictures are ones from early in my career."

The old man lifted a hand and swept it slowly down the length of the bamboo frames. "To you, these are pictures, memories of the beginnings of your success. To me, these are places where your grandmother and I made memories." He tapped his forehead. "Your grandmother is here, always with me. I don't need a picture to remind me of her."

She nodded, and he gathered up his teacup and got to his feet. Ransom followed him. She watched him wash out the teacups and pot, then put them carefully away. He turned to face her. "I'm going to the garden. Will you join me?"

"Yes."

The garden was small, like the house, and had been built and groomed by her grandparents. It was a place of peace and security. Lacquered wood shone under the moonlight. Barefoot from being in the house, she felt the sanded smoothness of the deck beneath her. The high fence surrounded them. As a little girl she had often thought the fence was strong enough to keep the rest of the world at bay. Now she knew it was no more than a collection of sticks, and that her grandfather was flesh and blood, not invulnerable to the evils that lurked on the other side.

He knelt and took out a tiny pair of scissors and began to trim a bonsai tree with practiced efficiency. He caught the clippings in his free palm and pocketed them as he worked. "What matters have brought you home again?"

"The business consortium Hosaka-san is assembling." The scissors never wavered from their task, but she saw a shadow pass across his face.

"You have heard of the violence the Westerners have used against the proposed members of the consortium?"

"Yes. I filed reports on some of them." Dark memories filled her mind. "I was at the assembly plant in Detroit within hours of the attack."

"I've heard that was very bad."

"It was. Many people were killed."

"Is this the kind of work you do now?"

"Some of it."

"I remember only the pretty pictures you used to take for the travel magazines, and the interviews you did with Japanese who had made their new homes in America."

"I also do special news reports, Grandfather, and have been doing them for years. Only a few months ago I helped police in San Francisco track down and capture a serial rapist in Chinatown. He was later tried and convicted, and people could return to the streets of their neighborhood without fear."

His silence told her she had embarrassed him with the sexual aspects of the story.

"I'm good at what I do," Ransom said, "and I'm proud of the effect I can have on people who are involved. My mother died at an early age after having me. Father died in Vietnam, and I never got to know him the way I got to know you and Grandmother. I am what I am because of you and her. At least the successful part of me. My shortcomings are my own."

"You are very generous."

"No. I only say it because it is so."

He turned from the tree. "And what do you hope to accomplish here?"

"I want to bring out the truth of the attacks."

"I see. And what truth is that?"

Ransom took a deep breath and steeled herself. "I think someone in the consortium helped plan them."

"Do you have proof of this?" The edge in the old man's voice was razor-sharp.

"No. Only thoughts."

He nodded, then resumed his clipping. "You know I have pledged loyalty to Hosaka-san for saving your grandmother's life years ago."

"Yes." It had happened over forty years ago, immediately after the war. Her grandfather had been a young man with a wife and young daughter. The fishing village where they had lived in Okinawa was too small to have a proper hospital. Joji Hosaka had been a big man in the black market at the time and, after realizing the skills the young Kiyosha Ogata had to offer, quickly arranged for his ill wife to be flown to the mainland for treatment.

After her recovery, Michi's grandfather had moved to Tokyo and built a house on the land Hosaka had provided, then set about providing those services. Ransom's grandmother had given her only hints about the types of things her grandfather did in Hosaka's name, but she had seen him come in injured at times, found his clothes stained with blood that wasn't his. "Obligation is a hard thing to bear," she said in a quiet voice.

"It is also the essence of everything I am. Do you understand this, too?"

She nodded, understanding only too well. It was his sense of honor and obligation that provided the unbreakable walls of the current maze she found herself in.

"It would be a hard thing for me to decide between my honor and family."

"I know," she said in a hoarse voice. "Remember what you told me when you decided to train me as your father had trained you? You told me that you'd felt you made a mistake by not sharing yourself completely with my mother, by not teaching her the things you had been taught. You said you felt this is part of what made her turn away from you and try to marry my father in hopes of going to America. Remember?''

"Yes. You were very small. I did not know if you would truly understand.''

"Maybe I didn't then, Grandfather, but I do now. And Grandmother understood. There aren't many like you left in the world, even in Japan." Ransom felt the tears well up in her eyes.

"Sometimes I feel that way, too." He took her tears away on his fingertips. "With your mother I was ashamed that I had no learning better to give her. This is a man's trade, handed down from father to son, and only a woman when there is a need. Defense is one thing. Learning to kill, quite another."

CHAPTER THIRTEEN

Yemon Hosaka left his Mercedes in front of the health club. Two men separated from the night shadows near the entrance and approached him. He identified himself in a tight voice and hurried through the sliding door as one of the men opened it for him.

"I am sorry, Hosaka-san," the man apologized. "I did not recognize you."

Yemon ignored the man. The guard was one of several Yakuza his younger brother insisted on keeping on a private payroll despite objections from their father and himself.

The interior of the health club smelled of leather, soap and cheap cologne. The atmosphere was muggy and misted his glasses. Irritated, he took them off and wiped them with a monogrammed handkerchief from his back pocket, never touching the one set so carefully in his jacket. He came to a halt at the narrow desk and slapped the countertop with his palm impatiently.

A young man with hair to his shoulders came around the corner. He put on a smile and waved to the empty chairs stationed around the pots of plastic plants. "As you can see, we are closed."

"Where's Saburo?" Yemon flicked a glance at his watch. It wouldn't be long before their father figured out where his brother was. Between them they had exhausted most of Saburo's usual haunts.

The young man put both hands on the countertop and shook the hair out of his eyes. He wore black chinos, a lightweight black jacket and a black T-shirt. If they hadn't been different sizes, Yemon would have believed the man had filched the clothes from Saburo's wardrobe. "I don't know you," the man said.

Unable to keep his anxiety and anger in check anymore, Yemon slapped his cupped palms over the man's ears, then grabbed the lapels of his jacket and hauled him over the counter.

The guy went down hard but came up immediately with a switchblade snapping into the locked position. Yemon didn't bother to feint. He swept a leg out and kicked the knife away, breaking several of the man's fingers in the process. He placed two fingers on the man's throat and shoved him backward into the wall beside the door. The counterman gagged, grabbing for his throat with his uninjured hand. Yemon closed in.

"Fool! This jacket alone is worth more than you are. Where's Saburo?"

The counterman shot a brief glance at the two guards outside the entrance and, seeing that they weren't interested in helping him, said, "In the pool."

"Is he alone?"

"No."

"Who's with him?"

"A couple of whores he brought with him."

Yemon nodded. "Much better. In a few minutes another man will arrive—an older man. He's Saburo's father. If you treat him with the same disrespect and insolence you've shown me, he'll have you killed. Do you understand?"

"Yes." The man gripped his broken hand, his features white with repressed pain.

Yemon curled a finger at one of the guards and waited until the man stuck his head into the lobby. "I've given this man fair warning that my father will be here shortly. If he continues to show disrespect at that time, shoot him. Or I'll have you shot."

The guard bowed. "Of course, Hosaka-san."

The counterman's eyes widened as the door closed. He released his injured hand and bowed without looking away from Yemon. "Someone should have told me who you were, Hosaka-san. Otherwise I would never have behaved as I did. Please accept my apologies."

"As a guard, you're a pathetic creature. You should know everyone who has cause to see my brother, and know everyone who hasn't." Yemon left the man, straightening his tie as he went. He glanced briefly at his reflection in a glass display case. Despite the exertion and violence, his appearance was impeccable. Satisfied, he pulled the door open and walked down the narrow hallway.

The stench of chlorine filled his nostrils as the swing door closed behind him. Someone had turned the overhead lights off, and he stood still while his night vision adjusted. Echoes of splashing water sounded ahead of him, followed immediately by feminine giggling. He moved forward, able to make out the perimeters of the indoor pool.

Garish blue-green underwater lights lit up the Olympic-sized pool. Three bodies, reduced by the lights to two-dimensional silhouettes, moved within the lighted rectangle. There was more giggling, then a man's voice saying something too low to be heard.

Yemon wrapped himself in silence, knowing he wouldn't be seen by the pool's occupants until he was practically upon them. A girl came up out of the water at his feet, shaking her hair out of her eyes. She was Korean, pretty, with long dark hair that floated on the water's surface behind her. Her thin lips formed an O of surprise, then she dived back under the water. A second later she broke the surface and called out Saburo's name in a panicked voice.

"Yemon," Saburo shouted. "Come on. Join us." There was no doubt that he was high on something.

Saburo lounged in the deep end of the pool, his back to the wall. He was bigger than Yemon, at least three inches taller and forty pounds heavier, though none of it was fat. Where Yemon had the delicate looks and dancer's physique of their mother, Saburo had inherited the gnarly bulk of their father. He was broad-chested, long-limbed, with almost no neck separating his head from his shoulders. Naked, the tattoos that covered his body from midforearm to neck to midcalf were clearly visible—warriors challenging dragons and other mythical beasts. Colorful fantasy figures from Japanese mythology twisted around his arms, legs and trunk. It had taken thousands of dollars and long years of painstaking work to embroider that indelible history on his brother's skin.

"Who's this?" asked the woman in the crook of Saburo's arm. She spoke Japanese, but with a British accent. Her ebony skin bespoke her African ancestry.

"My brother," Saburo replied, reaching for a wine bottle that sat at the edge of the pool.

The black woman raised an arm from the water and waved Yemon in with her scarlet-nailed fingers. "Come in, brother." She smiled. "I promise that I'm more than enough woman for the both of you." She breathed deeply, causing her large breasts to rise from the water.

Saburo roared with laughter, and Yemon felt his cheeks burn with embarrassment. "Yemon, I'd like you to meet Fuzzy Knight—" the black woman nodded regally "—and Cinnamon Spice." The Korean woman bowed her head. "They work together."

"Of course. But unless you want Father to meet them, as well, I suggest you get them and yourself out of there."

A frown darkened Saburo's face, and he cupped one of the woman's breasts in defiance. "You think he hasn't seen women such as these? Our father's no saint as you would believe him to be. He's a man of the earth, of the people, no matter how he would like others to forget this."

Yemon said nothing. He had learned long ago there was no use arguing with Saburo when he was high.

"Father has had dozens of women like this," Saburo said. "Even while mother was alive. I know this isn't a surprise to you. You learned to turn your face even as she did." A gloating smile lifted the corners of his mouth. "I've had some of the same women, and they tell me I'm better than my father ever was."

"Father's very angry with the way your man tried to handle things at Foreign Affairs this morning," Yemon said patiently. "He's been searching for you most of the day."

"I'm sure he has," Saburo said sarcastically. "In between bouts of reassuring the different members of his precious consortium."

Yemon was surprised at the anger in Saburo's words. "He's striving to further the economic interests of Japan," he stated in a reserved voice.

"And letting the Americans get the better of him." Saburo shook his fist. "I'm not going to let them trample over me, no matter what Father says. I'm going to take my stand against them and not let them push me away as if I'm a dog begging for table scraps."

Yemon held out a towel he'd picked up from the floor. "Please." He tried to say it with sincerity.

"Why are you here?" Saburo demanded, making no move to swim across the pool.

"Because you're my brother."

"Is that the reason, truly?"

"Yes."

Saburo shook his head. "I don't believe you."

Yemon dropped the towel.

"You lack ambition." Saburo smiled lazily. "You lack drive and stamina, and the simple courage to reach out and take something you want. Instead of finding your own world to conquer, you wait patiently for the one Father will hand down to you. You have much at stake here. If Father's consortium goes through, you stand to inherit a kingdom whose boundaries are governed only by fiscal sheets rather than physical confines. Don't you think I know that?''

"I don't know what goes through your mind. I haven't since we were children.''

"Yes, you do. You know me better than our own father.''

"Who will be here at any time,'' Yemon reminded him.

"Did you tell him I was here?''

"No, but it won't take him long to figure out.''

Saburo drank wine from the bottle. "Tell me something. If this consortium goes through as Father plans, and you do inherit it at his death, will you cut me in for a piece of it?''

"The consortium will be an entity that will decide its own future,'' Yemon replied. "It will require a strong hand at the helm, but it will have a life of its own.''

"Do you intend for that hand to be yours when the time comes?'' Saburo's words taunted.

"I think it could be so.''

Saburo's eyes gleamed. "So, perhaps you have ambitions after all, brother. But would you seek to defend it yourself as actively as I have? Would you attempt to kill the Americans who have cowed our government into allowing them into our country? Would you put a price on the heads of the men who were part of the attack yesterday morning?''

"You have done that?'' Yemon felt the anger surge up inside him again.

Saburo laughed. "Yes, and I'm paying whether they're dead or alive. I won't retreat before the enemy as you and Father seem intent on doing. I'll fight back until I'm dead.''

"You're worse than a fool,'' Yemon said in a hard voice. "We don't even know if it's the Americans who have been attacking the businesses in the United States. It may be someone else.''

"Who?''

Yemon waved the question away as he thought about the consequences of his brother's irrational actions. "As always, you're too impulsive."

"How quickly Father's words come to your lips." Saburo's tone was mocking. "Yet when your wife was killed three years ago, who did you come to when you wanted vengeance?"

"He would never have agreed." Yemon looked at his brother and wished he would shut up. The whores would learn too much if this kept up, and one thing he had learned very early, from his father as well as others, was that people who knew too much were simply too dangerous to keep around.

"No, he wouldn't have. And when he found out what we had done, his wrath seemed to know no bounds toward me, yet he was forgiving of you. You have a very secure place, brother. You're the first son and you've promoted yourself to a very solid third position in the proposed consortium. Your future seems assured."

Yemon gazed at his brother in surprise.

"Oh, yes. I've been keeping informed of how things are developing there." Saburo lifted the bottle. "To your successes. May they be many." He drank.

"Now is not the time to be taking action against the Americans in general," Yemon said. "You must wait until we see what develops. What you have been doing may hurt trade relations."

"Do you think it will hurt them worse than what has been done to us? Action and reaction, Yemon. Remember the lessons you ingrained in my mind when you taught me to play chess? Remember how you and old Kiyosha Ogata worked to teach me the way of the sword? I have learned, brother, and learned well. Things that work for me might not work for anyone else, but they do their job well for me."

"This isn't about you. This is about Father and about Japanese business."

"You say." Saburo knotted up a scarred fist. "I had six million dollars' worth of cocaine go up in those publishing offices in L.A. when they were bombed."

Yemon returned his brother's gaze. "So much?"

"Yes. It took me a long time to get together that kind of money. The coffers of my businesses aren't nearly as deep as those of Hosaka Industries. It will take me many months to begin accumulating that kind of cash flow again." Saburo glared at the darkened ceiling. "And I don't believe that it was just circumstances that my cocaine was blasted along with that building. Father's consortium has a spy within its ranks, and if you and he don't do something about it soon, there will be nothing left for you to inherit."

Saburo dropped the wine bottle into the pool and swam across. He came out of the water in one lithe bound and picked up a towel. After patting his face dry, he wrapped the towel around his waist. He stared at Yemon intently. "Work with me." He held his hand out. "Work with me as I worked with you. Help me find out who's been striking against the Japanese people in America."

Knowing his brother was more interested in discovering who had cost him the six million dollars in cocaine, Yemon said, "We'll talk later."

Saburo let his hand fall to his side. The friendliness left his features. "You're still a fool, still afraid to seize the day for yourself. I wonder, if you hadn't had me with you to help you track down your wife's killers and slay them, would you have done it yourself?"

"Yes." Yemon's answer was flat and uncompromising.

Footsteps sounded in the hallway. One of the guards came into view, gripping a small Uzi, followed by Joji Hosaka. Two more guards trailed behind.

Yemon bowed instantly, watching the intent look on his father's face. The elder Hosaka returned the bow curtly, his eyes focused on his unbowing younger son.

Joji Hosaka was at least seven inches shorter than Saburo, but Yemon never ceased to marvel at the way the older man seemed to tower over him. Silver hair glinted in the darkness. He reached out, faster than Yemon would have believed, and slapped Saburo's face. The sound reverberated in the enclosed space.

The prostitutes, their faces devoid of the enthusiasm that had been there earlier, clambered from the pool and picked up towels to wrap around their nude bodies.

"You show no respect for your father?" Hosaka stated in his gravelly voice. His eyes were cold and hard.

Saburo bowed slowly, his angry gaze locked on his father's face.

"You brought these women here?" Hosaka asked.

Saburo nodded.

Hosaka spoke to Yemon without looking at him. "What have they heard?"

"Enough, Father."

The women stood close together at the pool's edge, unsure of what to do or say.

Hosaka nodded and looked away from them. He pointed at the guard carrying the Uzi. "Kill them now."

The women screamed and tried to run, but the guard stepped forward and cut a blazing figure eight that stopped the screaming. The sound of the autofire was deafening in the enclosed space. Nine-millimeter bullets sliced through soft flesh and punched the crumpled bodies into the pool. A dark cloud of blood spread outward from the floating corpses.

"Saburo, I want you to clean this mess up with your own hands," Hosaka said in a soft voice. "I want you to touch the mortality of yourself with this penance, and be glad I still love you enough at this point that I don't want to see your body join theirs. When you're finished, I'll see you out in my car. We have much to speak about."

Saburo bowed. "As you wish, Father."

"Yemon, please accompany me."

"Yes, Father." Yemon followed, seeing the naked hatred blazing in his brother's eyes. Something would have to be done about Saburo soon before all their plans went awry.

CHAPTER FOURTEEN

"Whose bright idea was it for us to wear these fucking white jackets?" Justice Agent Darrel Wilson asked in disgust.

"Mine," Bolan answered without hesitation. He wore a white dinner jacket, too. All of the garments had been secured through the American embassy and had been tailored to cover the shoulder rigs the Justice team wore. The Beretta 93-R was tucked under Bolan's left arm. The Desert Eagle had been left at the embassy's temporary Justice office. He let his gaze rove over the immense floor space where the consortium meeting reception was taking place. Dozens of men in black business suits clustered in little groups and around tables covered with catered food.

"Why white, for God's sake?" Wilson continued to grumble. "We stick out in this crowd."

"Exactly," Bolan replied. It was the most basic military maneuver and, in this crowd, one of the most effective. The microsized walkie-talkies Brognola had requisitioned for the meet had been all but useless inside the building. Between other radio networks that the various divisions of security the Japanese police had set up, and systems that had been designed to limit such transmissions, the radio bands were filled with garbage. "This way we'll be able to locate one another instantly."

"Doesn't matter," Wilson said. "There's so much goddamn hardware floating across this floor that it's going to be a massacre anyway if somebody decides to pull their piece."

"We're here to do a job, Wilson," Bolan said in a grave-yard voice. "You want in, that's fine. You want out, get out now and don't let the door hit you in the ass."

A nerve twitched at the side of the agent's face. "No, sir." His back straightened. "I'm in."

Bolan nodded and walked away. He hadn't liked being hard on the man, but he'd be damned if he'd entrust the lives of the rest of the team to someone who had already given up. True, security on the consortium meeting would have been ridiculous if it depended entirely on the American sector. But it didn't. There were a lot of good Japanese cops here, too. And Bolan counted on that even though the relationships between the groups were strained.

Brognola and Tucker, who was dressed in a white jacket as well, stood in one corner. Bolan had noticed the CIA man mumbling into the lapel of his jacket often enough to be assured the Agency had access to a communications system that was operable even through the static. Where exactly Tucker's secret group was deployed was a mystery.

Bolan filled a porcelain coffee cup. The Justice people had been up late helping Fujitsu and the Metropolitan Police fill out reports on the attack at the hotel. Hours later they'd installed themselves in another hotel and set up watch shifts. Bolan had gotten several hours of sleep between the excitement of last night and planning tonight's security detail.

There hadn't been a lot of planning. With their already small numbers reduced by two, with their negative relationships with the Japanese officials, their status was no more than that of a color guard. They were gathered here, watching to see if the pot boiled over, and if it did, to see if there was anything they could do about it afterward.

He circulated through the crowd, his combat senses fully alert. He'd committed photographs of the top officials of the consortium to memory in the wee hours of the morning. Kokan, looking younger than his sixty-plus years of age, held court in one corner of the room around an ice sculpture of a rearing dragon.

Bolan sipped his coffee and moved into position beside Ron Roberts. The agent looked almost relaxed as he sipped Coors Gold from a can. Bolan didn't say anything about having alcohol while on the job because he'd learned snap, polish and regulations didn't always measure up with the soldier in the jungle. And this was definitely a jungle.

Roberts tilted the can in Bolan's direction and smiled. "Roberts's revenge," he said, displaying the brand name. "With all this free beer, I'm going to help boost the American economy. Want to pull a tab and help offset the trade deficit?"

Bolan held up his coffee cup and shook his head. "Are you on Hosaka?"

Roberts nodded and pointed with his chin. "There. The whole Hosaka clan. Papa, big brother and baby brother."

One of the women Justice agents excused herself from an elderly Japanese man and joined them. She wore a bright smile and a long evening dress. The handbag drooped heavily from the weight of the Delta 10 mm pistol and extra clips that it carried.

Bolan studied the Hosaka family over his coffee cup as he took another drink. Joji Hosaka held at least two dozen younger men in obvious thrall with whatever statements he was making. Yemon Hosaka looked thin and immaculate stuck between his heavyset father and hulking younger brother. The expression on Saburo's face was anything but contented, and a bruise peeked from beneath the skin of his left cheek.

The woman agent reached out to pull on the lapel of Roberts's jacket with easy familiarity. "These should be made standard, Ron. It gives you that dashing Roger Moore look."

Roberts captured her fingers in one hand. "Thank you, Janet, but you might drift down there to tell Darrel Wilson your view on these things. He isn't too enamored of his at the moment. He thinks it makes us look like servants. I tried telling him that's what we are, but it didn't seem to help any."

"It's his Southern breeding," the woman said with a smile. She shifted her gaze to Bolan and dropped her voice to a near whisper. "I don't know what's going on, but while I was evading that old goat's horns, I overheard a conversation between Saburo Hosaka and one of the news people that sounded decidedly unfriendly. I thought you should know."

"What news person?" Bolan asked.

"A woman named Michi Ransom." She looked over her shoulder. "She was just behind them a few minutes ago. I don't know where she is now."

Bolan nodded. "I'll check into it."

The woman moved back into the crowd.

Bolan glanced uneasily at the large windows overlooking the Tokyo skyline as he moved around the crowd. The back of his neck prickled. He glanced at his watch and saw that it was only a little after 7:00 p.m. He had a definite problem with the windows and the exposure they offered, but Fujitsu and others were supposed to have secured the area.

Still the Executioner knew there was no security net that could be set up to keep out assassins. The only true safety lay in taking out the person controlling the attempts, but that wasn't possible until that person's identity was known.

The silent feel of someone's eyes on him caused Bolan to pause and glance back at the Hosaka assembly. He locked gazes with the old man standing slightly behind and to Joji Hosaka's left. The man wore a black business suit like the people around him, but his mannerisms set him apart. And there was an aloofness about him, the kind Bolan was sure he would see in himself if he looked into a mirror. The man was a part of the assembly, but serving a different function, just as Bolan was.

The warrior's trained eye noted the alterations that had been made in the suit, and realized that it could hide handfuls of deadly objects. He mentally summoned up the file that had been put together covering Hosaka's security crews, but drew a blank.

After spotting the other members of his team, he joined Brognola and Tucker in their corner. He confronted the CIA man directly, noting the small wireless receiver in one ear. "Who's the old man with Joji Hosaka? I make him as a guard, but he's not on file."

Tucker's smile was thin and brittle. "His name is Kiyosha Ogata, and his title is something like a family retainer. The Agency maintains an open file on the guy. No one's been able to uncover the history between him and the Hosaka, though there's a story that Joji helped Ogata's wife after the war and Ogata became a servant to Hosaka to work out his debt of obligation."

"What does he do?"

Tucker shrugged. "Pretty much whatever Hosaka tells him to. Ogata maintains a small home west of Tokyo and seldom goes to Hosaka's estates unless called for. During the seventies, he trained both Yemon and Saburo in martial arts." He paused. "There's a myth in the Japanese section that Ogata's a trained assassin, but people who could substantiate that don't. Or they disappear. From what I hear, in Hosaka's black market days, Ogata sometimes took out people who leaned on Joji, or stood in the way of the empire Joji wanted to build."

"They'll start dinner before long," Brognola said. "If anything's going to go down tonight, it's going to go down soon."

Bolan nodded in agreement. He took up a place next to the big Fed and surveyed the crowd again. Saburo was talking to a young woman who evidently wasn't interested in what he had to say. She stood with her back to him, her profile vaguely familiar. The woman's hair was neatly piled on top of her head, and lights shimmered from the green dress she wore. "Are you familiar with any of the media people present?" he asked Brognola.

"I've turned down interviews with three people I know who cover the Washington beat," Brognola replied, "and I've seen a few others from the national news mags. I don't know them all. The attacks in the States have sharpened interests on this thing, from the financial people to the world news reporters looking to make a mark for themselves. Why?"

"Do you know a woman reporter named Michi Ransom? From the name, she could be affiliated with either an American or a Japanese network." Bolan watched Saburo put his hand on the woman's arm. She tried to shrug it away. The woman left the crowd, with Saburo trailing after her.

Brognola shook his head.

"There she is," Tucker said. "The woman there, in the green dress. The one Saburo is following."

Bolan watched as the woman halted at one of the catering tables. Saburo grabbed her elbow.

"Guy must have a lot of confidence," Brognola commented dryly. "He's not taking no for an answer."

"They know each other," Tucker told him. "Michi Ransom is a free-lance reporter, writer and photographer who works out of the States. She's also Kiyosha Ogata's granddaughter. She grew up around the Hosaka family."

Michi Ransom turned to Saburo, her face vivid with repressed fury. Bolan recognized her at once as the ninja woman. He moved into the crowd, intending to get some answers.

"THANKS," Ross Tuley said as he accepted the cup of coffee Vardeman handed him. He straightened up from his slumped position over the scope of the Weatherby Mark V hunting rifle.

Vardeman picked up a pair of binoculars and studied the drama in progress across the street. "How does it look?"

"Like shooting fish in a barrel," Tuley replied. He sipped the coffee and found it too hot. Setting it to one side to cool, he returned his attention to the Weatherby's scope. He scanned dozens of people in the room. The cross hairs of the scope briefly touched on each of the Hosaka clan, then settled on the old man, who promptly stepped to one side as if he had felt the whisper-touch of the magnification.

"Have you found Kokan?"

"Not yet." Tuley moved the barrel of the big rifle on, making its weight a part of him. He still felt uneasy from the unexpected save in the alley the previous night. So far he hadn't had the opportunity to contact Sacker to find out if their rescue had been arranged, or if someone else was taking an active part in the game.

"Doesn't make sense to take out the number two guy in this little business empire Hosaka and his chums are trying to build," Vardeman commented. "Not when you can just as easily take out father and son Hosaka and probably do more damage in that respect."

"Sacker has his reasons. Somewhere in that little black puzzle book of his everything we do is written down and charted out as close to perfection as he thinks it needs to be. We're going to dismantle this thing piece by piece, and he picks the pieces."

Vardeman grunted. "Wonder what his playbook has to say about this Belasko guy now?"

"Whatever it is, I don't think it's nearly enough." Tuley continued to squint through the scope. "That guy's dangerous. He's not operational on this the way the other Justice people are. If he had been, he would have waited for the police and cleared things up instead of avoiding them. And it was only a few hours before Belasko got to the guy who fixed one set of passports for us."

"Did you ever find out who fielded the team that took Shigeru out?"

"No." Tuley brought the cross hairs to a halt on Kokan. "I haven't talked to Sacker lately. I just found our pigeon."

"I got him, too. And a bonus. Take a look at nine o'clock from Kokan."

Tuley raised the rifle. Belasko, dressed in a white jacket, stood beside two men who were already known to him through Sacker's briefing. "Brognola and Tucker are with him."

"I see that."

Tuley's finger curled around the trigger of the high-powered hunting rifle. The cross hairs were centered on Belasko's right temple, then the target was gone. He blinked open his other eye and caught sight of Belasko moving toward Saburo Hosaka and a woman who was turning away from him.

The groups of men started to break up as they took their seats at the tables covered with silverware and white linen.

"Ross."

Tuley ignored the man as he trailed the Weatherby along with Belasko. "If I had any sense," he said in a soft voice, "I'd take Belasko out now and try to make the score on Kokan before everything turned to shit."

"You can't guarantee the hit on Kokan if you move on Belasko first."

"I know."

"Then get that thought out of your head, buddy, 'cause it's almost show time. When the toast goes down, Kokan's supposed to go down, too."

Tuley took the scope off of Belasko with regret. "Somehow I think I'm making a mistake."

"It's Sacker's play," Vardeman stated. His voice seemed lighter now. "Thought I'd lost you there for a minute."

"No." Tuley broke open the big weapon and thumbed in the two cartridges it held. "I may question Sacker's orders, or his reasons for doing something, but I follow them. The man's good at what he does, and his planning has gotten me out of some tight situations. I'll do it his way until his way doesn't work anymore."

Vardeman resumed looking through the binoculars.

"Besides, maybe the secondary team will take him out during the confusion." Shouldering his weapon, Tuley put the cross hairs on his target's right eye and waited.

"GET AWAY FROM ME," Michi Ransom gritted between clenched teeth.

Saburo's hand closed on her wrist with bruising strength. He smiled at her, dark eyes glinting above white teeth.

Ransom tried to jerk her hand away without being conspicuous. The last thing she wanted to do was alert her grandfather. Her stomach threatened to empty at Saburo's touch, and her heart beat rapidly. She felt weak and vulnerable as he took another step toward her.

"Don't be silly, Michi," Saburo whispered, his breath warm in her ear.

She felt the nausea rise and struggled to restrain it. Nightmares from the past beat at her self-control with taloned fists.

"Tell me," Saburo said with his smile casually in place, "have you had a man better than me yet?" His words taunted and tore at her.

Clamping down on the feelings of revulsion that threatened to explode out of her, she turned to face him. She smelled the alcohol on his breath, and it made her head spin with the memories that threatened to overwhelm her.

"You're more beautiful than I remember," Saburo said. He reached up to trail his fingers across her cheek. "I like the way you wear your hair now."

Ransom steeled herself not to flinch at his touch, breathing in through her nose the way her grandfather had taught her to do when she was faced with a difficult task. She reached up for his hand, touched it gently, then applied pressure to the nerve clusters under his thumb. She heard the breath wheeze out of him as the pain gripped him. It was a struggle not to increase the pressure to the point of real pain, perhaps to the point of snapping the bone.

Saburo's face blanched, and his eyelids closed slightly. He moved his fingers away from her cheek, but she didn't relax the hold. Curling his fingers over her hand, he tried to get away from her grip.

She increased the pressure, eliciting a small cry of pain. "I'm no defenseless girl anymore," she said. "Don't make the mistake of thinking I am." She gave the thumb a final twist, then released it. "It could get you killed."

Nostrils flaring with pain and rage, Saburo took his hand back and rubbed it.

Billy Wu, her cameraman, approached them, his camera resting comfortably on his shoulder like a parasitic growth. "Is there a problem, Michi?" the photographer asked.

"No, Billy, thank you."

The little cameraman was dwarfed by Saburo, but the scars on his face, arms and hands told of a long knowledge of violent life. Wu bowed to Ransom, carefully balancing his camera, then returned his attention to the consortium guests.

Ransom peered over Saburo's shoulder and saw his father staring at them. "I think your father wants you."

"I don't care," Saburo replied. "He doesn't run my life anymore. I do what I choose to. I take whatever I want. Maybe you should remember that when you look at me."

"A moment ago you couldn't even take back your own hand."

Saburo bared his teeth in a mirthless grin. "Next time I may use someone else's hands. I'm used to taking what I want from life now."

"You've always thought you could," she said, returning his gaze full measure, "so that part of you hasn't changed."

"Other things have." His words were cold and full of challenge. He turned and walked away, joining his father at the table. Yemon Hosaka sat immediately to the right of Joji Hosaka, Saburo sitting directly across from him.

"How do you want to handle these next few shots?" Billy Wu asked.

She looked at him, forcing her mind to return to the window the photography would give her viewers. It was easier to think in terms of the story, giving her more distance from the past she had hoped to avoid. "Just shoot it," she said in a quavery voice. She made an effort to firm it up. "We'll do the editing later. We can use these scenes to intro the different people involved in the founding of the consortium. The voice-overs will be mine, short and to the point. Give me a selection of shots, some in obvious good humor and others that reflect the seriousness of what they're planning. This is big news, Billy."

The cameraman nodded. "Especially considering what's been happening stateside." He shrugged into the weight of the camera again. "You never did say how you black-mailed the network into giving you this story."

"That's right," she said in a calmer voice. "I didn't."

"Hey, take it easy, you're among friends now. This is Billy you're talking to."

"Sorry."

"It's okay." Wu looked at her, and she tried to avoid the honesty she found in his gaze. "What is it, kid, the story or the jerk you were talking to?"

"Perhaps a little of both." Ransom looked past the cameraman and saw her grandfather sitting behind Hosaka at another table. He didn't acknowledge her, just as she knew he wouldn't. He never did when he worked.

"It seemed like you knew that guy from before," Wu persisted.

"A long time ago," she replied.

Wu accepted that after a moment. He patted the camera and took a peek through the viewfinder. "If he causes any more problems, just give a whistle. I'll be around."

"You've been watching Bogart again, haven't you?" she asked.

Wu smiled. "Hollywood never made pictures better than they did in those days." He moved off, following the camera as if it had a life of its own.

Ransom turned her attention to the punch bowl on the table behind her. Her hand shook as she filled the cup, and some spilled on her fingers.

"Let me," a deep male voice said.

Glancing over her shoulder, she saw the big man who she now knew to be a Justice agent. She had recognized him earlier, but had hoped that her different hairstyle and clothes would hide her identity. Mind racing, she allowed him to take the ladle and cup from her hands.

He filled her cup and gave it to her. "Thank you," she said.

He nodded and refilled his coffee cup, then turned to look out over the floor. "Your friend Akemi said you were in trouble."

Ransom took a sip of the punch, not looking at him. Waiters moved among the tables serving drinks. "Akemi worries too much."

"He didn't give me that kind of impression."

"You don't know him."

"True. And I didn't know you yesterday, either." The warrior sipped his coffee and studied her with ice-blue eyes. "But you didn't let that stop you from coming to my aid."

"You were capable of helping yourself."

"But you still dealt yourself in."

"Only to make sure."

"Why?"

Ransom didn't say anything. Joji Hosaka stood, raising his glass high, and spoke to the assembled men at the tables. A cheer filled the room as they joined the man in a toast to their combined futures.

"I need to know," Bolan said. "Did you follow me, or did you follow the men who attacked me?"

"What do you think?"

"I think you followed the men." His statement was flat and final. "I knew I was being tailed almost from the beginning. I counted eight different men at different times. I never saw you."

Ransom glanced at him coolly. "It appears we both have unanswered questions and unsolved problems awaiting us in our respective jobs."

"Lady, I know what my job is, and I know what a reporter usually goes through to get a story. What I need to know is how you're involved in this. I'm not a betting man, but I'm willing to wager there wasn't a story filed in any of the news services by a Michi Ransom on yesterday's fire-fight."

"That wasn't the story I signed on to do."

Bolan nodded. Ransom felt trapped and wanted to avoid the encounter.

"I think you've gotten yourself in over your head," the man said in a soft voice. "I think you've got your own resources concerning what's happening with the Hosaka Consortium, and who's pulling the strings. That makes you dangerous." She looked away from him. "You've got a past history with the Hosaka family," he continued. "Your grandfather is here, in whatever capacity he serves Joji Hosaka. You're here. The conversation you had with Saburo was short and unfriendly."

"And you think that means something?" Her words were curt.

"Sure I do."

"Then you're a fool."

"Look, there are a lot of variables in this operation, a lot of things to try to watch while dodging around and hoping the sky doesn't fall in on you. What you know could help."

"Help you, you mean?"

"Help all of us."

"There's where you're wrong." Ransom looked at her grandfather and thought of the possible ramifications of what would happen if she were to tell any of the Americans or Japanese everything she had uncovered. She forced back the tears, wondering where guilt ended and how obligation continued to be so much a part of her life even though she lived in the United States now. "There's nothing you could do that would help me."

He was silent for a moment, his mouth a thin, hard line. "I could have some people apply pressure on your employer to pull you off this investigation."

She smiled at him bitterly and shook her head. "The American media? If one of your Justice Department people starts applying pressure at the network, they'd only work that much harder to make sure I stay with it."

Satisfied that she had at least broken even in the conversation, Ransom looked back at the floor. Yemon Hosaka was standing now, offering his glass in a toast to Shoji Kokan who was seated at the other end of the main table.

She looked back at the Justice man, thinking that things would have been different if she could open up to some of the people involved in the conspiracy she had uncovered, beginning with her grandfather.

The sound of shattering glass burst through the over-large room, followed immediately by the harsh boom of gunfire. Kokan's glass exploded in his hand a split second before the side of his head erupted in a torrent of blood and brains that spread across the table.

Before she could move Ransom felt the big man's arm slide around her neck as he pulled them both to the floor. She had panoramic impressions of people in motion, of the Justice agent tugging a pistol from under his white jacket, of her grandfather covering Joji Hosaka with his own body, then she was shoved under the table as the big man pushed himself to his feet. She crawled back out from the table, the professional part of her watching Billy Wu kneeling behind a chair and working the camera, while the personal side of her felt chilled to the marrow when her grandfather ran with surprising speed to one of the room's exits into the hall. The Justice agent opened a nearer door and stepped out just as her grandfather did.

Autofire cut loose in the hall and shredded one of the doors the American had vanished through only a heartbeat earlier. She was in motion before she realized it.

CHAPTER FIFTEEN

The Executioner was all movement, dropping under the sudden barrage of autofire as he extended the Beretta 93-R in front of him. He thudded to the linoleum with both elbows and continued skidding across the hallway. Pieces of the door scattered around him like falling toothpicks.

Three men, dressed in dark turtlenecks, gloves, slacks, ski masks and military webbing, stood at the fire escape. One covered their retreat while the other two shoved through the door. Chunks of flooring danced into the air as the MAC-10 flared to renewed life.

Bolan rolled out of the way, coming to a halt on his stomach as he aimed at the man covering the retreat. The 93-R stitched a row of holes across the man's face, his head twisting violently with the impacts. The gunner went down as Bolan propelled himself to temporary cover in a doorway across the hall. The two gunmen had disappeared, leaving the dead man behind.

The warrior moved into the hallway. A door opened in front of him, and he came face-to-face with Kiyosha Ogata. The old man glanced at him briefly. Steel winked within his fingers, but Bolan couldn't tell what the old man held.

"Belasko!"

Glancing over his shoulder, Bolan saw Ron Roberts standing in the shattered door he'd come through less than a minute ago. "Get Tucker and Fujitsu," Bolan ordered, "and see if we can get this building secured." Roberts nodded and withdrew.

When Bolan looked back at the fire escape, Ogata stepped out into the corridor. He hustled after the man, keeping the Beretta pointed up and ready. He didn't know where the man fit in or why he seemed intent on following the gunners.

The fire escape was empty. The door to the hallway closed and shut off most of the screams that came from the banquet room. Ogata pressed himself against the far wall, short throwing knives in both hands. His hazel eyes gazed at Bolan in open speculation. Keeping careful watch on Ogata, Bolan moved to the center of the spiraling stairs. He gazed down and saw nothing.

"Move!" The hoarse command ripped from Ogata's throat.

Bolan hurled himself to one side instinctively, reading the pattern of movement above him even as the old man yelled. He caught himself against the far wall as a flurry of large-caliber rounds ricocheted from the railings. Sparks flew from the metal bars as echoes of the autofire ripped away the sensation of sound.

Already in motion, Ogata kept to the outside of the stairwell as he charged up the steps. Fisting the Beretta in one hand, Bolan threw himself after the bodyguard, finding himself hard-pressed to keep up with the old man. Ogata's feet moved silently as Bolan's shoes spanged tightly against the metal steps.

Another burst of autofire ripped through the air, followed by a scream of pain from below. Four flights of stairs farther up, the fire escape dead-ended, showing a sheet metal door with the lock shot away. The door moved slightly with the outside breeze.

Bolan took one side of the door, Ogata the other. The small rectangle of glass inset at eye level was reinforced by wire mesh. Beyond was an expanse of roof marred by silver air-conditioning ducts big enough to conceal compact cars. Nothing moved, but there was no doubt in the Executioner's mind that the two men he pursued were close by. They had cut themselves off from escape—or perhaps they only wanted it to appear that way.

Ogata leaned forward and pushed the door open. Crouching, he signaled that Bolan should take the left side while he took the right. The Executioner nodded, shrugging out of the white jacket.

Sprinting from the door, Ogata made for the nearest air-conditioning unit. Autofire chewed tar and pebbles near his feet.

Bolan swung around the door, squeezing the Beretta's clip dry in continuous 3-round bursts that ripped fist-sized holes through the air-conditioning ducts where he judged the gunner to be hiding. He changed clips and looked for Ogata as he ducked back behind the door. The old man had vanished.

The Executioner moved out along the twelve-story battle zone. It wouldn't be long before police or Foreign Affairs personnel put in an appearance. Once they did, Bolan knew his chances of interviewing one of the assassins alone would be nil. He moved through the duct work carefully, letting the Beretta lead him through the sheet metal maze.

He looked around the corner of a three-ton cooling unit, his back set against it. At the far end of the roof was a tennis court marked off in green and white concrete. A rope door sagged, blown by the wind. Sunlight gleamed on metal for a moment to the right. Bolan dodged, throwing himself down as .45-caliber slugs shredded the corner of the air-conditioning unit. The fan motor gave a banshee shriek as it fluttered to a stop and died.

Bolan zeroed in on the man's position only to see him stumble from his hiding place seconds later. The hilt of a knife protruded from the assassin's throat when he fell onto his back.

"Belasko!"

Bolan recognized Roberts's voice as he got to his feet again. "Here, Ron. Shut down that entrance. Nobody in, nobody out."

"You got it!"

Moving on, the sounds of the stricken air-conditioning fan still in his ears, Bolan shifted to the outside perimeter of the rooftop. He continued his search in a crouch.

The familiar whirling beat of helicopter rotors sounded below his side of the building, then rose dramatically as the chopper suddenly became visible.

Bolan tracked onto the Plexiglas nose of the helicopter and made out two men dressed in jeans and shirts. He centered the 93-R over the pilot's heart, unwilling to pull the trigger until he knew whose side they were on.

The helicopter swiveled, bringing the passenger into view. The long tube in the man's hands became identifiable as he hefted it onto his shoulders.

"Incoming!" Bolan yelled as he dropped the Beretta into target acquisition and stroked the trigger.

The helicopter was thirty feet away and climbing with a steady drone of rotors. The man in the passenger seat went down under the 93-R's assault, but not before the LAW had disgorged its contents. The resulting explosion shook the building.

The warrior looked back over his shoulder and saw smoke belching from what was left of the fire escape exit as the empty magazine hit the rooftop. He rammed another one home and released the slide.

Evidently the helicopter crew decided whatever rescue attempt they had been set up for was too costly because it streaked away. The aircraft paused over a building twice as high as the one the Executioner was standing on. A rope ladder was kicked free and two men scaled it.

Bolan watched, unable to do anything to prevent the snipers' escape. He turned away, returning to the hunt of the last man.

"Hey," a man's voice called out. "I'm ready to give my-self up."

Bolan leveled the Beretta at the point where the voice came from. "Throw down your weapons and come out with your hands on your head."

A MAC-10 clattered onto the pebbled rooftop. "Don't shoot, man. I'm dead serious about giving myself up. I had a ticket to ride. They canceled, not me. I didn't sign on to pull a fucking Butch and Sundance scenario." A .45 slid out next, followed by a Gerber knife. "All right, I'm unarmed. Just ease back on the trigger finger."

"Come out," Bolan ordered. "Slowly."

The man stepped out, his hands behind his head. He stopped when he was in full view.

"Down on your face."

The man complied at once, breathing rapidly and watching the Executioner's careful approach.

Bolan quickly frisked the man and found nothing. "Get up." He kept the Beretta centered between the man's eyes.

The assassin grinned good-naturedly. "I've got nothing to lose, cop. Twenty to one I'm outta this country before you are. This is a class operation."

Bolan stepped forward, taking the assassin's privacy away from him with a fist knotted in the material at his throat. "We're going to talk about this operation," he said in a wintery voice. "Just you and me."

The gunman's composure seemed to be slipping. "You're going to have to turn me over to the Japanese cops, Belasko. You and me, we both know the Justice Department's as worthless as tits on a boar hog on this assignment."

Bolan flicked the hammer on the Beretta back with a thumb as he shoved the flash-hider hard into the man's nose. "How worthless do you think that makes you, tough guy?"

The assassin didn't say anything.

Bolan shook him. "I know Ross Tuley runs your team from this side, and sooner or later we're going to cross paths."

Eyes focused entirely on the 93-R, the man said, "Tuley will piss on your grave."

Ignoring the taunt, Bolan asked, "Has Tuley got somebody on the inside of the Metropolitan Police Department?"

"Not so you'd notice."

"Who?"

"That's not my department. I'm hired help. Just like you."

Bolan shoved the man ahead of him as they followed the roofline, training the Beretta on the guy's back as he squinted through the swirling concrete dust. Bricks and chunks of mortar shifted on the rooftop where the fire escape door had been.

Ron Roberts forced his way through the wreckage, .45 fisted in one hand. "What happened to the helicopter?" he asked. Streaks of blood leaked from the corner of his mouth.

"Got away," Bolan replied tersely. "Made a stop across the street to retrieve the sniper crew."

"This one of the assholes in the hallway?"

Bolan nodded. "Where's Ogata?"

Roberts shrugged. "Beats me. I saw him leave the banquet room, but I didn't know he was with you."

"I am here," the old man's voice said.

Bolan saw Ogata come from behind one of the huge cooling units. The old man's dark suit was covered with a light film of concrete dust, and his face was ashen and devoid of expression.

Ogata came to a stop in front of the prisoner. "This is the last man we pursued," he said as he stared at the man. He shifted his gaze to Bolan. "Why did you stop halfway?"

Before Bolan could reply the old man launched into a whirling reverse kick that caught the assassin under the chin and lifted him from his feet. Material ripped in Bolan's fingers as he grabbed for his prisoner.

Screaming hoarsely, the man went over the side of the rooftop, his arms flailing uselessly. Seconds later he hit the street and didn't move.

"Son of a bitch, that's a long way down," Roberts said as he holstered his weapon and looked into the street.

A dozen plainclothes Metropolitan Police, guns drawn, came pouring through the opening Roberts had made in the demolished fire escape. Bolan kept his eyes on Ogata as the old man passed among the policemen undisturbed, wondering if the last death had just been retribution, or a means of keeping American investigators from learning anything useful.

"HOW DID DE LUCA get away?" Dale Corrigan asked.

John Winterroad looked his superior square in the eye over the big desk that separated them and shrugged. "It was dark."

Corrigan pushed himself out of his chair and walked to the narrow office window sandwiched between ranks of filing cabinets. He pulled at the slats of the shade and let in some of the premorning glow. "Bullshit. I've personally seen you take out three men in the dark back when we were field agents together."

"That was a long time ago," he said in a quiet voice. He took in the shelves of books, the carefully arranged prints on the walls, the orderly fashion of the desk set. A picture of Corrigan shaking hands with the past President hung just behind the desk. "This is a nice office."

Corrigan shook his head in disbelief. "Besides losing the major lead we had on this investigation, Vachs has filed a grievance against you for misconduct. Did you know that?"

Winterroad shrugged. "I figured it might happen."

"You figured it might happen," Corrigan repeated. "Don't you understand the seriousness of this?"

"The kid was out of line. Way out of line."

Corrigan leveled a forefinger at him. "That's your opinion. And Vachs is no kid. He's damn near thirty years old."

Leaning forward across the desk, Winterroad said, "Harry Vachs is a punk."

Corrigan sighed. "You say this is a nice office?" He waved at the room. "One like this could have been yours. If you'd only learn to play by the rules."

"Some of the rules are wrong," Winterroad stated.

"Again, that's your opinion." Corrigan took a deep breath. "This is a heavy-duty situation. I shouldn't have to tell you that."

"You don't."

"Then why the hell do I feel like I need to?" Corrigan shouted.

Winterroad returned the angry stare and remained silent.

"Aw, shit, I didn't call you in here to jump on your ass," Corrigan said in a milder tone. "I just want you to know what you're getting yourself into."

"I know. I knew that when this assignment landed in my lap and I was told to work the angles on this one stateside. CIA activity within the borders of the continental U.S. of A. is frowned upon."

Corrigan sat in his chair again and laced his hands before him. Winterroad couldn't help but notice how much the man had seemed to age since taking the promotion. "Alan Tucker's being stonewalled in Tokyo by the Foreign Affairs people and the Justice Department operating over there under Hal Brognola."

"Brognola's a hardass."

Corrigan raised his eyebrows. "You know him?"

"We've met."

"In effect, it seems we've been cut out of this operation by the Japanese and the Justice Department. I want us back in. The director wants us back in. As you know, some of this trouble stems from the Agency. De Luca was a prime example of that." Corrigan paused. "I'm not going to put on the kid gloves for you. You've been around the block enough times to know the score. If we don't turn up something on this pretty damn quick, we're going to end up getting a black eye, and heads are going to roll. Tucker's, mine, and maybe yours. We don't have time for the prima donna bullshit anymore.

"I want you on this," Corrigan went on, "and I want you on top of this from now on. We need to find De Luca, or someone else who's been involved with the teams hitting the Japanese businesses here. I want you to find out who and why before it's too late to stop the walls that are going up between America and Japan. I'll tell you right now, off the record, that if you thought the Wall Street crashes of '29 or '87 were something, you haven't seen a damn thing yet." He shuffled papers on his desk and spread out a dozen folders with the sweep of his hand. "I've got breakdowns on what could possibly happen in the next few months if Japanese investing continues to dry up. We're talking about an economic panic here."

"We're talking about a cash flow junkie going cold turkey," Winterroad said.

"We're talking about people's lives."

"We're talking about selling the United States out one little piece at a time." Winterroad tapped the folders. "I've seen those figures for myself, and to tell you the truth, they scare the hell out of me. I didn't know other countries owned such big chunks of us. I've been just as guilty of ignoring what's in the newspapers and stock reports as the next man."

Corrigan slumped back in his swivel chair. "Go home and get some sleep. We'll talk later this evening when I get a final analysis in on some things we've got working."

Winterroad nodded and stood. He walked to the door and opened it.

"John."

He glanced back at Corrigan, who was straightening the files scattered across his desktop.

"I'll see what I can do about Vachs's grievance." Corrigan smiled. "Chances are it'll end up in the circular file by mistake. Just leave the kid alone."

"Do yourself a favor and find something else for him to do. Anything that will keep him away from me."

"All right."

Winterroad closed the office door behind him and walked to Corrigan's secretary. He gave her an honest smile as he patted the slim young woman on the shoulder. "Do you still keep antacid tablets up here for Corrigan?"

She smiled at him with lights dancing in her gray eyes. "Sure do."

Winterroad noticed the single yellow rose in a white vase in one corner of her desk. "Things getting serious between you and the boyfriend?"

She shrugged. "Maybe, but you know I still only have eyes for you."

He tapped her under the chin with a scarred knuckle, noticing, not for the first time, how kissable her lips looked, then remembered she was young enough to be his daughter. Feeling even more depressed, he walked to his desk in the bullpen and locked up the drawers. He didn't want to go home to the empty apartment he maintained near the Wolf Trap Park Farm for the Performing Arts, but he cared even less to stay here. He looked around the bullpen, realizing for the first time in a long while how much he would miss it if events forced him out of the Agency. He had given a lot to his country, and he couldn't help but wonder how much he had left to give. And wasn't it strange how the right things to do could so easily turn out to be wrong things?

His phone rang and he considered walking out on it, but couldn't because he never had. "Hello?"

"Good morning," Sacker's unforgettable voice said.

Winterroad froze, not knowing what to say. He glanced back through the glass walls at Marie, who was talking on her phone and smiling. "You realize this phone could be tapped," he said.

"Rest assured that it isn't."

Winterroad didn't miss the double meaning that the man still had other friends among the Langley staff.

"I think it's time we talked."

Winterroad took off his hat and twirled it on his finger. Corrigan's words still rested uneasily in his mind, sifting through the economic dilemmas nesting like malignant tumors in the information assembled on Japanese investing. He couldn't help thinking that doing the right thing might only amount to doing something a man could live with. He said, "Where do you want to meet?"

"At Wolf Trap in, say, an hour and a half. That way you'll have time to go home, shower and dress. Wear something casual and dump the shoulder holster. Use an ankle rig if you feel naked." Sacker's voice was calm and confident. "I'll bring breakfast."

"You're in town? You must still have balls of iron."

Sacker chuckled, and it sounded as chilling as ever. "Some things don't change, no matter what else does. Be sure you come alone." The connection broke without warning.

"Shoji Kokan was the only guy they tried to take out," Bolan said. He stared at the glossy pictures of the dead men Brognola's team had put together. There were dozens of them scattered around the hotel room, more than one shot of each, some taken before they had been killed. "Why, with Hosaka just as available, and clearly in a higher position in the consortium?"

Brognola sat on the sofa studying the latest pictures of the dead men. He moved the Polaroid snapshots with a forefinger as if they were pieces in a puzzle. "Maybe they considered him to be the greater threat," the big Fed suggested.

Moving on to the wall where they had used masking tape to adhere the faces at eye level in almost straight rows, Bolan glanced at each in rapid reflection. "How was Kokan's security here in Tokyo?" he asked.

"We can't even say for sure he was in Tokyo that long before the meet," Tucker replied.

"The Agency had a team on him?"

"They've had a team on all of the consortium's big guys," Tucker replied, "but it hasn't done a lot of good. Most agents are too damn conspicuous to go poking around everywhere these guys go, and they can't hang very close without tripping over Metropolitan Police or Foreign Affairs people."

"Did we get anything on the team that hit our hotel rooms last night?" Bolan asked.

"Bear's still working it," Brognola replied.

"They're strictly street talent," Tucker added.

Bolan looked away from the wall. "Yakuza?"

"Maybe."

"Any idea who they were assigned to?"

"No."

The CIA agent's answer was too blunt, but Bolan let it pass. "There's only one tie with the Yakuza we know of," he said. He looked at Tucker and Brognola. "Saburo Hosaka."

"You're barking up the wrong tree, Belasko," the CIA man said. "Saburo Hosaka has no interest in this consortium at all."

"That you've been able to determine," Bolan said.

Tucker shrugged.

"Maybe he has an interest in seeing the consortium fail. Have you considered that?"

"No, but how the hell would Saburo Hosaka have the resources to do everything that's been done in the States?"

"He wouldn't need them if he was working with someone," Bolan replied.

"Still, Saburo isn't the type to cross his father."

"You don't think he is."

"What are you driving at, Mike?" Brognola asked.

Bolan pointed at the two covered walls. "On one hand, we've got Caucasian teams of ex-CIA and Air America guys. On the other, we have definite links to the Yakuza. We can choose to pursue the CIA connection, or we can move on the more homegrown one. I'm betting on the Yakuza because this is their turf. They don't have to operate here without being noticed like the ex-Agency teams do."

Tucker wasn't smiling. "Those men wouldn't exactly be called high-profile."

"No, but they're used to the hit-and-git method of strikes." Bolan looked back at the collection of photographs. "No, the answer, at least part of it, is on the streets."

"And that's one area Fujitsu wants us to stay out of," Tucker said. "The emotions are running high in Tokyo at the moment. It might not be long before Americans and Europeans are attacked in the streets."

"He's right," Brognola added. "The President's getting ready to ask American citizens to come home as soon as possible until we can get a handle on this situation. And you can bet our stay in-country is going to be curtailed before long, as well."

Someone knocked at the door. Brognola levered himself to his feet with the cane and limped over to it. His free hand was on the butt of his .38 as he peered through the peephole. "It's Roberts," he said as he unlocked the door.

The Justice agent came into the room and gave Brognola a manila envelope. "From Interpol," he said. He glanced up at the photographs. "Redecorating?"

Bolan ignored the man's grim humor. "What about Michi Ransom?"

"She dropped out of sight while Fujitsu ran our guys through the wringer."

"What about her hotel room?"

"The desk clerk said she checked in yesterday morning, but she hasn't been in since."

"So she obviously has some place to go when she runs to ground," Bolan said.

"Why are you interested in the Ransom woman?" Tucker asked.

"She's another common link between East and West in this operation."

"She's just a reporter."

"Who has a unique way of killing a story," Bolan assured the CIA man.

Brognola slit the envelope open with a thumbnail and extracted the contents. "Take a look at this," the big Fed said, holding the packet out to him.

Bolan examined the corpse's face. "Who am I looking at?"

"The guy who tried to put Tucker and me on ice yesterday morning."

The warrior flipped through the reports, leafing through mug shots from Interpol, and secondary data supplied both by Interpol and Kurtzman from Stony Man. The last arrest noted was for transporting cocaine to Hawaii, and the name of the probable trafficker he worked for at the time was Saburo Hosaka. He closed the file and gave it back to Brognola. "If the Ransom woman turns up," he told the big Fed, "I want her followed if we can arrange it. Nobody is to talk to her. Just keep an eye on her until I get in touch with you."

Brognola nodded. "Where are you going to be?"

"In the streets," Bolan said as he pulled a brown bomber jacket on over his turtleneck. He took up the handles of the suitcase containing his blacksuit and the Desert Eagle. "I'm going to rattle a few cages of my own and wait to see who falls out.''

"You're not going out there like some goddamn vigilante," Tucker growled, stepping in front of him. "That's only going to make matters worse."

Bolan's gaze was pure ice-blue penetration. "I came over here because I was asked to do a job," he told the CIA agent. "Evidently the rules I was supposed to play under have been rigged against us, so it's time to throw in a few new rules. Mine."

Tucker reached for his pistol.

Bolan had the Beretta out in an eye blink.

Tucker left his weapon holstered and pulled his hands above his shoulders. He locked eyes with Bolan. "Is this the kind of operation you're running, Brognola?"

The big Fed sat down on the sofa. "I've got two dead agents on this thing so far. I could have lost some more today. I don't give a damn what it takes, but I want a handle on this operation now."

"You got him, Ron?" Bolan asked.

Roberts pulled his .45 and leveled it at Tucker. "Yeah, I got him."

Slipping the Beretta back into the shoulder rig, Bolan moved out. The next battleground would be defined by the Executioner.

CHAPTER SIXTEEN

Bolan watched the first drug buy go down in the men's room of an upscale nightclub in the Roppongi district within twenty minutes of his arrival. He washed his hands and kept surveillance on the dealer via the mirror above the sink. When the slender Oriental pocketed the cash and left, Bolan followed.

The nightclub was packed. Blue-gray cigarette smoke swirled toward the ceiling from the close-set tables, filtering the color of the whirling lights that bathed the dance floor.

The dealer stopped beside a rubber palm tree, took a cigarette from inside his jacket and stuck it between his lips. Bolan thumbed his lighter and offered it to the dealer. The man gave him an uncertain smile, then lit the cigarette and inhaled deeply. He nodded his thanks. "Do you speak English?" the warrior asked.

"Yes."

Bolan gave him a thin grin. "That makes things easier." He showed him the business end of the Beretta. "Outside, guy."

"Who are you?"

The Executioner nudged him with the 93-R and pointed him toward the side door. A young man got up from one of the tables and walked toward them with folded yen notes between his fingers. "Tell him you're out of business temporarily," Bolan whispered, "or I'll put you out of business permanently."

The man stopped in front of them, forcing Bolan and his prisoner to halt. He pushed the yen notes forward and said something in Japanese. Holding his hand up, the dealer shook his head and replied in the same language.

Bolan watched the crowd, picking out the club's bouncers, watching two of them drift in his direction slowly. He'd been made, but he wasn't sure if it was because he was escorting the dealer out or if the bouncers had noticed one of the dealer's cocaine buys. He pressed the barrel of the Beretta into the man's back. "Move."

"He doesn't believe I'm out of product," the dealer said. "He thinks I'm only refusing to sell to him."

The bouncers were closing in. Bolan maneuvered the two men behind the brief shelter of rubber foliage and swung the Beretta's butt into the young man's temple. He caught him by the shirt before he fell and lowered him into a chair without anyone being the wiser. "Let's go," he told the dealer.

"Shit, man, maybe we make deal, okay?" The dealer's voice was higher, tight with panic.

Gripping the man by the upper arm, Bolan hustled him through the side door. The bouncers had complicated matters, especially if they were trying to shut the dealer down.

The side door opened onto an alley. Raising the Beretta, Bolan aimed at the cluster of lights halfway down the alley. He pulled the trigger and listened to the silenced *phuts* of the shots as they extinguished the lights. He shoved the dealer into a run and headed toward his rental car, which was parked nearby.

The bouncers burst through the side exit. Bolan lifted the 93-R and flamed a tri-burst at the wall beside the men. Sparks flew from the bricks, and the bouncers dropped to the ground and began to crawl back into the club. He opened the driver's side door and shoved his prisoner inside and over, then climbed in after him, the Beretta centered on the guy's chest.

"Look, man, I don't have much money." The dealer put his hands on his head, showing he knew the routine. "If this is a shakedown, you got me too soon. You know?"

Bolan took the key out of his pocket and put it in the ignition. He jerked the car into gear as people came out of the side door and around the front of the club. Without turning his lights on, he put his foot hard on the accelerator and aimed the car at the street in front of the club. Tires spun and shrieked.

He overcontrolled the rental and fishtailed out onto the street, shooting into a gap in the late-night traffic. The dealer cried out and covered his face with his hands as they slid across the lanes of oncoming vehicles. The warrior let go of the steering wheel long enough to switch on his lights.

"I'm looking for Saburo Hosaka," Bolan said.

"I don't know him."

Lifting the Beretta, the Executioner pressed it into the side of the man's neck with enough force to pin him against the window. "I didn't ask if you knew him. I want to leave a message."

The dealer nodded, swallowing with effort.

"You tell him I want Tuley and the other Americans he arranged passports for. You tell him I know he arranged the hit in Foreign Affairs yesterday morning. You tell him I'm going to keep looking until I find him or them. Understand?"

"Yes."

"Give it back to me."

The dealer did.

Satisfied, Bolan pulled over to the curb in front of an all-night movie theater. "Out of the car," he ordered.

The dealer crawled out, his lower lip trembling.

Bolan pointed the 93-R at the man's face. "There's a grate at your feet," he said in a graveyard voice. "Throw down the cocaine. Quick."

People in line for the movie started to get interested. The dealer knelt and dropped glassine envelopes through the slots of the grate.

"Is that all of it?" Bolan asked.

The man nodded.

"Good. Now the money."

The dealer looked at him unbelievingly.

The Executioner thumbed back the Beretta's hammer.

Yen notes drifted into the gutter in record time.

"Don't forget the message," Bolan said as he pulled the door shut and surged back into the traffic. He watched the rearview mirror and saw the dealer get to his feet. He slipped out of his bomber jacket, reached under the seat for the primed Uzi, shrugged the sling over his shoulder, then put the jacket back on. He checked the street at the light, placed himself on the mental map he'd made of his strike area, then plotted his course to his next message drop. Tokyo was a city that thrived on nightlife, and tonight it was being graced with the presence of a new kind of party animal that would add its own variation to every beat known. Saburo Hosaka was being put on notice.

"LOOK, BILLY," Michi Ransom said, holding a palm over the ear that wasn't covered with the telephone receiver, "I don't have time to explain now, but I want you to stay on top of things for me." She stood at the public telephone in front of the Ginza subway station and watched the people watching her.

"This is hot stuff we have here," Wu was saying. "I'm talking about film that's turning to solid gold even as we speak. I had my camera right on Kokan when he took the bullet. I need you to get in here and do the voice-overs."

"I can do it over the phone."

"The hell you can." Desperation entered Wu's voice. "Hey, we go back a few years, remember? I helped you get your start in this business. We're supposed to look after each other. Isn't that what you told me when you came to me to set this deal up?''

"The story's breaking faster than you think it is," she said.

Wu fell silent for a moment. "What are you working on? Besides irate news directors, I've also flagged calls from the Metropolitan Police wanting to know where you are."

A chill coursed through Ransom. She'd known interest by the authorities would only be a matter of time now that the Justice agent had recognized her. "Who's been calling?"

Papers shuffled at the other end of the connection. "A Detective Sergeant Yemana with Tokyo Special Services. And another guy, Goro Fujitsu of Foreign Affairs. Do you know either of these men?"

"No."

"Well, they sure as hell know you. Fujitsu didn't take my word that I didn't know where you were. He sent an unmarked car here to watch me."

"What about the Americans?"

"What Americans?"

"Has anyone tried to contact you from the American Justice Department?"

"No, but the last I heard, they were coordinating their activities through Foreign Affairs. Whatever you're working on, it isn't worth risking your life or pissing off the police. You should give it up and let those guys do their jobs."

Ransom forced herself to chuckle. "Is that what you would do?"

There was a pregnant pause, then, "No. You know it isn't."

"I'm a reporter," she said with false lightness. "It's the skill I depend on to earn a living. And this is my story. If Foreign Affairs gets the chance, they'll shut down everything I'm trying to do with it."

"The people who killed Kokan aren't kidding around, and the word I'm getting is that they're the same people responsible for the massacre at the Sumida River yesterday morning.''

"They are."

"How deep are you into this thing?" Wu asked.

"I'm not in over my head."

"Are you sure about that? I was told your grandfather killed a couple of the assassins himself."

Ransom's stomach tightened. She forced her voice to remain relaxed. "I didn't know that."

"Well, know it now. I got that straight from one of my contacts in the Metropolitan Police. The last man your grandfather killed was a man who had already surrendered. If it wasn't for Joji Hosaka's considerable influence, your grandfather would have been taken into custody for murder."

"Where is he now?"

"I don't know."

Ransom silently damned Hosaka. Her grandfather had killed those men on Joji Hosaka's orders. Why Hosaka would give those orders remained to be seen. "I've got to go. I'll be in touch when I can."

"Wait." Wu sounded frantic.

"What?"

"Keep in touch with me. Please. I'll do what I can to hold off your network."

"Thanks." Ransom broke the connection, filled with confusion and rage. She'd left the banquet room as soon as the Justice agent had, knowing the man would expose her for what she had done the previous day. And once knowledge like that had been released to the authorities, it was only a heartbeat away from Joji Hosaka's ears. There was still much to do, and the time to do it grew shorter.

WEARING A TRENCH COAT with the Uzi slung underneath it and four grenades tucked into the deep pockets, Bolan left his rental car parked at the side of the street and walked back into the darkness of the alley. He leaped and grabbed the lowest rung of a fire escape ladder and hauled himself up. The warrior made his way along the metal skeleton until he reached the sixteenth-floor landing, where he used a lockpick to open the metal door.

When the door closed behind him, Bolan was alone in a dark corridor. According to the current intel in his war book, the top three floors of the building were part of a Yakuza-operated pleasure palace, complete with several interlocking rooms used for making porno films that had international distribution. The first twelve stories were leased to legitimate businesses.

He bypassed several doors and moved toward the electronic nerve center of the operation. Surveillance cameras were out because too many of the house's "guests" were in the public eye, from Japanese business officials and politicians to their international counterparts.

Holding the machine pistol in one hand, the Executioner stepped into the lighted area around the corner. The beautiful redhead behind the high-topped counter looked at him in surprise, her light green eyes flaring at the sight of the weapon. Her left hand inched toward the underside of the counter.

Bolan pointed the Uzi at her. "I wouldn't," he growled.

She forced a slight smile and nodded. Her hand dropped away from the counter.

"Step back," Bolan ordered, closing in.

The woman moved back to the wall behind her, holding her hands above her head. "I don't suppose you'd care to tell me what this is about?" she asked. "Since you haven't shown me a badge and appear to be alone, I assume you're not with the local police."

"You assume pretty good," Bolan said as he stepped around the counter and ripped the wires from the silent alarm. The phone rang on the desk as a man walked into the reception area. Bolan dropped the Uzi out of sight under the folds of the trench coat as an answering machine took the incoming call.

The man straightened his tie and smiled at the woman. "Everything was exquisite, Gina," he said in accented English. "You'll give my regards to Ishikure-san?"

The woman smiled sweetly. "Of course."

The man whistled all the way to the private elevator across from the counter and gave a last wink to the receptionist as the door closed before him. Gina stared at Bolan.

"I want to know where your fire alarm is," he said.

"Why?"

The Executioner gave her a grim smile. "You're going out of business tonight." He showed her one of the grenades. "I want to make sure we have no casualties, so we're going to evacuate the building. Now."

"What the hell is this all about?"

"It's about a guy named Saburo Hosaka."

"I don't know anyone by that name."

"Somebody will. You give them the message that I'm looking for him and that I'm not going to stop until I find him."

The woman didn't move.

"If I have to do this myself, things aren't going to be as orderly as if you ring the fire alarm and get these people in motion. I don't have the time to wait while you consider your employment future."

Sighing, the woman reached behind the oil painting behind the desk and flipped it outward, exposing a recessed button. "You're going to make a lot of enemies with this move, Yank."

Gina pressed the button and a strident buzz filled the corridor as emergency lights flared to life. Shouts followed immediately as two dozen people in various stages of undress evacuated the rooms.

Bolan stepped forward, taking Gina's wrist in one big hand to lend credibility to his presence. He let the Uzi hang by its sling under the trench coat. "Use the fire escape," he shouted, then repeated the command. Once the people were moving in the right direction, he turned to the woman at his side. "Who's running this operation?"

"Mochihito Ishikure."

"Is he here?"

She shook her head.

"Who's in charge now?"

"Me."

Nodding tightly, Bolan pulled her after him, moving toward the elevator. "How many guns are on these three floors?"

Gina shrugged. The elevator doors shut them off from the pandemonium racing through the hallway as people evacuated the immediate area. "I don't know. Most of the guests who come here bring their own security staff."

The elevator dropped quickly, slowing abruptly as it stopped at the next floor. Bolan fisted the Uzi, pulling the woman to his left so that she wouldn't be in the line of fire. "How many of Ishikure's people are here now?" The doors opened and revealed another corridor filled with screaming men and women.

"I don't know. Ten or twelve."

A tall man in a dark suit jogged into the hallway from another corridor with a H&K pistol in one hand. He gave a quick glance around at the confusion and focused on the woman at Bolan's side. "Gina, what the hell's going on?" Then he noticed Bolan and lifted his weapon.

Already moving out of the elevator cage, the Executioner raised the Uzi, squeezed off a burst that lifted the man from his feet and deposited him in an ungainly heap against the wall. The fear-filled screaming reached an even higher level as men and women scattered before Bolan like rats caught in the sudden glare of a flashlight.

Bolan shoved his foot between the closing doors of the elevator cage. Elbowing them apart, he grabbed the woman's wrist and yanked her out. He kept the machine pistol in sight now, using it as crowd control to keep the group of prostitutes and johns out of the way. The woman fought against him as he dragged her.

"Where are the tapes and camera equipment?" Bolan asked.

"Let me go," the woman yelled as she swung an open-handed slap at his face. "You've got no right to do this."

Bolan blocked the slap with his forearm. Before she could try again, he pulled her next to the dead man lying in the middle of the hallway and forced her to her knees. "As far as I'm concerned, you gave up those rights when you signed on as part of this." He forced her to look at the corpse's face. "This can be easy or hard. It's your choice." Angry tears streamed down Gina's face. Bolan pulled her to her feet. "I want the photography lab, the sets and whatever inventory Ishikure keeps on hand."

"They'll kill you for this," the redhead gasped between sobs.

"They'll try," Bolan responded. "There's no time left now. Get moving."

Pulling the woman behind him, Bolan glanced around a corner. Three armed men in suits, two without jackets so that their shoulder rigs showed, walked briskly up the hallway, nervously checking the row of empty rooms. Bolan didn't understand the language, but it wasn't hard to figure out the topic. Stepping out from behind the corner, one hand securing the woman and the other on the Uzi, he squeezed the trigger and swung the weapon in a lethal figure eight. The 9 mm tumblers kicked life from the three guards, sprawling them across the carpet.

"Move out," Bolan commanded. He dropped the empty magazine and popped in a new one. The snap of the slide chambering the first round made the woman jerk apprehensively. She stepped over the bodies and shivered. A door behind them exploded against a wall and sent echoes racing down the hallway. The elevator groaned to renewed life as the door closed.

Heads bobbed into view back at the main corridor. The Executioner triggered a series of controlled bursts that drove their pursuit to ground, taking one of them out of action permanently. Muzzle-flashes flamed yellow against the dimness of the hallway lights, shredding the walls of the corridor. A fluorescent tube above Bolan's head rained down in pieces as the escaping gas cloud briefly gleamed, then dissipated. Holding the machine pistol at waist-level, he swung into a full-frontal attack on his enemies and emptied the clip. Another man went down even as Bolan turned and raced after the fleeing woman.

Ahead of him, a flashing emergency light exploded, then they were around the curve of the hallway. Bolan caught up with the woman easily. A neon nightscape of Tokyo hung on the walls, framed by the long windows.

"Here," the woman gasped. She pointed to a series of doors.

Bolan tried the first one, found it locked. "Get back," he told the woman. He squeezed a burst from the Uzi that left the lock a splintered, smoking wreckage. He lifted a foot and drove it into the door, opening the way. The interior was dark, but there were enough residual lights from the hallway to show him the camera equipment inside. He listened for footsteps in the curving hallway and found them advancing cautiously. Taking a grenade from the trench coat pocket, he pulled the pin, counted off the numbers, then tossed it into the corridor.

There was a thump, a scream of what he assumed was recognition, then a concussive blast that traversed the length of the hallway to shove the windows from their frames in an explosion of shattered glass.

Partially deafened from the blast, Bolan reached for another grenade, pulled the pin and heaved it into the middle of the room. The explosion sounded just as he triggered another burst from the Uzi that let him into the second room. This room was immense, honeycombed from the rooms behind and around it, and filled with furniture that allowed it to become a bedroom, living room, kitchen or anything else a director wanted it to be.

He moved on to the next room, ears ringing from the two grenades, sweeping his eyes back and forth in case the blast hadn't taken out all of the pursuit. The woman remained huddled against the wall, covering her head with her arms. The third room contained developing chemicals and equipment. He tossed a grenade inside and ran toward the woman, wanting to make sure she got out of the building in one piece. He locked his fingers around her elbow just as the grenade went off. The blast seemed to shake the building.

"You're dead, Yank," Gina reminded him.

"Not yet, at any rate."

"How will they get in touch with you?"

"I'll get in touch with them. Give me a number where I can reach you."

She hesitated, then gave him one.

"Tell Ishikure that I'll call once and only once every hour. If I don't get an answer, something else burns. Hosaka isn't part of the Yakuza family. He wants to be, but they won't protect him. Tell Ishikure I know that, too."

Dragging her toward the exit, Bolan mentally moved on to the next strike. The pressure was now on, and the Executioner wasn't going to let up.

CHAPTER SEVENTEEN

Wolf Trap Park Farm was just about deserted when Winterroad arrived. He kept the windows up and the air-conditioning on high. The quick shower and change of clothes had done wonders toward reenergizing him, but a tremor at the core of Winterroad's Agency persona troubled him over the meeting with Sacker.

He shifted in the bucket seat again, struggling to find a comfortable position where the Chief's .38 Special tucked into his waistband wouldn't scrape against his backbone. He didn't want to attempt hiding the pistol there as he got out of the car because Sacker's trained eye would spot the movement immediately, and he definitely didn't want to go unarmed.

His palms were sweating, and he rubbed them across his thighs to dry them. The physical reality of the tension he tried to conceal from himself amused him.

He followed the winding road past the red cedarwood amphitheater that was the park's primary attraction. Ballet, jazz, opera and dance were all there during the heavy season, followed by and preceded by an impressive schedule of nationally known folk and acoustic acts in the Barns. Usually, when he got the chance to attend, he skipped the big productions and favored the smaller groups. The atmosphere was more intimate and rustic, qualities he found himself in need of after getting back from international assignments that took him away from home for long periods.

He switched off the radio, stroked his pants pocket where the extra five rounds for the .38 were mixed in with three dollars' worth of quarters he'd purchased at his bank to disguise their presence, and let the silence push him into the professional thinking that had kept him alive. Almost ten minutes later he found Sacker just where the man had said he would be.

Winterroad pulled his car into the parking area provided at the side of the byway beside the new gold-colored Lincoln Continental. He took a moment to study the lay of the land before getting out. The Chief's felt like an iron taped to his spine.

Sacker sat in a lawn chair under the spreading branches of an elm tree. Winterroad felt he could have picked the man out of a crowd of a thousand people within an eye blink. Sacker wore loose slacks, a golf shirt, sunglasses and brilliant white tennis shoes.

As the agent closed the door behind him, he tried to remember how long it had been since he'd seen the man. It shocked him to realize almost twelve years had passed.

Sacker smiled and stood. "Hello, John."

Winterroad shook the man's hand. "Hope I didn't keep you waiting."

"Not at all." The creak of age was noticeably absent from the man's voice.

Glancing at the foliage surrounding them, Winterroad couldn't help but search for the people he was sure Sacker would have watching them.

A slow grin spread across Sacker's face. "They're there. There's no need to check." He held up a hand with three fingers extended. "There's three of them, all crack shots, all positioned so that at least two of them will have a clear shot at all times." He let the hand drop away. "You wouldn't have expected anything less, would you?"

Trying not to show how the thought of three snipers looking at him through their scopes affected him, Winterroad shook his head. "No, I guess not."

"Just as I didn't expect you to come unarmed."

Winterroad felt his cheeks burn.

Walking back to the Continental, Sacker retrieved a small red-and-white ice chest and a blanket from the back seat. He gave them to Winterroad while he stored the lawn chair in the trunk and locked the car, then took them back.

Falling in behind the older man, Winterroad tried to pick out the positions of the snipers.

"Have you found them?" Sacker asked without turning around.

"No."

The man laughed. "If you knew where they were, would it make you feel any better?"

"Probably not."

"It might even make you feel less secure."

Sacker stopped, not surprising Winterroad by choosing an area that was relatively free of low-hanging branches that would interfere with a sniper's line of fire. He spread out the blanket and sat down in a lotus position with ease. "Sit down. We came here to talk, remember? We're just two old friends." Winterroad sat. "And take that pistol out of your waistband. It must be uncomfortable as hell." Sacker held up a hand.

Winterroad pulled the .38 into view quickly and tucked it under his thigh. Sacker lowered his hand. "Please don't try to touch it again without telling me first."

"All right." Winterroad's throat was dry as his mind tumbled through queries concerning what fraction of a pound of pull he'd been away from death while moving the Chief's.

"I took the liberty of selecting a wine," Sacker said as he pulled a wine bottle from the ice chest. He held it out, displaying the label.

Winterroad glanced at it but didn't feel enlightened. Wine had never been his drink of choice. His taste ran more to beer and wine coolers.

"Rye bread or white?" Sacker asked, holding up two loaves.

Feeling silly for making a decision like that while three snipers kept him in their cross hairs, Winterroad said, "Rye." But this whole picnic scene fitted in with the way Sacker handled his affairs—always simple, and he was always in control.

Sacker shook out a small red-and-white checked tablecloth and littered it with mustard, mayonnaise and ketchup, covered dishes containing sweet and dill pickles, onions, sliced tomatoes and lettuce, packages of cheeses, pastrami, ham and salami. A plastic pouch held silverware. The wineglasses, individually wrapped, were chilled, as well. Sacker poured without spilling a drop. Winterroad hoped his hand didn't shake as he accepted the glass.

"To your health," Sacker said, lifting his glass.

"And yours." Winterroad sipped, finding the wine almost too dry for his taste.

Sacker assembled a sandwich as he spoke. Winterroad watched the man, his eye drawn to the small red-and-yellow kite fluttering in the morning breeze over Sacker's shoulder. Other people, couples, families, a few individuals, occupied different areas in the distance. "I've talked to Eric De Luca recently," the man said.

"How recently?" Winterroad couldn't keep the suspicion from his voice.

"Since the night you let him go."

"Maybe that was a mistake," Winterroad said as he picked up two pieces of bread.

"Letting him go?" Sacker shook his head. "Probably the smartest thing you've done in the past few years. It reminded me that you were out there and let me know you might be interested in our cause."

Winterroad didn't comment as he finished making his sandwich. "The cause being the Japanese economic base in the United States?" he finally asked.

"Yes."

"When De Luca told me that, I thought you'd have to be insane to try to fight Japanese profits."

Sacker smiled, taking no offense. "We've fought for a lot of lost causes over the years. Why should this one be any different? Vietnam, Nicaragua, El Salvador, the list goes on. Only now the war's finally starting to take shape here in our own backyard."

"You really believe that?"

"You bet your ass I do. Look around you. Everywhere you look someone in this country is trying to get into the pockets of some foreign investor. It isn't just the national government, either. State governments, hell, city and town councils are just as guilty of trying to sell their souls for the wealth the Japanese and other countries have to pour into our empty coffers. Japan, in recent years, has become the third largest investor in this country, after the British and the Dutch. They buy the third largest amount of U.S. Savings Bonds, own banks, car dealerships and assembly plants, half of the National Steel Corporation, twelve and a half percent of Goldman Sachs & Co., thirteen percent of Shearson Lehman Brothers, and a whole cross section of American businesses and real estate. The Japanese have invaded politics in a big way, and it's getting larger. By having plants and businesses within the continental United States, they've assured themselves of lobbyists to take care of them before both houses of Congress. Remember the Tennessee senatorial election a few years ago that sparked the debate over the Nissan U.S.A. people?"

"No."

"The Tennessee junior executive up for reelection discovered that his opponent was receiving political and financial support from the Nissan people through the American executives. The junior exec was on the outs with the Japanese because of his neutrality on a bill that would require a portion of every car sold in the United States to be manufactured in the United States. Their guy opposed such legislation. And that's only the tip of the iceberg. What are we going to find out when we start kicking over the rest of the rocks?''

Winterroad watched the man in silence, feeling the old and familiar pull of the words.

"What I'm trying to do is get the American people to start looking, to start kicking over those rocks and seeing the slugs beneath. They should get mad about it. They should see how much of this great land has already been sold out by people who are living for today and to hell with tomorrow. I want to wake them up. We're suckling a parasitic viper, and it's becoming a drug even more dangerous and even more addictive than any chemical dependency could be.''

Winterroad finished his sandwich and felt it sit at the bottom of his stomach like a lump of grease. The thought of all the deaths connected to the man sitting across from him swirled through his mind. "Where do I fit into this?''

Sacker refilled their glasses. "I need good people. This country needs good people. For my money, you're one of the best. You always have been, even though those assholes in Langley have trouble understanding that.''

Winterroad kept his face neutral. He had forgotten how persuasive Sacker could be, how the man could play to a person's vanities.

"The post-cold war existence is over,'' Sacker continued. "The chess game between the behind-the-scenes armies of the United States and Russia have outlived their usefulness, and their affordability. There's a new world emerging out there, and for America to become a part of it, we're going to have to play catch-up for a while. The good life's over, and it's going to take work to put us back on top. It's back to basics. The bottom line is the dollar—and people are beginning to see that now.''

"Why have you been staging the hits on the Japanese businessmen in the States?'' Winterroad asked.

"If you go back to the files and look," Sacker said, "you'll see that every one of those businesses was owned by a member of the proposed consortium Joji Hosaka is assembling in Tokyo. If Hosaka is able to weld those people into a cohesive unit, it could spell a sudden demise for the American economy. Ever since the 1987 save by the Japanese, economists have been warning that a sudden sellout by those same people could trigger a fall that Wall Street would never recover from." He paused. "People used to fear the atomic bomb. Can you imagine what it would be like for the United States to suddenly go belly-up?"

The words created harsh and frightening images inside Winterroad's head.

"People would be out of work. Things like televisions, radios, other technological devices that we take for granted in our everyday life, would be gone. You'd see this country ripped apart by looters, criminals and whoever else decided to cross our borders to pick the bones." Sacker made a fist. "That's what I'm fighting for—our right to survive. By attacking these people, by exposing them for what they really are and the fact that they couldn't care less about us, I'm going to wake some people up to the threat of their existence. To recover, the American economy would have to have a new infusion of capital to get back into assembling a lot of the things we need every day, but where would we get it? Other countries invest in us now because they can make money off the deal. What if they couldn't? Do you think they'd be interested in helping us?"

Winterroad didn't reply. The nightmare Sacker had described seemed all too real, too near.

"It's your fight, too," Sacker went on. "And I can promise you'll get more out of it than the pension you're hanging on to your Agency job for. You were never one to wait around for the glory. You've dwelt in the shadows for a long time, nurturing yourself with the thought that you did the best job you could on something that really mattered. I want to give that sense of honor and self-respect back to you. This is where the real battle for America's future is, and I'm guiding the front line."

Winterroad rolled up the napkin, carefully brushing the crumbs onto the blanket.

"What's it going to be?" Sacker asked.

A small boy topped a hill in the distance, tugging a stubborn kite after him that refused to get airborne. Winterroad tried to imagine the park filled with the desperate people Sacker had described. "I'm in," he said quietly.

PHILIP PICARD, aka Sacker, pulled into the early-morning traffic coursing through Vienna, Virginia. He lifted the mobile telephone, punched a two-digit number programmed into his speed dialing and said, "Report."

The man's voice at the other end was crisp and efficient. "Winterroad's leaving now, sir. There are no other vehicles in sight that appear to be covering him."

Picard pressed harder on the accelerator as he steered around a silver travel trailer. "Good. Stay on him. Make sure the four teams move in constant rotation. Winterroad is good. Don't think for a moment he isn't."

"Yes, sir."

Breaking the connection, Picard dialed another number. Cherie answered, her voice cool honey. "Miss me?" he asked, unable to avoid the grin reflected in his rearview mirror.

"Of course."

"We have the next two days to ourselves," Picard said, "and a Lear jet. Where would you like to go?"

"How about some place Oriental? Maybe Singapore?"

"Why Singapore?"

"I've never been there, and *National Geographic* had a special on it a few days ago. Did you know that sixty-five percent of the country's population live in the capital city? Did you know that the people there enjoy the highest per person income in Southeast Asia? Then there was the footage the photographers took. It sounded like the perfect place to go for a quiet few days.''

Picard laughed at her obvious enthusiasm. ''I can't promise that it will be all that quiet,'' he said. ''I've still got business going on that will require my attention.''

''When you sit down to do whatever it is you do, I can go shopping. It will be marvelous.''

''Tell Jensen to lay in the quickest course he can to Singapore and to plan on a three- or four-day layover before we have to get back to the island.''

Picard said goodbye and broke the connection and dialed another number. Singapore would work for him, too. It was only a few hours by jet to Tokyo. When the phone was answered, he said, ''Tell our boy in Tokyo he can take care of the local problem now. I've got everything secured at this end.''

''Yes, sir.''

Picard hung up the phone. The acquisition of John Winterroad hadn't been necessary, but it certainly started matters on a downhill slide toward the success he had plotted for. It also hadn't been surprising. A lot of the people Picard had culled from the CIA's ranks had been disgruntled employees looking for something to believe in again. And usually that something included an enemy to fight. Now, once Tuley liquidated Tucker in Tokyo, the Agency would move to place Winterroad in his position, giving Picard an even firmer grip on the events he controlled in Japan. And in the world market. He smiled to himself again, luxuriating in the feel of success that he had become accustomed to over the years.

MOVING THROUGH the darkness, clad only in the formfitting blacksuit with the Beretta in a speed rig and the Desert Eagle on his hip, the Executioner closed in on the warehouse. Perspiration trickled down the tiger stripes of greasepaint that darkened his face—the night air had thickened with humidity.

He carried the Uzi as his lead weapon, cradling it in one arm as he vaulted a low fence surrounding the warehouse and became a part of the shadows filling the empty parking area behind the building.

Remaining motionless at the side of a flatbed truck behind the closed bays of the warehouse, Bolan studied the lights visible in the building. Besides the truck, a total of five other vehicles sat in the parking lot—three older sedans and two American luxury cars. Both luxury cars announced the presence of Yakuza members.

Bolan left the truck, edging into the deeper shadows that surrounded the building like a moat. Pain thudded into the Executioner from the wound in his side, reminding him that the blitz he had embarked on was taking its toll on him as well as the people he pursued. He brushed perspiration from his eyes as he pressed into the weathered wood of the warehouse.

He peered in through a dirty window and saw the tarp-covered shapes of motors, hulls and sailboats scattered across the warped planks of the floor. A wooden staircase led upstairs to the small second story. Intel gleaned earlier revealed that the warehouse was a repair shop that barely made ends meet. The real money was turned in the upstairs room as Yakuza bookies set odds on everything from baseball to sumo wrestling, domestic and international events.

Easing the window up and out, Bolan threw a leg over the sill and stepped inside. Voices carried to him from his right. He moved forward, and seconds later found the two men stationed at the foot of the stairs. Both were armed with silenced Ingrams canted against their waists. Apparently word had gone out on the streets that Yakuza operations were being hit.

The door at the top of the stairs opened, letting bright light splash against the dark interior of the warehouse. The two men at the bottom of the stairs came to attention at once. A man in an expensive dark suit stepped onto the landing, stared down at them and said something. They responded at once. The man nodded and flipped a cigarette butt out over the edge of the stairs. The orange coal exploded against the side of one of the boats into a flurry of embers. Satisfied, the man turned and went back into the room, closing the door behind him.

Bolan lifted the 93-R from its shoulder rig as the two men at the bottom of the steps separated and walked the outer perimeters of the warehouse. As the first guard came abreast of Bolan's position, the warrior raised the Beretta and stroked the trigger. He caught the body and lowered it to the planking. When he looked back up, he'd lost the other man.

He slung the Uzi over his shoulder, choosing the Beretta's silence over the machine pistol's firepower, and set off to find the missing man. The unwary scuff of his target's foot alerted him to the man's whereabouts. The warrior catfooted to the guard's position, reached out and tore the weapon from the unsuspecting man's grip.

The man whirled around, the momentum of the movement knocking both men into the repair berth. The guard started to yell as the water closed over his head, but Bolan covered his mouth with a big palm. The guard struggled and reached for something under his jacket.

Still holding the man by a fistful of hair, Bolan holstered the Beretta and slipped the broad-bladed combat knife from its upside-down sheath in his rigging, chopping it in a short swing between the man's ribs and into his heart.

Bolan surfaced, drawing in a deep breath of air. He secured the body in the air pocket left between the bay water and the wooden planking. Hauling himself out of the water, he made his way to the fifty-five-gallon fuel drums stacked on pallets in one corner of the warehouse. Working quickly, he released the taps on several, the smell of gasoline becoming all-pervasive.

He took a five-gallon jerrican from the wall, fisted the Uzi and took the stairs two at a time to the landing. After sloshing a quarter of the can's contents across the landing, he positioned himself in front of the door with the jerrican at his feet. Then he rapped his knuckles on the wooden surface.

When the door opened, he caught a glimpse of long, narrow tables covered with phones and index files. More than a dozen men were working inside.

Before the man who answered the door could react, Bolan hit him with the Uzi. He reversed the machine pistol and sprayed the room with 9 mm tumblers, sending the men inside scurrying for cover. Then he booted the jerrican into the room, waiting until it reached the center of the room before emptying the Uzi's clip into it.

Sparks from the bullets ignited the gasoline, and fire spread out in an ever-widening pool as some of the men inside the room unlimbered weapons. Then it was racing back toward Bolan, following the trail he'd made by spilling it over the landing.

Bolan seized the unconscious man and dropped him into the open berth immediately below. As the fire crossed the threshold of the room and flared across the broad pool soaked into the staircase, the Executioner dived after the man. He hit the water cleanly, arcing back up almost at once to grab the jacket of the man he'd thrown in. He stroked for the clearance under the bay doors, noticing the bright stabs of bullets penetrating the dark water.

Then the fire reached into the pool made by the draining fifty-five-gallon fuel drums. The explosion ripped the warehouse apart, scattering puddles of fire. The rapid fire of the weapons abruptly ended as men scrambled for their lives.

Bolan pulled his prisoner under the bay doors as the interior of the warehouse turned into a fiery hell. Fire roared out from under the bay area like dragon's breath. There was a moment of intense heat, then it evaporated, withdrawing back into the inside of the warehouse.

The man gurgled and spit, suddenly flailing at the water. Bolan treaded water an arm's length away, leveling the Desert Eagle at his prisoner's face. He waited until the man saw him, then thumbed back the hammer. "Do you speak English?" the Executioner asked.

The man shook his head and said something in rapid-fire Japanese.

"It doesn't matter. You'll understand enough. Saburo Hosaka." He motioned with the big .44, then repeated the name.

Eyes riveted on the Desert Eagle's large bore, the man said, "Saburo Hosaka."

Bolan nodded. "Just tell them that. They'll get the message." He swam for shore, leaving the man treading water. Dark plumes of smoke from the burning warehouse stabbed into the night sky and washed away the brightness of the stars.

CHAPTER EIGHTEEN

"Hello?"

Bolan didn't recognize the voice. "I expected a woman to answer at this number." He leaned into the phone booth, keeping a watchful eye on the street.

"Unfortunately she isn't out of the hospital yet. Perhaps I may be of service."

"What happened?"

"She's suffering from smoke inhalation after reentering the building to try to recover... some sensitive documents."

"That's too bad."

"Yes," the man agreed, "but better than other people who didn't make it out of the building at all."

Bolan ignored the thinly veiled sarcasm. "I'm looking for someone."

"So I've been told."

"Where is he?"

"As yet my superiors are trying to decide whether to aid you in this. The Hosaka family is attempting things that are beneficial to our efforts. We wouldn't want to see Joji Hosaka's dreams die before they have a chance to take root."

Bolan hardened his voice. "I closed the waterfront gambling room in the warehouse on the Arakawa Hosuiro River less than twenty minutes ago. If you want to continue to up the ante, I'm staying in the game. It's your choice."

The phone was covered at the other end, leaving only the dead buzz of static. Seconds later the man came back on. "I have just been authorized to release the information to you. Do you have a pencil?''

"Just give it to me.''

The man repeated the address.

"If this information is false, another one of your businesses will suffer losses tonight," Bolan warned.

"We understand that. We—''

Bolan hung up.

"The guy's a menace, Hal," Alan Tucker yelled, slapping the steering wheel for emphasis.

Brognola looked at the younger man and sighed. The argument had been off and on for the past few hours, flaring back to full strength each time special reports broke into regular radio programming to announce another incident of violence.

"Look at that," Tucker said, pointing at the building beyond the police cordon.

On the other side of the cordon, yellow fire trucks converged on the blazing building. Ambulances rolled slowly through the congestion of people, cars, emergency vehicles and fire hoses.

Brognola fished another antacid tablet from his shirt pocket and popped it into his mouth. He glanced to the right side of the street and saw members of Fujitsu's staff from the banquet security. He looked for Fujitsu but didn't see him. The Foreign Affairs man had appeared extremely interested in Bolan's disappearance and had ordered a special bulletin put out on Bolan despite Brognola's protests.

"Do you remember the Egyptian hijacking?" Tucker asked as he pulled the car to a halt. "That's what Belasko reminds me of. And do you know what they said about that after the Egyptians went through the plane and killed the terrorists despite the resulting high rate of civilian deaths? The only thing worse than being hijacked is being rescued by the Egyptians."

"We don't have a handle on this operation," Brognola said. He pushed himself up from the seat and out onto the street, coming to a stop beside the CIA man.

Flames rushed into the night sky twenty feet above the top of the building. A cloud of smoke wreathed the top two floors.

Tucker pointed at the building. "So this is your answer? You're just going to unleash this mad dog of yours and hope he kills some of the right people?"

Brognola turned, thrusting his face to a point within inches of Tucker's. "You're out of line."

Tucker didn't back away. He shoved a finger at the head Fed. "Out of line, hell. Your boy was out of line back there at the hotel when he pulled his gun on me."

"Belasko pulled his piece before you did," Brognola said. "Don't go getting sanctimonious on me. And if you shove that finger in my face again, you're going to have to put a splint on it when you get it back."

Tucker's jaw muscles worked, and he blinked with restrained fury. Brognola leaned back against the car. The voices of the crowd, combined with the rescue efforts by the emergency people, created an undercurrent of sound punctuated by the hissing rush of the fire hoses, the bullhorn used by the fire department and the winch motors of the hook-and-ladder trucks.

"You're keeping something back," Brognola said softly.

Tucker didn't respond. He rested his hands on his hips, allowing his jacket to gape enough to reveal the rubber-banded handle of his .44.

"Every department involved in the baby-sitting job on the Hosaka Consortium has been made," Brognola continued. "You know it, I know it and the Japanese know it. The thing that's keeping you on the prod right now is that you're worrying that whatever it is you've been keeping under wraps is about to fall into public view."

More police cars arrived, parking at the sides of the street while the uniforms clambered out with fiberglass shields and other riot gear. They fell in with other policemen forming a wedge to get an ambulance through the crowd.

"I wouldn't be the only one with something to hide if that was true. It wouldn't do for anyone to find out who your boy really is, or to know that the Justice Department brought him over here to kick the shit out of everything."

"We can sit here all night and throw mud at each other," Brognola said tiredly. "What we can't do is do something about this assignment. At least not if we play by the rules."

Tucker looked at him sharply. "Have you ever thought that maybe those rules are the only things that keep us from being like the people we're hunting?"

"Yeah. I used to think about that a lot when I first met Belasko. Lost a hell of a lot of sleep over it from time to time. Nowadays I realize things haven't changed that much. I still don't like bending the rules when it becomes necessary, but I realize it *is* necessary, so I sleep a little better."

"Sounds like a cop-out to me."

"That's from where you're sitting, buddy. Let me define the difference in rules between the CIA and law enforcement. In law enforcement you worry about how you take the guy down, the legal ramifications, the social ramifications, the precedents you set when you nail the guy, the whole ball of wax. In the CIA you boys decide who needs to be taken out, then you do it. The only thing you're worried about is getting caught. That's what you're worried about now. Somewhere, in all the bullshit files Langley has buried on this thing, there's somebody who's still pretty tight with the Agency." Brognola paused. "Now tell me I'm wrong."

Tucker shook his head. "You got an extra cigar?" Brognola gave him one. Tucker lit it, inhaled, then started choking. "Damn, Hal, these things are terrible."

Brognola chuckled. "I wouldn't know. I never light them. But they taste okay."

Tucker puffed away.

Firemen in the upper stories of the building threw bodies out of the windows to land in the nets below. Brognola could tell they were bodies from the way they dropped instead of fell. "The President is about to call Americans home," he said.

"I wasn't told about that," Tucker replied. "It probably hasn't helped that we're getting our asses kicked over here."

"No."

Tucker blew out a stream of smoke. "Suppose there was a guy Langley's afraid will crawl out of the woodwork?" He looked at Brognola. "What would you do about it?"

"I don't know. Depends on how I might be able to get to him."

"Let's suppose a little more. Let's suppose this guy has been like a ghost for the past ten years or so. That his file was eradicated years ago, that everything we think we know about him seems to contradict itself somewhere. Suppose we could almost tie him to Hosaka's black market dealings during the occupation after World War II, but we couldn't prove anything. Maybe some of these mercs who have been brought down almost have ties to this guy, too, but nobody knows where he is or how he got in touch with them." Tucker squinted against the cigar smoke. "Let's say Langley's even afraid to address the situation because they're not sure how deeply the guy's resources still run in the Agency. What would you do then?"

Brognola shook his head. "I'd have to know more."

"That's all you get—a vague collection of rumors and half-truths, and nothing solid for years. Would you be interested?"

"In following a trail of bread crumbs?"

Tucker looked toward the burning building. "It might prove better than attempting to piss off the Yakuza, since they're not a part of the immediate problem."

Brognola was silent. He looked over Tucker's shoulder as a sports car maneuvered in behind one of the police vehicles thirty feet away.

"I've put together a file," Tucker revealed. "The Agency doesn't even know I have it."

"Why are you telling me this?"

"Because I know Belasko is really Mack Bolan, and I know he won't bow out if we're told to." Tucker's eyes glittered brightly. "Don't get me wrong. I believe there's a right way and a wrong way to do something, and I don't want to be pulled out of this operation. But with this situation it just needs doing any way we can get it done."

Brognola stuck out his hand. "You've got a deal."

Tucker took the hand and smiled grimly. Metal glinted in the window of the sports car as Brognola's beat-cop instincts went haywire. A speck of ruby light touched Tucker's shoulder, then raced toward his neck. Yelling, "Sniper," Brognola pushed the other man, knocking them both to the street. There was no sound, but the CIA man jerked from impacts.

Brognola rolled over, dragging the .38 into view. Smoke surrounded the sports car's tires as the driver reversed and sped away.

Brognola squeezed off two rounds at the windshield where the laser scope was still visible. A bullet whined from the street surface only inches from his gun hand. Then the car disappeared around a corner. Keeping the revolver fisted, Brognola limped back to Tucker.

Twin bloodstains leaked from the CIA agent's abdomen. He held his arms across his stomach, pain whitening his face, rolled into a fetal position.

Sitting down, knowing policemen were already on their way, Brognola cradled Tucker's head in his arms. "Just hold on, kid, help's already on the way."

"Too late," Tucker said grimly. Blood dribbled from the corner of his mouth. "I've been shot before. This is different." He coughed, spitting up more blood.

Brognola held him tightly, watching the younger man's eyes rapidly losing muscle control.

"I've been . . . expecting this," Tucker gasped, "but you never . . . really know until you know . . . do you?"

"No. You don't."

Tucker swallowed hard. "The files, Hal." He swallowed again. "That's one thing they hadn't counted on." He coughed. "Key...around my neck...train locker...Ginza station."

Four uniformed policemen in riot gear surrounded the car and trained their guns on Brognola. The big Fed slid his .38 away and held Tucker.

A convulsion shook the CIA man. He closed his eyes, barely opened them back to unfocused slits. "Code word...disks...is Rosebud...thought it fit." He coughed, then wheezed wetly. "Get the son of a bitch."

"We will," Brognola promised.

Tucker stopped breathing and lay still. Without being seen, Brognola continued to hold the man long enough to tug the rawhide thong from around Tucker's neck and drop the key into his own pocket. He laid the body gently down. When he looked back up, Fujitsu was there. Covered with Tucker's blood, the big Fed stood and said, "Looks like those pictures of yours were faked after all." He shrugged out of his jacket and covered Tucker's face.

GUSTS OF WIND swept across the rooftop, creating miniature dust storms that died as soon as they tipped over the edge of the building.

Bolan crouched in the darkness, adjusting the binoculars. He counted from the bottom up, and once he found the floor he wanted, he started scanning the large windows of

the offices. It took the second series of searching to uncover the one he wanted.

The huge bulk of the air-conditioning unit behind him
kicked on, and the rooftop vibrated under his feet. He
moved away. Long seconds later he became part of the
building's shadows, lying prone as he studied the movement inside the office.

Expensive furniture filled the suite, and the bright lights
were muted by the magnification of the polarized glass. It
also bent the light in a manner that told him it was bullet-
proofed, as well. But that didn't concern him because he
wasn't there to take out Saburo Hosaka. However, it did let
him know Papa Hosaka had spent plenty of money on security for the building.

Inside the office Saburo Hosaka nervously paced along
the windows, chain-smoking. Three men stood or sat in the
spacious conference room behind him, all marred by scars
that testified to previous violent encounters.

Bolan put the binoculars down and watched the guy with
his naked eye for a moment. It wasn't hard to guess from the
pacing that Saburo Hosaka was waiting on someone.

There had been plenty of time for word to hit the street.
Saburo knew he was being stalked, and Bolan was guessing
the man knew the Yakuza had given him up to the stalker.

Lifting the binoculars again, Bolan scanned the street.
There were four hard vehicles below. Two of them were
American luxury cars denoting the interest the Yakuza
continued to show in the future of Saburo Hosaka. A black
minivan was parked directly across from the entrance. The
small sedan on the other side of the street could hold at least
four more soldiers.

Those were the numbers on this side of the building. Bolan reasoned the other main entrance probably held a crew
about the same size.

As Bolan watched the street, a limousine pulled to a
rocking stop in front of the building. He trained the binoc-

ulars on the people getting out, not terribly surprised when
he saw Yemon Hosaka in the middle of four men acting as
security. He'd thought Joji Hosaka might be the one Saburo contacted, then he reconsidered. If Saburo wanted a
meet with his father, he would have gone to the Hosaka
home. The thought added an auspicious flavor to the mix
rumbling through the Executioner's suspicious mind. Or
perhaps Papa Hosaka hadn't shown simply because he believed the situation concerning his son had reached some
kind of critical point.

Yemon Hosaka and his security crew disappeared inside
the building.

Bolan kept to the darkness as he evacuated his position.
The recon was done, and the target had been verified. Now
it was time for the warrior to kick open the engagement.

ARMS ACHING with the strain, Michi Ransom continued her
hand-over-hand climb along the nylon cord between the
buildings. The arrow holding the cord vibrated with her
movements but maintained its bite into the wooden sign
advertising the lawyer's offices at this level.

She wore gloves covered in resin to help maintain her grip.
Inside, her hands sweated and her fingertips felt like prunes.
As she swung forward for the next handhold, the weapons
positioned over her body thumped softly against her. She
forced her breathing to remain regular, not thinking about
the distance still before her until her feet touched the ledge.
Once there, she rested a moment, drawing in her breath
sharply, feeling the cloth of the mask covering her lower face
press against her mouth and nostrils.

Leaning forward to spread her weight across the building
rather than keep it dangling from the nylon cord, she
reached into a concealed pocket of the black uniform she
wore and removed a glass cutter. She pressed it against the
dark window of the office beside her, inscribing a circle,

halting only when a police car slid quietly through the alley, shining its lights into the dark corners.

She finished the circle, put the cutter away, took out a roll of double-sided tape she'd brought expressly for this purpose and made an X of two long strips, looping them in the middle to form a handle. Using the slack in the loop of tape, she rapped the heel of her palm against the circle in the window and pulled back. The glass squeaked and came away in her hand. Reversing it, she stuck the glass to the side of the building, then clambered inside.

A quiet scrape let her know the weight of the glass circle had gotten too great for the tape strips. She leaned out the hole as it started its downward slide, trapping it in her gloved hand. Then, pulling the glass inside, she placed it against the wall.

She used the sword strapped across her back to cut through the nylon rope. Escape would have to come by other means if it became necessary. The rope fell against the dark side of the building and disappeared into the shadows. She took the time to use the glass cutter to remove the rest of the glass from the window. It would be more difficult to notice a whole pane of glass missing than to notice a hole cut through one. She laid the pieces next to the circle.

The lawyer's offices smelled of stale paper, herbal room deodorants and lingering traces of strong tea. Bookshelves containing massive tomes covered one wall.

Ransom placed the office in her mental map of the building as she scooted the swivel chair over to the wall with the air duct. She used a small knife to remove the screws, put the screen on the floor and climbed inside. Metallic air blew into her face as she forced her way along on hands and knees.

The building had been old when Joji Hosaka bought the floor his offices were located on, and the new skin of reflective glass and brick had been grafted on at a later date. The cooling system remained the same—a monolith in architecture that didn't perform as well as newer systems, unreplaced because tenants of the building couldn't agree on who would pay how much.

Ransom made her way to the end of the duct and found herself looking out over the central cooling shaft. Cooled air pushed up at her. The duct had widened to three feet at this point and she stood, hunkered over. She leaned out, holding on to the metal lip of the duct work. Another duct was directly above her.

She took out a collapsible grappling hook with padded ends, whirled it and launched it toward the opening. Then she began her ascent.

DRESSED IN THE WHITE coveralls and cap he'd found in the maintenance room of the building's underground garage, Bolan crossed the street with the light. He'd had to let the hem out of the coverall legs to get them to drop to within three inches of his boots, and the cap was canted forward to help disguise the fact that his features weren't Oriental. He'd also found a red toolbox the Uzi would fit inside once it was broken down. The coveralls had belonged to a big-chested man with short legs and provided adequate coverage for his weapons.

He walked like a man worn down by the hours, dreading one last, unexpected assignment. The hardmen in the cars glanced at him but didn't appear interested enough to ask questions. He timed his arrival with a handful of young men obviously feeling no pain.

Bolan followed them inside, taking care to trail behind just far enough to get in the locked doors on their key.

Plexiglas-covered boards in the lobby listed the businesses occupying the office suites in Japanese and English. Plastic plants, scattered rows of seats in alternating red and ivory that carried out the lobby decor, and a small group of men clustered near each elevator fleshed out the surroundings.

Bolan didn't hesitate once inside. He marched straight over to the elevators and stepped inside one that already held an older couple. None of the hard teams tried to follow him.

He tipped his hat to the couple, then pressed a button two floors above their stop at the twenty-third floor. He held the toolbox in front of him and didn't look anywhere in particular, giving off the appearance of a man in no hurry to do his job.

The couple got off without anyone else getting on. Bolan hit the stop button after the elevator doors slid to a close, felt it lurch to a sudden halt, then reached up and rapped the heel of his hand against the emergency exit. He put the toolbox through first, pressed the button for the bottom floor, then restarted the elevator. It came to a jerky halt two floors up just as he hammered the emergency exit back in place. Fisting the toolbox, he heard the elevator doors ping closed and stepped off the cage just as it started downward again.

Clinging to the side of the elevator shaft, he stepped out of the coveralls, dropped the hat and started moving upward, climbing through the maze of steel supports. He paused at the floor that housed the offices of Joji Hosaka, slipped the combat knife from his harness and pried the elevator doors open a fraction of an inch.

Five men occupied the corridor, three of them carrying Heckler & Koch MP-5 submachine guns with curved 30-round boxes. Evidently the Hosaka brothers had decided to pull the gloves off for any encounters that might take place inside the building.

Bolan didn't doubt they had placed guards in the fire escapes, as well, effectively sealing off the building. The problem was, with this much security on tap, it would prove even harder to take Saburo Hosaka while the man was on the move.

The numbers were falling too fast on this one to let it slide. People were dying through carefully orchestrated plans by a still as yet unknown enemy. The Executioner's only choice was to keep the heat on until something collapsed from all the pressure.

He slipped the knife from between the doors and sheathed it. It took less than a minute to reassemble the Uzi and sling it over his shoulder. He left the toolbox on one of the support beams, reflecting on the layout of the room he'd seen during his recon. It wasn't necessary he leave the building with Saburo Hosaka. All he had to do was obtain a name, then get the hell out.

The elevator shaft hummed with the renewed movement of the cage. Bolan glanced down, watching it rise.

"WE MUST TALK," Saburo announced as Yemon stepped into the large conference room.

Tightening his grip on the anger threatening to explode out of him, Yemon walked into the room, ignoring his brother's gunmen. His own guards automatically took up positions on both sides of the main door. "Of course," he said in a controlled voice. He lifted a hand toward his private office.

Two of Saburo's guards made as if to enter, but his brother waved them back impatiently.

Yemon opened the door and stepped aside. His gaze touched that of the lieutenant of his private security team. Both of them nodded imperceptibly as Saburo passed through the door.

Inside, the immense office was a mixture of opulence, technology and antiquity. Persian rugs covered the floor; oil paintings hung on the wall; vases of exquisite color and shape, some dating from the Ming dynasty, sat in niches made into two of the walls. A pair of samurai swords hung over the back wall under the sunburst flag of Imperial Japan.

"Modesty has never been one of your strong points, has it?" Saburo asked with a broad smile.

"The businessmen I deal with expect a show when they speak with me," Yemon said, ignoring the sarcasm. "I see to it they get it." He walked around his brother and headed for the large, ornate cherrywood desk sitting off-center in front of the aquarium.

"And this is merely the opening number."

"Yes."

"Is it effective?"

Yemon took his seat in the swivel chair. He could tell by the glow in Saburo's eyes that he had been using drugs. The knowledge tightened his stomach, threatening to unleash the hostility he felt. "Yes."

Saburo walked closer, pausing to touch one of the vases. Yemon had to bite back a command for it not to be touched. He laced his fingers in front of him, presenting a calm exterior, waiting for Saburo to come to the point.

"All this," Saburo said, replacing the vase, "and I wager Father hates it."

Yemon nodded. "It is so."

A grin twisted Saburo's lips. He seated himself in one of the three chairs before the desk. "Do you know why?"

"No," Yemon answered honestly. It had been a point of contention between them for years.

"Because Father believes in the old ways. He believes a man should be taken for who and what he is rather than what he surrounds himself with. This—" he waved at the room "—shows nothing of you. Only shadows of who you may be. Are you an appreciator of fine paintings? Your collected paintings say so. Do you like fine things? The rugs, the selection of liquors in the bar in the center of the room say so. Are you attracted by the past? The swords, the vases, these things say so." Saburo paused. "So, who then am I talking to when I take this seat across from you? Am I dealing with someone who has a taste for art, for good living, for history, or perhaps someone who lets his introspection guide him?"

"The people I deal with expect this," Yemon said.

"Maybe they do, but you don't have to give it to them. Father doesn't."

"Father lives in the past."

"Don't the samurai swords, the vases and the flag suggest the same thing about you?"

Yemon remained silent, curbing his impatience.

"That's why Father's office has remained unchanged after all these years," Saburo said. "He displays nothing of himself save the businessman. His office is stripped of personal possessions except for a few that speak of his successes in the business areas. The furniture is the best functional pieces money can buy, yet they aren't art. He shows no extravagances. He communicates his stance and never wavers from it."

"Why are you here?" Yemon asked, annoyed with his brother's beliefs. Their father had voiced almost the same line of thinking about the decor of the room. It was amazing to see how closely his father's and brother's rationale could be, yet leave them seemingly stranded in opposite worlds.

"Have you listened to the news tonight?"

"Only on the way over here in the car."

"Did you hear about the fire-bombed building or the destruction of the warehouse on the Arakawa Hosuiro River?"

"A little, but I didn't pay attention to it. It has nothing to do with me, or us."

"That's where you're wrong." Saburo reached inside his jacket.

Yemon watched the hand closely, his gaze locked with Saburo's. The hand came away with a twisted cigarette. "I don't permit smoking in my office."

"Permit me, just this once." Saburo flicked a lighter to life and ignited the marijuana cigarette. Blue-gray smoke whirled around his head and he waved it away. "I have never darkened the doorway of your office here before and I plan never to again. But now we must talk.''

Yemon reached into his desk and took out a plastic case filled with paper clips. He poured the paper clips out and set the case in front of Saburo.

"There's a man hunting me," he said in a quiet voice, "a man I don't know. The building and the warehouse were Yakuza holdings, an esteemed whorehouse with an international clientele, and a nerve center that does a lot of gambling business. This man destroyed both places, then let Yakuza members know he was only doing it to find me. They were to tell him where I was.''

Settling back into his swivel chair, Yemon said, "And do you think they'll try to protect you?''

"No. I'm no fool, and I've seen the Yakuza vehicles parked below. If they haven't already sold me out, it will be soon.''

"Then this unknown man may be in the area even now.''

Saburo inhaled deeply, held the smoke then let it out in a gentle stream. "What difference would it make? I have my people, you have yours, and there are Yakuza out there, as well. If this man does come here, he'll never leave.''

"Why did you bring these troubles of yours to my doorstep?''

Saburo squinted against the smoke. "An interesting question, brother, and one I only have questions to answer with. I don't know this man, nor why he would have reason to seek me. Yet of his presence there can be no doubt. People who have seen him and survived say he's an American.''

Masking his anxiety, Yemon turned from the desk and slid open a panel above the huge aquarium set in one wall. He took a box of fish food from the recess, then took pinches of it to spread among the numerous hexagonal tanks built within the larger one.

"I have no dealings with Americans," Saburo continued. "My business is here within Tokyo."

"But it travels to different continents," Yemon commented as he continued moving slowly down the length of the aquarium to feed the fish. "As the cocaine did that was found in the L.A. publishing offices. Father is still hunting for the heads of the shipping people who allowed that to happen." He looked at his brother. "It's no secret that you use the legitimate connections of our company to squeeze in deals of your own."

"And you and Father have worked diligently to make sure my attempts to do this have become increasingly less profitable."

"We have been successful."

"Yes. Extremely so."

Yemon put the box of fish food away.

"Yet, in this case, one of your dockworkers solicited me, saying he was sure he could get a package of my merchandise through. This, after months of which I have been unsuccessful at bribing any of the people within Father's company."

Studying his brother's reflection in the aquarium, Yemon decided the reference to the company as their father's had been intentional. Suddenly his stomach felt as if it delicately balanced on a knife blade. He turned to face Saburo. "Give me this man's name."

"It won't do any good. After I started thinking about some of the events that have happened of late, I had someone check on this man. I found out he'd been transferred to one of Father's British offices. With a promotion."

Yemon kept his face neutral, not revealing any of the emotions flitting beneath.

"I thought it also interesting that it was your name on this man's promotion papers, not Father's."

Shrugging, Yemon said, "I have my faults as well as the next man. I've been known to make mistakes."

"Not very many."

The words hung in the air, suspended by possible threat.

"In fact, I think that Father and I have both been guilty of underestimating you." The grin on Saburo's face was as blankly menacing as a shark's. He stood and approached the aquarium. He tapped on the glass with a forefinger. A Siamese fighting fish wavered through the water like an indigo-blue heartbeat until it bumped into the glass. "These fish have always fascinated you, haven't they?"

Yemon remained silent.

"You have had ones like these since we were children. Maybe, then, you do have something in this office that reveals the inner man. The Siamese fighting fish, once it reaches adulthood, claims the water as its own, challenging to the death any other fish that attempts to enter its area. Even its own family." Saburo smiled again. "Interesting, isn't it? But everything makes sense once you have the key to its operation."

Glancing at the expensive watch on his wrist, Yemon said, "It's getting late and I'm tired. If you have something to say, get on with it. There's still much to be done in the morning."

"You and Father are the only people in this family who have direct dealings with the Americans. I find myself now being stalked by an American. I ask myself how this can be. How can this man know me? Then I realize he doesn't know much about me. He doesn't know where to find me, or even where to look. He moves only on information about me, attacking the Yakuza holdings, hoping to force me into the open." Saburo took a hit of the marijuana.

Yemon felt the knife slide under his stomach ever so slightly, puncturing, spilling a familiar coldness through his body. He sat at the desk. Things had obviously gotten out of hand, and he felt more in control. What to do became obvious.

"I asked myself how this American might have come to know my name. I thought of the attack I made on the CIA agent and the Justice representative in the Foreign Affairs building. But I quickly dismissed that. That would have only provided an introduction at best, not given the man a reason to pursue me. Then I thought of the American mercenaries who had been killed on the Sumida River, of Shigeru who sometimes worked with me and was in the business of providing false passports. Shigeru was killed by an American Justice agent. I asked myself if it was possible Shigeru provided passports for the American mercenaries. Then I called his wife. Can you guess what I found out?"

"No."

"She told me Shigeru had provided the passports, and that he had been paid by me. Knowing I hadn't commissioned the work, I realized someone had used my name, and that brings me to you, Yemon." Saburo dropped the marijuana on the carpet and crushed it under his foot. "You remember, of course, that Shigeru was the man who constructed false identities for us when we hunted the killers of your wife. I told him then that if you ever needed anything, you could go to him and he would help you."

"You're suggesting I had something to do with that?"

"I know you did. Those ninjas who killed Shigeru were men in your special employ, men you trained yourself as Ogata trained us. Father doesn't admit to knowing of their existence, and perhaps he doesn't. But I do. Those men were the ones who put a quick end to the different outlets I had for shipping in Father's business. It took me months to find out who they belonged to. I was impressed at the time."

"This is all idle speculation."

"Is it?"

Yemon met his challenging gaze wordlessly.

"Would Father think so? After all, if you're involved in this as I think you must be, it has caused him considerable problems, as well."

"Why did you come to me with this instead of going immediately to him?"

"Because I wanted you to know I held your future in my hands as you have tried to make me feel for all of our lives. I was always the youngest, the most headstrong, the one Father could never take pride in. Yet I seem to remain the most loyal." Saburo smiled broadly. "I like that feeling."

"So you intend to tell Father of your beliefs?"

"Yes."

"It won't make him feel any differently about you."

"I think it will."

"You're making a mistake."

"Far smaller than the ones you've obviously made." Saburo turned to go.

Yemon called out to him. "There is one thing you should know."

"What?"

"My wife's killers never existed. I killed her myself because she found out things I didn't want anyone to know." Yemon paused. "And I loved her very much."

Saburo shook his head. "Such villainy."

"We come by it honestly, though. Father brought us into this world with hands soiled by the blood of others."

"But he never turned on his own."

"Because they never had anything worth taking," Yemon replied. "You were a fool to come here." He withdrew a Walther automatic pistol from a desk drawer and fired on his brother, emptying the clip.

CHAPTER NINETEEN

Bolan scrambled through the steel supports, hauling himself up to the next floor as the elevator closed in on him. He paused, rammed his combat knife through the slit between the doors and twisted. The metal grated as the doors parted grudgingly.

Slipping his fingers through the crack, he pulled the doors open just as the elevator cage grazed his foot. He leaped, rolling across the carpet as the door closed behind him, then got to his feet with the silenced Beretta in hand. Ready or not, the opening numbers on the play had been kicked into motion.

He jogged to the fire escape door, combat senses flaring wildly, searching for the security net that had settled around the Hosaka clan. Easing the door open with his fingertips, he peered around it, looking down, then up. One man stood in the landing below, cradling a MAC-10 in his arms. Another man, seen through slits of the metal stairs, was two more stories up.

Lining up his target from the doorway, Bolan flicked the 93-R on single-shot and gently squeezed the trigger. Two floors up the 9 mm parabellum took the guard in the chest, punching him back into the wall. Even as he took his first staggering step, the Executioner followed with a second only a couple inches under the chin.

The corpse hit the ground with a thud, and the MAC-10 slid across the carpet to bang end-over-end down the stairs. The guard two floors down looked up, bringing his weapon into target acquisition. Bullets chopped into the concrete walls of the fire escape, ringing from the metal and throwing sparks.

Bolan put the Beretta's sights on the guard just as the man found him. He triggered three rapid-fire shots, spacing them across the guard's chest and driving the man down. The elevator dinged open behind him. A quick glance showed him four or five armed men clustered inside the cage as he eased into the fire escape.

One of the men shouted something Bolan couldn't understand, then pointed directly at him. The warrior didn't hesitate, knowing something had happened that he wasn't aware of, or someone had made him and was slow in reacting. He banged into the wall as he made the corner turning down the stairs. Bullets thudded into the metal door of the fire escape, punctuated by yelling.

On the twenty-seventh floor he peered through the wire-meshed window of the fire escape door just as the five guards in the hallway rushed into the conference room. Judging from what he saw, the move wasn't a covering one for an external problem—rather a response to quell an internal one.

He pushed through the door, holstering the Beretta as he readied the Uzi for the attack force that would come at him from the fire escape. The elevator doors at the other end of the hall opened. Two men stood against the walls of the cage, concealed by the corners of the doors.

Bolan fired a short burst into the cage to keep the men honest, then shifted to the man coming out of the conference room. A row of 9 mm tumblers caught the guard in the chest and flung him away. The elevator doors began to close, and one of the men stuck out a foot to prevent it from doing so. The Executioner put a 3-round burst into the foot. As the man yelled and dragged his foot back into the cage, the elevator closed and began to descend.

With one avenue of the three-pronged attack shut down momentarily, Bolan charged the conference room, coming to a halt to one side of the door. He changed clips in the Uzi, caught a flash of clothing coming through the entrance to the conference room and swung the buttstock of the weapon. The foldout wire stock caught the man in the face and drove him back inside.

Two gunners slid across the floor from the fire escape, unaimed shots from their automatic weapons chewing hunks from the carpets and knocking holes in the plaster walls. Something bounced on the carpet ahead of them, there was a hollow pop, then white smoke filled the hallway and cut them from Bolan's view.

THE CRACK of semiautomatic gunfire sounded like rolling thunder in the air duct. Able to make her way in a hunkered-down position, Ransom continued on through the duct work. She paused at a T in the duct, identifying the direction the sounds had come from. The mental map she'd constructed of the floor told her the gunfire had come from the same direction she was heading for.

Perspiration covered her body under the black material of the suit despite the cooling air that surrounded her. Her leg muscles trembled from the long moments of sustained exertion.

The duct work narrowed again as she neared Hosaka's offices, forcing her to crawl. Her rib cage, bruised and battered already, burned in renewed agony. Moments later more gunfire sounded. This time it was from fully automatic weapons that didn't let up.

Confronted with a sudden choice of three directions, she took the middle route, squeezing into the darkness. She wondered if her weapons would catch on anything. A full-grown man wouldn't have been able to make the crawl, even without the weapons. The thin welds joining the duct work sections scraped against her breasts, cut into her hips, raked liquid fire across her back. Biting her lips against the pain, she forced herself forward on her elbows. Her sword caught. She paused to release it, then continued on.

Her hand found a curve in the duct work made invisible by the blackness. The gunfire died away. She considered going back, choosing another direction, then realized there were no guarantees the others would be any different. Gunfire erupted again. She reached through the darkness, found the ridge of a weld and pulled herself forward.

Light shone through a rectangle on the bottom of the duct ten feet away. Rising to her hands and knees, she made her way over to it, filling her lungs with air gratefully.

Below, through the crosshatched view permitted by the screen, she saw the Justice agent, Belasko, against the outside wall near the Hosaka conference room. She took in the blacksuit the man wore, the weapons hanging from the military webbing, and was suddenly reminded of her grandfather. She realized the Justice man was in his natural element. Clothes didn't make the man—the man made the clothes.

Two men raced from the fire escape, firing their weapons blindly. Reaching into the concealed pockets of her suit, she pulled out a smoke bomb and dropped it through the slits of the screen. When the white smoke billowed up, she drew her sword, kicked the screen from its moorings and dropped through the opening behind the two guards.

Ransom hit the carpet without making a sound. Unable to see the men enveloped in the cloud as they were unable to see her, she listened, remaining in a squat, her legs shifting like springs to take her instantly in whatever direction she decided to go. She let instinct and training guide her. Bringing the sword around in both hands, she slashed at what she thought to be knee level.

The keen blade cut through something, and someone yelled. Bullets streamed in through the white smoke. Dropping flat against her bruised rib cage, keeping the cry of pain locked tight inside, she saw a foot materialize near her face.

She seized the foot, yanked and yelled. Bullets crashed into the man's body as he went off balance.

Rolling out of the quickly dissipating smoke, Ransom gathered her feet under her and stood, finding a place against the wall. Farther down the hallway she saw Belasko whirl around the doorway to unload two quick bursts inside the conference room. A man's death scream was cut off midway.

The man she had cut with the sword stared at her over his shoulder as he scrambled for his dropped weapon. Ransom stepped forward, moving by reaction loosely guided by thought. Using the sword one-handed, she cut through the man's throat, turning away instantly as movement from the fire escape drew her attention.

A man peered around the doorway and brought his weapon up. The smoke was gone now, leaving her a clear target for the gunner. A *shaken* was in her fingers before she knew it, then gone just as quickly. The whirling star imbedded in the man's hand and drove him back inside the fire escape.

Another pocket of her uniform yielded a small handful of caltrops designed to penetrate shoes. Ransom threw them at the floor, scattering them in the path of the people taking cover in the fire escape.

Sword in hand, she turned back around, only to find herself face-to-face with Belasko's weapon. She reached for a throwing knife, knowing she'd be too late.

"DOWN!" Bolan yelled, and the woman obeyed instantly.

The field of fire now clear, the Executioner swept a withering burst over the fire escape door, driving long scars across the metal and emptying the rectangular glass window.

Ransom rolled to her feet and took up a position on the other side of the door. Breathing rapidly, she held the sword straight up in front of her in steady hands. Perspiration gathered around her dark eyes.

Bolan smelled the whisper of perfume around the woman, so out of place with the other sights, sounds and smells of the carnage that had overtaken this section of the floor.

"Saburo?" she asked. Her voice was slightly muffled by the mask.

"Inside," Bolan said. He shelved the questions he wanted to ask, accepting the woman as unplanned backup, though he planned to watch every move she made. She had acted in his defense twice, but he had no intention of fully trusting her until he understood her motivations.

He glanced back inside the conference room, seeing one of the two remaining guards left alive try to streak across the room. He emptied the last of the clip as he took the man out, the bullets chopping out the large glass windows of the room as they overtook him.

With no magazines left for the Uzi, he slung it upside down across his back as he drew the Desert Eagle and pulled back out of the room. Glancing at the elevator light indicator, he saw the cage on the rise again.

Bullets smashed into the doorframe next to Bolan from the gunner concealed behind the overturned metal table. Dropping to one knee as the gunfire died away, the Executioner extended the Magnum in a Weaver's grip and started blowing holes through the table. The harsh, flat boom of the .44 filled the hallway. The third round caught the hidden man and spilled him into view. Before he could bring his weapon to his shoulder, Bolan moved into the doorway and sent a 240-grain hollowpoint through the gunner's face.

The body fell as he went into motion. He lifted one of the H&K submachine guns the hallway guards had been armed with and held it out to Ransom. "Can you use this?"

"I've never used firearms."

Bolan pushed it into her hands. "Point it in the general direction and pull the trigger in one- or two-second counts.

You've got at least one elevator full of replacements coming from that end."

She wiped her sword clean on a dead man's shirt and sheathed it, then stepped back to the doorway as Bolan turned his attention to the door. He tried the handle and found it locked. "Do you know whose office this is?" he asked.

"Yemon's."

Bolan nodded and pointed the Desert Eagle at the lock, standing to one side of the door. "Watch yourself, because he and Saburo are missing from the head count I've done. I imagine they're not in here alone." He pulled the trigger, checked the torn metal, then aimed and pulled the trigger again. Pieces of the lock scattered across the carpet at his feet. Surprisingly no one fired at him from inside.

Behind him, the H&K submachine gun chattered to vibrant life. "They're here," Ransom called in a cool voice.

Bolan tested the door and it swung inward. He eased it open a little more and jammed the toe of his boot into it as he continued to stand to one side. "How many men?"

"At least a half dozen, maybe more." Ransom fired the submachine gun again, drawing return fire.

The Executioner flipped the door open and peered around the corner. The only body he saw was the one slumped on the other side of the door. The office was empty. He heard the H&K run dry and glanced at Ransom. "Fall back, away from the door."

The woman nodded, drawing the sword again. "There are others at the opposite end of the hall. My caltrops have discouraged them, but it won't be long before they attempt to pick their way through."

Bolan led the way into the room. Pausing at the door after Ransom entered, he took out his Ka-bar and jammed it into the doorjamb. It wouldn't hold long, but it would slow down the gunners once they reached the office.

Ransom knelt and flipped the body over. Saburo Hosaka's head rolled loosely back and forth, coming to a rest against the woman's leg.

Bolan watched a shudder course through her, remembering the way she'd struck out at him with the stiletto during their first meeting. He gazed around the inner sanctum, finding no answers to the questions that filled his head.

Ransom pushed herself up from the floor, still holding on to the sword. "Someone killed him," she said needlessly.

Glancing at her, Bolan saw indecision blacken her dark eyes.

"Who?" she demanded.

He shook his head. "I don't know. You got here the same time I did."

She shivered again, tightening her grip on the sword as she looked at the dead man. "Yemon was here?"

"He had to be," Bolan said. "He wasn't out there." A drumbeat of gunfire rumbled against the door. Bolan glanced at the woman. "Any ideas about how we get out of here?"

YEMON HOSAKA STARED at the Justice agent and the woman ninja through the one-way glass concealed by the aquarium. In the darkness of the hidden passageway, the lights and the fish seemed to be unreal, another world enclosed in a glass skin. He watched as the woman turned Saburo's body over, feeling the anger rise inside himself at his brother's stupidity. If the Justice agent hadn't chosen this time to attack the offices, there might not have been a way to explain this to his father. His plans, carefully nurtured and calculated for years, would have been for nothing.

He continued to watch, drawn by the woman's reactions to his brother's corpse. Something familiar pulled at his consciousness, giving him the feeling that he somehow knew her. He studied the brief slash of features presented through the hole cut in the mask.

Then memory rushed to fill the uncertainty in Yemon's mind. He remembered how Michi Ransom had acted earlier the previous evening at the banquet. He stared into the brown eyes and knew her for who she was.

Yemon gripped the Walther tighter in his fist. He had fed a new clip into the automatic before pressing the hidden button that opened the sliding door and gave access to the passageway. Taking his gaze from the woman, disdainful of the figure she cut in the black uniform and the way she held her sword, he focused on the man. He easily recognized him as the one who had tracked the assassins from the banquet room.

Recalling Saburo's words that someone was challenging the Yakuza for his brother's whereabouts, Yemon had no doubts that he was looking at the man who had done that. That he was obviously successful in his quest, that he was here now and had penetrated through the guards he, Saburo and the Yakuza had posted, marked him as a dangerous man.

Michi Ransom could be dismissed. She knew of the offices. Her grandfather had brought her here when she was a child. Uncertainty touched him as he wondered if she had been there for Saburo or for him. The Hosaka offices were home to him, not Saburo. The unexpected turn of his thoughts unsettled him.

He lifted the Walther and pointed it at the two warriors dressed in black. He squeezed on the trigger. The bullets would go through the aquarium, perhaps not as true as he wished, but maybe close enough. He focused on the big man's face, narrowing his eyes, staring at him down the length of the short barrel.

Then the indigo-blue Siamese fighting fish glided before him and broke the spell. Yemon released the trigger, released his pent-up breath. If the bullets didn't fly true enough, he could be risking everything. He pocketed the small automatic and smiled.

"Another time, then," he promised in a soft voice that wouldn't go beyond his ears. Turning, he made his way back through the passageway to the ladder that led to the building's roof.

LONG SPLINTERS FLEW from the office door to bury themselves in the Persian rugs. Bullets continued to pelt the door, more of them penetrating.

Bolan checked the room quickly. Ransom left the corpse, still buried in whatever thoughts held her, but helped him in the search. "Yemon was here," he said as he glanced out the windows overlooking the street. "I saw him arrive."

The woman's reply was flat and noncommittal. "He will have a way out of here. He was trained by my grandfather." She ran her hands along the ornate shelving built above and below the aquarium. Fish darted inside it, reacting to the vibration of gunfire filling the room. Water jetted through a hole made in one of the aquarium's sides by a stray bullet and splashed onto the floor.

A glint of metal caught Bolan's eye as he moved into position beside Ransom. He knelt, picked the spent pistol magazine from the carpet and identified it as belonging to a .38.

The gunfire died away.

Abandoning the shelving, Ransom made her way to the wall opposite the windows, tapping it with the butt of her sword. Bolan looked at the desk drawer. He pulled it open and found a box of .38-caliber bullets tucked behind a rubber-banded group of pencils. The lock at the front of the drawer hadn't been broken. He filed the information away, dropped the magazine inside the drawer and joined Ransom.

"Here," the woman said at his approach. She tapped the wall again with the sword. The hollow cavity on the other side was evident. "There has to be a latch or a trigger somewhere." Her fingers flew along the wall.

Something crashed into the office door with impressive force. The woman looked at Bolan.

"Battering ram," he said tersely. He picked a spot on the door about five feet up, then fired the remaining rounds in the Desert Eagle. The banging died away, replaced at once by gunfire. He fed a new magazine into the .44. "Let me over there."

Ransom stepped aside. The battering started again. "They'll be through in a moment."

Bolan nodded. He raised a foot, aimed it to the right of the hollow's center and kicked. Plaster cracked, but the hidden door held. He kicked it again, feeling the shock go all the way up to his hip. The wound in his side ripped open, and he could feel blood seeping into the blacksuit. The third time his foot crashed through the door, tearing a large chunk from it. He reached inside, found the bolt that had been thrown from the other side to seal it off, pulled it back and pushed on into the cavity. Ransom immediately followed, pausing only long enough to slip the bolt back into place as a delaying tactic.

Soft light filtered through the aquarium waters, shot through with larger-than-life shadows that swam and darted, and made a long rectangle against the back wall. Bolan trailed his empty hand along the wall and found the ladder built into the duct work. The rung in his hand vibrated slightly, letting him know someone was still inside the tunnel. "Up here."

She nodded and sheathed the sword on her back. Leathering the .44, Bolan took the lead, pulling himself up into the darkness. The rungs continued to vibrate in his hands. He didn't doubt the double vibrations now coursing through the construction had alerted Yemon Hosaka that he was being followed. The tunnel corkscrewed as it went up, providing coverage from anyone trying to fire straight up into it. Sharp angles filled the sides that would turn back any bullets.

The guards were at the hidden door now. More shots followed, pierced by the strident ringing of a telephone. The door gave with a loud crack. The telephone went silent in midring.

Bolan threw himself up the rungs, striving to catch his quarry, taking them two at a time. His breath came in ragged gasps, echoed by the softer, quicker intakes of Ransom.

More vibrations joined the ones already going through the ladder. Sensing the woman stop, Bolan paused and looked down. If she was too tired to go on, he couldn't just leave her there.

Ransom dug a hand into a concealed pocket, then flung the contents down, following it immediately with another. Metal clanged against metal. Agonized screams erupted from below. "Caltrops," she said, pulling herself up again. "It should buy us some time."

The thought of what the razor-edged balls would do to anyone looking up caused Bolan to rethink his own position. Then he realized there was no real choice if he expected to gain something from the strike.

Someone fired up into the tunnel. The resulting ricochets started another series of screams and high-pitched invective. There were no further shots.

Long minutes passed, filled with nothing but the seemingly unending series of pushes, pulls and shoves. Liquid fire seemed to be packed into the joints of Bolan's arms and knees. Then the tunnel came to a dead end. He paused to take a penflash from his pocket. Flicking it on, he gave the opening a thorough search. He caught the trip wire the first time through, quickly tracing it to the small deposits of C-4 at the sides that would have ruptured the tunnel and killed whomever was attempting to raise the door. He disconnected the wires and threw the door back.

Wind whipped across the top of the building, part of it from the coming storm, part of it from the helicopter lifting off from the rooftop. Raising the heavy .44 into target acquisition, Bolan focused on the tail rotor, the weakest part of the craft, as he ran to the edge of the building. Then he thought of the streets below and the other buildings. He let the Desert Eagle fall to his side, watching helplessly as the helicopter heeled over and vanished into the night.

CHAPTER TWENTY

Winterroad clawed his way up through the bed sheets and reached for the phone. "Yeah?" he grunted. He rolled onto his back, blinking bleary eyes at the bright early-afternoon sunshine colliding with the drawn shutters of his bedroom.

"It's me," Dale Corrigan said.

"Is this important?"

"If it wasn't, I wouldn't call."

"Give me a minute to get it together."

"Are you alone?"

Winterroad laughed bitterly. "You've been reading too many espionage thrillers, Dale. Either that or I'm the only spy who missed out on having a woman in every port."

"I'll call back in fifteen minutes. Don't go back to sleep." The phone clicked dead.

Winterroad stared at the receiver in his hand. A moment later it started to beep. He cradled it and forced himself up from the bed, moving into the small bathroom. As the shower water ran, he wondered where the days had gone when he could simply get up from five minutes of sleep and keep on moving at top speed.

Feeling refreshed, he stepped from the shower, dried and wrapped a towel around his waist. With an economy of motion learned from living on the go, he lathered his face with shaving cream while wiping at the steamed mirror with the other hand. After finishing the morning rituals, he dressed then sat on the bed, watching the clock tick down the last minute since Corrigan's call.

He considered the possible reasons for Corrigan's call. The scene in the office earlier that morning made him sure Corrigan wouldn't have gotten in contact unless it was damn important. The man would have let him sleep at least a few more hours before trying to mend any bridges of communication. And Winterroad felt sure that whatever mending needed to be done this time needed to be done by him, not Corrigan.

His thoughts turned to the meeting with Sacker, and he wondered if they had been spotted together. He quickly dismissed that theory on two counts. One, if they had been seen together, the Agency would have wasted no time in trying to apprehend Sacker. And two, if Corrigan had heard about such a meeting taking place, he'd have surrounded the apartment with agents rather than calling to confirm it.

The phone rang, and he picked it up before it had the chance to ring again.

"Are you awake now?" Corrigan asked.

"Yes." Winterroad massaged his eyes, feeling the familiar sharp ache of not enough sleep, thinking the eyes were the first part of the body to tell a man he was getting old. Eyes showed it and felt it.

"You know it's not my way to pussyfoot around things," Corrigan went on, "so I'll just come out and say it. Somebody killed Alan Tucker in Tokyo last night...this morning." The man sighed. "Shit. It was little more than an hour ago. These goddamn time zones still give me hell. I have to work through them on a globe to make any sense of it."

Winterroad felt the need for a cigarette and automatically patted his empty pockets. He'd put them down one day in 1972 and never picked them up again. The spot on his lung X rays had disappeared shortly after that.

"They want to send you in as his replacement," Corrigan said.

Winterroad stood, pacing back and forth in front of the bed, barefoot. His mind raced. "Who's they?"

"Nobody knows for sure. There was a Justice agent, Hal Brognola, on deck for the shooting."

"I know Brognola."

"Yeah, I remember now."

"Was anyone else there?"

"From the squads? No."

"Any chance that Tucker intercepted a bullet meant for Brognola?"

"Not from the report. You might check that out when you get over there. From what I read here, it was a straight hit on Tucker only, with no attempt made on Brognola at all."

"That doesn't make a hell of a lot of sense."

"That's what I said, too. Whatever the case is, you're up as his replacement, if you want it." Corrigan hesitated. "It'll mean something to the people upstairs."

"Screw the people upstairs. The last thing I want to hear right now is the promise of some kind of promotion by walking in over Tucker's dead body."

Corrigan fell silent.

"What else do you have on this?"

"Just scattered reports of some kind of activity in the ranks of suspected Yakuza. The Foreign Affairs people are trying to make it sound like some kind of intergang war, but I'm not buying it. This kind of activity starts, and somebody kills Tucker. They might not be related, but I'm definitely going to take it at more than face value."

Winterroad stopped pacing and pulled a battered suitcase from the closet. "Have you got a plane lined up for me?"

"It leaves within the hour."

"When and where?"

Corrigan gave him the information.

Winterroad wrote it down on a page in the telephone book lying beside the television, tore it out and tucked it into his shirt pocket.

"Take care of yourself over there," Corrigan said with real sentiment. "And give me a call as soon as you get settled."

Winterroad hung up, sat on the bed and stared at the phone in his lap. He wasn't surprised when it rang only moments later. Nor was he surprised to find the caller was Sacker.

SHRILLING SIRENS filled the night air, reminding Bolan that the numbers had all but ran out on the mission. The helicopter containing Yemon Hosaka and at least some of the answers he'd come for had disappeared around a distant skyscraper. He ran to the fire escape door on the rooftop, smashed through the lock and went inside. Ransom stayed almost on top of his shadow.

"They're going to be all over the building looking for us," the woman said as they jogged down the hallway of the top floor.

"I know." People peered out of their apartments, dodging back inside when they saw the two warriors in black.

"Yemon killed Saburo," Ransom said as they swung around a corner.

"Yes." Bolan listened for sounds of pursuit. Their own footfalls were muffled by the carpet.

"Why?"

Bolan drew up short, fisting the Desert Eagle in both hands, surveying the lobby in front of the elevator. "It didn't appear to be self-defense," he said dryly. The elevator doors remained closed, but the light over the top of them clicked off the floors as it rose.

"Saburo knew something," Ransom said.

"I think so, too."

"And Yemon killed him because of it."

"From what I've heard, Yemon appears to be every inch his father's son."

"Maybe," Ransom replied cryptically.

Bolan glanced at the woman, wishing he had the time to question her. He moved to the fire escape, looked down and, finding no one, led the way inside. They made it two floors down before an eruption of gunfire flamed from the metal stairs. Screams of people attempting to leave the building by the fire escape echoed in the narrow enclosure.

Not wanting to pull innocents into the firefight, Bolan slammed back through the door of the thirty-sixth floor. The small crowd of people filling the hallway shrieked and ran toward the other end of the building, vanishing around corners. Aware that the building was rapidly turning into a deadly little maze with no way out, he glanced at the elevator numbers. The flashing light had steadied at the thirty-fourth floor. He took another Ka-bar from its sheath on his right thigh, kneeled, and quickly cut two almost yard-wide squares from the carpet. Sheathing the knife, he yanked them up, giving one to Ransom.

She took it without question, covering their backs.

Bolan levered the elevator doors open and looked down. The elevator cage sat motionless below them. "They're trying to cut us off," he told her. "Come on." He leaned out into the opening and wrapped the section of carpet around one of the elevator's support cables, holding the doors open for the woman.

Ransom sheathed the sword and imitated him, gripping the carpet tightly in her hands, soft side outward. She swung out, clamping her feet to the thick cable as she slid down.

Bolan followed, tightening his grip on the hoist cable as he controlled his slide downward. The doors closed behind him, shutting out the light. The whir of machinery filled the shaft and overrode the swishing sound generated by the carpet. "Don't touch the cage," he said.

Angling her body, Ransom came to a stop at the side of the shaft. Bolan slid down and came to a rest on the other side. Unleathering the Desert Eagle, he released the cable and shifted his weight evenly across the cage. Using his Ka-bar, he pried the escape hatch from the elevator and thrust the .44 through immediately.

There was only one gunner in the cage. A 240-grain bullet punched him back against the wall of the elevator and knocked him away from the doors before he could bring his weapon up, allowing the doors to close. The elevator started down immediately.

Bolan dropped through the hatch, checking to make sure the man was dead. He holstered the .44 and picked up the Uzi the man had been carrying, dropping his onto the floor. Ransom was beside him a heartbeat later. She didn't give the corpse a second glance. He unclipped the walkie-talkie from the dead man's waist and listened briefly to the conversation going through the channel.

The elevator came to a stop. Bolan stepped back as the door opened, covering the hallway with the Uzi. They were within the office areas now and the hallway was dark. Two men bearing weapons were the only people in sight, and they dodged away when the warrior aimed a short burst at them. The elevator doors closed again as the communications over the walkie-talkie increased.

"They know where we are now," Ransom said.

"That's fine. The ride's over, anyway." Bolan used the Ka-bar to rip off the cover of the elevator controls, then cut some of the wires. Sparks flashed and the cage came to a stop. He forced the doors open.

They hung suspended between floors. Taking the section of carpet, Bolan ducked under the floor, dropping into the hallway below. Ransom slithered out behind him.

"It's fourteen floors straight down," Bolan growled. "Think you can make it?"

She nodded and quickly moved into the shaft. He joined her, wrapping the carpet around the suspension cables. "Keep your grip loose," he advised. "Let gravity do the work. All you have to do is control it."

"I know." Her voice sounded strong.

Bolan glanced down at the darkness below as they dropped through the bowels of the building. His fingers heated up as he matched his descent with that of the woman, his greater weight increasing the friction.

Then they were down, almost so suddenly that they crashed into the car buffer at the bottom. Recovering from the impact first, Bolan scrambled toward the doors and forced them open slightly. The dimly lit interior of a parking garage spread out before him.

The Executioner led the way into the garage, letting his combat senses take full measure of the area. The smell of oil and gasoline permeated the area, shot through with the odor of disinfectants and detergents. Shadows clustered around the yard-wide support beams that became part of the low-slung ceiling.

A foot shifting on the concrete alerted Bolan, and he spun, bringing up the Uzi. Lightning flashed at him as he spotted the two men approaching through the rows of parked cars. The windshield of the vehicle in front of him spiderwebbed, and bullets screamed as they skipped over the bodywork, leaving sparks in their wake.

The Executioner's deadly figure eight took out one of the men instantly and drove the other to cover. He turned his attention back to Ransom in time to see the woman underhand a *shaken* at another man's face. The guard's weapon spit fire as it traced an uneven line across the ceiling, scattering broken light fixtures.

Bolan triggered a tri-burst into the man's chest, and the guy collapsed into an untidy heap. The warrior sprinted after Ransom, the hollow footsteps of their pursuers echoing on the concrete floor.

A man stepped out of the shadows, leveling a handgun at Ransom. She ducked under the line of fire, disemboweling the man with a glittering swipe of her short sword.

"Here," Bolan called as he pulled open the door of a van. He slid inside, dropping the Uzi into the space between the seats. Reaching under the dash, he hot-wired the ignition system and got the engine going as Ransom clambered through the door and picked up the Uzi. He jerked the vehicle into gear and stomped on the accelerator as four men raced into view.

The Uzi chattered through the window and Ransom leaned out and hosed the group with 9 mm parabellums. One man was hit and dropped to the ground, while the others opened fire.

Bolan reached for the woman as the windshield shattered. He grabbed a fistful of her black uniform and pulled her into the seat. He heard a choked cry of pain, then Ransom fell back on him, the Uzi dropping away from her limp fingers. Her loose weight thudded against him as he fought the steering wheel.

The van crashed into one of the support beams, coming to a sudden stop. Bolan reversed the machine, backing away to get room to maneuver. Bullets tore through the thin sheet metal of the van. Ransom didn't move. The warrior glanced at her and saw the blood covering her face from a head wound. He wasn't sure if she was breathing.

Bolan powered the vehicle into a collision course with the yellow-and-black striped wooden pole blocking the entrance. The pole splintered as he roared up the incline leading to the street.

THE GINZA TRAIN STATION was doing a fair business when Brognola arrived. Early-morning workers clustered in the waiting areas reading newspapers, comic books and business reports.

He limped across the floor to the rows of bus lockers, knowing the cane would already draw some attention, trying to keep his tired eyes open. The .38 was in its customary holster, but he'd added a .45 automatic from Ron Roberts's arsenal when he'd returned to the hotel to change clothes. The big pistol dragged at his trench coat.

The characters on the key were Japanese. He moved slowly through the locker area, searching for a match. Two rows farther on, he found it. Seating himself on the wooden bench in front of the lockers, he stretched out his wounded leg, appreciating the relief.

Four young men, dressed in leather and red bandannas, occupied a corner of the locker area, talking quietly among themselves. An endless stream of men dressed in dark suits filed past Brognola, some giving him more than casual glances. They also gave a wide berth to the leather boys at the rear of the locker room.

Glancing up, Brognola scanned the immediate vicinity, using the mirrors hanging from the wall. The tail caught his eye at once. The guy couldn't have been more obvious than if he'd been reading his magazine upside down. To the big Fed's trained eye, the man might as well have worn a sign with Cop on it.

Brognola picked up the cane and limped into the rest room at the back of the lockers. He worked his way across the slippery tile floor and took a stall, removing his hat so that it would make his tail's job of finding him harder.

The four leather boys entered first, no longer talking, walking in a predatory fashion. No one else was in the rest room. The gang spread out across the urinals, one youth taking up a position at the sink.

The big Fed stood there for a few minutes, waiting patiently. He had time on his side for the moment. Fujitsu's man would get nervous soon and begin to wonder if his quarry had simply left by another route.

The leather boys at the urinals zipped up, glanced at one another, then moved toward Brognola. The door opened and the undercover policeman entered, folding his magazine under his arm.

Brognola crouched, his head below the privacy wall of the stall, lifted his cane and stood to one side of the door, waiting. When the man reached his door, the big Fed pulled the door in quickly and wrapped a hand around the guy's tie, rattling him against both sides of the stall as he yanked him inside.

The policeman groaned as Brognola rammed him into the rear wall of the stall. He frisked the dazed man quickly, turning up a pistol, a pair of handcuffs and their key. He pocketed the pistol and the key and snapped one end of the cuffs to the man's wrist and the other to the plumbing of the toilet.

"Who put you onto me?" Brognola demanded.

The policeman shook his head. "You're under arrest, Brognola."

"Thanks, but I believe I'll pass this time." The Fed straightened his clothing. "When you see Fujitsu, tell him to start cooperating before this thing blows up in our faces. I don't have time to trip over his Boy Scouts everywhere I go."

The leather boys were against the wall when he limped out of the stall. One of them had a knife in his hand, frozen by the explosion of activity in the stall. Brognola lifted the .38 and pointed it at him. "You'd better be planning on doing your nails, sonny, or you're going to walk out of here in worse shape than I am." The youth made the knife disappear.

Safely out of reach, Brognola slid the cop's gun to him under the stall. The leather boys didn't miss the action. "I'll call someone to get you out of there," he said as he put the .38 away and walked through the door.

Back at the lockers, Brognola unlocked the door and found a cheap briefcase inside. The briefcase was empty. Then he noticed that the top lining bulged slightly. When he pulled it back, Brognola found two computer disks. Satisfied, he closed the briefcase, then limped hurriedly to the subway train, filing in with the early-morning commuters to escape the undercover man's backup.

The car was standing room only. He grabbed the loop hanging overhead and looked out the windows. Hefting the briefcase, he wondered if there was enough information on the disks to warrant Tucker's death. Then he considered the possibility that the information the CIA man had turned up was purely wild-card material, and that Tucker's death was part of an even larger scheme. The thought left him feeling cold and uncomfortable. The image of Tucker dying in his arms wouldn't go away. He wondered where Striker was.

"IS SHE ALIVE?" Akemi asked as he stepped out of the small temple.

"So far," Bolan replied. He held Ransom in his arms.

"Come inside," Akemi said, moving back into the temple.

Bolan followed the man.

"Put her there," the Japanese said when they entered the room where he'd treated Bolan.

The warrior knelt, placing the woman gently on a mat. She moaned softly, shifted, but didn't wake up. He sat beside her, tucking his legs up under him. He unleathered the Desert Eagle and laid it beside his thigh. Fisting the material of his shirt, he pushed it against the wound in his side, struggling against the sudden rush of pain. His hand felt slick and warm as he attempted to help the clotting process.

Akemi returned within moments, kneeling as he set a pan of water near Ransom's head. He spread first-aid equipment to the other side, then lit candles. The warm yellow glow filled the room.

Blood stained the woman's features, hanging in clumps from her hair. She breathed deeply, tried to sit up, then passed out again.

"What happened?" Akemi asked.

In terse sentences Bolan outlined the assault on the Hosaka offices. When he finished, Akemi shook his head and continued his ministrations.

"I tried to tell her it would come to this," the man said. The woman's face was almost clean now. Bolan saw the erratic rip along her left temple where a bullet had skated across her skull. "She felt she had no choice, and in truth, perhaps she did not."

"What does she know about what's been going on?" Bolan asked.

"You would have to ask her."

Bolan's voice was harsh. "Look, I don't know what loyalties you two have for each other, but it's almost gotten her killed. Whatever you know, I need to be told."

Akemi looked up, his features placid. "You speak of loyalties, and here you sit, wounded, in perhaps graver risk than Michi is. The only thing pushing you into this is a loyalty for a country that forces you to hide in shadows."

Bolan didn't say anything.

Akemi turned his attentions back to his patient. He mixed an evil-smelling powder into the water and made a poultice to put on her temple. "Yes, I know the kind of man you are. My life was not always devoted only to this temple. You are a man of passion, of fierce loyalties, who has a need to make things as morally right as you can. These are the things that have involved Michi in the present affair, though on a much smaller scale. Still, the passions are the same and fill the whole person. Though you fight for ideals of differing sizes, you fight no harder for yours than she does for hers."

"She's out of her league."

"Ah, yet you think you have the ability to take on armies by yourself? Surely you have realized that is what is involved here."

"I don't know everything that's involved."

"Neither does Michi."

"I need what she knows."

"Then talk to her. Perhaps she needs what you know, as well." Finished with the poultice, the man looked at Bolan.

"You have already been won over to her cause in some respects."

"How do you figure that?"

"You brought her here, to a place of safety for her rather than taking her back to your compatriots where she would not have the freedom to continue her fight."

"Maybe I didn't have a choice about it."

"Maybe you did not."

Dropping the subject, the warrior asked, "How is she?"

"I believe she has a concussion. Combined with her own frenzied state of mind these past few days, I think that is what is keeping her unconscious. We will have to keep watch over her the next few hours. After she has some rest, I think she will recover well."

Bolan nodded. "I need to make some phone calls."

"There is a rain slicker by the door."

The warrior forced himself to his feet. "I'll be back." He took the rain slicker and let himself out into the night. Dawn stabbed gray fingers through the eastern sky. Morning life stirred in the marketplace as shopkeepers prepared themselves for another day.

He dropped change into the pay phone and dialed the number of the hotel where the Justice team was staying. He heard Ron Roberts's voice come on the phone, and the click of phone-tapping devices a moment later. He asked for Brognola, counting off the seconds on the tracing effort.

"I can't help you, buddy," Roberts said. "And you can bet this line's wired."

"I heard them come on. Tell Hal I'll be in touch." He broke the connection, then he went back to the temple because there was nowhere else to go. Yet.

Ransom was under a thin blanket when he returned, her breathing deep and regular. Akemi knelt by her head, patiently watching her, his face unreadable. He looked up at Bolan's approach.

Black comets flamed in Bolan's vision, and he struggled to keep himself upright. He reached into the pocket of the blacksuit where he had placed the anti-inflammatory tablets the emergency room doctor had given him. Tossing four into his mouth, he chewed them dry.

"Your wound needs tending."

Bolan nodded, stripping out of the harness and the blacksuit. Taking the water basin Akemi had been using, he sat with his back to a wall and started cleaning the wound.

"Allow me." The Japanese took the basin and got fresh water.

"How is she?"

"She sleeps." Akemi's touch was gentle, soothing.

Bolan leaned his head against the wall, closed his eyes and fought to make the pain go away. "Hosaka will be looking for us," he said. "I don't know how much help my people will be able to offer."

"Did they see Michi?"

"Yes, but she was masked."

"Maybe it will be enough." Akemi rinsed out the towel. "You believe Yemon killed Saburo?"

"Yes."

"It does not surprise me, but it will certainly make your quest harder. Joji Hosaka will not take the death of his son lightly, and I am sure Yemon will not volunteer the information of who actually killed Saburo."

Akemi went on. "You are in a war, a very terrible war with people who should be allowed to simply kill each other. The problem is that, should any of them win, the effect on the rest of the world could be devastating. And there are many sides to it, each interested only in furthering its own goals."

"What are you talking about?"

"I cannot say any more. You need to talk to Michi."

"And if she won't talk?"

"Then I will be forced to carry a heavier burden."

The man's words didn't sound promising. Bolan tried to sort through the few facts he had. Joji Hosaka was putting together a consortium for the benefit of Japanese business in America. Someone else with access to American mercenaries and ex-CIA agents was out to stop him, as well as discourage continued Japanese growth in the United States. And where was Yemon Hosaka now that he had killed his brother? Who commanded *his* loyalties?

"You have trusted me this far," Akemi said. "If you would be willing to trust me still further, I have a place where you and Michi can be safe."

Bolan considered his few options. "All right."

"Michi will need care, and I do not want to involve anyone else in this unless it becomes necessary. You need care yourself, but you have been in this position before. I feel you are strong enough to handle your own health, but she will require aid for a day or two."

"For as long as I can."

"With everything that has happened of late, events will have to take their own course before you can plan your next move."

"I know." Bolan watched the candle flame dancing lightly on the sleeping woman's face, wondering what secrets her mind held, and if the information could help him put everything together. Then, with his hand curled around the butt of the Desert Eagle, he dropped into a much-needed sleep.

"IT WAS ONE of the American agents who killed Saburo," Yemon said as he followed his father through the crowd of rescue workers gathered around the office building.

Joji Hosaka shoved a yellow-slickered fireman out of his way, earning a scowl from the man until he saw who had pushed him. The fireman moved away and bowed. "Do you know the man's name?" Kiyosha Ogata was a reed-thin figure in black at his father's side.

Hurrying to catch up, jumping lithely over the fire hoses, Yemon said, "I think he's called Belasko." He watched his father give the old man a look and saw Ogata nod in immediate response.

"Why did you not call me when Saburo asked you to meet him?" his father demanded.

"I didn't think it was important enough to bother you with, Father." Yemon almost collided with his father as the man came to a sudden stop. "And he had asked for me, not you. Even though he's your son, he's also my brother. I've helped him before when I was able."

"And tonight?"

"I had no opportunity." Yemon returned Ogata's flat black gaze, knowing he had never been able to lie to the man. Still, Ogata would never mention his suspicions without the proof necessary to back them up.

Joji Hosaka froze one of the ambulance attendants with a look. "I want my son brought to me," he ordered. "I do not want him taken to a morgue to lie there until the butchers start on him."

The man nodded and walked away quickly, waving to one of his colleagues.

A news crew pushed its way toward Joji Hosaka. When the team was twenty feet away, he raised his hand. The lead reporter dropped his microphone and herded the cameraman away.

Yemon watched the process with interest. Ever since he'd been a boy, he could only remember it being this way. No matter what the situation, no matter who was involved, it had always been Joji Hosaka in control. Until now. The thought made him feel good, and he realized Saburo's unplanned death had actually moved things along much faster, as had the unexpected pressure from the American Justice agent.

"What did Saburo wish to speak to you about?" his father asked.

"I never had the chance to find out. We had just gone into the office when the American broke in on us and shot him." His men would all swear to that. Again he faced the look from Ogata and didn't flinch.

Two ambulance attendants approached Hosaka with a gurney, pulled out the legs and set the gurney before him. Yemon watched his father pull the blood-spattered sheet back and stare at the face beneath. Saburo's features had been untouched by the bullets. It looked as if he were only sleeping.

"I'm sorry, Hosaka-san, but the body must be taken downtown."

Yemon turned and saw Goro Fujitsu standing to one side.

"I will not allow them to cut him."

"It is the law," Fujitsu said, walking forward until he was on the other side of the gurney.

"The law?" Joji Hosaka repeated incredulously. "It was the law who was supposed to keep this from happening."

"I am sorry, Hosaka-san, but that is the way it must be."

Without facing his bodyguard, Joji Hosaka said, in a voice loud enough to be heard by Fujitsu, "Kiyosha, I want the man who is responsible for this dead. I want you to bring me his head on a stick."

"Yes, Hosaka-san." Ogata bowed and melted into the shadows.

"That will not make matters any better," Fujitsu stated calmly.

"Yes," Joji Hosaka said with slow deliberation, "it will." He spread his hands. "Now, if I may, I'd like to spend a few moments with my son."

Fujitsu responded with a grudging nod, then stepped away.

Someone touched Yemon on the shoulder. He turned and found one of his private guards at his side.

"There is a call for you in the car, Hosaka-san," the guard whispered. He looked lean and hard, wearing black sunglasses and black gloves.

"Take a message," Yemon said impatiently, intending to show support for his father.

"It is from Singapore."

"I'll take it."

The guard nodded and fell into step beside him.

"The old man, Ogata. Have you got someone on him?"

"Yes, Hosaka-san."

"I want men following him constantly, and reports given to me regularly. If he can find Belasko, I want both of them dead."

The guard nodded.

Sliding into his father's limousine, pleased with the way things had turned out and the fact that Ogata was now gone from his father's immediate defense, Yemon lifted the receiver and said hello.

CHAPTER TWENTY-ONE

Philip Picard took breakfast alone on the balcony of his luxury motel in Singapore. Below, broad boulevards and towering skyscrapers contrasted with narrow winding streets crowded with rows of homes and shops. The section of the harbor within his view was filled with shrimp trawlers and pleasure craft of all sizes. One of them was his, but he couldn't see it from his present position.

He buttered another croissant, then poured a fresh cup of coffee. The telephone rang, and he picked it up before it could wake Cherie.

"Picard," he said.

Keith Caputo identified himself at the other end. "Christ, do you know what time it is here?" the investments manager complained.

Picard consulted his watch. It was shortly after 11:00 a.m. in Singapore. "It should be a little after three in the morning for you," he told the broker. "You're late."

Caputo sighed. "I overslept," he confessed. "But I have the stock reports concerning the Japanese market. As expected, the stock market is showing stress from the Japanese problems. The Dow Jones took another plunge yesterday when news of Kokan's murder hit the wires. Trading is at an all-time low since the fall in 1987." Caputo sounded worn and haggard. "Truth to tell, I'd been considering dusting off the old résumé, then realized I've never really done anything other than work in fast-food restaurants and deliver newspapers."

Picard smiled and added honey to the croissant now that the butter had melted. "It will get better before long."

"I'm glad you've got all the faith you have, but I'm not going to hold my breath. I wish I had the millions to lose that you seem to have. You could damn well bet I wouldn't be putting them in American stocks right now."

"Think about it, though. With as much buying as I'm doing in the ever-weakening stock market, how much could it possibly be worth when the market comes back into shape?"

"We're talking 'if' here, not 'when.'"

"It will."

"One of these days you need to tell me where you get all your money, and what it's like to be one of the incredibly rich. The last place I expected you to be is Singapore, or anywhere out of the United States, with the markets crumbling the way they are. What are you going to do if the dollar suddenly turns up worthless?"

Picard looked through the gauzy balcony curtains and saw Cherie beginning to show signs of life. "Take the day off," he advised, "before you end up on an operating table."

"I wish I could, but I've been spending ten and twelve hours a day on the phone talking to frantic people who think I'm personally responsible for what's happening to their investments."

After a few more sympathetic exchanges with the broker, he hung up and ate the croissant, savoring the postponed flavor, reflecting that the best things in life were the ones you had to wait on.

Finished with breakfast, he poured a final cup of coffee before reaching for the phone. Tuley wasn't in so he left a message for the man to return his call.

A few minutes later the phone jangled. When he answered it, Tuley was on the other end. "Winterroad will be there within hours," Picard said. "I want to see to it that we keep him covered at all times. I want nothing to happen to him.''

Tuley was silent for a moment. "John actually signed on?''

"You were the only one with doubts. He's a good man, like you, and tired of not getting any recognition for his efforts. I won't say that he'll take up our fight as readily as you have, but at the moment, it's enough to have someone inside the enemy camp. By the way, that was good work with Tucker. My sources at Langley tell me nobody has any idea of who took him out or why. Don't worry about being replaced. You're the only man I want handling the enforcement arm of this operation.''

"I wasn't worried about that," Tuley said quickly enough to let Picard know that the thought had been on his mind. "I just couldn't picture John turning on the Agency so fast.''

"Just keep in mind the fact that he didn't burn you when he could have. He stood by you like a partner should.''

"I know.''

"Trust me on this. I know what I'm doing. It's almost downhill from here. But the time has come for Brognola to bow out of the picture, too. Once Winterroad arrives and makes contact with you, I want your team to ensure the Justice team is left leaderless. The more confusion we can build in the next few days, the better.''

"I'll handle it myself.''

"Good. Then I won't have to worry about that." Picard hung up and went to find out what Cherie wanted from room service, deciding to order something else for himself in celebration. Tonight he would put the finishing touches on the Hosaka angle. Personally.

THE SMALL HOUSE SAT on a verdant hill surrounded by a forest of oak trees. Akemi drove the four-wheel-drive Suzuki Samurai up the steep, winding dirt road that was little more than an overgrown trail.

Bolan rode in silence, his leg stretched out to take the pressure off the wound in his side. He studied the countryside through the windows, catching Ransom's reflection occasionally in the glass. Her color still hadn't returned to normal, making her look ashen and gray. She gritted her teeth from time to time as the Samurai crawled over a bumpy incline.

Akemi braked the 4X4 in the small yard and waved toward the house. "This was my father's home. I visit it occasionally as I find time from the temple, but I have not been here in months. I apologize for any inconvenience."

Bolan gave the man a ghost of a smile. "A safehouse has more important qualities than hot and cold running water and an indoor toilet."

Akemi nodded. "True, very true."

The warrior opened his door and stepped out. Red stone lanterns sat in a semicircle outlining a rock garden on either side of the entrance. The slight wind carried the sweet fragrance of flowers and the after-odors of early-morning rain. As Bolan reached for the suitcase containing his blacksuit and his weapons, a second Samurai roared over the final hill and sputtered to a stop. Akemi walked back to speak with the driver.

Ransom disembarked carefully, obviously trying not to move her head. She wore a canary-yellow dress that showed generous amounts of shoulder and thigh. Akemi had apologized and blushed when he had given it to her, saying that it was all he could find on short notice that would fit her. She carried the matching high heels in one hand. The green duffel bag in her other hand looked totally out of place. She caught Bolan staring at her and didn't look away.

Bolan moved forward and reached out a hand. "I'll carry your bag for you."

Her voice was soft and firm. "Thank you, but I have it."

Bolan nodded and turned his attention back to the house.

Akemi returned, carrying a portable radio. "There is no electricity," he said apologetically as he led them to the door. "To heat water for a bath you must first light the heater in the bathroom, then draw your bath in buckets. Likewise, there is no phone. This radio will keep you up-to-date on the news, and I have brought extra batteries."

Inside, the house was hot, humid and musty. The furniture was of dark wood, handmade, and serviceable. Colorful knitted spreads adorned the sitting cushions.

Bolan made a circuit around the house while Akemi talked to Ransom, checking the visibility from each window. The house was no hardsite, but it didn't have to be as long as no one knew they were there. So far even Brognola didn't know where he was.

Leaving his suitcase in one corner of the living room, Bolan returned to the 4X4 for the sacks of groceries Akemi had purchased earlier in the morning.

Akemi returned from the bedroom he had shown to Ransom. "If there is anything else I can do, please don't hesitate to get in touch."

"You've done more than enough already," Bolan said.

"Still."

"I will."

Akemi tossed over the keys to the Samurai they'd arrived in. "Take care of her," he said in a low voice.

Bolan nodded. He took the Beretta 93-R from his suitcase, shoved it into the waistband of his pants and followed the man outside, staying under the shade of a spreading oak tree as the Samurai bounced back down the way it had come.

Farther below, at the foot of one of the hills ringing the area, was the small town where Akemi had told him a phone could be found. Bolan turned and found Ransom standing ten feet away. The look on her face revealed nothing of what was on her mind. Her sheathed sword was in her hand.

"The news reports list you as Saburo's murderer," she said.

"I know."

"That has made things even more complicated. My grandfather will be looking for you now, and Joji Hosaka will have told him to kill you."

"What will he do when he finds out you're involved?"

"I don't know." Ransom looked at him with wet eyes. "We need to talk now. Before things get any worse."

Bolan nodded and followed her into the house, not sure if anything concerning the operation could take a turn for the worse.

"YOU'VE GOT your hands on some dynamite," Aaron Kurtzman told Hal Brognola. "Provided it's all true, and provided you can prove it."

The Fed cradled the phone to his ear as the fax machine he had commandeered in the Tokyo American embassy continued to spit out page after page from the computer disks he'd sent to the Stony Man complex by modem hours earlier. "Tell me what I'm looking at, Aaron," he said, putting the sheets of paper to one side. A picture faxed through, and he looked at it with interest, seeing a much younger Joji Hosaka in the middle of what looked like a labor strike. The reproduction was a grainy black-and-white, and Brognola judged it to be sometime in the early 1950s.

"According to the files you transmitted, Joji Hosaka was an agent of American G-2 forces after World War II," Kurtzman said. "I won't go into everything he did, but there are plenty of ties to the black market and the Yakuza."

"I take it he was a busy boy."

"You take it right."

Another picture emerged from the fax. Hosaka, in the middle of a marketplace, was in animated conversation with a lean, raw-boned man. Someone had written August 21,

1962, in one corner of the picture. "I just got the picture of Hosaka talking to an unidentified man."

"He's still unidentified, and he's the subject of Tucker's investigation. You'll find a list of his known aliases on page nineteen of the document."

Brognola found the page and dragged his thumb down the dozens of names. More pictures spilled through, showing Hosaka with the same man. "What's the story on this guy?"

"He was CIA during the occupation," Kurtzman replied, "and, under the code name Sacker, he was responsible for engineering a lot of the Yakuza-oriented strike breaks and various other activities G-2 undertook after the war."

"Through Joji Hosaka?"

"Hosaka was his main man, but by no means his only. Sacker has always operated under a layer of controls, from what I gathered of the files, and always as an aggressive covert chief."

Brognola sat down in the chair behind the desk holding the chattering fax machine. "He liked it."

"Yeah."

Spreading the sheets out before him, the big Fed tried to take it all in. "So where does that leave us now?"

"Tucker believed Sacker was ramrodding the purge in the States, using men whose loyalty he'd culled from his time with the Agency."

"Is this guy still with the CIA?"

"Tucker wasn't sure. I'm still running down the aliases, but most of them are dead ends. I think it's safe to assume the guy has built a new identity for himself and dropped into it."

"But why come out now?"

"Tucker thought Sacker was after a piece of the pie Hosaka's assembling in Tokyo."

"Blackmail?" Brognola scanned the sheets again. "That doesn't wash, Aaron. This guy was a player, he thrived on the excitement. I can't see him turning this operation just to get his hands on a few dollars."

"A few million dollars," Kurtzman corrected. "Possibly more. Let's not forget how big Hosaka's piggy bank is."

"That may be, but it doesn't feel right from this end."

"Those were Tucker's feelings. Don't forget, you're also dealing with a guy who's undoubtedly seen the best years of his life. Maybe his bank account's running too low to suit him."

The sheets quit feeding through, then a heartbeat later the fax machine turned itself off. Brognola looked at his watch, automatically checking the one on the wall. "Is there any indication whether Tucker went to anyone with this?"

"No."

"Apparently he's been sitting on this information for some time," Brognola mused. "Why?"

"According to these files, Sacker dropped entirely out of sight in the early eighties. What would you do if you were looking for an invisible enemy?"

"Keep my head down and keep a low profile." Brognola shifted in the chair uneasily. He took a cigar from his pocket, unwrapped it with one hand, then chewed on it. "So what brought Tucker to their attention?"

"If there's an answer, I don't think it's these files. If they had known about them, Sacker's wrecking crew would have made sure they disappeared, too."

"Yeah." Brognola turned it over in his head, juggling it around as he tried to get it to fit the pattern of logic he was attempting to build. "Unless Tucker's assassination was planned to develop something else. Did you run down the names of the people Striker took out over here?"

"Yeah, and a lot of them dead-ended where Sacker's name did. It looks like they're his people—if you allow your imagination to make the jump that proof can't."

"What about Ross Tuley?"

"Recruited for the Air America program," Kurtzman replied. "The Agency isn't aware they donated the files I have here, by the way. I might have left a few fingerprints in their computers, so that could be something we'll be dealing with later. Smash-and-grab isn't my specialty. I usually go in more for the subtle entry. But comparing the time of Tuley's hitch in Air America to the knowledge of Sacker's record that Tucker was able to outline, I'd say Sacker recruited him."

"There was no mention of Sacker in Tuley's files?"

"No, but one of the aliases Tucker mentioned is."

"How did Tucker make this guy?"

"I don't know, but judging from the different entries, it took Tucker a few years to come up with the intel he did have. Another thing—according to Tuley's files, Tucker was instrumental in having Tuley thrown out of the Agency for unsanctioned hits scattered across Europe and Asia. It's possible Tucker came across Sacker there."

Brognola sighed. "We may never know for sure."

"No. But it doesn't really matter, does it? I mean, if Tucker was correct, and Sacker's behind the strikes against the Japanese, this gives us a shot at him."

The big Fed dumped the shredded cigar in the wastebasket beside the desk, checked his watch again and said, "Take a stroll through those files of yours and see what you get when you enter the name John Winterroad."

Computers keys clacked in the background. A moment later Kurtzman came back on the line, his voice subdued. "Winterroad was recruited during the Phoenix Program in Vietnam. He was also Ross Tuley's partner when Tuley was shelled out of the Agency after Tucker's investigation. Why?"

A sour taste filled Brognola's mouth as he leaned back in the chair. The chain of logic his mind wrestled with had been completed. "Winterroad is Tucker's replacement on the

CIA end of things," he said. "I'm supposed to meet him at the airport in less than an hour."

RANSOM BUSIED HERSELF at the wood-burning stove in the small kitchen, heating water for rice and tea. "The Hosaka family has been a part of my life ever since I was born," she said as she measured the tea into cups.

"Grandfather pledged himself and his life to Joji Hosaka after World War II when Grandmother was sick. Hosaka knew my grandfather for what he was, so I don't think the offer was made out of the kindness of his heart. You saw him the day of the banquet. I'm sure someone at least mentioned Kiyosha Ogata."

Bolan nodded. "I was told he was a bodyguard."

"That's only part of the truth." Ransom dropped rice in the boiling water and covered the pot as she put it to one side. She made the tea automatically, then poured it into small, handleless cups and handed one to Bolan. "The whole truth is that my grandfather is an assassin." Ransom looked at him, as if to judge what his reaction might be.

Bolan confronted the issue head-on rather than trying to dodge it. "I'm after the people responsible for the deaths in the United States. Did your grandfather have anything to do with that?"

Ransom shook her head. "No. Those things were done by whoever sent those men to ambush you. There are two enemy camps here. One belongs to Hosaka, because you are now believed to be the murderer of Saburo. The other belongs to the American interests."

"But Hosaka's the common denominator?"

"More precisely, the consortium Joji Hosaka is proposing is the common denominator. Let me tell the story from the beginning. I've found it's always the best way for me." Ransom cleared her throat. "I've known since I was a little girl what services my grandfather has provided for Joji Hosaka. It didn't stop him from being a loving person, a good husband, a good father to me when my parents died.''

Bolan listened to her, hearing the emotions behind her words, willing himself not to be swayed by them.

"Until Joji Hosaka, my grandfather had never taken a life. His art was taught to him by his father and has been passed on in such a fashion for generations. My ancestors were spies for the emperors in the past and gave their services when they felt their allegiance was owed or when fishing was poor. Perhaps it's something you can't understand as a Westerner. America has such a limited history.''

"I understand," Bolan said. The fires of his own honor hadn't been extinguished in the personal hell that came after Vietnam.

"Tradition, obligation, loyalty, these are powerful cornerstones in the Japanese mind," Ransom explained. "And I have found them nowhere if not in my grandfather. That's why I knew he wouldn't leave Joji Hosaka's side when this began. What do you know of the consortium?''

"Not much," Bolan admitted.

"How can you involve yourself if you don't even know what's at stake here?''

"Why don't you tell me?''

"Business is a tool," she said in a more neutral voice. "A very dangerous weapon in the right hands. The United States has been using it effectively for years. Now they suddenly find themselves at the mercy of that same weapon, only they refuse to open their eyes and acknowledge its presence. You see media coverage about Japan and other countries buying into American lands and businesses. People shake their fists at the thought of the United States being owned by the French, the Japanese, the Middle East, and others, but they don't stop to realize the steps it would take to tip the world trade balance back in their favor. Those who do see it seem to be more willing to close their eyes than anything else. American financial independence is being stripped away with every pound, franc and yen they borrow. And with the financial independence, often goes the political." She looked into his eyes. "That's what this is about. The consortium Joji Hosaka wants to create could conceivably crush America's financial security in weeks. Do you know the havoc that could wreak back there? What would the American people be willing to sacrifice to keep that from happening?"

"Do you think that's what Hosaka is trying to do?"

"I don't know." Ransom eyed him critically. "But if it was, what would you be willing to do to prevent it?"

Bolan didn't reply. The question was moot at this point.

"You see, everything Joji Hosaka and the consortium could do would be perfectly legal. There are no laws about a creditor requesting a debtor to repay money the debtor has been lent. That's called foreclosure. And if there's ever been a country hovering on the brink of foreclosure, it's the United States at this point in time. And in this war there will be no Geneva Convention or Marquis of Queensbury rules, only Dun and Bradstreet listings and Dow Jones quotes."

"You paint a bleak picture," Bolan told her.

"It's a bleak world."

"Where do you fit into this?"

"I'm a reporter, covering the Orient and the Middle East in general, and Japan in particular. I've lived in the United States for ten years now. I got my break as a photographer because I'm good with a camera. After a year of hand-to-mouth existence in New York City waiting tables, I parlayed my pictures into a photojournalist's career. I followed that with some magazine articles, eventually a few books. I'm good at what I do. Damn good. Now I work as a free-lance reporter and I make a good living. A month ago I was tipped about the consortium by a friend in the business district of Wall Street. He wanted to know what I knew about it, which was nothing at the time, but I discovered enough to arrange an assignment over here. I could have come alone, on my own, but I wanted the cover."

"Why?"

"Because of the Hosaka family." Ransom paused. "I told you they had always been a part of my life. Even by going to America it seems I haven't been able to get away from them."

"How did you know about the assassination attempt on my life?"

"I have friends, contacts, associates, or whatever you wish to call them, over here. No doubt your agency can say the same thing." She put her empty tea cup down. "At first, when the violence began to erupt in the States, I believed, as did most of the Foreign Affairs people, that it was some kind of covert action to break up the courage of the people in the consortium. I thought it had backfired, because Hosaka's influence in the shaping of it became even more powerful." She looked at him. "Instead, I'm told there's a group of American mercenaries in the shadows of Tokyo vying for control of the consortium through Joji Hosaka."

"How?"

"Threat of death, or of blackmail. My informant wasn't sure. There's a man, someone who's known to Joji Hosaka, who knows much about him. I was told their relationship goes back a number of years."

"To the occupation?"

"I'm not sure. The information is sketchy at best. But I did know about the attempt on the Justice agent that was upcoming."

"Hosaka had a lot of Yakuza connections after the war," Bolan said as he finished his tea and set the cup aside. "Would that have been enough to open him to blackmail?"

"No, I think he was being set up from inside his own family. I'd heard about the passports the Americans arranged through one of Saburo's men."

"And you figured Saburo as the inside man?"

"No, that didn't make sense. Saburo was an animal, reaching out and taking what he was powerful enough to take, then throwing it away when he was done."

With her words, an image of Saburo Hosaka talking to Ransom came to Bolan's mind, followed swiftly by the first day they had met, when she threatened him with the stiletto.

"It wasn't until I saw Saburo's body—that he had been given no chance to defend himself—that I knew for sure who was behind the internal struggle of the Hosaka family."

"Yemon."

"Yes. Saburo was loyal to his father, disobedient perhaps, but he would never allow anyone to speak against Joji Hosaka. I saw him cut a chauffeur with a knife for cursing his father when I was just a girl. Violence came naturally to him."

"And Yemon was able to operate through Saburo's channels?"

"Some of them. Yemon never had anything to do with the drug deals Saburo handled. Even Joji handled some matters through Saburo."

Bolan focused on her eyes. "So why didn't you go to someone about this?"

"I was afraid for my grandfather. If officials moved too slowly, and they would with the scanty information I would have to provide, chances were good that my grandfather would be killed with Joji Hosaka." She turned away from him. "The Hosaka family has had control of my grandfather's life for too long already because of his loyalty and honor. I don't want his beliefs to be the death of him, as well. I'm not altruistic, and I'm not out to save the world. Only my grandfather. He's the only true innocent I see involved in this."

"So why have you decided to trust me with this now?"

She walked to the wood-burning stove and put the rice back on to heat. "Because I've seen you in action, and I know of you. You have honor and, even more, you understand how it can be twisted and manipulated against the person who bases his life on it. You aren't so very different from my grandfather."

"If your grandfather's hunting me," Bolan said softly, "continuing what I'm doing is going to increase our chances of a confrontation. What will you do then?"

Her eyes were flat, dark mirrors of her soul. Her face was unreadable as she ladled rice onto a plate for him. "When I was seventeen," she said in an emotionless voice, "I was brutally raped by Saburo Hosaka. I had been training in the arts with my grandfather, and maybe I could have killed Saburo for what he did. If I had, my grandfather might have been ordered to kill me, leaving him no choice but to take his own life for failing Joji Hosaka. In Japan it isn't unusual for rape victims to take their own lives in the name of honor. I wanted to. I felt dirty, unclean, and I've never forgotten the feel of Saburo's hands on my body. My grandmother knew. She helped me hide what had happened from my grandfather. I was trapped. If I told Grandfather what had happened, he would have killed Saburo, then himself. It took Grandmother's reasoning to talk me out of the knife I held to my chest, to make me realize that taking my own life would have the same results. The hardest thing I've ever done was to let Saburo Hosaka live after that day. But I did. Because of my grandfather."

Ransom stood, and Bolan watched her walk to the bedroom and slide the door closed behind her.

"HELLO, JOHN."

Winterroad turned toward the whisper, automatically reaching for his pistol.

"The gun's not necessary," the voice insisted.

The CIA agent peered through the dim lighting of the hotel lobby and saw Ross Tuley standing next to a ceiling-to-floor window that overlooked downtown Tokyo. His ex-partner looked as lean and whipcord tough as ever, making him conscious of the extra pounds he'd put on himself since the last time they'd seen each other. He released the butt of his pistol as he walked over to the man. "How did you get in?"

Tuley shook his head and laughed. "Hotel security's a joke," he replied. "The Justice Department's less than worthless in this operation."

"I heard a guy named Belasko kicked the hell out of one of your teams," Winterroad drawled. He came to a stop a few feet in front of Tuley. "It's in all the reports I received when I arrived."

Footsteps sounded behind them. Winterroad glanced over his shoulder and spotted a big man standing to one side of the hallway. He looked back at Tuley.

"New partner," the merc offered. "We take care of each other."

"Is that supposed to be a dig?"

"Was the crack about Belasko?"

"You don't like me very much, do you?" Winterroad asked.

Tuley smiled broadly. "I might say the same thing to you."

"I wasn't supposed to like you," Winterroad replied. "You were my partner."

"You kind of forgot that at the Agency hearing a few years back."

"I did what I could."

"Sacker believes you did, or you wouldn't be here now." Tuley breathed in through his nose and let it out in a whistle between his teeth. "You're playing in the big-time now, guy. You're going to like it. No more red tape, no more people pulling you away from doing something you know is right, no more bullshit. Sacker always does what he sets out to do.''

"I know," Winterroad said. "That's why I came."

"Have you met Brognola yet?"

"He brought me in from the airport."

"What do you think about him?"

"We've met before."

Tuley looked at him without saying anything.

"He's a good cop," Winterroad said. "I knew that going in."

"He's also the one backing Belasko. Brognola isn't playing this operation strictly aboveboard."

"Seems to be in keeping with the general guidelines laid down by this operation."

A white-jacketed room service waiter rapped his knuckles on a door down the hall.

"I didn't want you involved in this," Tuley said with honesty, "because I don't trust you the way Sacker does. You still believe in America first, the same as I do, but you have your own way of going about things. I tried to tell that to Sacker, but he wasn't listening." He smiled. "So here I am, the welcoming committee to let you know Sacker's backing your play while you're here. And just a personal note from me to you, to let you know I'll be watching."

Winterroad put on a fake smile. "I'll keep that in mind." He walked away, waiting until he was inside the elevator to pull the walkie-talkie from his pocket.

CHAPTER TWENTY-TWO

Bolan started with the Uzi, breaking it down and cleaning it with the gun kit Akemi had been able to acquire. There were only eight rounds left in the clip. When he was finished reassembling it, he loaded the clip with ammunition from the case Brognola had brought over in the diplomatic pouch. He laid the weapon aside and glanced through the window.

Darkness stained the forest beyond the small patch of yard claimed by the house, growing deeper and blacker with every passing moment. He felt better. He'd eaten twice since Ransom had made the midday meal, both times rousing from a slumber. His body still ached, but stretching exercises had relieved most of the cramps and kinks from the muscles.

He sat with crossed legs, his internal clock ticking away the seconds. Soon it would be time to call Brognola.

He reached for the Beretta, fieldstripping and cleaning it automatically, letting his mind wander elsewhere, vectoring in the numbers on the mission.

"My grandfather often sits cleaning his weapons as you're doing now," Ransom said. "Seemingly without conscious thought, as if they're old friends."

Bolan looked up. "I didn't hear you come in."

She stood in the doorway, still wearing the yellow dress. Her eyes looked clearer. "That's because you were attuned to noises outside the house. You've accepted that you have nothing to fear inside."

He smiled. "There's tea in a pan on the stove and some leftover rice. You need to eat something before you take the anti-inflammatories Akemi left with you. The tea's nothing to write home about, but it's got plenty of caffeine." He laid the separate pieces of the 93-R before him, then began the cleaning process.

"I only wanted to apologize for my behavior earlier. I had no right to be so hard on you. It's just that—"

"I was convenient."

"Yes." She smiled, and it was the first genuine one he could remember seeing on her. But the weight of fear still rolled restlessly behind it.

"Apology accepted."

The silence that followed was full of tension.

"Where do we go from here?" Ransom finally asked.

"I've still got a mission to complete," Bolan replied. "I'm going to make a call in a few hours and see if I can find out where the rest of the Hosaka clan is."

"I can tell you where they might go."

He looked up at her.

"Joji Hosaka keeps a house on Oshima Island. Actually it's more of a fortress. But I think, given the uncertainty of the present circumstances, he'll go there."

"And Yemon?"

"I don't think he'll leave his father's side at this point."

"I'll mention it to my friend."

"I want to go with you."

Bolan shook his head.

"I can help." Her look was pleading.

Softening his voice, Bolan said, "You've helped enough. It's time you cleared out of it. This situation's going to get a lot uglier before it gets any better."

"And what of my grandfather?"

"You need to remember that your grandfather and I have been taking care of ourselves for a long time."

"He's hunting you. If you find him before you find Ye-mon, what then?"

Bolan had no answer.

"Grandfather will listen to me, and I can take care of myself." Ransom returned his stare full measure. "If you choose to go without me, I'll make my own way. I'm giving you a choice now because two together will have a better chance than one alone. I've earned the right to go, even in your eyes."

As the warrior reassembled the Beretta, he knew he'd have a fight on his hands if he disagreed. And she was correct about earning the right. Ransom had proved capable of taking care of herself, as well as willing to go the distance. The warrior had learned a long time ago that that was all you could expect of your teammates.

DRESSED IN BLACK and wearing a .45 on his hip, Philip Picard climbed out of the helicopter and bent low under the whirling rotors as he made his way to the waiting yacht docked at the pier.

Once he and the other five men were clear, the helicopter took off, throwing blinding sheets of sand in every direction. Picard took the lead, jogging down the shore and across the wooden pier to the waiting boat. He felt jubilant as he stepped onto the deck. This night would see the culmination of years of planning.

He climbed the stairs leading to the wheelhouse, taking them two at a time. The yacht's engines kicked to life and they headed out to sea. Behind him Picard could see the lights of Atami. He looked back at the blackness sandwiched between the cloud-filled sky and the dark expanse of water, knowing Oshima Island and his quarry were just ahead of him.

Two men were in the steering area, also dressed in black. He joined the man standing by the railing. "Does he suspect anything?" he asked. The prow of the vessel smashed through the waves and saltwater sprayed over him. But he felt exhilarated rather than discomforted.

"No," Yemon Hosaka replied. "He doesn't suspect a thing. It was a good plan. A very good plan."

"THERE'S A MAN you need to know about," Brognola growled.

Bolan tucked the telephone under his chin as he stared out the narrow window of the village inn at the deserted gravel and sand road that ran through the heart of the town. A few lights were visible from his position, but most of them were lanterns left outside to illuminate different doorways. "I'm listening."

Brognola outlined the information Kurtzman had given him concerning the man code-named Sacker.

"Sacker," Bolan repeated thoughtfully.

"Do you know the guy?"

"We've never met, but I've got some intel on him in my journals. I first heard of him in Vietnam when he worked the Phoenix Project under Casey. He had a reputation for being able to walk through walls." Bolan shifted, looking out the window again. The man behind the innkeeper's desk was trying to watch him without being noticed. "But it doesn't scan as easy as Sacker trying to protect the United States from an economic takeover bid by Japan." He related the information Ransom had given him.

"Sacker's planning to run the consortium himself through Joji Hosaka?" Brognola asked when he finished.

"No, through Yemon Hosaka. Think about it. That's why Kokan was assassinated instead of Joji Hosaka. Yemon's the third in line for succession as head of the consortium. By taking Kokan out now, before Hosaka, there was no chance for the different business interests to become split over picking their new leader. Once Joji Hosaka is out of the way, Yemon will naturally step into the position."

"You think Yemon's going to kill his father?"

"Yes. He killed Saburo when his knowledge became dangerous. I don't think he'll have any compunctions about killing his father. Saburo was a split-second decision. His father's death is something he's been planning for some time."

"Where do you go from here?"

"Oshima Island," Bolan replied. "Joji Hosaka has a house there. I intend to take Yemon out of the play and squeeze him for information about Sacker."

"You'll be going up against an army, Striker."

"There's no choice. You're out of this for now, Hal. At least we were able to put all the pieces together first. And I won't be entirely alone." Bolan thought of Ransom waiting in the Samurai outside.

"Leave it alone until I can get something put together on this," Brognola said. "There might be something I can do to put some pressure on now that we know what it's all about."

"It'll be too late. And you don't have any real evidence. You've got a handful of guesses from Tucker, and even less from me. Sacker and Yemon Hosaka have tied this thing up nice and neat to frame the United States. Japan won't allow American military personnel free run of their countryside."

"Still, I'm going to push and keep on pushing until something gives," the big Fed said stubbornly. "Somebody will have to listen when—"

Bolan's hearing registered the sound of a gunshot, another less than a heartbeat later, then the phone connection broke. He dropped money in the phone, dialed the number to the restaurant Brognola had left in a coded message from Roberts. There was no response, only static.

Hanging the phone up, Bolan walked outside. Ransom wasn't in the vehicle. He melted into the darkness at the side of the inn, unleathering the Desert Eagle. A chunk of brick slammed from a corner of the building above his head as a cloud of brick dust settled over him. He ducked and ran, hearing the not-too-distant rolling thunder of a high-powered sniper rifle.

Moonlight gleamed on the edged blade that seemed to come from nowhere in front of him. The Executioner lined up the .44 on the black-clad figure with the sword even as another ninja closed in on the heels of the first.

"MISSED HIM!" Sliding the van door open, Ross Tuley bolted from the vehicle, dropping the sniper rifle he'd used in his attempt on Brognola and unslinging the MAC-10. He sprinted across the street, closing in on the man from Justice. Vardeman was a shadow at his side.

He flagged Vardeman to the narrow alley at the side of the building. "The side, the side. The back door leads that way."

Vardeman nodded and veered off.

Tuley triggered a sustained burst across the window that had been punctured by the rifle bullets, showering bits and pieces of glass over the people diving for cover. A slow-moving man took a 3-round burst in the throat as Tuley came to a stop in the shelter of the door. Even as the man went down the merc looked for Brognola. The man was on a cane. He couldn't have gotten far.

Emptying the clip across the walls to keep the customers down, Tuley reloaded and dashed across the eating area, knocking tables out of his way. The back door was sliding shut as he came up on it. A man dressed in a cook's apron and hat swung unexpectedly from the kitchen, clasping a heavy meat cleaver.

Tuley blocked the blow with the MAC-10, drawing the .45 holstered at his belt before the man could swing again. The heavy bullets slammed the cook against a stainless-steel table.

A single shot sounded in the alley. Tuley holstered the .45 and wheeled around the corner, the MAC-10 up and ready.

The weapon was knocked from his hands as a gun muzzle slammed against his forehead.

RANSOM FELT PANIC tearing at her with the sharp beak of a hawk at the knowledge that her grandfather must be somewhere in the night. She forced it away, forced her legs to carry her up the side of the wooden building toward the sniper who had shot at Belasko.

She wore black clothing again, as Belasko did, and had strapped her sword across her shoulders. Leaping up from the rickety eave overhanging the first floor, she threw a hand over the top of the second floor and forced her body to follow.

Her head topped the roof's edge as the sniper started to turn toward her. A knife suddenly pierced the man's left cheek, nailing his face to the stock of the rifle. His scream was bloodcurdling, continuing even after a shadow ran from the darkness of the roof and kicked him over the edge.

Recognition swept over Ransom as she clambered onto the roof. "Grandfather."

"Michi," the old man acknowledged, drawing his sword. "Are you all right?"

"Yes." She joined him at the railing and looked down at the road. Besides the body of the man in the road, there were two other corpses near the inn where Belasko had gone to use the phone. "These men are not yours?"

"No, they belong to Yemon. I thought I had lost them, but he has trained them better than I believed."

"When I saw this man up here, I thought you were behind the attack."

The old man led the way to the side of the building, uncoiling a thin nylon rope from a pocket inside his uniform. "Because of Saburo?"

"Yes."

"Faugh," he said with a shake of his head. "Yemon lied about this American killing Saburo. He has never been able to lie to me. His father might believe him, but I do not.'' He slid down the rope.

The woman followed him a moment later, relief coursing through her because her grandfather wasn't pursuing Belasko. ''Yemon killed Saburo.''

''Yes, that is what I believed.'' The old man made himself a part of the darkness.

Ransom was surprised to find her sword in her hand. Her heartbeat was regular. Perspiration stained her hands. ''And what of Belasko?''

''The man you were with?''

''Yes.''

''I found out from Akemi that you were here. I came to take you away from this. With the things Joji Hosaka and his consortium have set into motion, the earth may open up and swallow all of us. I want you to be safe.''

''I can't leave Belasko to finish this by himself.''

''He is a warrior. It is what he must do.''

''And I also, Grandfather. You trained me to be a warrior as well, remember?''

His eyes met hers. ''I remember. It was all I had to give you.''

''You gave me much more than that. You gave me love, and a sense of honor that saw me through a time more barren than anything I have seen since. Belasko's fight is mine. I made it mine before he even knew of it.''

The old man studied her in the darkness. ''Yes, I suppose you did. Let us go find this American of yours.'' He moved away silently.

Face burning because she believed her grandfather had read more into her words than she had wanted, Ransom followed.

''COME OUT HERE, you son of a bitch,'' Brognola growled, keeping the .38 leveled at Ross Tuley. He held the cane in a clenched fist, fingers still numb from the swipe that had taken the MAC-10 from the man's hands.

A cut on Tuley's forehead dribbled blood down his nose. "It's okay, General. You caught me." He smirked and laced his hands behind his head. "I'm your prisoner."

Lowering the cane, Brognola limped back to the first man he'd shot. The man was sprawled back over a row of metal trash cans, a single bullet hole over his heart.

"That's some shooting," Tuley said admiringly. "Vardeman was a good soldier. It says something that you were able to take him."

"He wasn't expecting me to be standing there when he came around the corner."

"Neither was I."

Brognola curbed the impatience running through him, centering the .38's muzzle on Tuley's chest. "Okay, smart guy, I want some answers."

"I want a lawyer."

"You're in Tokyo, clown. I don't think their justice system is as lenient as ours in the States."

"You might be surprised. There are any number of things that can be arranged here." Tuley smiled. "Already have been, in case you didn't notice."

"Where's Sacker?"

"I don't know." A grin spread across Tuley's face. "Hey, John, glad to see you could make the party."

Footsteps sounded behind Brognola to let him know Tuley's words weren't a ruse. He turned slowly, keeping the gun trained on his prisoner. Winterroad stood in the mouth of the alley with a pistol filling his hand.

A foot-long muzzle-flash exploded from the weapon even as Brognola glimpsed Tuley going into action behind him.

BOLAN TRIGGERED the Desert Eagle twice, the impacts nearly decapitating the first man. The next somersaulted over the corpse, moving too fast for the Executioner to get target acquisition.

A blade flashed toward Bolan's throat, and he dodged away from it. Before he hit the road, the warrior lifted the .44 and put a round into the man's chest, staggering him. The next round punched through the ninja's head and whined off the brick wall behind him.

Then the Executioner was up and running for the protection of the shadows clinging to the single-story shop next to the inn, unwilling to quit the battle zone until he found out what had happened to Michi Ransom. His combat senses flared around him, marking off fields of fire, probable hiding places and avenues of escape should that become necessary.

Autofire rang out, driving the warrior over a low fence next to the shop. He switched magazines on the Desert Eagle, wanting a fresh one for any more confrontations. As he surveyed the road, looking for the unseen gunman, a shadow broke free of the building across the street, flanked by another one carrying a bow.

The bowman let an arrow fly, hardly pausing at all before reaching for another. A scream cut through the night as a ninja fell from hiding and lay unmoving on the rooftop of a nearby building.

The first ninja reached the Samurai, and it fired up a moment later. "Belasko!" Ransom screamed, pulling her mask off so that he could see her.

Autofire tracked onto the bowman running toward the moving vehicle. Bolan stood and fired several shots toward the muzzle-flashes. Whether they hit or not, the bullets drove the gunner to the ground. The Executioner vaulted the fence, changing clips on the run as Ransom brought the 4X4 around. He saw the bow-carrying ninja race over to it and catch hold of the rear, standing atop the bumper as he armed his weapon again.

The warrior sprinted to the middle of the road, aware that another vehicle was in motion. A long sedan tore from hiding, aiming for the smaller Samurai. Drawing the driver's side into target acquisition, the Executioner flamed three shots into the windshield, causing it to veer out of control.

The sedan slammed into the 4X4 with enough force to threaten the control Ransom had over the vehicle. The Samurai skidded for a moment, and Bolan could see the woman fighting desperately with the steering wheel. The 4X4 hit the corner of a brick building, showering sparks in its wake. The sedan didn't fare so well, colliding head-on with the unmoving wall. The front end crumpled.

An explosion rocked the ground near Bolan, its concussive force blowing him off his feet. He rolled, coming up into a standing position. He tasted blood from a split lip, the dirt of the road.

The bowman lifted his weapon, aiming at the ninja fifty feet away, who was readying another grenade. The arrow pierced the man's throat, causing him to drop the deadly egg. A moment later the corpse was ripped to bloody shreds.

Bolan ran to the felled sniper and checked the long-barreled rifle for damage as he took momentary cover in a doorway. He wiped dust from the Star-Tron scope mounted on the Steyr-Mannlicher Model M Professional and holstered the .44. Working the bolt, he slid a fresh round into the chamber, then raised it to his shoulder as the Star-Tron took away the night. The weight was like an old friend, the ability to see his enemies clearly a refreshing change.

Autofire chased the archer from the road, kicking up dust and gravel as it tracked back toward Ransom and the 4X4. The Executioner squeezed the trigger gently, worked the bolt, then squeezed gently again. Two men died. He was back in his element now, as unforgiving as the gunsight he used. The bolt pulled back empty.

Slinging the rifle, Bolan ran to the dead sniper and cut the ammo pouch from his waist. He glanced toward the archer, finding the man with sword in hand dispatching a final attacker.

Then the road was quiet.

Bolan loaded the rifle, slid the bolt home and drew the Desert Eagle. He walked toward the waiting Samurai, seeing the pockmarks of bullets scattered across the hood and the windshield. "Are you all right?" he asked Ransom.

Her smile was streaked with dirt. "I am now. Maybe our problems aren't as large as I thought. I'd like to introduce Kiyosha Ogata, my grandfather, who came here to rescue me, and who doesn't believe you killed Saburo Hosaka."

Understanding the meaning behind her words, Bolan holstered the .44 and faced the man. Ogata tugged off his hood, his eyes hard and glittering. "I understand from Akemi that I am indebted to you for saving my granddaughter's life." He bowed.

Returning the bow, Bolan said, "I think we're about even. She didn't need as much rescuing as Akemi might have made you think."

"*Hai*, so I, too, have learned."

Bolan swung into the driver's seat as Ransom moved into the back. Ogata took the passenger seat. The warrior released the clutch and started the vehicle in the direction of the road leading to Atami almost twenty-five miles away. The town was also the fastest route to Oshima Island, according to the maps Bolan had studied.

"Where to?" Ransom asked.

"First, I find a safe spot to drop you and your grandfather. Then I've got to find Yemon Hosaka and the man behind the American mercenaries."

"You know who he is?" Ransom asked.

Bolan nodded.

"You're not leaving me," Ransom said defiantly.

"Yes, I am," Bolan replied with conviction.

"And you're wrong about leaving Grandfather behind, too. He's still as involved as you are."

Bolan looked at the old man, seeing the truth of the woman's statement in the wrinkled features. "What if Joji Hosaka tells you to kill us?"

"Bolan!" Ransom sounded furious.

Ogata spoke up. "I do not think that will be a problem. Those men back there had instructions to kill Michi and me as well as you. They belonged to Yemon." He paused. "I am sure Yemon has taken care of all the loose ends now. He used Saburo's murder as a means to get me away from his father. I used my instructions as a means of securing Michi's safety. I did not know Yemon had killed Saburo. Otherwise I would have stayed and protected Joji Hosaka, as my honor demanded. Now I think I will find myself in the position of avenging his death, which will align our goals."

Bolan nodded. "I think you're right."

"Can you afford to let Yemon and his partner get away with this?" Ransom asked. "Now that things have progressed to this point, there's no turning back."

"I know," Bolan said.

"And," Ransom added, "we know the island."

Bolan sighed, realizing he had no real choice, not if he wanted to better his chances for completing the mission. The Samurai continued rolling through the night.

WINTERROAD SAW the surprised expression on Tuley's face when the man realized the gun was directed at him instead of Brognola. The big-bore slug caught Tuley in the forehead and spread-eagled him in the alley.

Brognola completed the move to bring the .38 around as Winterroad raised his weapon. "It's okay. Tuley was going for a sleeve gun. He used to carry it all the time when we worked together at the Agency."

He watched the Justice agent hobble over to inspect Tuley's body, the .38 still in hand. Brognola raked at something with the cane, exposing the large-calibered derringer cupped in the dead man's hands.

The big Fed looked up and took a cigar from his pocket after putting the pistol away. "I had some doubts concerning you after I heard about Sacker."

Winterroad let his surprise show. "I wasn't aware you knew about Sacker."

"Tucker left me some intel. When I had it researched, your name came up. I thought he might have recruited you."

Winterroad sighed and put his weapon away. "He tried and I almost went for it. I'm getting old, too goddamn old to be playing cowboys and Indians out in the field anymore, and I don't have anywhere to go from here. Sacker tried to make it sound like I was saving America from the Yellow Peril. Straight out of the comic books kind of heroism. But it's the kind I believe in, at least, the kind I want to believe in."

"I understand." And the look in Brognola's eyes told Winterroad the man *did* understand.

"If it hadn't been for this sudden field promotion as a result of Tucker's murder, maybe I would have let myself believe in it a few days longer. But it was too goddamn coincidental. I couldn't ignore the fact that Sacker had him killed just as he's set everything else into motion here." Winterroad gazed down at Tuley, trying to make sense of how cluttered honor, duty and heroism could become when a man started doubting that any of them existed. "Anyway, when Tuley contacted me earlier, as arranged through a phone call from Sacker, I had an agent put on him with orders not to act until I gave clearance. I almost got here too late. I wasn't expecting them to move against you as quickly as they did."

"Do you know where Sacker is?"

"I had the call traced, but all I could find out was that it originated from somewhere in Tokyo."

"So he's here?"

"Yeah. Somewhere."

Brognola limped off.

Winterroad fell into step beside him. "So what do we do now? I'd say I've pretty much broken the angle I was planning to work."

"Are you willing to tell the Japanese about your contact with Sacker?"

"I don't think it's something the Agency would be particularly fond of," Winterroad said. "But then I've never been one to stay on Langley's good side."

Brognola raised an eyebrow. "Do they have one?"

"Yeah. Me."

They turned the corner, squaring off against the irate crowd gathered in front of the restaurant.

"What does telling the Japanese have to do with anything?" Winterroad asked.

"I know where Sacker probably is," Brognola said. "I'm sure they'll be interested, too. You can corroborate my story. Together we're going to have to leverage an army from a guy named Fujitsu before I lose one of the best men I've ever known."

CHAPTER TWENTY-THREE

Switching off the engines of the speedboat they had liberated near Atami, Mack Bolan took a small pair of night glasses from a pocket of the blacksuit and surveyed the shore of Oshima Island less than a mile away.

Small gray boat houses lined the beach on this side of the island, and was a replica of what lay on the other side according to Ransom and Ogata. In the greenish glow of the vision afforded by the night glasses, there weren't many people moving around. A few boats, mostly fishing boats and the occasional houseboat, sat out the night in deeper water.

From the outside looking in the island appeared as the tourist attraction it was supposed to be. Tropical vegetation grew furiously over every untouched piece of land, highlighting the houses, Japanese-style ryokan inns, and the roads. In the center of the island, towering almost twenty-five hundred feet into the night sky, was the impressive bulk of Mount Mihara, formed by a volcanic reaction years before.

"See anything?" Ransom asked as Bolan put the night glasses away.

He shook his head and dropped back into the seat. Ogata sat in the stern, feet crossed in a lotus position as he waited. With the grayness reflecting from the ocean surface barely penetrating the cowl of his clothing, he looked like a medieval representation of death. Instead of the scythe, he carried the short sword slung over his back.

Bolan touched the controls, listening to the powerful engines kick to life, then felt the propellers bite deep into the ocean and push them forward.

Navigating between the houseboats and fishing boats, the Executioner took advantage of the concealment they offered. "Where's the Hosaka estate?" he asked, not taking his eyes from the shoreline.

"On the north side of Mount Mihara," Ransom replied.

"What's the terrain like?"

"Mountainous, rugged, and he has spared no expense on security. As you have noticed, Joji Hosaka made a number of enemies on his way to his success."

The warrior picked out a spot on the beach, then reduced the boat's forward speed until they coasted to a crunching stop in the loose sand.

They quit the boat silently. Ransom carried the Beretta with three extra clips, and Ogata carried only those things he had hidden on his person. In the dark, stalking their way into Hosaka's estate house, the primitive weapons the old ninja carried would be as effective as a round from the .44.

Bolan followed them into the darkness of the forest a moment later, his Uzi up and ready. The sniper rifle was slung upside down over his back and tied so that the barrel didn't interfere with leg movement.

Oshima island was less than three miles wide, and the plan was to make the two-and-a-quarter-mile distance to Hosaka's estate on foot rather than risk involvement with the local population by taking a car.

Fifteen minutes later Ogata waved them to concealment, taking refuge behind a tree and fading so quickly that even the Executioner's trained eye could no longer pick him out. Ransom went flat behind a rocky shelf jutting from the uneven terrain. Bolan dropped behind a cluster of bushes, moving the snout of the Uzi into position.

Three men appeared in the darkness farther down the slope. Bolan watched them approach. Unable to understand what was being said, he judged that one of the three was arguing with the others and they weren't taking him seriously.

The men came to a stop in a clearing Bolan and his team had skirted. The arguing got louder, with the man holding to his own convictions finally walking off into the brush by himself.

Bolan put the Uzi aside for the Ka-bar in his harness, fisting it tightly as he moved forward. He stayed low to the ground, watching the two men left behind as they continued talking between themselves. Both wore black, leaving their ski masks rolled up as they smoked. They carried machine pistols as well as swords.

Circling behind them, Bolan rose to a standing position less than fifteen feet away, part of the trunk of the oak tree that reared toward the dark heavens.

Reversing the knife so that the blade pointed downward, Bolan took a step forward. A sound in the brush where their companion had disappeared drew the men's attention, and they reached for their guns.

Bolan leaped, smashing into his chosen target and taking the man down. He rolled to his feet and saw the remaining guard wheel in his direction. The knife left his hand and thudded through the guard's heart. Returning his attention to the man beneath him, Bolan grabbed the guard's chin and jerked, the sound of the snapping spine seeming to fill the clearing. Then it vanished as quickly as the life itself.

He stood and walked over to the man impaled by his knife. Ransom rose from the darkness, and Ogata walked into the clearing with his sword in his fist. Besides the knife an arrow had penetrated one eye and a slim stiletto jutted out from under the man's jaw.

Ogata put a foot on the dead man's chest, pulled the arrow out and returned it to his granddaughter. He pocketed his own stiletto after cleaning it.

Bolan removed his knife and the extra clips the guard had carried for the Uzi. Then they went on into the darkness.

YEMON ESCORTED his father across the sweeping veranda toward the rooms he had commandeered as his personal offices on the island. The sky was oppressive, thick with the coming rain. Usually he found it depressing as well. But tonight, everything was coming together for him. He had to keep the smile from his face and the lift from his voice.

"Who is on the phone?" Joji Hosaka asked as he stepped through the whitewashed double doors Yemon opened for him.

"I don't know. I thought it might be Ogata, but it isn't his voice."

His father looked rumpled in the expensive suit, still lost in his thoughts over Saburo's death. Yemon tried to remember if the man had slept since last night but found he was unable to. Of course, he'd had distractions of his own. As for himself, he'd had no sleep at all. Even with everything coming together as it was, there had still seemed so much to do. Now it was done. Only the dying remained.

The office was divided into two parts: one was dressed in elegance as a waiting room for guests entering from the veranda, the other as an electronic network that connected Yemon to the businesses he constantly oversaw. He felt a wave of jealousy consume him when he saw that Picard had taken his chair behind the desk, but he squelched it before it could become a problem. Everything would turn within the hour, and the fall would be that much harder for his enemies if they thought they held the upper hand.

Picard switched the light on, catching the elder Hosaka by surprise. Joji Hosaka blinked as he turned toward the light, looking like an owl with the intensity of his gaze. Two of Picard's men stepped from the darkness near the floor-to-ceiling bookshelves.

"You!" Hosaka made a visible effort to control the rage that filled him.

Picard smiled, leaning forward to place his elbows on the desktop. "Hello, Joji," the man said in fluent Japanese. "It's been a long time."

"You are a fool to be here," Hosaka said. "I have an army waiting outside. One word from me and you're not only a fool, but a dead man, as well."

Picard's smile grew wider. "I think Yemon might have something to say about that."

Yemon felt his father's eyes on him, saw them widen when the father sensed the truth in the son.

"You're with him," Hosaka said in a quiet voice. He took a step backward, his hand clawing at the door that led to the waiting room. It was locked.

Yemon walked to a chair in front of the desk and lifted the remote control for the electronics around the office. He cradled it in his lap, waiting for the proper time. Picard pushed himself up on his knuckles, seating himself on the corner of the desk.

"You have disgraced your family," Joji Hosaka accused, staring at his son.

Yemon returned the gaze full measure, letting some of the anger and rage he had harbored for so long show through. "No. I am not the disgrace. I am everything you raised me to be. And more. You have prostituted yourself for the Americans far too long and have helped keep this country under their control for four decades. I am trying to make amends for that."

Consternation narrowed Picard's eyes. Yemon turned his head and smiled. He pointed the remote control at the wall behind the two American mercenaries and flicked a button. Panels slid aside, allowing four ninjas to enter the room before the mercenaries could bring their weapons to bear. They operated as two-man teams, one bringing their man down with a sword blow while the other secured the weapon.

Before Picard could pull the holstered .45, Yemon moved from the chair into a spinning kick that knocked the older man headlong into the library shelves behind him. With a roar of rage, Picard got to his feet, blood trickling from his broken nose.

Almost effortlessly Yemon blocked the wild overhand punch with the back of his arm, responding with a chop to Picard's throat that took the man's wind away. While the man tried to recover, Yemon pulled the .45 from Picard's holster.

"Search him," Yemon commanded one of the ninjas. The black-clad man responded immediately, turning up two small knives and a derringer. The ninja's knife flicked in quick flashes that removed the pockets and lining from Picard's clothes. "Sit him there," he said when the man had finished, pointing to one of the chairs in front of the desk.

Moving behind the big desk, Yemon placed the .45 on the desktop and picked up the remote control again. He watched as Picard, with the bloody blade of a sword under his jaw, was made to sit in the chair. The man's eyes were nuclear furnaces of pure hatred.

Yemon pointed to the other chair. "Sit down," he commanded his father.

Joji Hosaka made no move at first, then, when another ninja started forward, sat by Picard.

Yemon permitted himself a smile as he looked at the older man. "As I said, Picard, it was basically a very good plan. I just made a few additions of my own." He flicked the remote control again and a forty-two-inch television set in the wall came to life. "We built an empire, Father. You, Kokan and me, and we started it a decade ago when Hosaka Industries became a legitimate business and broke away from the dirt Picard had us do."

"You didn't think the business was so bad at the beginning," Picard said. "Neither did your father."

"No, but times change. So do fortunes. Hosaka Industries became quite successful in its own right. Then the consortium came about."

"It wouldn't have without my help," Picard reminded him. "I blackmailed some of the larger investors your father and you couldn't persuade. You wouldn't have gotten any of this off the ground if it hadn't been for me. I provided the strikes in America that made them feel even more united."

"For which I thank you." Yemon bowed his head. "I couldn't have achieved those effects without your help."

"You knew those people would be killed?" The look on Joji Hosaka's face was incredulous.

"Of course. Who do you think helped provide Picard's men with target areas that would achieve the most notice?" Yemon shook his head at his father's squeamishness. "This is war. People die in war."

"This is quite a boy you've got here," Picard said with heavy sarcasm. "We've been in on this together for four years, and I'd never even suspected he had enough guts to put something like this together." He smiled. "It's a shame, though, that you're still going to have to deal with me to make sure you keep your flock together. And I've kept notes on this whole little operation as insurance."

"I don't think so, Picard. I've known you too long. You keep the most self-damaging information in your head, and that will die with you. And just in case..." Yemon triggered the wall panels again, allowing Cherie to step into the room. "One of the additions I made," he said softly, trailing his fingers down the woman's white arm. He enjoyed the look of utter defeat that flashed across Picard's face. "You've gotten soft in your later years, Picard, and that's what's getting you killed."

BOLAN UNFOLDED a collapsible grappling hook from his blacksuit, took a couple of swings to build momentum, then let it fly to the top of the twelve-foot stone wall in front of him. He pulled on the nylon rope, securing the hook's hold, then glanced to where Ransom was performing the same maneuver twenty feet away. Thirty feet behind them Ogata crouched in the brush left by the landscapers, bow in hand.

The warrior scaled the wall soundlessly and halted near the top, cautiously pulling himself up until he could see over the edge. The courtyard of the estate was shrouded in darkness, but the night vision glasses had revealed that the area was patrolled by men dressed in black who carried automatic weapons. He had timed the passage of the guard beneath this post and discovered the man made his rounds once every minute and a quarter. Numbers dropped softly through the Executioner's mind, as natural as breathing.

The courtyard was lavishly landscaped, filled with pruned pine trees, a stone garden on the north side of the house, flower beds and three different fountains. Outbuildings for storage and servants' quarters were spaced around the main house. The house was three stories high, with red-lacquered tile roofs turned up on the corners in pagoda style. Only a handful of lights showed in the windows, and more guards kept watch on the courtyard from positions on the top floor. A veranda, facing north and west to the open sea, was open and exposed, the curtains twisting in the breeze.

The Executioner drew himself up to the top of the stone wall and lay flat. Ransom did the same, never once betraying her position by sight or sound. Numbers continued to click through his head, urged on by the dawn, which was ready to break in the black eastern sky.

The guard walked his round, dressed in the familiar black, his hood pushed back while he smoked a cigarette. Seconds later the man was past them.

Bolan slipped over the edge of the wall and dropped to the ground, unlimbering the Uzi. No matter how much recon work he could have done, it was only a matter of time before they were discovered once the probe went hard. Silence would buy them perhaps minutes, but not much more.

Ogata was over the wall in a rush, flipping over in a tight ball, then landing with his sword drawn. He nodded, letting Bolan know that their approach had gone unnoticed, then took the lead, aiming for the house in a circuitous approach.

The plan was simplicity—close in on the house, take out the Hosakas and Sacker if possible, then make their escape in the confusion.

A few moments later Ogata waved them down, then crept forward with his sword in both hands. Bolan watched the man step out suddenly, trip the guard he heard coming around the corner of the servants' house and drive the sword home. The Executioner was in motion again before the choked gurgle of the dying man reached his ears.

The warrior looked up at the veranda, drawing Ogata's attention. "That's where Yemon's offices are?"

Ogata nodded.

Bolan glanced up through the darkness at the second-story veranda and the guard on the third floor. He pointed. "I need that man taken out."

Ogata nodded again and unslung his bow. Bolan listened for the *twang* of the bowstring, then took off running, not waiting to see the results of the arrow's flight.

Bolan slung the Uzi before launching himself up into the lower branches of a tree that grew close to the corner of the building. His side flared with renewed pain as he pulled himself up into its branches. When he was high enough, he reached out and threw a leg over the veranda railing, unslung the Uzi and took refuge beside a potted banana tree.

Voices reached his ears.

He moved leaves on the banana tree and peered through the open sliding glass doors. Seeing no one there, he moved inside toward the voices. He recognized Yemon Hosaka's, then Joji Hosaka's. There was another man, with an American accent, whom Bolan assumed to be Sacker. He listened as Yemon Hosaka took over the conversation again.

YEMON STUDIED his two captives. His father showed no signs of hope, but Picard was too calm. It unnerved him slightly, making him want to pull the trigger. But his desire to explain the success he had wrought overcame his unease.

"You were both instrumental in creating the vehicle I have taken control of," he announced, rising from the chair. He stepped over one of Picard's dead guards. "You both saw the potential of the consortium concerning world business, and you both wanted to twist it to your own greed. By causing the schism between Japan and the United States, by causing the fall of the financial dependency the Americans have given to us, I will make Japan a giant in the world. An acknowledged giant."

"You're insane," Joji Hosaka said.

"Am I?" Yemon glared at his father. "No, it's you who have been insane. You have been guilty of raping this country for four decades with the help of your CIA friends after the war. We have operated as their satellite since then. Now, with the tides of financial freedom being stripped from their country, with the American people not even aware of what they're doing to themselves, now is the time to strike."

"What do you know of business?" Joji demanded. "If you try to destroy the American market, think of the void it will leave for Japanese business."

"I have. We can survive it. They cannot."

"Do you actually think the American people are going to take this lying down?" Picard asked. "If you do, you've got another think coming. Your old man's right—you're crazy."

"Really, Picard?" Yemon faced the man, meeting his gaze unflinchingly. "And wasn't that why you were seeking control of the consortium through me? So you could play better politics in your own country? In your language, bullshit. You know the kind of power the consortium can wield over the United States right now, and it draws you like a magnet to steel because that is true wealth to you. How does it feel to see someone come along and take that from you?''

''You haven't done it yet.''

Yemon slapped the desktop with a palm. ''Yes, I have. And I'm going to use it to further Japan's future. The land of the rising sun is going to rise to heights no one ever dreamed of.''

''You figure on cutting yourself a deal right in there near the top, don't you?'' Picard asked.

Yemon grinned. ''Why not? I'll be leading a large block of this country's wealthiest people. Retaliation by pulling out of the United States financially is going to seem tame, but it will have the most impact.'' He pressed the remote control and a picture appeared on the television of the flag with the rising sun. ''America left us in ashes after World War II, and we came out of it. It will be interesting to see if they have the resources and strength to do the same.''

An explosion rocked the house, followed quickly by another. Cherie screamed. Lifting the .45, Yemon faced Picard.

''One thing I forget to mention,'' Picard said as he threw himself out of the chair. ''Trust or no trust, I didn't come to this little shindig alone.''

RANSOM WATCHED in disbelief as the front gates of the estate blew without warning. Then a buzz saw of noise started up, flowing through the opening with the motorcycles that flooded the courtyard. There were two men on each motorcycle, one to handle the steering while the other kept up a steady barrage of gunfire that chopped through the black-clad estate guards.

Her grandfather pulled at her sleeve, motioning her back into the shadows.

"We can't leave Belasko," she said stubbornly.

"We'll do him no good at all if we're dead."

Ransom drew her bow and nocked an arrow, pausing to glance up at the empty veranda, then followed her grandfather. She watched, unable to take her gaze away as the carnage and destruction continued. A motorcycle roared to a stop forty feet from the house, sliding to a standstill as the rear man dismounted and fell to one knee. A bulky tube took shape on his shoulder. A second later fire belched out of the rear of the tube and an explosion blew the front doors from their hinges. The driver of the motorcycle reloaded the bazooka, then patted the shooter on the helmet. The second round smashed into the upper story, opening a gaping wound in the wall.

A motorcycle roared at them. Her grandfather stood and ran, weaving, making himself a difficult target for the gunner. Bullets kicked up grass as they pursued him.

Moving instinctively, Ransom nocked the arrow back to her cheek, targeted in as her grandfather had taught her with the body instead of only the eyes, then released the shaft. The feathers brushed her cheek as it left her fingers, plunging through the clear visor covering her target's face, and knocking the gunner away.

She saw the sword in her grandfather's hands flicker once, then the helmeted head of the driver was rolling across his leather-jacketed shoulders. The motorcycle was out of control and smashed into a small building containing the estate's gardening equipment.

Men abandoned the motorcycles in front of the house, roughly half of the assault team taking the building by storm. The man with the bazooka wreaked havoc on the lesser buildings as his loader fed him round after round. The small pagoda-style structures went up in orange and yellow flames, staining the darkness of the morning sky.

Ransom took another arrow from her quiver, trusting the bow more than her unknown abilities with the Beretta Belasko had given her, drew it back and sighted for the bazooka man. Releasing half her breath, she held the rest and let go of the string, immediately reaching for another arrow.

The shaft sped true, burying itself in the man's chest, dropping him forward on his face. His companion went down under a sudden burst from one of the guards. Ransom put her next shaft through the ninja's eye as he turned to face them, the point coming through the back of the man's head.

Grenades increased the chaos and destruction in the courtyard, destroying one of the fountains and leaving an uncontrolled jet streaming straight into the air. Trees were felled by others. Orange and gold flames clung to awnings, dropping them in flaming kite tails to dash sparks against the ground and quickly flutter away.

The whining drone of the motorcycles seemed unstoppable, punctuated by the rattling roar of automatic weapons. A sudden burst dropped Ransom and her grandfather into the protection of the nearest flower bed.

Looking out across the flames, explosions and corpses, she said, ''This is madness.''

Her grandfather was beside her, fisting his sword in both hands. ''No, this is a deathground where survival is possible only through the courage of desperation.''

Ransom's thoughts turned to Mike Belasko, remembering him as the warrior in black whose convictions ran as deeply as her grandfather's. She couldn't help but wonder if he would find the courage of desperation her grandfather spoke of. Then a new, louder drone filled her ears, pulling her attention skyward.

Four large helicopters filled the sky.

CHAPTER TWENTY-FOUR

Bolan watched the procession of motorcycles stream through the mangled front gates. Shots rang out inside the room occupied by the Hosakas and Sacker. Bullets penetrated the door, ripping out chunks of wood.

A man raced from an adjoining room, gun held at waist level. The Executioner cut him down with a burst from the Uzi. He whirled, slammed a big foot on the door near the lock, felt it give and go crashing back inside.

Autofire raked the doorway, forcing him back. Reaching into his webbing, Bolan took out a spare clip for the Uzi and tossed it into the room. The ruse worked. The men thought a grenade had been thrown inside and scrambled for cover.

The Executioner swung around the door, hammering several rounds through the two guards trying to squeeze through the open panels behind the desk. Their bodies fell across the threshold, blocking the attempts the sliding door made to close behind them.

Three dead men were in the room in addition to the ones he was responsible for. One of them was Joji Hosaka, slumped backward in a chair with a bullet hole in his forehead. Two were American. A screaming woman huddled in the corner of the room, her arms held protectively over her head.

The Executioner crossed the room in long strides, lifted her up and asked, "Where are they?"

The woman screamed louder, pushing at his face with a hand. Her fingers came away bloody.

Bolan repeated his question.

"Through there," the blonde said, pointing through the secret doors.

"Who?"

"Yemon and Picard."

Bolan charged through the open doorway, determined to stop Yemon Hosaka dead in his tracks. He gripped the Uzi tightly, following the sloping passageway toward the rear of the building.

A faint *whup-whup-whup* rattled through the passageway, overtaking him as he ran, a familiar sound heard above the constant yammerings of autofire and explosions. Helicopters. Big ones.

BROGNOLA GRABBED Fujitsu by the shoulder and pulled him away from his field of view. The Hosaka estate was just below, the setting for a major fight. There were dozens of fires scattered about, and coils of black smoke rose toward the helicopters.

"Son of a bitch," he heard Winterroad say.

"Here's your proof," Brognola said to Fujitsu. The satisfaction in being proved right that the Hosaka family wasn't a wholly innocent victim in the stateside terrorist action was no compensation for the knowledge that Mack Bolan was somewhere below in the conflagration.

"I see no proof," the Foreign Affairs man said. "I see only more death." He turned a weary but iron-hard face toward Brognola. "And if I find your agent Belasko is at the root of this, consider yourself placed in my custody. And I'll have you shot if you try to escape."

Brognola lifted the cane ruefully. "As if I could get very far. Get these choppers down there, damn it. I've got a friend down there who's put his neck on the line to get to the bottom of this."

Fujitsu motioned to the pilot to land, talking in rapid Japanese over the open channel shared by the four Bell helicopters. Their chopper landed outside the estate, and the four teams disembarked with crack efficiency as each of the squad leaders followed Fujitsu's orders.

Brognola forced his injured leg to let him keep up with the Foreign Affairs man. It was more than a matter of pride. It had taken too much time to persuade Fujitsu to undertake the mission. And that just might have cost Bolan his life.

The first man of their team reached the inner courtyard, holding his riot shield in front of him. A heartbeat later a motorcycle roared into him, the front wheel high in the air. The man went down as the motorcycle tracked over him.

Feeling clumsy in the body armor Fujitsu had insisted he wear, Brognola drew the motorcyclist into target acquisition and dropped the hammer on his .38. The motorcycle went out of control, and the unnatural angle of the rider's neck told the big Fed it wasn't necessary to check for vital signs.

Then the battle was joined.

RANSOM STREAKED toward the back of the house, followed by her grandfather. She tucked the Beretta into her sword belt, reaching for the grappling hook concealed in her clothes. Chances of getting in through the front were virtually exhausted. The squad in riot gear had broken all attempts at retreat, turning ninjas and American mercenaries back with astonishing success. It left only the rear.

One of the mercenaries peered out at her from an inside room through a glass stained by blood, swinging his weapon around to bring her into his sights. She ducked, reaching for one of the smoke pellets in a concealed pocket. She crushed it underfoot as she kept moving. White smoke rose to engulf her.

Bullets missed her by feet as she freed the Beretta. With the man in her sights, she squeezed the trigger and kept it up until the corpse jerked out of sight.

A motorcycle careened around the corner of the building, and the rider jammed on the brakes when he spotted them, changing direction as he set up the rear man for the shot. Ransom saw her grandfather slide toward them with a thick branch in his hand.

The branch caught in the rear wheel as the gunner tried to bring his weapon to bear, stopping all forward motion and slinging the two men off like a bucking stallion. Her grandfather killed them both with his sword before they were able to get to their feet.

A door opened farther down, reminding Ransom of the garage containing the limousine Joji Hosaka had kept there from the old days when he had been more connected to the Yakuza. She ran for it, the 93-R tight in her fist.

PICARD WIPED at the blood streaming down his chest. His breath was ragged, raspy, too wet sounding to be anywhere close to normal. His hand, holding the .45 he'd stripped from one of his men, was slick with blood, as well.

The secret corridor he traveled turned onto an upstairs bedroom that had been hit by the bazooka. He gazed down through the wreckage at the bodies littering the courtyard under the increasingly lighter sky. Sunrise was only moments away.

Memories of Cherie bounced against the walls of his mind, finding them collapsing in on themselves. He had been so wrong, so soft, about both of them. Cherie and Yemon.

Gritting his teeth against the pain growing in his chest, he made his way out of the room, finding a staircase that led down, leaning on the railing hard. The worst part was that no one would know how close he'd come to controlling so much.

But if he got away, there was still the chance that he could somehow make things go right for him. He had changed things around plenty of times before. There was no reason why he couldn't do it again.

He forced himself to walk faster, tightening his grip on the pistol in his hand. He didn't have to die from the bullet wound in his chest. He hadn't given in to it when Yemon had first shot him, and he damn sure wasn't going to now. All he needed was a few minutes to get to the forest, then he could rest and wait out the day, until he could find a way to get out of the country. He had money, a whole belt full around his waist. It would be his ticket, more than enough to get the job done.

He walked toward the rear of the house, stepping over the bodies in his way. His hand touched the doorknob at the side of the house. Someone called his name.

YEMON STEPPED through the panel in the garage, waving the bloody .45 in his hand at the two men taking cover near the garage door. "Into the car. Now."

The men climbed into the front seat of the limousine without question.

Yemon got in the back, then reached forward for one of the machine guns that belonged to his hardmen. The driver hit the electric garage door opener, and the door slid up with a squeal. The rear tires shrieked as they spun on the concrete and pushed the armor-plated vehicle up the short incline.

Buckling in as the car started uphill, Yemon glanced up, saw Michi Ransom at the side of the garage and yelled, "Stop the car!"

Anger burned in him as the luxury car spun in a half circle. The woman had been with the big American, and if she was here, it meant that the American was to blame for the sudden turn of bad luck. And she might know enough to testify about his murder of Saburo. She was a reporter and commanded a large audience. He rolled down his window and aimed the .45 at the woman as she pointed a gun at him. He flinched, even knowing the bulletproof windshield would stop the rounds, then triggered his pistol.

At least one of the rounds hit Ransom and punched her to the ground. The .45 clicked dry, and he was out of ammo. A squad of riot-garbed men crowded around the front of the vehicle.

"Get us out of here," Yemon commanded.

The driver threw the car into reverse, backing over a line of stone lanterns delineating a flower bed. The bits and pieces clacked against the undercarriage, louder than the bullets that began to ping against the armor plating. The luxury car wheeled around, rocking on its special springs like a boat at sea. Then it shot forward, smashing into bodies, streaking for the front gate.

Yemon lifted the mobile phone in front of him and dialed the number of the warehouse on the northeast side of the island. "Get the plane ready," he ordered. The voice at the other end acknowledged him and he hung up.

He allowed himself a small smile of satisfaction. Everything would be all right. Even at the worst his plans would only be delayed, not set aside. The red sun of imperial Japan could still dawn over the world.

BOLAN RUSHED OUT of the passageway and into the garage in time to see Ransom go down. He triggered the Uzi as he charged up the incline, but saw that the parabellums had no effect on the white limousine.

He dropped beside Ransom just as Ogata reached her. Together they turned her over gently. Blood spurted from a wound in her left shoulder.

A handful of men in riot gear jogged around the corner, pointing their weapons at them as the team secured the garage.

"Yemon was in that car," Ransom said.

Bolan nodded. "I've got to stop him."

"There's a warehouse on the northeast side of the island," she said. "Joji kept a seaplane there."

"You're going to be all right."

"I know." She forced a smile. "Go."

Bolan looked at Ogata. The old ninja stripped his face mask away and nodded. "I will take care of her. Go. Your mission is not yet finished."

Bolan stood, drawing the immediate attention of the men in riot gear. Brognola joined the warrior as they commanded him to put down his weapons, and identified him as a Justice agent. "Take care of these people for me, Hal," the Executioner said as he brushed past the big Fed and picked up one of the motorcycles. He mounted the vehicle, kicked it to life and sped off in pursuit of the white limousine, dragging a foot as he made the corner outside the gates.

He pushed the motorcycle, listening to the engine keening its protest. The Steyr tugged at its sling, shifting in the wind. The road curved suddenly, and he had to gear down and skid through a tangle of trees before returning to the road.

Gearing back up, he raised the speed to seventy miles an hour, then eighty. The handlebars felt light, spongy.

The road dipped down without warning as he topped a rolling hill. The motorcycle left the ground, thudding hard when it returned to earth.

Bolan studied the winding path the road took to the beach and noticed the seaplane already warming up alongside a dock. Knowing he wouldn't be able to overtake the vehicle by staying on the street, he pulled the motorcycle off the road and fought the handlebars as he chose the straightest path possible.

Trees whipped at him, and he dodged them as well as the volcanic boulders that suddenly seemed everywhere. The motorcycle became inspired with a life of its own, wanting to slip, slide and jump with every heartbeat.

But he was gaining on the limousine.

The motorcycle left the ground again, rear tire spinning dirt when it landed. He geared down, shot around the spreading pine tree that suddenly loomed in his way and brought the front wheel up as he jumped a ditch.

The motorcycle's engine whined as it flew through the air, startling a small flock of birds from the trees. Less than a thousand yards from the shore something caught in the motorcycle's wheels. Bolan flew over the handlebars.

SACKER TURNED toward Winterroad, and the agent saw an easy grin spread across the man's face. Blood covered Sacker's shirt, dripping down the barrel of his gun. He spit out a mouthful of blood, not taking his eyes from Winterroad's.

"I thought it was you," Winterroad said softly. His own gun felt solid in his hand. He kept it pointed at the floor. So far no one had noticed that he'd left the group.

"You turned on me, too, John?" Sacker asked. He laughed. "Damn, I must be losing my touch. Getting soft. I get bamboozled by a broad for the first time in my life, outfoxed by a kid young enough to be my grandson and sold out by somebody whose politics I thought I knew."

Winterroad didn't know what the man was talking about. He watched Sacker's eyes. "It isn't about politics," he said. "When it came down to the wire, it was about me doing the job I knew I was supposed to do. All the wishing in the world isn't going to make it what I want it to be."

"A man's got to have vision," Sacker said. "He's got to believe he can take on the world and win."

"You took it on," Winterroad commented, "and it kicked your ass."

Sacker grinned again. "Not yet it hasn't." He steadied his grip on the gun.

"It doesn't have to be that way," Winterroad warned.

"Yeah, I guess I could give myself up, right? How long do you think I'd last in a cage?" Sacker shook his head. "No, it has to be this way." He lifted the blood-slick gun.

Winterroad fired from the hip, putting two bullets squarely through Sacker's heart, watching the man fall back across the sink, then crumple to the floor. He holstered his gun and looked down at the dead man, not knowing exactly how he had turned out different from Sacker after being brought up in the same mind-set at the Agency, but glad he was.

BOLAN SPILLED across the rough terrain, losing skin from his face and hands. The motorcycle died behind him. He pushed himself to his feet, walked gingerly to the bike and found that the front wheel was now in the shape of a half-moon.

He looked down the slope, seeing Yemon Hosaka's limousine had less than a half mile of road left before it let him out near the seaplane.

The warrior shrugged out of the sling for the Steyr and raced down the slope, losing sight of the limo from time to time as the trees swept it from his vision. Thoughts of what Yemon Hosaka intended to do with the consortium, that even now the United States Justice Department and Japanese Foreign Affairs might not be able to wade through everything that had happened over the past few months, dogged him. Visions of the kind of pandemonium that would overtake America if the stock market suddenly crashed again, with no hope of recovery, flashed through his mind. At worst, such action might give birth to a whole nation of savages with no future. At best . . . He drew a blank. There would be no "best."

He ran and vaulted over a boulder, resting one bloody hand on it for an instant. He shed more gear, getting rid of the weight. Within seconds he was stripped of all equipment other than the sniper rifle.

Rotors beat overhead, letting him know Brognola and Fujitsu had sent at least one of the helicopters in pursuit. A figure stepped out of the seaplane and raised something to his shoulder. There was a puff of smoke, then a loud explosion overhead as the helicopter blew apart. Pieces rained to the ground.

Bolan ran, never glancing away from his target and the path that would take him there. Blood seeped into his eye, but he didn't take time to brush it away. He tripped over hanging lianas on a jump that didn't clear the necessary distance, rolling and shoving himself back to his feet.

The limousine sent sand flying as it skidded to a stop on the beach.

Knowing the numbers had ran out on the play, Bolan dropped to a prone position, stretching the rifle out before him. It felt impossibly heavy. He wiped the blood out of his eyes, squinted through the telescopic lens and found at least one of them broken from the motorcycle wreck.

He loosened the screws holding it in place and threw it away as Yemon Hosaka opened the back door of the limo.

Steadying his arm, the Executioner took a full breath, facing the lightening sky in the east, and let it out slowly, following Hosaka with the barrel through the open sights from at least three hundred yards out.

The seaplane continued to bob on the ocean's surface. White sails coasted slowly across Bolan's field of vision. He shut them out, narrowed his field of focus to the back of his target's head. Hosaka zigzagged as he ran, presenting a difficult target.

Bolan waited, knowing he would have the opportunity when the man climbed down the ladder to the waiting seaplane. The Executioner watched intently as Hosaka grabbed the top of the wooden ladder, took up slack on the Steyr's forward trigger. Hosaka started down, his movement now constant.

The rifle banged against the Executioner's shoulder as he touched the rear trigger.

A heartbeat later Hosaka's body left the ladder like a leaden weight jerked by an invisible string, sinking under the ocean surface as the morning's red sun rose and scattered a baleful glare over the azure sea.